The Happiness Plan

Susan Mallery

MILLS & BOON

Mills & Boon
An imprint of HarperCollins*Publishers* Ltd
1 London Bridge Street
London SE1 9GF

www.harpercollins.co.uk

HarperCollins*Publishers*
Macken House, 39/40 Mayor Street Upper,
Dublin 1, D01 C9W8, Ireland

This paperback edition 2023
1

First published in Great Britain by Mills & Boon,
an imprint of HarperCollins*Publishers* Ltd 2023

Copyright © 2023 Susan Mallery, Inc.

Susan Mallery asserts the moral right to be
identified as the author of this work.
A catalogue record for this book is
available from the British Library.

ISBN: 978-1-84845-929-8

MIX
Paper | Supporting
responsible forestry
FSC™ C007454
www.fsc.org

This book is produced from independently certified FSC™ paper
to ensure responsible forest management.

For more information visit: www.harpercollins.co.uk/green

Printed and Bound in the UK using 100% Renewable
Electricity at CPI Group (UK) Ltd

The Happiness Plan

To my Facebook All Access Group. You always come through for me, whether it's naming a marketing group (thanks, Deb!!) or a town or even a pet. Your love and support are always the highlight of my day and I love that we get to hang out together.

So many of you have asked for Heather's book, so here it is. Enjoy!!

one

"Is it possible you're overcommitting in your personal life because you don't want to feel your emotions?" Tori Rocha asked, her tone more concerned than judgy. "Kittens? Really? Because you needed one more thing?"

Heather Sitterly glanced down at the three sleeping two-week-old kittens she'd just agreed to foster, thought about the client she'd signed that morning and the kitchen remodel she was considering.

"Possible?" she repeated, grinning as she spoke. "No. Not possible. I think we can agree it's likely. Very likely."

Tori's mouth twitched, as if trying not to smile. "Admitting you have a problem is half the battle. How can I help?"

Heather shifted her wrist so her friend and the head graphic designer at 206 Marketing Group could see her smart watch.

"In forty-two minutes these little guys will need feeding."

"The conference room in forty-two minutes. I'll be there."

So would the rest of the senior staff, Heather thought, because forty-two minutes from now was the weekly update meeting.

"Thanks."

Heather walked to her large corner office where she had an oversize executive desk, a small conference table and a seating area. The traditional furniture contrasted with the soft-sided playpen in the back corner.

She set the box of kittens on the coffee table and pulled a couple of soft blankets from the closet, along with a large heating pad. She set the heating pad on the lowest setting and covered it with one of the blankets, then used the second one to make a little nest. Carefully, she transferred the sleeping kittens to the playpen where they mewed for a few seconds before falling back to sleep.

"I'll take good care of you," she whispered. "In a few weeks you'll be old enough to go to your forever homes. You'll have a great life."

Between now and adoption day, Heather would be their surrogate mother. While time consuming, the task wasn't a stretch. She fostered on a regular basis. Once she got the kittens back to her place, she would be aided by her crabby, mistrustful cat, LC, who loathed her but was an amazing foster dad to all the kittens she brought home.

Heather crossed to her desk and uploaded the signed contracts from Mountain Goat Northwest, their newest client. She'd been courting them for eighteen months, so having them sign on the dotted line was a sweet victory. MGNW specialized in outerwear for various sports but emphasized sustainable fabrics and bright colors, often decorated with faux fur. Many of their jackets and pants could be custom ordered with personalized details such as patterns and trim.

She'd sold MGNW on an experiential marketing campaign—one that would help form a relationship with their customers to create brand loyalty for a lifetime.

Once she'd sent the contracts to accounting, she answered her email briefly, fingers flying over the keyboard. She'd nearly finished when a new email appeared with a familiar subject line.

More detailed DNA results. See who else might be related to you.

"I already know who's related to me," Heather murmured, clicking on the link. She logged in to her Ancestry account and stared at the familiar information.

Potential blood relatives included a few distant cousins, some old lady in Belarus and a married man with two daughters living about forty-five minutes north of Seattle. Her gaze lingered on the last entry.

Fletcher Causey, age fifty-two. From what she'd learned in a cursory online search, he was a high school history teacher, had never been in prison and according to his Facebook page, which for reasons not clear to her wasn't private, was a devoted dad to two girls. He liked sports, grew his own vegetables and had been married to his wife for fifteen years. More compelling than all that was the fact that according to Ancestry, there was a 97.5 percent chance he was also Heather's father. The result of a one-night stand when he and her mother had been eighteen.

She'd learned about the possible DNA match six months ago but had yet to reach out. Her mother was enough of a pain—Heather wasn't interested in another clingy relative. Only Fletcher seemed like a good guy and she'd always wondered about her father and...

"Is it true? Are there kittens?"

She looked up and smiled at Sam, her head of market research. Sam was a genius when it came to understanding demographics and trends, often creating his own algorithms to dig down into the numbers. Heather didn't understand the how of what he did, but she appreciated the results.

"Three of them and you're the first one here."

"I washed my hands," he said as he crossed to the playpen. He slowly removed one kitten, getting a mew of protest as he carefully turned it over before putting it back.

There were two black-and-white kittens and one gray one. The second kitten barely stirred as he lifted it. Once he'd determined the gender, he sat down on the sofa and carefully put a tiny blue collar around its neck.

"Let me guess," she said drily. "Russell Wilson?"

"My hero."

"You know he's no longer a Seahawk. He left the team and our beautiful city."

Sam shook his head. "Don't care. Ten years after he's retired, he'll still be my man."

Heather's watch beeped a five-minute warning for the meeting.

"Time to heat the formula," she said.

"I'll bring these guys." Sam put Russell Wilson into the box and collected the other two kittens.

Heather walked to the break room where she found Tori collecting towels, feeding syringes and cotton balls. A can of formula was on the counter along with a cup of water.

"I warmed the water already," Tori told her. "But check the temperature."

"Thanks. Sam's already claimed his kitten. Did you want to name one?"

Her friend grinned. "Unlike Sam, I'm not comfortable giving kittens the same name over and over again and I've run out of creative options. I'll let someone else give it a shot."

The house rule was the first to help with a kitten got to name it—at least until its adoption.

Heather mixed the formula and tested the temperature before carrying it into the conference room. Her director of digital marketing had already claimed the gray girl. Tori passed out supplies while Heather filled each syringe.

"I hear we're due for a celebration," Elliot Young, her mentor and business partner, said as he walked into the conference room. "Someone signed Mountain Goat Northwest this morning."

He was followed by one of the marketing staff pushing a cart piled high with cupcakes, sparkling water and coffee.

Elliot sat next to her and reached for the kitten she held. "You worked hard for that account. You deserve to celebrate."

Everyone not holding a kitten applauded. Heather felt a flush of pride and gratitude.

"It was a team effort," she told them. "We're going to be good for them and they're going to be good for us."

Elliot set the kitten on the towel and picked up the syringe filled with formula. Like everyone at 206 Marketing Group, he was well practiced in feeding and caring for motherless kittens. It came with the job. During the interview process, all prospective employees were warned that there were nearly always cats in the building, along with Tori's dog. Those with a severe pet allergy might want to think about working elsewhere.

Once everyone had their cupcakes and drinks, Heather took control of the meeting.

"We'll start with experiential marketing," she said, glancing to her left.

As she listened to the update, Heather thought about how fortunate she was in her work life. With Elliot's wise counsel, she'd avoided many of the pitfalls that came with starting a new business. She'd been well funded and had been able to lure away top talent and clients. Four years after opening its doors, the company was thriving and so was she. At least professionally. The rest of her life was a disaster.

Well, not all of it—just the romantic part, driven by her inability to commit. Or say the L word. Okay, and she had trust issues. There was also the confusion of equally wanting and not wanting to meet her birth father. Plus, her mother. Other than that, she was the picture of mental health.

And while most of those problems could be solved—with the exception of her mother—dealing with them made her uncomfortable. Which was why she had a new batch of foster kittens with which to distract herself.

Better kittens than emotional self-exploration, she thought. Maybe, at the end of the day, business success was enough and the relationship stuff wasn't necessary. A lie, of course, but one she thought she could embrace fully. At least for now.

"Is she asleep? Dad said not to bug her if she's asleep."

"She's not asleep. She can hear us."

"We're going to get in big trouble if we wake her. She worked really late last night."

Daphne Brown stayed perfectly still, doing her best not to smile as she listened to her stepkids loudly whispering from just outside the master bedroom. Usually, the three of them slept in on weekends, but they were excited to go hiking with their dad and uncles, so they'd bounced out of bed at six. She'd ignored the pounding of their steps as they raced downstairs, but there was no way to sleep through their talking.

"I want to say good morning," Alexa, the youngest of the three, said more loudly.

Daphne rolled onto her back, bumping into Albert and Vanessa. Albert, a Siamese mix, raised his head and stared disdainfully at the children in the doorway. He was very much a one-person cat and Brody's three were not his people. In contrast, Vanessa, a beautiful calico, loved the world and expected it to love her back. She stood with an obvious expectation of cuddles and pets.

She was not disappointed. The kids threw themselves onto the bed, wrestling with each other to see who could snuggle closest, Alexa dragging Vanessa with her.

"You're awake! You're awake!"

Elijah, ten and the oldest, spoke for the siblings. He was a natural-born leader and Daphne thought he had the potential to be president. "We already had breakfast. Dad made pancakes. But don't worry. We cleaned up the mess."

She sat up and shoved the pillows behind her back. Elijah settled on her left while Cadin and Alexa shared her right side. Vanessa climbed on her lap and Albert moved away to a safe distance where he could observe and judge.

"You cleaned up?" Daphne asked with a grin. "On purpose?"

They all laughed. Alexa proudly explained, "I started it. I cleared my plate and put it on the counter. I got an extra disk."

"You did? That's amazing!"

In their house, good behavior was rewarded with a small plastic disk. Elijah's were green and Cadin's were blue—the Seattle Seahawks colors—while Alexa's were bright purple for the University of Washington Huskies. Disks were collected in a box and every few weeks, one was drawn. The kid whose disk was drawn got to be king or queen for the day, choosing dinner and the evening's entertainment.

"How were the pancakes?" Daphne asked, putting her arms around her brood. "Excellent?"

"Superior," Cadin said.

"Outstanding!" Elijah told her.

Alexa looked up at her and grinned. "They were very, very good."

"Did you leave any for me?"

Smiles faded as the kids stared at her in confusion.

"Dad said you didn't want any," Elijah told her.

Her good mood drained away, leaving the exhaustion that came from only five hours of sleep. Just as unpleasant was the proof that Brody was still pissed at her and showing it in every passive-aggressive way possible.

Aware of the three watching her, she faked a huge smile as she said, "But I do want my coffee."

They scrambled off the bed.

"I'll pour," Elijah said, beating the others to the top of the landing.

"I'll get the milk."

"I'll get the mug."

"No running on the stairs," she called, then turned to her cats and softened her voice. "I didn't want his pancakes, anyway. Maybe I'll go out to breakfast. Because men are stupid poopieheads."

Albert rubbed her face with his in agreement.

Daphne pulled her robe over the T-shirt and yoga pants that she slept in when the kids were with them. Sexy nightgowns only happened on alternate weeks. Since the change in the parenting plan three months ago—with every other weekend replaced by shared custody and the children here alternating weeks—she'd been living a strange half-life. Half the time she and Brody could do what they wanted without worrying about soccer or summer programs. The other half they were harried working parents and she had to deal with meals for five and doctors' appointments, not to mention homework, playdates, shopping and activities, while maintaining her seventy- to eighty-hour workweek. She loved having the kids around and looked forward to spending time with them, but she was exhausted. Making partner within a month of the custody change had been exciting but had added to her stress level. And now she and Brody were fighting.

She went downstairs to the kitchen. The scent of pancakes and bacon lingered, but there was no evidence of the meal. Brody hadn't even saved her a couple of pieces of bacon. The kids had her coffee ready. She smiled and thanked them, then took a sip.

"Heaven," she told them.

They laughed.

"What time are you leaving?" she asked Elijah.

"Nine," he told her. "Grant and Campbell are coming here and we're going to the deli for sandwiches. Dad said it's a two-hour drive to the trailhead, so we won't be back until four or five."

Daphne did the math. Two hours there and back, so four hours in total. Say a half hour for a lunch break, which left three and a half hours for hiking. Not her idea of a fun day, and she wasn't sure Alexa was going to be up for that much, either.

"You going to be okay with all those men?" she asked the six-year-old, careful to keep her voice teasing.

"I'll be in charge." Alexa batted her eyelashes.

Daphne grinned. "You go, girl." Her humor faded. "You'll tell your dad if you get tired."

"She'll be fine."

Brody had entered the kitchen. Most days the sight of his dark hair and broad shoulders still made her swoon a little. He was a handsome man with an easy charm that had caught her attention immediately. Their courtship had been fast, intense and everything she'd dreamed of. She'd fallen for his kids, too, adored his brothers, got along with his ex-wife and until two weeks ago, had thought they had a solid marriage.

"Is it a steep trail?" she asked him. "She's small and she can't always keep up. Maybe she should stay home with me."

His dark eyes sharpened. "You said you'd be *working*."

Daphne held in a flinch. There it was again—that tone. Why did he have to be so difficult?

"I am, but here and only for a couple of hours." She looked at Alexa. "We could go to lunch and a movie."

Alexa glanced between them as if not sure what to say. Judging from their concerned expressions and tense body language, Brody's kids had figured out there was something wrong.

"Alexa, you're coming with us," Brody said firmly. He pointed to the doorway. "All of you, go get dressed. Layers. It'll be cool when we start, but hot as we hike the trail."

They trooped out of the kitchen, leaving the adults by themselves. Daphne picked up her coffee, then set it down.

"Alexa shouldn't go. She's going to fall behind, then she'll cry and you'll get mad and yell at her, which will make things worse. She's only six. She can't hike for three hours."

Her husband glared at her. "I think I know my children a little better than you do."

Her temper rose. His "I'm the real parent and you're not" attitude was new and annoying.

"Why?" she asked. "I spend as much time with them. But sure, if you want to be a jerk, go ahead. You're getting good at it."

He crossed his arms over his chest. "I'm not being a jerk. I'm taking my kids out for a hike with their uncles."

"Oh, Brody, come on. Making breakfast for everyone but me? Being stubborn about Alexa? You know I'm right about her being too small, but you'd rather she suffer than admit that." She pressed her hands against the island. "At some point you have to stop being pissed long enough to have a conversation with me."

His eyes narrowed. "I'm not pissed, as you describe it, Daphne. I found out my wife had an affair with someone she works with. *Pissed* doesn't come close to explaining what I feel."

The exhaustion returned and with it a need to defend herself for the thousandth time.

"I didn't have an affair," she said quietly, aware of three sets of ears upstairs. "You know I didn't. Miguel and I are colleagues and friends. We have lunch. I have lunch with lots of people and many of them are men. If you hired women in your department, you'd have lunch with them. It's a business thing. It's what happens."

Brody moved closer to her, anger radiating from him in waves. "He sent you flowers."

She tried not to flinch, aware that the flower thing was bad. "He did and I was as surprised as you."

"I doubt that."

She ignored him and kept talking. "I told him he shouldn't do that."

She'd been very direct in the note she'd dropped off at his office, first thanking him for the flowers, but then telling Miguel sending them wasn't appropriate and that he should never do it again.

"You kept them!"

She threw up her hands. "Yes. My assistant thought they were from you. Throwing them in the trash would send all kinds of messages that would create trouble."

"You didn't tell me about the flowers."

Score one for him, she thought grimly. "I didn't. I've already apologized for that and I'm happy to do so again. I was wrong. I should have said something. I was surprised and didn't know what to say. So I kept quiet."

And had put the flowers on her credenza and forgotten about them until Brody had showed up to take her to lunch two days later. Her assistant had complimented him on flowers he hadn't sent and it had all been a shit storm ever since.

"Brody, please. Miguel and I are just friends. There's nothing between us. There never has been. I'm not interested in anyone else and even if for some crazy reason I was, I have no time for an affair. As you're always pointing out, I run from work to home and back. I love you and the kids and our life. We're happy together. At least we were."

She thought about adding they rarely fought, only lately that was all they did. First about the baby and now this.

"You want me to let it go," he said bitterly. "But you won't even admit what it was. You can pretend all you want, but you had an affair with that man. Until you stop lying to me and possibly yourself, this can't be fixed."

He stalked out of the kitchen. Daphne held in a scream. Why was he being so unreasonable? An affair? Seriously? The last thing she wanted was more stress in her life. Why did Brody have to be like this?

She drew in a breath, then exhaled sharply. The stupid flowers, she thought resentfully. She should have tossed them and let Irena, her assistant, think what she wanted. Then none of this would have happened. But she hadn't and now Brody was determined to make her pay for something she hadn't done.

She and Miguel were work friends, nothing more. They had lunch and okay, the occasional drink in one of their offices when they worked late, but she did the same with some of the other partners. Less often, perhaps, but it happened. She was friends with lots of people at the office. As for the flowers, Miguel had apologized for overstepping and that had been that. Or so she'd thought.

But God forbid Brody should believe her very rational explanation. Instead, he accused her of having an affair and was turning into an unreasonable goat of a man.

She dumped her cold coffee. After feeding Albert and Vanessa, she went upstairs to shower, only to find Alexa waiting in her bedroom.

The little girl ran to her and hugged her tight. "Are you mad at me?"

Daphne dropped to her knees. "Sweetie, why would I be mad?"

Tears filled Alexa's big brown eyes. "Because I said I want to go with Daddy instead of staying with you. But I want to do both, cross my heart."

"I know." She smoothed her hair off her forehead. "I want you to go with your daddy if that makes you happy. I'd never be mad about that. I'm just worried that it's too much. So you need to be able to say when you get tired."

"I will. I don't want to be left behind. They always leave me behind because I'm the youngest and I'm small."

"But mighty in spirit," Daphne told her.

Alexa grinned. "I'm powerful." Her smile faded. "Can we go to lunch and a movie next Saturday I'm here?"

"We can." Daphne pulled her close. "It's a date."

Order restored, Alexa broke free. "I have to get dressed."

"Yes, you do."

She ran out of the room. Daphne walked into the master bath where she locked the door. Once she'd showered, she would take a look at her to-do list. With everyone gone until late afternoon, she could focus on work for a few hours, then get everything else done and possibly have time for a quick nap. Far better than what she really wanted to do, which was curl up and have a lengthy cry as she tried to figure out how to get her marriage back on track when her husband was furious with her for something she hadn't done.

two

"You look beautiful tonight," Kyle said with a smile. "You look beautiful every time I see you, but there's a little extra sparkle tonight."

"Thanks," Tori said with a laugh. "I feel sparkly."

Some of it came from the ten additional minutes she'd spent on her makeup, and some of it was because after almost three dates with Kyle, she was starting to feel the tiniest whisper of hope. Maybe, just maybe, for once, she'd picked a good guy. Not a deadbeat loser who would hit her up for a loan or a man who'd fathered five kids with five different women and didn't bother with any of them, or a guy who said he loved her, then left because he felt too much. Because the truth was, Tori seemed to attract—and be attracted to—less than perfect men.

She held in a sigh. Okay, more than less than perfect, but so far two and a tenth dates in, Kyle seemed different.

"How was your day?" He leaned toward her as he spoke, as if he was really interested in what she had to say.

"Good. I'm starting on the campaign for a new client."

"How does that happen? Do you come up with the ideas yourself?"

"Usually, we brainstorm directions as a team. I do some preliminary designs so we can decide on a style. Contemporary, nostalgic, cutting edge? Who's the target audience? In a perfect world, I'll come up with something that spans demographics, but initially, there's a more specific group I'm trying to reach."

Their server appeared and took their drink orders.

"What did you do today?" she asked when the man had left.

"Three dental cleanings and a couple of well-puppy visits," he told her.

Kyle was a veterinarian. They'd met at the dog park a couple of weeks ago when she'd taken Scout and Zeus for some playtime. He'd been there with a beautiful black lab. While the dogs had made friends, she and Kyle had started talking.

"Don't talk about puppies," she said with a laugh. "I'm always tempted. My friends are all into cats, but if it were up to me, there would be puppies every day."

He chuckled. "They're a lot of fun. Today I saw a three-month-old beagle. He was a cute little guy who—"

"Hello, Kyle."

Tori glanced at the woman who had stopped by their table. She was in her midthirties and casually dressed for the upscale restaurant. But it was her expression—part disbelief, part resignation, overlaid with vibrating anger—that most caught Tori's attention.

"Olivia." Kyle paled. "What are you doing here?"

"I followed you."

Tori's *oh crap, this is going to be bad* radar kicked in. Something was happening and things were about to turn yucky.

Olivia looked at her. "Where did you meet?"

The random question surprised her. "At, um, the dog park."

"Of course." Her expression turned pitying. "It's not his dog. We were pet sitting for a friend."

Tori's throat tightened as her stomach lurched. Apprehension morphed into dread. "We?" She looked at Kyle, who was staring at the table. "We?"

"He's married, with two kids," Olivia told her. "He's a truck driver for a local delivery company. And he cheats. A lot."

No. Just no. Tori looked at Kyle. "Married?"

"I'm sorry."

Sorry? He was sorry?

There were a thousand things she could say. The cutlery was heavy—she could throw her fork at his head. But to what end? Once again, her hopes and dreams had been crushed by cruel reality. All she wanted was to find a good guy, fall in love and live a happy, albeit ordinary, life. A couple of kids, dogs, vacations. Growing old together and being able to look back on years of good, solid memories.

Which was, she thought as she rose, too much to ask. At least in her little corner of the universe. Humiliation burned. She'd been a fool. Again.

"I didn't know," she told Olivia.

"I guessed that." Her tone, like her expression, was pitying. No doubt she thought Tori was pathetic—something Tori found herself agreeing with.

She slipped on her coat and quickly walked outside. A light misty rain fell, but she didn't bother with her umbrella. She hurried to the valet stand and handed over her ticket, grateful she'd driven herself. Better to be able to leave right away than to have to wait for an Uber, terrified she would have to face Olivia again.

Married. That was bad, even for her. She expected a loser, or at the very least, a guy who would leave, because if they weren't jerks, they left. But married? Why?

She tipped the valet and got into her small SUV. As she drove toward her condo in Bellevue she wondered if she'd missed any signs. How could she have not known he was married?

She parked at her building, then took the elevator to the third floor where she had a good-size one-bedroom with a den condo. There was a large south-facing deck and plenty of windows to let in light. But instead of entering her own unit, she went next door, knocked once, then used her key to let herself in.

"It's me," she said, going for cheerful but knowing she'd fallen flat.

Scout, her mini Labradoodle and Zeus, Grant's golden retriever, raced to greet her. They whined and spun and nosed each other out of the way so they could be petted first. The enthusiastic greeting eased a few of the sharp edges of her shame.

"Hey, guys," she said, petting them both before shrugging out of her coat and stepping out of her heels.

Grant stepped out of the kitchen, a bowl of cereal in one hand. He frowned.

"You're home early."

"I know."

"Too early." He put down the bowl on the breakfast bar. "What happened?"

"I don't want to talk about it."

One dark eyebrow rose, but he didn't speak. She told herself she could outwait him, that while they were friends, she wasn't required to share any part of her personal life with him. Five seconds later she said, "He's married."

Grant's expression softened into concern. He held open his arms.

She crossed to him and let him give her one of his *everything is going to be okay* hugs.

"Asshole," he muttered.

"And worse." She stepped back and told herself to just get the telling over with. "I thought he was a good guy. A possibility. There we were, ordering drinks and having a good time, when his wife showed up."

Scout leaned against her. Tori scratched her ears. "It was so humiliating. He lied about everything. He's not a vet. That wasn't even his dog."

She felt her eyes starting to burn and willed herself not to cry. Kyle wasn't worth the tears. "I'm such an idiot."

"You're not," Grant said, walking into the kitchen. "There was no way you could know he was a lying shit who cheated on his wife."

As he spoke, he poured her a cup of coffee. She was about to protest that she would never sleep if she drank coffee this late, but then he added a couple of ounces of Jameson Irish Whiskey to her mug. She got the can of whipped cream from the fridge and squirted on a generous dollop, then took the Irish coffee from him.

In the living room, Grant took his undoctored coffee and settled on one of the big club chairs. She sat on the sofa, tucking her legs under her. Both dogs jumped up to get comfortable.

"Tell me," Grant said, his voice kind. "What happened?"

She recounted the brief but painful encounter. When she'd finished, she said, "What's wrong with me? I either pick guys who leave or I find jerks like Kyle. I just want a normal, nice man to fall in love with."

"You say you want that, but the truth is you look for guys who leave because they reinforce your belief that people you love won't stay."

"Ouch," she said, but without a lot of energy. She'd heard Grant's theories on her inability to find "the one" for over a year now. The man did love to psychoanalyze. One would think that being an ER doctor would keep him in his medical lane, but no. He was forever speculating about her love life.

"Even if you're right," she added, "and I'm not saying you are…"

He smiled. "Of course not."

"Explain Kyle. He wasn't giving out 'I leave' signals."

"That was just bad luck. He sounds like a player and you got caught up in the game." His dark gaze was steady. "You didn't do anything wrong."

"I know."

"You say the words but I don't think you believe them."

"I feel stupid."

And humiliated and small, but why get into that? She sipped more of her coffee. It went down way too smoothly. On the bright side, all she had to do tonight was wash off her makeup and put on jammies. So what if she got a little buzzed? Netflix wouldn't care. She didn't even have to walk Scout. Grant would take her out with Zeus, right before his shift at the hospital.

"Don't waste a lot of mental energy on Kyle," he said. "You need to get back out there."

She rolled her eyes. "Seriously? You're telling me to not give up on dating? You, Mr. I-haven't-been-on-a-date-or-had-sex-since-my-divorce-fourteen-months-ago? You're not someone I want to take dating advice from."

"Those who can, do," he said calmly. "Those who are still healing from a bad divorce, advise. Tori, you want to find someone. You want to be connected and in a family. Don't stop looking because of Kyle. He doesn't deserve that much power."

She sagged back against the cushions. "I know you're right." She shifted her gaze to his. "Want to know the worst part? I didn't feel any sparks. I told myself that it was better to find someone decent than worry about attraction. I was willing to settle."

"Don't. You deserve better."

"I deserve to win the lottery but do you see that happening?"

"You don't play."

"There is that."

"Eight-thirty," he said. "Time for me to walk the dogs."

She nodded and stood. As she passed Grant on her way to the kitchen, he stretched out his hand. She ducked out of reach and glared at him.

"Stop trying to ruffle my hair. It's annoying."

"You look cute with mussed hair."

"I look cute all the time. I swear if you do that again, I'll kick you in the balls."

His lopsided grin was familiar. "Cheap talk."

"It is. Eventually, you're going to want to start using them again and I don't want to be the reason you can't."

He was still laughing as she grabbed her coat and slipped on her shoes. Scout glanced between her and Grant, as if unsure where to go.

"Grant's taking you, baby girl," she said, touching her dog's face. Scout moved next to him.

Tori waved, then walked the short distance to her own condo. She flipped on lights as she went inside. Grant's huge corner unit was about twenty-one hundred square feet, with two bedrooms and two and a half baths. She had sixteen hundred square feet, which was plenty for her and Scout.

She changed into pajamas covered in dancing daisies, then washed her face. She'd just finished braiding her long, curly hair when she heard a knock on her front door. Grant entered seconds later, both dogs with him.

Scout and Zeus made a beeline for her. Grant stayed by the door. He'd already changed into scrubs and athletic shoes, and had an insulated lunch tote in one hand.

"Usual shift?" she asked.

"Ten to seven."

Which often meant not leaving the hospital until closer to eight in the morning. "I'll drop off Zeus on my way to work."

He nodded. "You okay?"

She sighed. "No, but I will be. In the meantime, I'll watch *The Queen's Gambit* again and eat too much ice cream."

He crossed to her, pulled her close and kissed the top of her head. "Hang in there, kid. We'll find you someone."

"I hope so. Now you need to get going. Lives are depending on you."

He grinned. "I am pretty special."

"Yes, but I'm pretty."

He was still laughing as he walked out and shut the door behind him.

Tori chose a half-full carton of Mukilteo Mudd ice cream. She carried it and a spoon to her bedroom. Scout and Zeus followed, politely waiting until she was settled before jumping on the bed. She turned on the Netflix app. As her programs loaded, she adjusted the pillows until she was comfortably propped up.

But instead of picking up the remote again, she stared at the screen and wondered how long it would take to think about tonight without feeling sick to her stomach.

It wasn't just herself she had to deal with. Tomorrow she would see Heather at work and her boss/friend would, of course, ask about the date. Then one of them would share the info with Daphne, who would tell Brody. Either Brody or Grant would tell their third brother, Campbell, so her entire circle of close friends would know about her humiliation.

She knew they would all be sympathetic, but wished that for once, she could be the happy, settled friend who was offering the strong shoulder instead of the one in need of moral support. Not that they would agree. They loved her—she knew that—just like she loved them. She was lucky when it came to her friends. Less lucky when it came to men.

Heather's alarm chirped at two-thirty in the morning. She forced herself to sit up before silencing the annoying sound. When she turned on the bedside lamp, she was greeted by a very sharp *meow*—one that implied LC had been waiting for her to get up for a while now and why wouldn't she cooperate more?

"I'm ignoring you," Heather told the cat. She went into the bathroom and splashed water on her face before going to the kitchen. Once the kitten formula was made, she grabbed all the supplies and walked into the second bedroom—aka the cat sanctuary.

LC's litter box was here, along with a huge cat tree. There were toys, beds and a large playpen where her current rescue litter was already stirring.

"Feeding time," she said softly. "How's everyone doing?"

LC watched as she carefully weighed each kitten and recorded the amount on her phone. An app told her how much formula they should get and if they were growing as expected.

"Come here, Russell Wilson," she murmured as she picked up the kitten with the blue collar. "Time for a yummy meal."

LC hovered nearby, watching her closely, as if ready to jump in if she did something wrong.

"Would that you could, big guy," she told him.

Russell Wilson latched on right away. When he was done eating, she burped him, then got him to do his bathroom thing.

"And we're done," she said as she put him back into the playpen on the blanket-covered heating pad. LC immediately jumped in with him and began grooming him, pausing every now and then to give her stink eye.

"You're a horrible creature," Heather told him as she picked up the second kitten. "After five years, you really should warm up to me."

Only she knew he wouldn't. LC hadn't liked her from the start, but he'd been part of a bonded pair and she'd totally fallen in love with his sister Willow, so she'd brought him home, as well. He was the opposite of his sister. Willow loved the world and Heather most of all. She'd been a snuggle bug, sweet tempered and a joy to live with. LC endured his time with Heather because he didn't have a choice. There were a few humans he liked and one he loved, but Heather didn't fall into either category.

Unfortunately, two years ago Willow had died of large cell lymphoma. She'd gone from a happy, healthy cat to dying in less than two weeks, leaving both Heather and LC stunned. She'd thought maybe the loss would bring them closer together, but LC remained firmly in the "I hate Heather" camp.

She finished with the second kitten, then picked up the last one. The night was quiet, the condo still. As she worked, she ignored the voice that whispered she was still lonely and maybe she should do something about that. That less than thirty minutes away was a very handsome man who had told her he loved her and wanted to spend his life with her.

Thinking about Campbell made her chest hurt a little. It was easy to be tough during the day but at three in the morning, well, she just wasn't. At this hour, while feeding kittens, she often wondered how things would have been if she could have said, "Sure, let's move in together." Or even some version of, "Yes, I love you." Only she hadn't done either. She couldn't. Taking a chance on giving her heart was beyond impossible. There was too much risk and not enough reward. But that didn't mean she didn't miss him.

"You loved him," she said to LC. Her grumpy cat had taken one look at Campbell and had fallen hard. With him, LC was a puddle of love, purring, snuggling. It had been a kind of joke between them. The last time she and Campbell had ended things, she'd offered him the cat because they were obviously meant to be together. But Campbell hadn't taken it that way at all. He'd looked at her as if she was the cruelest person ever born and had told her to "stop throwing away hearts that love you."

Even now his words made her shrink inside. That hadn't been what she'd meant at all. She hadn't been throwing away LC, she'd been offering what she'd seen as a way to make both him and Campbell happy.

She'd tried to explain but he wouldn't listen, then she'd gotten defensive because she always did and they'd said things and she'd left and that had been the end. And even after all this time, she still missed him and sometimes, at three in the morning, she wondered if she'd been wrong to let him go.

She finished with the last kitten and put her next to LC. After making sure the heating pad was at the right temperature and was completely covered by the blanket, she lightly patted LC.

"You could come sleep with me."

LC shifted slightly so his back was to her, the message very clear. The rejection wasn't new but for some reason, it stung more than usual. She collected her supplies and walked out of the cat room.

After cleaning up, she got back in bed and willed herself to go to sleep. But instead of closing her eyes, she found herself staring at the ceiling and wishing she'd tried harder with Campbell. The man loved her and wanted her to move in with him. Was that so awful? Why hadn't she been able to cooperate a little?

But the thought of committing, telling him she loved him, had terrified her. In truth, outside of her two cousins who helped raise her, she'd never told anyone she loved them. Not a girlfriend, certainly never a man. It was too big a risk. Too awful to consider. Which left her in the horrible position of wanting the very thing that terrified her and in the process, losing Campbell completely.

three

Tori quickly exchanged her dancing daisy pj's for yoga pants and a sweatshirt before sliding her feet into clogs. Zeus and Scout watched from the soft comfort of her bed, with identical expressions of "We're fine. Let's sleep longer."

"I'm ignoring you," Tori told them both as she headed down the hall, toward the front of her condo.

It was barely after six in the morning, but in late July in the Pacific Northwest, that meant the sun had already been up for two hours. Even better, the skies were clear with the promise of a beautiful day.

"Let's go," she called as she collected poop bags and leashes. The dogs joined her, then the three of them went down the elevator to the ground level and their familiar morning route.

Tori didn't mind the early-morning walk. Scout and Zeus

were good company and the quiet neighborhood was pretty. The only thing that could make it better would be if someone parked a coffee kiosk on a corner. Sadly, that had never happened. As they crossed the street, she checked in with her heart and found it was untouched by the Kyle disaster from the previous evening, however, her pride was still battered. She knew she'd been played and wasn't responsible for yucky Kyle, but she couldn't escape a sense of shame and embarrassment for not figuring out he was married.

An hour later both dogs were fed and she'd texted Grant that she was nearly out of Zeus's food. She'd showered and dressed for work. By seven-thirty she was letting Zeus into Grant's condo.

"Your dad will be home in a little bit," she said, petting the dog. Zeus wagged his tail in agreement and settled on the sofa for a nap while Scout went with her to the parking garage. The mini Labradoodle settled in the back seat of Tori's small SUV.

A forty-minute fight with traffic later, she pulled into an upscale office complex and slipped into her parking space. She and Scout went into the building and up to their floor where Scout made the rounds to greet everyone already there before returning to Tori's office and her big, fluffy bed in the corner.

Tori turned on her three computer screens and pulled up the work she'd started for the Mountain Goat Northwest campaign. While what she'd come up with so far was good, it wasn't great. She was hoping for inspiration.

She went onto her favorite photography sites, focusing on mountain shots and pictures of skiers, but the poses were all too familiar. She wanted edgy, young and inclusive. The campaign would be experiential, but it all started with an idea. She looked at pictures from extreme winter sports and found an interesting image of lone ski tracks in a blizzard.

"Somebody always takes the long way," she murmured,

quickly drawing on her sketch pad. "Or maybe sometimes you *need* to take the long way."

She purchased the license for the image and loaded it onto one of her screens, then returned to her drawing. Mountain Goat Northwest wanted their first campaign to revolve around some kind of party. Not a unique concept, but workable, Tori thought, her hand flying across the paper as she did a down and dirty storyboard of young, fit people arriving at the MGNW party in various modes of transportation. Including the lone skier because sometimes the long way was... What? Worth it? Important?

Scout nudged her hand. Tori forced her attention away from the pad and looked at her dog.

"Really? Already?"

Usually, Scout only had to go out a couple of times a day. But as Tori stood, she realized she was stiff from sitting in one position for—she glanced at her clock. Yikes. Four hours.

"Out we go," she said.

On her way to the front of the building, Heather fell into step with her.

"I haven't seen you all morning," her boss/friend said.

"I've been storyboarding. I'll have something in a couple of hours. It's rough but has potential."

"I can't wait." Heather smiled. "So how was last night?"

With her head still stuck in campaign mode, it took Tori a second to understand. Last night as in...

"What?" Heather asked anxiously. "Was he a jerk? Did he expect sex too soon?"

Tori walked to the grass alongside the building. "Worse. He's married. His wife showed up." She detailed the nightmare. "He lied about everything. That wasn't even his dog. I feel so stupid."

"Why? You had no way of knowing."

"He seemed too good to be true. That should have been a clue. I have terrible luck when it comes to men."

"You do seem to find the bad ones. I'm sorry for what happened but it's not on you."

"I hear the words and I believe them, but in my gut I think it has to be me. I'm the common denominator in all these relationships." She moved so Scout could sniff a few bushes. "I just want somebody nice, who makes my heart skip a beat every now and then. Why is that too much to ask?"

"It's not. He's out there. You'll find him."

Tori smiled. "I mean this with love, but you are the most emotionally stunted person I know. I'm not sure your advice is helpful."

Heather laughed. "Fair enough."

Tori paused, not sure if she should mention the weekend or not. "We're having brunch Sunday."

Heather's expression tightened. "I'm busy."

"You're avoiding us." Tori touched her arm. "We miss you. It's not the same without you."

Once or twice a month, her group of friends met for brunch. She and Grant were the non-couple friends, Daphne and Brody came, along with Campbell. Back when he and Heather had been dating, she'd always showed up, but lately...

"I miss having you around with everyone else," Tori admitted.

"It would be too awkward. Didn't you say Campbell's dating someone?"

"Yes. I don't think it's serious, but even if it is, you said you're totally done with him. So can't we all be a family again?"

"The seven of us?" Heather asked drily. "That would be fun."

"It could be. Or you could start dating someone and bring

him along. Just think about it. We're meeting at Life's a Yolk at ten."

"I'll think about it."

Tori wanted to believe her, but in her heart of hearts, she doubted Heather would be there. The once-tight group was changing—something she didn't like, or know how to stop.

Sunday morning Heather couldn't shake the sense of restlessness that had gripped her for days. She'd fed the kittens early and had made a to-do list for the day. She would do laundry, go for a run, get groceries and care for the kittens. Busy, busy, that was her. But even as she went through the refrigerator to figure out what she needed, she found herself glancing at the clock and thinking about what Tori had said about brunch.

She missed hanging out with everyone the way she had when she and Campbell had been together. She missed the sense of belonging and how they all treated her like she was totally normal. She missed the closeness, the laughter, having Campbell come over after so they could spend a couple of hours in bed.

She missed him and after all this time, she couldn't help wondering if maybe she'd made a mistake when she'd ended things. The man had wanted them to move in together with the idea of getting married eventually. Was that so wrong? So twisted? She should have said yes. She could possibly, maybe, think about almost living with someone. How hard could it be?

She glanced from the unfinished grocery list to the clock and back, then tossed down her pen and ran to her bedroom. She dressed quickly, put on a little makeup and brushed her shoulder-length blond hair. Would he notice her new bangs?

"Does it matter?" she muttered to herself. She grabbed her

purse and her keys, called out to LC that she was leaving and walked purposefully to her car before she could talk herself out of going.

She nearly turned around three times, but managed to drive all the way to his townhouse. As she parked, she wondered if he was even home. She no longer knew his schedule, so he could be spending the night in Wichita before flying home.

"One way to find out," she said as she walked up to the front door and rang the bell.

Seconds later the door opened and Campbell stood in front of her, looking tall and handsome in jeans and a polo shirt.

Her heart unexpectedly fluttered and her palms got sweaty. The visceral reaction startled her, but also made her even more determined to just spit out the truth and get things right between them.

His brows drew together. "Heather? What are you doing here?"

"I, ah, wanted to talk to you."

"This isn't a good time."

His voice was unexpectedly stern, which surprised her. "It'll only take a second. Please?"

He hesitated, then stepped back to let her in. "I have five minutes."

She nodded and followed him into the townhouse. He looked so good. Familiar. Campbell had always been there for her, had fallen hard, had spoken his feelings easily. She'd been the one who held back and the one who had walked away.

"I know I have issues," she told him, twisting her fingers together. "It's hard for me to trust anyone." She drew in a breath. "Okay, nearly impossible, but the thing is I miss you."

She paused, hoping he would say something, but his slightly impatient expression didn't change.

"I thought maybe we could try again," she continued,

thinking she should have planned what she was going to say more than she had. Or at all. "I've changed."

Which was a complete lie, but maybe if she worked on changing starting now, she could make some quick progress.

"I want to be like everyone else," she told him. "You know, normal. With connections to people and feelings. I'm open to us living together if you still want that."

Which was the most she'd ever offered. Would it be enough? Because if he asked if she loved him, she had no idea what she was going to say. She cared about him and wanted to get back together with him, but honestly, what was love?

He stared at her for several seconds, then shook his head. "You ended things three months ago and you're just now thinking you miss me? What about the time before that when you announced, at my brother's wedding, that we were finished? You've dumped me twice."

He took a step back. "I'm done, Heather. I've moved on and even if I hadn't, you're too broken for me. I know a lot of the problem is what your mom did to you while you were growing up. I know it's probably not your fault, but I can't deal with you. Not again. You're not what I want. I've found someone else and we're happy."

His mouth flattened. "I'm not trying to be a jerk. I'm telling you the truth. There's no third chance. I hope you find what you're looking for but it won't be with me."

The harsh words hit her like fists and she nearly doubled over from the unexpected attack. Air rushed from her lungs and the room spun. But on the heels of the pain came a need to run and hide. Standing there, she was too exposed, too out in the open. What else would he say? What other flaws would he bring to light?

She lunged for the door, pulled it open, ran to her car and got inside. She barely checked for traffic before heading onto the quiet side street. Home was her only safe space. She had to get there before she lost it completely. Not that there would be tears. She didn't believe in them.

Too broken. Too broken. *Too broken.*

The words echoed over and over in her head. Shame engulfed her, nearly bigger than the hurt. All this time she'd thought he cared about her. He'd told her he loved her, he'd talked about forever, but he hadn't meant any of it. He couldn't have. Not when he'd figured out the truth she'd done her best to hide. She *was* too broken. Whatever mechanism made it possible for people to love was missing in her. Or it had been crushed by her upbringing. Or maybe both. She wasn't sure it mattered. All she knew was that she'd both lost Campbell forever and had her deepest, most painful flaw laid out for all to see. And she had no idea which was worse.

Tori and Scout walked the few steps to Grant's condo. She knocked once, then opened the door.

"It's me."

Scout joined Zeus on the sofa. Seconds later Grant walked out of the master. "Morning," he said with a smile. "Ready to go?"

"Yes, I'm starving."

"You're always hungry."

"Not always. Just at mealtime, and breakfast should have been two hours ago."

They walked toward the elevator.

"I'll drive," he said.

"You always drive. Why is that? I have a nice enough car."

"I have a nicer SUV. It's doctor nice."

She rolled her eyes. "Yes, you make more than me, but my job is more fun."

"I save lives."

"Show-off."

"I can't avoid my greatness."

They reached the garage and he held open the passenger door. After she slid onto the seat, he touched her arm.

"How are you feeling?"

"Fine. Oh, you're asking if I'm still licking my wounds about Kyle." She reached for her seat belt. "He was an asshole and I'm better off without him."

"You are, but are you all right?"

"I'm fine. I feel slightly less stupid. Last night I did a beauty mask." She motioned to her face. "How could you not notice?"

"That you're glowing?"

"Yeah, it was a ten-dollar mask."

He chuckled. "I have no idea what to say."

"Then feed me."

Once he was in the car, she said, "Are you exhausted? I don't know how you keep switching up your schedule. You work four nights, then have three days off when you live on a more normal schedule, then back to nights. I couldn't do it."

"I have a lot of practice."

"Your circadian rhythm must look like a pretzel."

"What does a normal one look like?"

"Kind of a loopy oval."

"You read that in a medical journal?"

She gave him a pitying look. "Everyone knows what a circadian rhythm looks like. You should switch to days." A familiar argument and one she never won.

"I'm thinking about it."

She stared at him. "Seriously? You'd change your shift?"

"Maybe."

"That would be weird. We have a whole schedule that totally works for us."

"We'd figure out a new one."

"Wow. Days. I'm all astonishment. Is Campbell going to be at brunch?"

"As far as I know."

"I wonder if he's bringing Nora. I hope he isn't."

"I thought you liked her."

"No. Don't say that. It's disloyal. Heather's my friend."

"She dumped him. Twice. It's okay to like Nora."

"So says the man. Nora is a sweetie, but I miss hanging out with Heather."

"You work with her. You see her every day."

"Not on weekends and not at brunch. I invited her, by the way."

"To brunch? When Campbell's with Nora? So it's like dinner theater?"

"Heather wouldn't make a scene."

"She wouldn't have to. The scene would occur without any help."

"Maybe we should break them up."

Grant groaned. "Campbell and Nora? No. Besides, if you did come up with a plan, which is doubtful because you're not that kind of person, knowing you broke them up would make you feel awful. Then I'd have to hear all about it."

"I just want my family back together."

"Maybe Nora can be part of your new family."

"Maybe."

But it wouldn't be the same. She'd always liked when Campbell and Heather were a couple. With them together, and Daphne and Brody married, she felt safe. Cared for, with a place where she belonged. Grant had his brothers, Daphne had Brody and his kids, plus her parents. Heather had her cousins and well, her mother, not that Amber was anyone's idea of a dream relation. But still, she was someone. While Tori's only relative was a sister who'd walked away the day Tori had grad-uated from high school. They hadn't spoken since.

"What are you doing this afternoon?" he asked.

"Taking Scout hiking."

"Really? A hike?"

She pressed her lips together. "Fine. We're going to walk a relatively easy trail."

"Want company?"

"Sure. Can we barbecue later?"

"Steaks?"

She sighed. "You're a doctor. You should know about the red meat thing. There are some really good plant-based options out there."

"So steaks?"

"Yes, steaks. I'll make that loaded potato salad you like."

"You're a good woman."

They pulled into the parking lot of Life's a Yolk. It was a few minutes before ten and the temperature was already into the seventies. Summers in Seattle could be amazing, she thought, shutting her door. Sadly, the beautiful weather would be off-set by months of gray skies and cold rain.

Daphne and Brody were already waiting at a table. In the second before they saw her and Grant, Tori noticed a distance between them. Not physically, but in the way they were sit-ting and not looking at each other. She hurried over to greet her friend, but there was no way to ask if something was wrong. They'd barely taken their seats when Campbell and Nora arrived.

After hugs and hellos, they placed their breakfast orders and passed around the coffee carafe.

"How was your week?" Nora asked her.

"Good. Busy. We have a new client at work. What about you?"

Nora, a pretty, petite blonde, who was the director of a large area preschool, smiled at Campbell before returning her attention to Tori. "Very nice."

Uh-oh. Tori didn't like that look. It was too intimate. Were they getting serious, talking about moving in together or worse?

"You mean it this time?" Brody asked Grant.

Tori turned to them as Grant nodded. "Yes. I want to go back to days."

"Finally," Brody said, while Campbell looked skeptical.

"I'll believe it when it happens," Campbell grumbled.

"Oh, he's telling the truth," Nora said with a smile. "I can see it in his eyes. And I even know why he's making the change."

"You said you were thinking about it. I don't want a new routine," Tori said.

"My little ray of sunshine," Grant teased. "It'll be fine."

"It'll be weird." She looked at Nora. "Why is he doing this?"

"He wants to fall in love."

The table went silent as everyone stared at Grant. Tori blinked several times. In love? Grant?

"Since when?" she asked. "You're not even dating."

"Close," Grant told Nora. "But no, I don't want to fall in love. I would like to *start* dating and it's hard to do that while working nights."

Brody didn't look convinced. "You said you never wanted to risk that again."

"I'm healed."

"No way," Campbell told him before turning to Nora. "Krissa, Grant's ex, was an emotional vampire. She was so dependent, she couldn't make a decision about anything without him. *Needy* doesn't come close to describing her."

Nora looked at Grant. "So you're afraid to risk love again because you don't want another Krissa in your life."

"Possibly, but I would like to get laid." He grinned. "No offense."

Nora laughed. "None taken. So you're actually looking to hook up with someone."

"I'm thinking more serial dating with a lot of sex thrown in."

Tori stared at him, not sure what to make of the revelation. "You never said anything."

"Telling you I want to get laid would make you think less of me."

"Why? We all enjoy sex. It's part of the human condition."

Grant dating? She wasn't sure how she felt about that. She liked their familiar routine. On the other hand, he'd been alone for a while now and he really deserved someone special in his life. Except...

She poked him in the arm. "You better keep it casual. We're the non-couple friends. If you fall for someone, where does that leave me?"

"You'll always have a place with us," Brody told her. "Plus, it's Grant. Who's going to be interested in him?"

He and Campbell laughed. Grant smiled good-naturedly.

"This is where I remind you I'm a doctor. That makes me a catch."

"You're a sad excuse for a man," Campbell told him.

Nora looked at Tori. "You and Grant have never..."

Never? "Slept together? God, no. We really are the non-couple friends."

Sure, he was fun to be around and nice-looking and yes, a doctor, but what she had with him was way better than anything she'd had with a guy she'd dated, and she wasn't looking for that to change.

"How did you meet?" Nora asked him.

"Brody and Daphne met first," Grant told her. "Along with Campbell and—" He stopped talking and the table went silent.

"I know about Heather," Nora told him. "It's okay."

Daphne leaned forward. "Brody and Campbell were going out to dinner. Heather and I were doing the same. There was a long wait and the four of us got to talking. We ended up sharing a table." She glanced at Brody. "And the rest is history."

Tori thought she heard something in her friend's voice, but wasn't sure.

"I met Heather at USC," Tori said. "And through her, Daphne, who was going to law school. Those two moved back up here while I got a job in LA. Three years ago Heather hired me, so I moved up here. About eighteen months ago Daphne suggested I talk to Grant about a condo in his building. I bought it and now we're next-door neighbors."

Nora sighed happily. "Nice. You really are a family."

On the drive home, Tori sagged back in her seat. "I like Nora."

"You say that as if it's a bad thing."

"It is. I love Heather."

"You can love them both."

"No, I can't."

"If Heather wanted to be with Campbell, she wouldn't have left. It's okay to like Nora."

"But it's not that simple. Heather has issues when it comes to caring about people." Tori didn't know how to explain the problem. "Her mom reminds me of how you've described Krissa. She depended on Heather for everything. The difference is Heather was a kid. Amber was capable, but she never bothered to take on any responsibility. Everything was always someone else's fault. Heather was stuck supporting them both from the time she was sixteen. If her cousins and Elliot hadn't intervened, she would still be taking care of her. Heather's afraid that if she falls in love with someone, he'll turn into her mother and suck the life out of her."

"That's not who Campbell is."

"I know, but her fears aren't rational."

"I still say if she had any feelings for Campbell she wouldn't have dumped him."

"I hope you're right." She sighed. "I feel guilty about Nora."

"Would stopping for ice cream make you feel better?"

She smiled at him. "It might."

four

Heather tried to keep busy until she was sure brunch would be over, then texted both her friends.

How serious are Campbell and Nora?

Not that their relationship mattered as much as what he'd said about her, but it was easier to worry about that than deal with the horrifying humiliation that threatened to engulf her.

A few minutes later her phone chimed.

Daphne's response, a rational Why do you ask?, was very much like her, while Tori's I know I said I don't think they're serious, but I'm less sure now was both painful to hear and yet an odd relief. Maybe Campbell said what he did because he felt guilty about being with someone else. Maybe it had been a distraction from what he was really feeling and wasn't personal at all.

She stared at her phone, then started typing. I went and saw him this morning. It didn't go well.

Dots appeared instantly. Daphne answered first. Do you need us to come over? Before she could answer, Tori said, I'm on my way.

Thanks.

Heather took care of the kittens, then sat on her large deck until she heard Tori at the front door. Her friend walked in wearing jeans, a T-shirt and hiking boots. Heather groaned.

"You had plans."

"Just to take Scout out for a long walk on one of the trails. I can still do that later."

Tori was tall, with long, dark, wavy hair and large brown eyes. Freckles dotted her nose. She constantly tried to be elegant or striking but always defaulted to simply adorable.

LC came running into the living room, making little mews of pleasure.

"LC!" Tori scooped him up and held him close. His loud purr practically echoed in the room as he rubbed his face against Tori's.

"Big guy," Tori murmured, stroking him. "You're so handsome. How have you been?"

Heather observed the over-the-top display by her cat and tried not to take it personally.

Daphne arrived a few minutes later and hugged them both before taking LC in her arms.

"What's going on?" Daphne asked bluntly. "It's been three months. Why are you going to see Campbell after all this time? We told you he was seeing someone."

Tori shot Daphne a warning look. "Maybe you could save the cross-examination until after she tells us what happened."

Daphne collapsed on the sofa. "Sorry." She cleared her throat and spoke more softly. "Wow, you going to see Campbell. That's a surprise. What's the motivation?"

Heather tried to find humor in the change of tone. She took one of the chairs and watched her cat drape himself between her two friends.

"I've been thinking about Campbell lately. Missing him. I know you said he was dating someone but I didn't think it was serious, so I went to talk to him."

Tori and Daphne exchanged a look.

"You said in your text it didn't go well," Tori said.

Heather stared at the carpet, trying not to remember their brief but painful encounter. "He said he was seeing someone and it was going great and we were through."

Tori winced while Daphne looked uncomfortable.

"You okay?" Daphne asked.

Heather debated lying, only her texting her friends in the first place was kind of the answer to the question.

"Is there something wrong with me?"

Tori's eyes widened. "No! Why would you say that? You're great."

Daphne studied her. "Heather, what's going on? What else did Campbell say?"

"He said I'd dumped him twice and he was totally over me." There was more, of course, but she wasn't ready to say the rest of it.

"Are you surprised?" Daphne asked gently. "Campbell's like Brody. Traditional, caring, wants a regular life. He's a one-man woman and he wanted you to be that woman. He adored you and you..."

"Kept breaking his heart," Tori murmured. "Sorry, but you

did. And we could never figure out why. Heather, you were so good together. You need someone solid like him. He thought you were amazing."

Thought…past tense, because he sure didn't think that now.

Daphne leaned toward her. "I don't want to be the one to say this, but I think he's serious about Nora. They've been together a while and she adores him. After what you put him through, I'm guessing that feels really good."

Not anything Heather wanted to hear, she thought grimly. But Daphne had always been the one to state the obvious. No doubt, part of her legal training. Tori led with her heart but Daphne was blunt.

"Do you like her?" Heather asked, wondering why she was torturing herself. Wasn't the day going badly enough?

"She's, um, you know, nice," Tori said, avoiding her gaze. "I don't want to like her. I talked to Grant about breaking them up but he said that was a bad idea."

Heather faked a smile. "You're too sweet to do that. You'd never forgive yourself."

Wow—so it had finally happened. Campbell had moved on, leaving her behind. Pain ripped her heart into little pieces.

She'd known she could end up here. She'd been the one to keep leaving, and no one enjoyed being dumped over and over again. It was just…

"I thought we'd find our way back to each other," she admitted. "I thought one day I'd be able to handle him caring about me and I'd tell him I wanted us to be together."

There weren't any tears, but her throat got tight and she felt close to throwing up. Campbell was gone. She'd never imagined she could lose him forever.

Tori hurried across the room and pulled her to her feet. "I'm sorry," she whispered, hugging her close. "He's stupid and I hate him."

"No, you don't. You can't."

"Then I'll hate Nora."

Heather stepped back. "Don't hate anyone for me. I created this problem, so I have to solve it." She pushed Tori toward the sofa and sat back in her own chair. "It's just going to take a while to get over him. I'll do what I always do, come up with a plan. A happiness plan."

"You are the plan queen." Daphne watched her carefully. "You okay?"

"Not yet."

Her friend's mouth twisted. "This is on Amber. She did this to you. Trapping you, using you, sucking you dry until you were terrified to trust."

"She does have mad skills," Heather said, going for humor but suspecting she only sounded pathetic.

"If she hadn't been so horrible, you'd be able to trust that Campbell was never going to treat you the way your mom did. You could be together."

"Instead, I'm stuck being broken," she said with a lightness she didn't feel, but more concerned about testing the word in front of a friendly audience.

"I wouldn't say *broken*," Tori began. "Maybe just damaged."

Daphne's gaze was sympathetic. "What else did he say? What aren't you telling us?"

"He said I wasn't what he wanted."

This time both her friends pulled her to her feet to hold her tight. She let their affection and caring wash over her, telling herself it was enough. Sure, she was broken, but at least she was together enough to have two great friends who obviously cared about her.

"We should get someone to beat him up," Tori murmured. "Not his brothers. I don't think they'd do it. Plus, I doubt Grant would be super great in a fight. He's too much into healing to take someone down."

Daphne stared at Heather. "You're in bad shape. I'm going to stay. We can order in food and do some serious day drinking."

Tori nodded. "Maybe we can find a good revenge movie."

Heather knew they would both give up their day to hang with her. She appreciated there was just enough wholeness inside her to inspire that much loyalty. But honestly, she just wanted to fall apart alone and feel sorry for herself.

"I'm fine," she said firmly as she pointed to the door. "You came, you listened and now you have to get on with your own lives. Please. You have stuff to do."

Tori looked doubtful. "But you need us."

"I need a good pity party and then to move on. Really. I'll be fine."

After a little convincing, her friends left. Once they were gone, Heather spent about eighteen seconds being brave, then collapsed on the sofa, wondering what on earth to do now. She had so much emotion, so much pain, and nowhere to put it.

She checked her watch, but had another hour until it was time to feed the kittens. Maybe she could rearrange her closet or—

Her gaze fell on her laptop. She couldn't have Campbell. That was done. She had never been the type to wallow. She had told her friends that she would come up with a happiness plan. Maybe step one was to stop being so afraid and to let more people into her life. Without considering the consequences, she sat down and logged on to Facebook.

Hi. My name is Heather and about thirty-five years ago, you spent the night with my mom, Amber. At least I think it was you. Ancestry says we're a 97.5 percent match. I'm not looking for money and this isn't a scam. I'm just curious about you and wondered if you wanted to know about me.

Before she could change her mind, she sent the message and closed her computer. Done and done, she told herself.

Her feeling of accomplishment lasted about twenty minutes before she spiraled from disbelief she'd actually reached out to some stranger who may or may not be her father, to worry that she'd probably gotten in touch with some loser who would latch on to her and never let go. What if he wanted money? What if—

"What if I stopped channeling my mother?" she said.

The sense of unease didn't go away but she had to admit it was a nice distraction when compared to the pain Campbell had caused. She watched a few shows on Netflix, took care of the kittens and only checked Facebook every twenty minutes. Close to nine, she had a response.

Heather. You're a surprise. I only did Ancestry one time and never bothered with a membership. I just joined and there you are. A 97.5 percent match. I don't know what to say. I would very much like to talk to you. We should meet. My wife, Jillian, is excited at the thought of a stepdaughter, which is pretty funny. Here's my number and my email address. Please get in touch with me.

Heather stared at the information, a knot forming in her stomach. Holy crap—what had she done?

Daphne glanced at the menu, then smiled. "Why do I bother?"

"You could order something different," Miguel said with a grin. "Surprise me."

"Not my style."

Their regular server appeared. "Ms. Brown, what can I bring you? Your usual?"

"Yes, Jonathan. The House Steak Salad, dressing on the side."

Jonathan made a note on his small pad. "Excellent, and for you, Mr. Rodriguez?"

"The same."

He nodded and left. They already had their iced tea and had refused the breadbasket. Everything was as it always was when she had lunch with Miguel.

She held in a sigh. All right—not everything. In the back of her mind was a tiny niggling sense of guilt, which was ridiculous. She was having lunch with a colleague, nothing more. A single, extraordinarily handsome colleague, but so what? Noticing he was attractive was just stating the obvious. She'd never been interested in Miguel that way. He was smart and funny and uncomplicated. She enjoyed his company. His being a man was immaterial.

Despite her attempts to convince herself all was well, the guilt lingered. Probably because she believed Brody would be furious that she was having lunch with Miguel. And while the rational part of her knew she should pay attention to that, the rest of her was just as pissed—not only at his assumptions, but for his part in the problem.

As if reading her mind, Miguel asked, "How are things at home?"

She sagged back in her chair. "Terrible. Brody's still angry and not talking to me. Now that the kids are gone, the house is so quiet."

"I'm sorry. This is all my fault. Should I talk to him?"

Daphne wasn't sure if she should shriek or burst out laughing. "No. That would be a very bad idea." Miguel talking to Brody would only send them into a deeper spiral of disaster.

"It's so unfair," she told him. "I have lunch with a lot of people. We're friends and he knows that. I've set you up on dates.

I've helped you buy presents for your various women. There's nothing going on."

"You're a beautiful woman. I understand why he would be jealous."

"Could I at least do something wrong before I'm punished?"

He leaned forward. "The flowers were a mistake. I wasn't thinking. I was in the shop, ordering some for my mother, and I saw the bouquet and thought of you."

Yes, the flowers had been a boneheaded move, but there was no point in making Miguel feel worse. She should have tossed them immediately. Or told Brody what had happened. They'd both messed up and they'd talked about the problem for too long. Time to lighten up the mood.

"You were ordering flowers for your mother and thought of me?" she said, her tone teasing. "That's not very flattering."

"At least now you know I wasn't coming on to you." His smile faded. "We should stop having lunch. At least for a while."

"No. I'm not having Brody define my life that way." She picked up her iced tea. That would be too much like Brody winning. She wasn't the one who had gone back on her word—he had.

"Good. I'd miss our lunches."

"I would, too."

Being with Miguel was easy. He had the same drive to achieve that she did. While his practice and hers rarely overlapped, whenever they did work together, the project always went smoothly. Miguel got her and made her laugh. Friendship was miles from an affair, but would Brody see that?

She sighed. "I wish things weren't so difficult at home."

"He's angry. He loves you and he's worried."

She rolled her eyes. "Anger I could respect. He's being petty. Saturday morning he made pancakes for everyone but me."

"I'm sorry. Marriage is hard at the best of times and I've made things worse."

She waved his comment away. "Brody and I will work our way through this." Somehow. Eventually, they would start talking and then they could figure it out.

"I think part of the problem is we don't generally fight," she said. "We've always gotten along. Oh, there have been minor disagreements, but this is the first big argument we've had. Worse, he's mad about something I didn't do and he's being a jerk."

"He's threatened. You and I share something he's not a part of." His mouth twisted. "The flowers rubbed his nose in that."

"You're taking his side."

"I would never do that. I agree he's being childish, but there's a reason. Like I said, marriage is hard."

Despite her annoyance at Brody and her concern about the situation, she smiled.

"You say that like you have personal experience. Is this where I remind you that you can barely handle having a girlfriend? You're commitment phobic."

"I can commit."

She laughed. "Oh, please."

He looked at her. "For the right woman I could."

"Cheap talk."

He grinned. "All right. Maybe I'm not the marrying kind, but I can be an excellent boyfriend."

Jonathan returned with their salads.

"You're missing out," Daphne told him when they were alone again. "Marriage is great. So's falling in love."

"You sound wistful."

"Not a surprise. Brody and I had a great courtship. We met in line at a restaurant."

She smiled at the memory. "Brody started talking to me and

Campbell introduced himself to Heather. By the time our table was ready, we decided to have dinner together. And that was it. Brody and I started dating. A few months later he proposed."

She looked at Miguel. "From that first night, I just knew he was the one. His kids were adorable." She grinned. "I even get along with his ex-wife. It was meant to be."

Or at least it had been until lately. First, him saying they weren't ready to have a baby, and then the problem with Miguel.

"I want that back," she admitted. "The way we used to be."

"It'll happen. Like you said, it was meant to be."

"I hope you're right."

"Was it the same with becoming a lawyer?" he asked.

She speared a piece of lettuce. "No. I was planning to get my MBA. But my junior year of college I dated a guy in law school. He wasn't very interesting but I loved hearing about his classes." She laughed. "My parents were thrilled when I told them I wanted to go to law school."

"Balloons and champagne?"

"And many happy tears. What about you?"

"I wanted to play baseball."

That made sense. Miguel was sports obsessed in all things, including his legal practice. He and his team represented star athletes from around the country, along with an impressive roster of local players from the Seahawks, Mariners, Sounders and Kraken teams.

"Professionally?" she asked.

He nodded. "An injury in college ended my career. I thought about becoming an agent, but I'm not that good at selling, so I went into law instead."

"That must have been tough."

He shrugged. "I was disappointed for a few months. Dreams die hard."

"They do," she said, thinking of how Brody had, until recently, made her marriage and family dreams come true. If that were to change...

She pushed that thought away. They weren't in that much trouble. Things were a little tough right now, but they would survive the challenge. Together they could learn and grow from what had happened.

"On the bright side," she told him, "you have great seats to all the games."

He grinned. "There is that. So what do you have going on this afternoon?"

"Redoing a will with a new client."

"Is this a client with a lot of billable hours or a few billable hours?"

"A lot," she said with a laugh. The fifty-something woman was recently widowed. Her late husband had been part owner in a small business and the company's key man life insurance policy had paid out six million dollars. Suddenly, her three adult children were clamoring for "their share" now and she wanted to put everything in a trust they couldn't get access to until she was gone.

"The other partners and I thank you."

"You and the other partners are welcome."

"I'm heading out of town to speak with a prospective client myself."

"You'll win him over," she told him.

He winked. "I usually do."

She waved her fork. "Speaking as the firm's newest partner, yay, Miguel."

He raised his glass of iced tea. "To billable hours."

She lifted hers. "And the clients who bring them."

five

Heather sat with Elliot in the small conference room for their monthly "how's it going" meeting—something he'd insisted on when they started the company. They met one-on-one with no interruptions. They discussed everything from clients to billing to growth plans. It was a chance to stay connected with the business and each other.

Elliot was one of the most influential people in Heather's life. They'd met fifteen years ago when he'd been hired to handle marketing at her cousin's company, Clandestine Kitty. Heather had been all of twenty, with zero experience in business and no knowledge about what it took to convince a consumer that they absolutely needed to buy the latest whatever. She'd been assigned to Elliot's department where she'd worked hard and had failed constantly.

But Elliot had seen something in her and had encouraged her to leave Blackberry Island to go to college. When she'd finally found the strength to walk away from her emotionally abusive mother, Elliot had helped her get into USC. He'd arranged for scholarship money and had found her a place to live. He'd been her mentor, her friend, surrogate father and the person she most wanted to be like. Seven years ago, when she decided to start her own business, he'd been the first one she'd called. Five years ago they'd opened 206 Marketing Group.

"Did you see Tori's storyboards for MGNW?" he asked.

"Yes. They're brilliant, as per usual. I love the idea of taking the hard way to the party."

They went through the details, then both signed off on the work. When they were done, Elliot glanced at her.

"What's wrong?"

"Nothing," she said automatically. "Why do you ask?"

He raised his eyebrows without speaking.

Heather did her best to outwait him, but as always, Elliot's silence made her squirm.

"My life sucks," she blurted. "My personal life. Work is excellent."

"You have great friends, a nice condo and kittens to care for," he said slowly. "So what sucks?"

Why had she started down this conversational path? She searched her mind for something to say to distract him, then smiled broadly when the perfect solution appeared.

"I got in touch with my birth father."

Elliot's look of surprise was almost comical. "Amber's one-night stand? How did you find him?"

"Ancestry. I sent him a message on Facebook." She paused. "I'm having second thoughts, because, you know, family."

"Did he answer?"

She nodded. "He seems enthused."

"Are you going to talk to him?"

"I don't know." Her desire to meet the man depended on her mood. "After all this time, I'm not sure I want a biological father."

"You get half your DNA from him. There's information to be had." He smiled. "Besides, you might like him."

A possibility she hadn't considered. "He's married with a couple of kids. The wife is much younger. I'm glad you married someone age appropriate."

"Thank you. So what about your life sucks?"

She groaned. "Why can't I distract you? The father thing is huge."

"I know you. Your avoidance means you're talking about your romantic life."

"Maybe. Probably. Yes."

"You and Campbell are still apart?"

Ugh. Not a topic she wanted to pursue. "He's done with me. He made that really clear. There's someone else. I'm sure she's lovely." Even she heard the bitterness in her voice.

"Regrets?" Elliot asked.

"No." She looked at him, comfortable with lying. Okay, not comfortable exactly... "Yes. Some. I just thought we'd figure it out, but he didn't and now he's with her. I hate her."

"Have you met her?"

"Of course not. I don't have to know her to hate her. It's what she represents."

"Someone who can make a commitment?"

His gentle tone took a little of the sting out of the words, but she flinched all the same.

"You need to work on your people skills," she told him.

"I'm the voice in your head, Heather. It's my job to say the difficult things. Campbell wanted to marry you."

Just the word made her look longingly toward the door. "We both know I'm incapable of marrying anyone."

"I don't believe that. You have great capacity to love. Look at how you feel about Tori and Daphne and your cousins." He smiled. "You love me and my family."

"That's different. I trust you guys. I know who you are and I know you'll never hurt me."

"Campbell wouldn't hurt you. Not the way you think."

"I want to believe you," she admitted. "But I can't. Say I do it. Say I move in with him and we're living together and then one day he gets sick or something. Then what?"

"Then you bring him tissues or whatever else he needs, possibly drive him to the doctor. He gets better and you move on."

She glared at him. "You know what I mean. What if one day he decides that my sole reason for being is to take care of him? What if he takes everything—my money, my time, my life? What if he traps me?" Because she knew that could happen. It had happened to her.

"You're not a little girl anymore," Elliot told her, his voice kind. "You have more skills. More resources. You're stronger. You could walk away."

"It doesn't happen all at once," she pointed out. "Sometimes it happens slowly, so you don't notice. Then, before you know it, there's no way out."

"There's always a way out. You found it before, you can again."

"You're being rational. This isn't a rational fear."

"And Campbell isn't your mother."

She looked at him. "Whether he is or not doesn't matter. He's moved on."

"Then you should, too. Find someone else who makes your

heart beat faster. You're a smart, funny, successful woman who happens to be beautiful. A lot of men would be interested."

"They haven't been so far."

"That's because you're not looking." He touched her hand. "Heather, you're like a daughter to me. I want you to be happy. You deserve love. Real love. The kind that gives more than it takes. Have a little faith—in the world, in love and most of all, in yourself."

"Or I could just get more kittens."

Heather dialed the phone number. The second she heard ringing, every fiber in her being told her to hang up. She didn't need more drama in her life.

"Hello?"

She clutched her cell phone more tightly. "Um, hi. Fletcher?"

"Yes?"

"It's Heather Sitterly. Your, ah, well, I'm the one who reached out on Facebook. About maybe being your daughter."

"Heather! I'm so glad you called. Hold on a second, please."

She heard him lower the phone, then call, "Jillian! Jillian! It's Heather." There was muffled conversation, then Fletcher saying, "I'm putting you on speakerphone so Jillian can join us."

Jillian? The wife?

"Hello, Heather," a woman said, her voice bright with delight. "We're so happy you called. We hoped you would. How are you? *Where* are you?"

"Yes, where are you?" Fletcher said. "I met your mother close to a place called Blackberry Island. It's in Washington State."

"I know the place," Heather said drily. "I grew up there."

"What?" Fletcher sounded shocked. "Do you live there now?"

"I'm in Seattle."

"Seattle?" Jillian's voice was thick with disbelief. "Oh, Fletcher, she's been right here the whole time and we never knew. We could have passed each other in the grocery store."

Jillian sounded dismayed at the prospect, while Heather found herself a little freaked out.

"You're around Marysville, right?" she asked.

"Yes, just north of the town," Fletcher told her. "I'm sorry I didn't know about you. Your mother and I had just the weekend. I never thought she was pregnant. She didn't reach out…"

"How would she?" Jillian asked. "Darling, she didn't even know your last name. He was back to college the next day," she added, obviously addressing her comment to Heather. "WSU."

"That was my last weekend with the rodeo," he said. "I finished work Saturday morning, met your mother that afternoon." He chuckled. "She was beautiful and funny. We had a great time."

Funny? Amber? Heather couldn't picture it.

"Is she all right?" he asked. "Now and before. I'm sorry you had to grow up without a father. Unless she married someone. Is that what happened? Is she happily married with a half dozen grown kids?"

"Not really," Heather said, having trouble following the conversation. Her mind simply couldn't take in that she was speaking with her biological father. "It was mostly my mom and me. She was married for a while when I was little, but it didn't last."

"I'm sorry," Fletcher murmured. "I wanted her to be happy."

A sentiment her mother wouldn't share when it came to her summer weekend boyfriend.

"What about you?" Jillian asked. "Are you married?"

"No. I'm more focused on my business."

"Oh, Fletcher, she has a business. That's amazing. What do you do, Heather?"

"Marketing." She was careful not to give any specifics. Yes, this man might be her father, but what did she really know about him?

"You went to college?" Jillian asked.

"Uh-huh. USC."

Jillian's voice rose in pitch. "Oh, Fletcher. Your oldest daughter went to college. And USC. You must be so proud."

He chuckled. "I didn't have anything to do with it, but yes, I'm a little proud. I'd like us to meet, Heather."

She'd been expecting the ask, but still, the shift in topic caught her off guard.

"Ah, sure. Maybe coffee sometime." In the future. The distant future.

"Are you free Sunday afternoon?" Jillian asked. "You could come here. To the house. The girls are with friends all afternoon, so it will just be the two of us. Of course we want you to meet them, they're your sisters after all, but I think it will be easier if it's just you, me and Fletcher for that first meeting."

Heather had never been a person who fainted, but she was thinking this might be a good time to take up the practice.

Sisters? They thought Fletcher's girls were her sisters? No. They were his kids and no relation to her. Well, except for the fact that they shared a father. So technically, possibly, they were half sisters.

"Heather?" Fletcher's voice was soft. "You still there?"

"Yes. Sorry. It's a lot to absorb."

"Take your time. Jillian's right. We want to meet you but if coming to the house is too much, we can meet somewhere else."

How could he not know the location wasn't the problem? It was the idea of a father and sisters and whatever Jillian was to her. It was too many people who may or may not want something from her.

"We could get lunch somewhere," Jillian added softly. "We really do want to meet you but the last thing we want to do is scare you away."

Lunch was easy, she thought. Safe. Only she wasn't sure she wanted to meet her father for the first time in a restaurant. What if she got emotional? Crying was unlikely, but she could still have some kind of outburst or maybe just some ragged breathing. Maybe their house was a better option. And if she got uncomfortable, she could leave anytime she wanted.

"Your place sounds okay," she said. "But only for an hour or so. This is a lot for me to take in."

For them, too, but they seemed to be handling it better than she was.

"That's wonderful," her father said. "I'll text you the address. How about two o'clock?"

"I can do that." She could ask Daphne to take the kittens for the afternoon.

"We can't wait to meet you," Jillian said, her voice filled with warmth. "Thanks for reaching out, Heather. We're so grateful."

"Sure. You're welcome. I'll see you Sunday."

Heather hung up quickly. Seconds later Fletcher sent over his address, along with Jillian's direct number. That was followed by a picture of the four of them, laughing together on what looked like the front porch.

She stared at the photograph. She'd seen images of the family before, on Fletcher's Facebook page, but this one felt different. She could see a little of herself in her father's features. More significantly, she could see herself in his daughters. They all had the same shape eyes and maybe their chins were similar.

Sisters, she thought in disbelief. She could know in her head it was possible, but believing was a whole other thing.

★ ★ ★

The weeks they didn't have the kids, Daphne put in more hours at work so she could be home at a reasonable time to have dinner with Elijah, Cadin and Alexa when they were over. But after three days of barely seeing Brody and not speaking to him at all, she decided it was up to her to do something to fix the problem. She left her office at six, stopped for Thai and walked into the house a little before seven.

"It's me," she called.

Albert and Vanessa both greeted her. They were friendly but not frantic, so she guessed Brody had fed them. She set the food on the counter, then petted the cats, waiting for him to come upstairs and say hello. That was their pattern. Whoever got home first—and it was usually him—came out to greet the other. But there was no sound of footsteps on the basement stairs. Just the noise from the television.

Daphne glared at the floor. "Stupid man," she muttered, before heading to the second floor. If he didn't want to talk to her, she could not talk more than he could begin to imagine.

The childish logic depressed her. Not talking couldn't fix things. Nor would getting upset all the time. They had to sit down and have a reasonable adult conversation about what was wrong.

She changed into jeans and a T-shirt, and slipped her feet into sandals, before heading back to the kitchen. Brody sat at the island. They stared at each other warily.

"You're home early," he said.

"I thought it would be nice to spend some time together. I haven't seen you in a few days."

"I fed the cats."

"Thank you." She motioned to the bag. "I brought home Thai."

His gaze slid from hers. "I ate already."

The possibility of a good evening slipped away. "You ate? Why didn't you tell me you were getting dinner without me?"

"Why didn't you tell me you were leaving work early? You work late when we don't have the kids and I always get dinner by myself."

"Not always. Just a few days a week."

"I had no way of knowing this wasn't one of those days."

"But you usually ask."

And here they were, she thought glumly. Back on the blame train, accusing each other of thoughtlessness, of rule breaking. There was no warmth between them, and without the affection that was the foundation of their relationship, no benefit of the doubt.

She sank onto a stool at the island. "I want us to like each other again."

"I want that, too." He sounded more resigned than hopeful.

"I don't know what to do," she admitted. "You're acting like I'm the bad guy, and I didn't do anything wrong."

His gaze locked on her face. "Seriously?"

"Yes. I've never been unfaithful. I've never considered being unfaithful. Since the night we met, I've only wanted to be with you. Just you."

"The man sent you flowers."

She held in a groan. "Yes, he did. I should have told you right away and I should have thrown them out. I was surprised and I didn't know how to handle the situation. I'm sorry. I wish you could believe me."

He looked away. "Me, too."

Sadness joined frustration. "So you don't trust me."

His gaze swung back to her. "I did. I thought everything was fine. Then I find out about this guy you've been seeing."

"It was lunch," she said loudly.

"He sent you flowers," he added, his voice louder than hers.

She told herself not to push back, that escalation didn't help anyone. She leaned back in her chair and tried to figure out why they kept going in unproductive circles. Yes, the flowers were bad, but she'd apologized a dozen times. She should have handled the situation differently. As for lunch with Miguel— that was exactly what she'd explained over and over. There was nothing between them. Nothing.

She looked at Brody, who was watching her cautiously. She'd never had relationships with a lot of quarreling. She didn't like it. He was easygoing, so until now, they'd managed to quickly work through issues. Only not when it came to the damned flowers and not when they'd talked about the baby.

In fact, the fight about the baby had come first. She blinked several times. Was that it? Was Brody making a big deal about the flowers to distract her from the real problem?

"What?" he demanded. "You've thought of something."

She stared at him. No way she could accuse him of that, she thought. He would be pissed. Worse, he wouldn't listen.

"Just say it." His gaze sharpened. "Or are you thinking about Miguel?"

She knew he was deliberately taunting her and if she wanted to be the bigger person, she shouldn't respond, but apparently she wasn't because she said, "This is all a distraction."

He frowned. "What?"

"Miguel and the flowers. You know nothing happened. You're making a fuss because you don't want to talk about the real problem."

His confusion seemed genuine. "What real problem?"

"We had a deal," she said, pointing at him. "You and I agreed we were going to have a baby together and now you've changed your mind. That's when all this started. I brought up us getting pregnant and you said no."

She tried to keep her voice strong but the more she spoke,

the harder it was to hide the quivers forming inside her. She'd been so shocked when he said now wasn't a good time, and had immediately wondered if he'd changed his mind, or worse, had lied when he'd said he wanted children with her.

He already had three from his first marriage. He didn't need more. She'd put off having children to get her career up and running, but she'd never given up on becoming a mother. She wanted that, and having such a great relationship with his kids only reinforced her decision.

Brody swore under his breath. "I didn't say no. I said it wasn't a good time. I said we should wait until things were a little more stable."

"And then you picked this fight."

"I didn't pick a fight. Another man sent you flowers. That's not on me. I suggest we line up fifty random people and ask each of them if they think Miguel sending you flowers is okay."

She rose and glared at him. "I never said it was okay. I said I was surprised and I handled it badly. Miguel and I are friends. Nothing more. You're the one blowing things out of proportion."

"Me? You're accusing me of manipulating you, and you're calling me a liar."

"You changed your mind about the baby."

"I said now was a bad time." He slapped both hands on the counter. "Dammit, Daphne, you made partner less than a year ago and you're still working seventy-hour weeks. With the change in the parenting plan, we have the kids every other week. It's a lot, plus, we've been married less than two years. So yes, I thought waiting to get pregnant might give us some breathing room."

His voice gentled. "I want us to be solid. Having a baby can strain a marriage."

She glared at him. "You're judging me by what your ex-wife did. You had three kids close together and it was too much. So because you and she couldn't do it, you're going to keep me from having a baby? Why do you get to decide what I can and can't handle? There are female partners who get it all done. If they can do it, I can do it. What makes you think you know best and I'm just the dumb little wife who won't listen?"

"That's not what I said."

Anger was easier than hurt, so she hung on to it with both hands. "Close enough. You want to wait? How long? I'm not going to be working less in a year. Or is it because I agreed to the adjustment in the parenting plan, all the free time is used up and now having a baby isn't reasonable?"

He closed his eyes and exhaled, then looked at her. "You know that's not what I meant."

"You said one of the reasons you didn't want us to have a baby was because we have your kids so much."

The mad slipped away, leaving a gaping hole that threatened to engulf her. Tears burned but she blinked them away. "You get all that you want and I end up taking care of everything, but no baby for me."

The unfairness of what he'd said, of the situation, twisted her stomach and hurt her heart. How could this be happening? They'd made a plan. He'd promised her. She'd believed him, loved him and married him.

"It's not an either-or situation," he told her.

"Of course it is. That's what you said." Her throat tightened. "You never planned on having a child with me, did you?"

"I want us to have a baby. I love you and that was always the plan."

"I don't believe you."

His shoulders slumped. "Is that true? You think I'd betray you like that?"

"You think I had an affair and I didn't. I guess we don't trust each other at all." Which was a sucky thing to have to admit.

He stood. "We're not going to solve this tonight. You must be hungry and tired. I'm going back downstairs."

Daphne watched him leave. When she was alone in the kitchen, she gave in to the inevitable and let the tears fall.

How had this all happened? she thought, wiping her cheeks as her breath came in choking sobs. How had they lost their way? A few weeks ago everything had been great, and now she didn't know where they were or what was happening. Worse, she didn't know how to define the problem, let alone how to fix it.

Eventually, her tears slowed. She splashed water on her face, then put the takeout she'd brought home in the refrigerator and climbed the stairs to the second floor, Albert and Vanessa at her heels.

But when she reached the hallway, she didn't turn toward the master. Instead, she went the other way, to Alexa's room. A safer, more neutral space, she thought, lying down on the twin bed. Just for a little while—until she figured out what to do next.

six

Heather reached for the TV remote. She pushed the off button, silencing the far too Zen and soft-spoken instructor right in the middle of her "Namaste." She loathed yoga—it was so slow and she wasn't very bendy—but somehow doing a routine always made her feel more calm and centered.

She tucked her mat into the hall closet, then walked barefoot into the kitchen thinking she should eat something. Only it was nearly nine at night and she wasn't sure going to bed on a full stomach was a good idea. She tried to remember if she'd had lunch and just wasn't sure. There had been meetings all day long and—

Her phone chirped. Her almost-relaxed mood evaporated when she saw a text from Campbell.

Do you have a minute?

She stared at the five words. What did that mean? He wanted to talk? About what? Based on their last conversation, there was nothing left to say. She doubted he wanted to dump on her again—their last meeting aside, Campbell wasn't a jerk.

Sure.

Right after she sent the text, her doorbell rang.

It took her a second to connect the text with someone being at her condo. When she realized who it was, her whole body went on alert. She glanced down at the shorts and T-shirt she was wearing, told herself Campbell wouldn't care what she looked like and went to let him in.

"Hey," he said. "I'm glad you're willing to talk to me."

Talking at that moment seemed unlikely, she thought, stepping back to let him in. He looked so good. He was wearing his Alaska Airlines pilot uniform and had the faint air of weariness that told her he was on his way home rather than heading to the airport.

She cleared her throat and said, "How was your flight?"

"Good."

"Wichita?"

He grinned. "And LA."

The smile was like a kick in the gut. Wanting stirred, but more painful was the way her heart seemed to surge toward him as if desperate for a little Campbell affection. Thankfully, LC provided a great distraction, crying out as he raced to Campbell.

He picked up the madly purring cat and held him close. "LC. How are you?"

LC frantically rubbed Campbell's chin with his head even

as he squirmed to get closer. His purrs got so loud, Heather worried he might choke.

"Obviously, he's missed you," she murmured, leading the way into the living room.

"He's a good guy."

Campbell settled on the sofa while she took a chair and watched the lovefest. LC continued to rub his head against Campbell's face, purring and kneading. Heather found herself in the awkward position of being jealous of her cat. She also wondered why Campbell was here. She doubted he'd realized he wanted that third or maybe fourth chance she'd offered.

She searched for some neutral topic to start the conversation, only to be interrupted by her watch alarm. Campbell's brows rose.

"You have kittens?"

"Three."

He set LC aside and stood. "Let's do it."

They walked into the kitchen and collected supplies. Campbell moved with the ease of a man familiar with where things were. Not a surprise—he'd been with her when she'd bought the place, had helped her unpack and later, had cared for kittens here.

"You're smiling," he said, collecting syringes as she measured out formula.

"I was thinking about you helping me condo shop."

He looked around. "This was the best one." His smile returned. "It's way nicer than mine."

"I make more money than you."

"It's the talent. You have mad skills."

The compliment helped her relax a little. She had no idea why he was here. Probably not to tell her more honest but painful truths. At least she hoped not.

They walked into the second bedroom. He weighed each

of the kittens while she recorded the number. After measuring out the formula, they each took a towel and carried the babies out to the living room. LC followed, ready to monitor the situation and step in if needed. When the first two were eating, Campbell looked at her.

"I wanted to apologize."

She turned away. "We don't have to talk about that."

"I was a jerk. I'm sorry. I was harsh and I hurt you."

She stroked Russell Wilson. "You told the truth," she said with a lightness she didn't feel. "I am too broken."

He winced. "I shouldn't have said that. I reacted without thinking. I was trying to protect myself."

She glanced at him. "From what?"

"You. What you said—it was a shock to me. I didn't know what to say. We were done. That last time, you made it clear you were never coming back and then there you were, saying you wanted another chance. Like I said, I reacted."

She appreciated the generous apology. Given how she'd treated him in the past, it was probably more than she deserved.

"You're right," she said softly. "Me showing up like that was a shock. I understand why you said what you did." She braced herself for the lie. "It's okay. I'm fine."

One brow rose. "I doubt that."

She gave him a faint smile. "All right, I'll admit I got my feelings hurt, but you weren't wrong to say what you did. Relationships are hard for me."

"There's an understatement."

"Excuse me?"

"Heather, you have a lot of good qualities and you're a genius at work, but the whole love thing flummoxes you. You don't trust easily."

He finished with his kitten and set him in the box on the

coffee table. LC jumped inside to sniff, then licked both kittens while Campbell picked up the third.

"I can't go there again," he said when the kitten latched on. "Not because it would inevitably end badly for me, but because we don't want the same things."

She wanted to protest that he was wrong—that she did want all of it, too. Only she wasn't sure she did. She looked at LC with the kittens and told herself there was no one else in her head so she could tell the truth. Sometimes she did want the regular stuff, only she wasn't sure how it was possible. He'd talked about getting married and having kids. He'd said it so casually, as if it was no big deal, but she knew otherwise.

"I still remember our first date," he said. "Not the night we met but when it was just the two of us."

"I remember that, too."

"You warned me you had issues. I couldn't see past your smile. I was all in, then Brody and Daphne got engaged and that freaked you out."

It had. The permanency of marriage, the idea of being linked with someone so completely, had terrified her.

"I was scared," she admitted. "I could tell what you were thinking."

"That I was madly in love with you and wanted to spend my life with you?" he asked drily.

She nodded. "Then at the wedding, I knew you were close to proposing and I just couldn't do it." She met his gaze. "I'm sorry I ended things at the reception."

"I'm not sure there was a good time to break my heart."

She flinched. "I know, but that was really bad. I was terrified and I needed to protect myself."

He finished and put the kitten in the box with her siblings.

"I want regular stuff," he told her. "A wife, a couple of kids.

That's important to me. I want a connection and memories and a good life. I can't give that up, Heather. Not even for you."

Her throat tightened. When he said it like that, every part of her hurt, because she could see it happening. Campbell was the kind of man who gave everything he had. He loved fully. She, on the other hand, spent all her emotional energy protecting herself.

In a perfect world she would say that she wanted that, too. Only she couldn't think it, let alone say it. What if he stopped being responsible and hardworking and suddenly expected her to be his everything? What if he tore away the pieces of her life, of her very being, until she was and had nothing?

He smiled. "I can see by the look in your eyes that if we weren't at your place, you'd be out the door in five seconds flat."

"Maybe," she murmured, then sighed. "I don't want to feel this way, but I don't know how to stop. I don't like running, but what's the alternative? I'm just so afraid you'll need more than I have. Not just you, of course. Anyone. You're asking me to take a huge risk."

He was nice enough not to point out he wasn't asking her for anything.

"How do you do it?" she asked. "Put yourself out there? Aren't you the least bit afraid the woman you marry will turn into my mother?"

He laughed. "No. Amber is unique. I'm sorry for what you had to go through, but most people aren't like her. In a relationship we all need things at different times. The one who needs something takes, then later, the other one has the needs. It's a partnership."

She understood the words—almost believed them—but she couldn't imagine acting on them. It was a matter of perspective—she couldn't get past the fear enough to see the situation clearly, so she would always respond based on her past, not her present.

"I'm sorry I was so difficult," she told him. "It wasn't on purpose."

"I know."

He stood, pulled her into his arms. The feel of his body against hers was so familiar, she thought wistfully. Strong and warm and safe. Except for wanting to love her, he'd always been safe.

He kissed the top of her head. "I am sorry for what I said."

"It's okay. I'm sorry for how I acted." She sucked in a breath for courage. "I regret losing you, but I get it. I really do wish you the best. I want you to be happy."

Emotions flashed through his eyes. She tried to guess what he was thinking, but had no idea.

"Thanks for helping with the kittens," she said.

He nodded. "Anytime."

He gave LC a quick pat, then walked out of her condo. Heather sank back on the sofa and covered her face with her hands. There weren't any tears—she didn't allow them anymore—but there was plenty of pain and a sense of having lost something precious for the very last time.

Late Saturday morning Tori put the clean towels in the linen closet. She was feeling virtuous, having finished all her weekend chores. There was food in the refrigerator, the laundry was done and she'd scrubbed the main bathroom until it sparkled. Grant was taking a rare day shift, so she had both dogs. After lunch she was going to take them on a long walk and have a serious talk with herself about her personal life.

The Kyle screwup had really shaken her. Dating a married man was horrifying. Okay, she hadn't known, but still. Thinking about it made her shudder and get a little sick to her stomach. She had to figure out the problem—which was today's goal. She would—

There was a loud pop followed by a deluge of cold water. Tori screamed and tried to get out of the flow, only it was everywhere. Both dogs came running, barking and bumping into her. She spun in place, trying to figure out what was happening, then looked up. The fire sprinklers had gone off. But there was no alarm, just gallons and gallons of water.

She grabbed her bag and both leashes. At the last minute she threw her tablet into her tote and raced into the hallway, the dogs at her heels. Her neighbors were already there, shrieking and trying to dodge water. Several were shouting to find the shutoff. She went into the stairwell, only to find there were sprinklers there, as well. Water followed her to the street level, where the rest of her neighbors collected. They were all dripping wet. Water poured out the front door and ran off balconies. She stared at the building, trying to comprehend what was happening as her neighbors pointed and cried.

"Everything's ruined!"

"Did anyone hear an alarm? Is there a fire?"

"We should call the fire department!"

"I'm on with the emergency number for the HOA."

Tori pulled her cell phone out of her jeans pocket. She sent a quick text to Grant to call her as soon as he could then called Heather to let her know what was going on. Her heart pounded and she wanted to both scream and cry.

Within five minutes the fire department was on scene, but it took them nearly twenty to get the water turned off and another half hour for them to assess the building. Grant phoned and she explained what had happened. He said he would be right there.

Tori sat on the lawn, a dog on each side of her, grateful for the warm summer day. Her clothes dried but her mind simply couldn't take in what had happened. The volume of water was going to be devastating, she thought, shaking a little, despite the bright sunshine. Every unit had been affected. What were the repairs going to be like? Was her stuff okay? What about the building itself?

"Tori?"

She saw Grant hurrying toward her. She ran to him, the dogs keeping pace. When she reached him, she threw herself at him. He caught her and pulled her close.

"What happened?" he asked, holding her tight as he surveyed the building.

"I don't know. I'd just finished my laundry when the sprinklers went off. I guess they went on everywhere in the building. There was so much water. I didn't know what to do."

He pointed toward the building. "One of the firefighters is motioning for us to come over."

He took Zeus's leash in one hand and kept his other arm around her. They walked toward the firefighter.

"All right, everyone," the woman said. "Here's what we know. There was an accidental discharge of the fire sprinkler system." Her expression turned sympathetic. "We're talking about pressurized water shooting out at about 75 gallons a minute. That's a lot of water. Our initial inspection shows that every unit was affected, as were all the common areas. We've turned off the electricity and the water to the building."

"When's it coming back on?" someone asked.

"Not anytime soon," she said bluntly. "The building will have to be inspected for structural damage. The main electrical lines will probably need to be replaced and every unit is going to have to be gutted."

Tori stared at the woman. The words all made sense, but their meaning was beyond her.

"You can't live here until the repairs are made," the firefighter continued. "We'll give you a couple of hours to carry out what you can salvage, then we're locking you out until the building is inspected."

Despite the heat, Tori shivered. She felt sick to her stomach. "We're losing our homes? I don't understand. How could this happen? What are we going to do?"

Just then Heather ran up. She hugged Tori and gave Grant's arm a squeeze.

He brought her up to speed while Tori stared at the building. She loved her place—she didn't want to leave. Worse, she didn't know where to go or what to do next.

"I'll call the insurance agent," Grant said. "She handles both our policies, so she can get the paperwork moving for both of us."

Heather eyed the water still flowing out the front door. "I want to say I'll call SERVPRO, but I think we're a long way from them coming in. First the building has to be inspected."

"This can't be happening," Tori whispered. "It can't."

Heather moved close. "Look at me."

Tori did as she instructed.

"You'll be fine," her friend told her. "You have insurance. Whatever went wrong is on the HOA. They have insurance, too. It's going to be a pain in the ass, but we'll get through it together. In the meantime, you'll come stay with me until we can find you a place for the next few months. I don't have a bed in the guest room, but you've slept on the sofa before and it's comfortable."

"Months?"

Grant nodded. "It's going to be a while." He pulled out his phone. "I'll see if I can bunk with Campbell for a few days."

Tori looked at Heather. "This isn't happening."

"I'm afraid it is. Come on. We'll put the dogs in my car, then go upstairs and see what we can salvage."

Her condo was worse than she'd imagined. The water was ankle deep and everything was soaked. Her furniture, her carpet, the drywall. She would guess the appliances were ruined as were the cabinets. She stood in the middle of her living room, not sure what to do.

"Any electronics will be toast," Heather said bluntly as she headed for the kitchen. "Where do you keep the trash bags?"

"In the pantry."

Heather got them and tossed the destroyed cardboard box on the counter, then began unrolling bags.

"Forget the food. That will all be drenched. I'll collect paperwork. We can dry that out at my place. You go in the bedroom and gather clothes and toiletries. Just take it all. We'll assess it later."

Grant walked into the living room. "You doing okay?"

"No," Tori whispered.

"We're fine," Heather assured him. "You go take care of your place. They're not giving us much time. We'll get it all into my car and yours."

"My car!"

Tori started for the door. Grant stopped her. He put his hands on her upper arms and stared into her eyes.

"Your car will be fine. You're at the highest part of the parking garage, so the water will run down. If I'm remembering correctly, there aren't that many sprinklers in the garage, so you were probably spared the worst of it."

Tears burned in her eyes. "I think I'm in shock."

"You are. It was a horrible thing to go through, but we don't have a lot of time."

"I know." She wiped away the tears. "I'm okay."

A lie, but they were on a serious deadline.

She and Heather spent the next hour collecting as much as they could. She shoved dripping clothes into garbage bags, along with shoes that were probably ruined. She emptied her bathroom of her skin care and cosmetics. Heather collected all the papers in her small filing cabinet, then stacked dripping linens next to cans of dog food. The dry food would have to be replaced, along with Scout's beds.

They filled Heather's car first, then her own. Grant had been correct—there wasn't any standing water by her vehicle and while it was wet, it started right away and there wasn't any water inside. The firefighters had opened the gate, so she was able to drive out with no problem.

As she followed Heather to her lakefront condo, Tori had the strangest feeling nothing was ever going to be the same again. Not her or her condo or anything else in her life. She told herself she would be fine, that she had friends, her beloved dog and good insurance. But the words didn't take away the fear of the unknown. In a few seconds she'd lost everything, and she had no idea what came next.

seven

Sunday Heather drove north on I5. After about forty-five minutes, the density of the Seattle Metro area gave way to open land and the occasional Indian casino complex. She eyed the large outlet mall and told herself she would stop there on her way back. Sort of a reward for good behavior. But as she neared the exit to her father's neighborhood, she found herself wanting to turn around.

Why was she doing this? She was thirty-four and she'd been totally fine without the man. She didn't need him now. There was also the issue of telling her mother about him, which she was going to put off as long as possible. Plus, he wanted her to meet his uncomfortably young wife. Really? At least the daughters wouldn't be there. Daughters, she repeated in her mind. Not sisters. She could barely deal with the idea of a father let alone siblings.

Maybe she should reschedule, she thought, even as she took the off-ramp. Tori was still shaken and could probably use the company. She couldn't use the kittens as an excuse—Tori was happy to feed them. And Tori had been the one to insist she go. Family first and all that.

She followed her GPS into a quiet, older neighborhood of modest homes. There weren't any McMansions to be seen, no flashy Teslas.

You have arrived at your destination. Heather parked in front of a house just like all the others and wondered if she was going to throw up. But before she could drive away, the front door opened and a middle-aged man stepped onto the porch.

He was about six feet and relatively fit. His dark blond hair had a bit of gray at his temples. He wore glasses and a smile big enough to power the west coast. Heather reluctantly turned off her engine, grabbed her bag and got out of her car.

Fletcher was joined by a tall, willowy woman with red hair. Daphne was a redhead as well, but her sleek bob was more auburn. Jillian's long hair was in-your-face bright and hanging to the middle of her back.

"You made it," Fletcher said. "Heather, it's wonderful to meet you. I was so excited, I could barely sleep."

Jillian laughed. "He's telling the truth. He kept me awake with his tossing and turning. How are you, my dear? This must be such a shock."

"Hi," Heather said weakly, thinking that mentioning the nausea would be a real downer for everyone.

As she approached the couple, she had the horrifying thought that they were going to hug her. Heather didn't hug people she didn't know. Fortunately, they only smiled and held open the front door.

She had a brief impression of a well-worn house, stacks of toys and an energy that made her slightly less cautious.

Jillian led the way into the kitchen where a pitcher of iced tea and a plate of homemade cookies sat on the rectangular table.

"Please," Fletcher said, hurrying to pull out a chair.

She sat down. He held out the chair for Jillian, then sat next to his wife and beamed at Heather.

"You're here," he said happily. "I can't believe it."

"Me, either. This is very strange."

"I can't imagine," Jillian admitted as she poured them each a glass of iced tea. "What did your mother say when you told her you'd found Fletcher?"

Heather shifted uneasily in her seat. "Yes, well, I haven't told her yet. I wanted to meet you first." Not that she had any plans to share the day with Amber—at least not for a while.

"How is she doing?" Fletcher asked. "You said she never had other children."

"No, just me."

"I'm surprised. I only knew her for that night, but she was so easy to be with. Sweet and funny. Her smile." He reached for his glass. "You have it, I think."

Sweet and funny? Her mother? Heather wanted to say that Ancestry must have made a mistake, only she could see a lot of herself in Fletcher, so what had happened to her mother?

"You were a rodeo cowboy, weren't you? When did you give that up?"

Under other circumstances, Fletcher's totally blank expression would have been comical.

"I was never a rodeo cowboy." He laughed. "I did meet your mother at the rodeo. It wasn't a real competition event— more of a demonstration show. I was home from college on break and took a job cleaning out stables."

"Amber always said…" She faked a smile. "I guess it doesn't matter. You were in college at the time?"

"WSU. I was a history major." His smile turned self-deprecating. "A geek major, but I can't help it. I love history."

Jillian touched his arm. "Geek or not, you had a way with the ladies."

"I'd be proof of that," Heather murmured.

Jillian laughed. "That's true."

Everything about this was surreal, she thought. Her being in this house, the man sitting across from her, his description of her mother. The fact that his hazel eyes were the same color and shape as hers. She couldn't wrap her mind around what was happening.

"How long have you two been married?" she asked.

"Fifteen years," Fletcher said.

"That long." She glanced at Jillian. "You were pretty young."

The other woman leaned toward Fletcher. "Such a polite way to ask about the age difference." She smiled at him before turning back to Heather. "Don't blame him. I pursued him. I was eighteen, but I knew the second we met that he was the one."

She reached out her hand toward Heather. "Have you ever felt that about someone? A knowing?"

"Not really."

"It was wonderful. Suddenly, everything made sense. Only Fletcher wouldn't admit he felt the same. He said I was too young and refused to go out with me."

"You asked him out?"

Jillian grinned. "I did. I told him we could have sex on the first date and he still turned me down."

Heather was grateful she wasn't drinking or she would have spit. Jillian was just a little too free with the information for her comfort.

But on the heels of that realization came an even more uncomfortable one.

"Wait," she said, hoping she didn't sound as horrified as she felt. "You were eighteen, and you've been married fifteen years?" So Jillian was younger than she was?

"Oh, we didn't get married until I was nineteen. I'll be thirty-five in October."

Heather swallowed hard. "Me, too."

"When's your birthday? Mine's the twentieth."

"The twenty-seventh."

Great. So her father's wife was a whole week older than she was.

"I'm not a cradle robber," Fletcher said firmly. "Until I met Jillian, I'd never dated a younger woman."

"And, like I said, if it'd been up to you, you never would have." Jillian turned back to Heather. "I was working in a diner. I was saving money for college. He took a table in my section and we started talking. There was an air of kindness about him, if that makes sense, with a hint of wicked. I was hooked and I asked him out."

Heather's gaze slid to her father. "Which you turned down."

"I did."

"But he showed up again three days later." Jillian's tone was triumphant.

Fletcher looked at Jillian. "I couldn't stay away." He returned his attention to Heather. "I asked her out and said we wouldn't be having sex on the first date. After that night, I knew she was something special."

"And then he refused to see me again."

"What? She liked you and you liked her?"

"I was a divorced man pushing forty. She could do a lot better than me. I told her that she should give it six months. If she was still interested, to call me."

"That was a risk," Heather said, picking up one of the peanut butter cookies. "She could have found someone else."

"He thought I would." Jillian took his hand in hers. "Oh, I dated, but none of them were him and six months to the day, I called. We went out that night and eloped three months later."

They shared another look that made Heather feel both envious and uncomfortable. The love between them was palpable. She'd seen it a few times. It was how Dugan looked at her cousin Sophie and how Daphne and Brody were together. But it wasn't anything she could imagine experiencing herself.

"We waited a few years to have our girls," Jillian added. "Ella is eleven and Layla is nine. They're going to be so excited to meet you. They've been after us to give them another sister and now here you are."

Sister? No. She wasn't anyone's sister.

"Tell us about you," Fletcher urged. "Are you married?"

"No. I'm not the marrying kind."

Jillian touched her arm. "Don't say that. Marriage is a blessing. The love of a good man can be…" Her voice trailed off as she frowned slightly. "Or any partner," she added quickly. "It doesn't have to be a man."

Heather laughed. "It's okay. If I were to get married, it would be to a guy. I just don't see myself doing that." Giving her life over to someone who would turn around and do his best to suck all the joy from her existence. Only that kind of thinking had cost her Campbell and that was still a loss she hadn't processed.

"I work a lot," she said.

"That's right. You're in marketing." He paused. "Did I understand that you own the company?"

Heather nodded.

Fletcher's eyes widened. "That's impressive. It's in Seattle?"

"Yes. I love what I do. My first job out of college was with a large marketing company, then a few years ago I started my own firm." She grinned. "Well, I'm still paying off investors, so mostly mine."

"You must be very talented," Fletcher said.

"I have a good team."

Jillian glanced at the clock. "You know, the girls will be home in a bit. Did you want to stay and meet them?"

Heather stiffened. "I think it's too soon."

Jillian started to protest, but Fletcher shook his head. "It's all right. This is a lot for all of us. Let's take a little time to get to know each other." His gaze met hers. "Heather, I don't want to scare you off, but I would like us to be friends. I'll admit my ultimate goal is to welcome you into the family, but let's start with getting to know each other."

His statement should have sent her running for the door, but while she was nervous about the whole *welcoming her into the family* thing, she liked the idea of knowing this man. He was nice and normal. And very likely, her biological father.

"We should take a DNA test," she said.

Jillian looked surprised. "You're not sure he's your dad?"

"A DNA test sounds good," Fletcher said easily.

"I'll arrange it." Heather pulled out her phone and made a note. "I'm sure I can find something online where they send us the test and we send it back."

"Whatever you'd like."

"Thanks."

She stood, then paused, not sure what to say or do. Jillian pulled her close for a hug. Heather tried to relax, but found herself offering a stiff, finger-tip-to-the-back, A-frame hug. Fletcher only patted her shoulder.

"I want us to stay in touch," he repeated.

"I do, too."

She spoke without thinking, only to realize it was possible she was telling the truth.

The drive home was uneventful. She bypassed the outlet mall without shopping but made a note to mention it to Tori. Maybe they could go together so Tori could flesh out her wardrobe. So much had been ruined by the flood.

She arrived at her place and found her friend with the kittens. Tori had a feather wand toy she was dragging across the carpet. The kittens watched it and tried to pounce. Scout and LC monitored the situation.

The kittens were nearly four weeks old and were down to only four feedings a day. They were starting to interact with their world and enjoyed playtime.

Tori saw her and scrambled to her feet. "How did it go? Are you okay?"

Heather waved her back to the floor and sank down herself. Scout came over to greet her while LC looked the other way.

"It was good," she said. "Strange. Fletcher is nice. He has a very soothing manner—probably from being a teacher. I liked his wife, too." She wrinkled her nose. "She's my age. I mean literally. Our birthdays are a week apart, which should have freaked me out, but on them, it works."

Tori watched her as she spoke. "You sound okay about it. That's good, right?"

"It is. I don't know what I was expecting. I felt awkward at first, then relaxed. He wants to stay in touch."

Russell Wilson walked over to her. She picked him up and stroked him. He immediately began to purr.

"Did you meet your sisters?"

Heather glanced at her friend. "They're not my sisters."

"Half sisters, then." Tori's tone turned wistful. "You're getting a whole new family. That's great."

Of course Tori would see it that way, Heather thought. She didn't have any relatives except for a sister she hadn't seen in years. Heather was less convinced she wanted more family, but it seemed she had found some.

"The girls weren't there," she said. "Maybe next time. Oh, we're going to do a DNA test, just to confirm everything."

"This is exciting." Tori rustled the feathers for the other two kittens. "Are you going to tell Amber?"

"I doubt I have a choice." She shuddered at the thought of what her mother would say about Fletcher. "I'm due to visit her. I'll tell her then. At least in person I can try to manage her reaction."

She would also talk to her cousin Sophie about it ahead of time. Sophie was always a great ally.

"Enough about me," Heather said. "How are you doing?"

"I'm still in shock. I'm not having much luck looking for a place to rent. I found a couple, but they won't take a dog as big as Scout. Who puts a twenty-five pound limit on dogs? I'm exhausted and scared and confused."

"It's a lot, but you're not in this alone," Heather said firmly. "You can stay here as long as you want. I mean that."

Having Tori around was easy. They'd been roommates at college and had always gotten along. LC enjoyed Scout's company, so sharing space worked for everyone.

"Thanks," Tori told her. "Daphne said I could sleep in their basement, which is sweet, but not a long-term solution. In the meantime, she's looking for places for us, as well."

The two kittens still playing collapsed onto the floor. Tori petted them both.

"These guys must be close to transitioning to regular food."

Heather nodded. "In a couple of days. They're also ready to start using a litter box. I'll introduce them to the process this afternoon."

"They grow up so fast," Tori teased, then her smile faded a little. "Daphne and I were talking earlier."

Heather immediately went on alert. "About housing for you?"

"There were other topics." Tori shifted slightly on the carpet. "We want you to come to brunch next Saturday."

Heather pressed her lips together. Brunch with her friends? She certainly wanted to hang out with them, but there were two big-ass problems. Campbell and his new girlfriend.

"We miss you," Tori added.

"You can't miss me. You see me every day."

"You know what I mean. I miss us, as a group. It's not the same without you."

"I don't know if I can do it," Heather admitted. "Sitting across from Campbell and what's her name."

"Nora," Tori murmured.

"Whatever. My point is I'd be uncomfortable and I'm not sure Campbell and Nora would be happy to have me right there."

"I care about you more than I care about them. Heather, if you can't deal with whomever Campbell is dating, then you're never going to be part of the group and I know you don't want that."

Give up the group? Heather hadn't thought of it that way. She couldn't. They were her family—at least that was how she'd always thought of them.

"You have me and Daphne, but it's not the same," Tori continued. "At least think about it."

She nodded. "I will, but you need to talk to Campbell. I don't want him thinking I'm there to make trouble."

Or trying to get his attention, even though he'd made it clear he was a thousand miles beyond over her.

"I'll talk to Grant," Tori said. "He can talk to Campbell."

"Coward."

"Grant's the brother I know best. If Campbell's okay with it, you'll come?"

Heather hesitated before nodding slowly. "You're right. This is my family and I don't want to lose what we had." Even if that meant watching Campbell fall in love with someone who wasn't her.

Promise you'll listen with an open mind.

Daphne stared at the text. "Seriously, Mom? You drive me crazy."

She spoke out loud, without fear of being overheard. Not only was she alone in her car, her mother was all the way down in Arizona.

She texted back. I love my job. I just made partner. I'm not looking for something different.

You haven't heard what Renee has to say. She's one of my oldest and dearest friends. Please hear her out.

"Like I don't know who Renee is?" Daphne sighed. "Mothers. There's a reason they get all the blame."

I promise to hear every word. Gotta go. Love you.

Love you, too.

Daphne slipped her phone into her bag and got out of the car. She was at a Starbucks in Bellevue, across from the downtown shopping center. The low, one-story building was an anomaly in a sea of high-rises.

She went inside and glanced around for Renee. Seconds later the attractive, well-dressed, fifty-something woman joined her.

"Daphne! You look amazing."

Daphne smiled and hugged her. "You do, too."

"I haven't seen you in, what, twelve years?"

"Thirteen. I think it was at my college graduation party."

Renee laughed. "I remember the big banner. It was some version of 'our daughter is going to law school.'"

"They were very proud."

"As they should have been."

They reached the front of the line and placed their order. While Renee waited for the lattes, Daphne claimed a quiet table by the window.

"I heard you made partner," Renee said as she sat down. "You must be so proud of yourself. Especially at your law firm. They work you hard."

"They do, but I love what I do, so the days go fast."

Renee smiled. "Your mother tells me you're married. And Brody has three kids from a previous marriage?"

"Yes." Daphne smiled. "Elijah's ten, Cadin's eight and Alexa is six. We share custody so we have them every other week."

Renee's brows rose slightly. "Plus eighty-hour weeks. How do you do it?"

"Brody and I work it together," she said. Until recently. Since "the flower incident," they were barely speaking and when they did, rarely were those conversations pleasant.

"I like to think I'm in pretty good shape," Renee said with a laugh. "I'm exhausted just listening to you." Her smile softened. "But you're happy."

"Very."

"Then I'm probably wasting my time, but indulge me."

"Of course."

"What do you know about *Velkommen*?"

Daphne glanced at Renee. "I'm sorry. Something came up at work and we have the kids this week, and I couldn't find the time to do any research."

Renee waved away the apology. "Not to worry. Now I

know where to start. *Velkommen* is Norwegian for *welcome*. As in, we welcome you and you are welcome with us. We're a licensed fiduciary. We're not a broker—we don't make investments. We act as our client's representative when they can't. We have power of attorney both financially and medically."

She set down her coffee. "So Mrs. Smith, age eighty-two, has a stroke. When the paramedics pick her up, they'll take her to the closest hospital, who will contact her doctor. Her doctor notifies us and a caseworker shows up at her bedside, day or night. From that moment on, we speak for Mrs. Smith until she can speak for herself. We make sure her cat is fed, pay her bills, water her plants. If she needs to go to a nursing home permanently, we manage that."

"Wouldn't her family do all that?"

"Mrs. Smith has no family. Her friends are also elderly. There's no one to take on the responsibility." She sipped her latte. "Or instead of a stroke, Mrs. Smith breaks a hip. Now that retirement community she's been resisting is looking better and better. But every penny she spends now is one less penny for her two adult children. They decide to have her declared unfit so they can put her somewhere cheaper, where she has to share a room and doesn't get the fresh flowers that she loves so much."

Daphne sighed. "Now I feel bad for her."

"Don't. We're there to protect Mrs. Smith from everyone, even her adult children. If she's declared unfit, she has already arranged for us to be her guardian. She's told us her wishes as far as the type of retirement community. We know she wants fresh flowers every week. We know her little dog will be adopted by that nice family across the street."

"How did I not know about your company?" Daphne asked.

"We're not large. Most people rely on family to take care of them, but for some, that's not an option. The majority of our clients are older, but we have a few young adults who are disabled in some way."

"Of course," Daphne said. "What if you're the single parent of a seriously handicapped adult child who can't fend for him or herself, but could live another thirty years, with no other family?" A nightmare scenario.

"That's where we step in. Size wise, we don't compare with your law firm. We have three principals, legal counsel, two care coordinators and a dozen caseworkers, based here in Bellevue."

Renee smiled. "We're also concerned about continuity for our clients. We work hard to hire the right people. We pay well and we offer generous benefits. It's been three years since we hired someone new."

Daphne felt her eyes widen. "In any position?"

Renee nodded. "However, our legal counsel wants to retire and that's where you come in." She leaned forward. "We're interested in you, Daphne. You already work with wills and trusts. You have a reputation for excellence." Her smile returned. "Plus, I've known you all your life, so I'm clear on your character."

"While I appreciate the compliments, I'm not interested in another job. I love what I do and I did just make partner." Why would she walk away from that? She was also well paid and doubted *Velkommen* could match her low mid six-figure salary.

"We're strong advocates of work-life balance," Renee said as if she hadn't heard Daphne's protestation. "Forty-hour weeks are common. You could also work from home a few days a week. You'd join our senior management team, just four of us." She grinned. "With Roger retiring, it's all women, so that's interesting."

The smile faded. "We're a good group of people doing satisfying work. I've stood by the hospital bed of a client who had a heart attack. I was able to say that everything was handled. The hospital had a copy of the client's medical directive, the people who needed to be called were being called, the stove was off, the pet was safe and later, someone would put gas in the client's car so it would be ready to go when the client was discharged."

"Or to be sold if the client didn't make it."

"That, too. We need a good lawyer. I think you're the one. I know you weren't considering this. You have a good plan. I'm simply asking you to think about it." The smile returned. "I'll casually mention our excellent medical insurance and generous maternity leave."

"If that's my mother using you to find out if I'm pregnant, please tell her the second I know, she'll know."

Renee laughed. "She did ask me to check out your stomach. She'll be sad to know you're as fit as ever."

Daphne shook her head. "That woman. I'm so grateful she's well over a thousand miles away."

"I don't believe that. You miss her."

"All right, yes, I do. But wow, can she make me crazy."

"It's one of the perks of motherhood." She rose. "Thank you for listening."

"Of course." Daphne stood with her coffee. "You do interesting work. Your clients must be so grateful you exist, but it's really not for me."

"I understand. I hope it's all right if I reach out in a few weeks. Just to see if you've been thinking about us."

"Of course." Because her mom would scold her if she said no.

They hugged goodbye in the parking garage. Daphne got in and started her car. While she had no interest in the job, she had to admit the Bellevue location would be great, closer to the house. Her commute would be cut in half. As for the forty-hour week—she honestly had no idea what she would do with herself if she worked that little. She couldn't remember the last time she'd been caught up with nothing pressing to do.

The company impressed her. She was used to family drama and arguments over wills and trusts. But she wasn't involved after. To be so intimately connected to someone's life, to give them incredible peace of mind, knowing they wouldn't be alone, didn't have to worry about wishes being ignored or a beloved pet being dumped at a shelter, that would be satisfying.

"If things were different," she said as she pulled out of the parking lot and headed for downtown Seattle.

But she loved her job—including the long hours. She liked the challenges, the sense of achievement. If the downside was seventy- or eighty-hour weeks and a less perfect home life, she'd always found a way to make it work.

eight

Tori stepped inside Heather's condo, Scout at her heels. Her dog immediately gave a little *woof* to let LC know she was there. The cat trotted out and started rubbing against Scout before heading to Tori for a greeting.

"Hey, Mr. Man," Tori said, picking him up and snuggling with him. He purred and gave her chin a quick kiss.

Tori set him on the back of the sofa and stepped out of her pumps. She rarely wore a four-inch heel at work, but these were one of two pairs that had, somewhat, survived the flood. She needed to go shoe shopping for sure.

That morning she'd taken her soaked clothing to her favorite dry cleaner. Myra had promised to do the best she could, but several of the winter blazers were probably damaged beyond repair, along with her two fancy dresses. Most of her summer things had survived. She'd already done six loads of laundry so far.

Sadly, her cosmetics and skin care were equally hit and miss. She'd started a replacement list. Her tablet was dead, so she needed another one of those. Fortunately, her laptop had been at the office, so spared.

A long conversation with her insurance agent had been re-assuring. They would coordinate with the HOA and all her contents were fully covered. Tori simply had to keep receipts of all her purchases.

She knew eventually she would be made whole. But knowing and believing were two different things. She hadn't slept much the past two nights and couldn't shake a low-grade sense of anxiety.

Her phone buzzed. She smiled when she saw a text was from Grant.

You home?

Just. I'm about to feed Scout and LC.

Good. I'll be there in fifteen minutes. I'm picking up tacos from that place we like.

Relief joined gratitude. Heather was working late with El-liot and had told Tori to eat whatever she wanted for dinner. Tori had planned to make a list of foods and hit the grocery store, but Grant bringing takeout was so much better. The kittens were at the office with Heather, so Tori didn't have to worry about them.

She changed into shorts and a T-shirt, fed LC and Scout, then set the table. She was taking Scout out for her post-dinner poop when he arrived, food in one hand and beer in the other, Zeus trailing behind him. Scout raced over to greet both of them. Tori joined him.

"Hey," he said as she approached. "How are you doing?"

The sight of his familiar face destroyed the last of her defenses. Her shoulders sagged, her throat got tight and her eyes began to burn.

"Terrible," she admitted. "I can't sleep, I can't focus and I've lost everything. Rebuilding seems too daunting and I don't know where to start."

His mouth twisted with concern. "Let's get inside. Once you have a little food in your stomach, you'll feel better."

She doubted that, but didn't want to be too depressing, so she nodded. Once inside, she washed her hands before helping him plate the food. He passed her an open beer. They sat across from each other at the small table. Zeus and Scout wrestled in the living room. LC watched from the safety of the sofa back, occasionally batting at the air, as if giving pointers to the dogs.

Grant had brought street tacos from a little hole-in-the-wall place they liked. There were shrimp, carnitas and chicken tacos, along with a crisp salad and guacamole and chips. Grant set one of each taco on her plate, then did the same for himself. He centered the guac between them, then touched his beer bottle to hers.

"It's going to be okay," he told her.

"You don't know that."

He smiled. "Of course I do. We have good insurance, the HOA reserves are funded and ours is not the first building to ever experience a flood. People have survived this. We will, too."

"You being rational doesn't work for me."

"I can't help it. Rational is my natural state."

She took a bite of the shrimp taco. The blend of flavors and heat were perfect. Just tasting the food reminded her she hadn't eaten much in the past couple of days. She devoured all three tacos in less than a minute, then wiped her fingers on a napkin and reached for a chip, only to find Grant smiling at her.

"What?" she demanded.

"You were hungry."

"Shut up."

He laughed.

She dug her chip into the guac. "Why aren't you at work?"

"I took a couple of days off to figure out how to get us going on reconstruction. Plus, looking for a place."

She groaned. "Tell me about it. There's a weight limit on dogs."

"I've seen that, too. At least you can get into places that go up to fifty pounds. Scout's only what? Thirty-five?"

"Uh-huh."

"Zeus is over sixty. Plus, some of the apartments are so small. I looked at one and knew that he'd be smacking the walls by wagging his tail."

"You've looked at a place? I haven't done that, mostly because I can't find anywhere good. There was a house that seemed promising but I can't afford the rent."

He stared at her. "Why didn't you call me? We could have rented it and split the cost."

She paused, a chip halfway to her mouth. "Together?"

"Why not? We practically live together now."

"No, we don't."

They didn't. Sure, his dog spent the night with her and he walked hers before he left for work and sometimes they shared the grocery shopping and he took care of any spiders she found, but that wasn't living together.

He pulled out his phone. "Do you remember the address?"

"No." She got out her phone and quickly found the listing. "Oh, it's rented already."

He set his phone on the table. "A house is a good idea. Let's start looking at those."

She was still processing the idea of them being roommates. She supposed he was right—it wouldn't be all that different.

"I'll check in the morning," she said. "I'm taking the day off to get organized. And do some shopping." She reached for another chip. "Any of your stuff survive?"

"My lone suit is at the cleaners, along with my leather jacket. The scrubs are okay and my jeans will wash. Everything else is destroyed. I know you're dealing with the same problem."

She told herself to stay in her head and not feel all the emotions. Dinner was too good to be ruined by an emotional breakdown.

"I am. Nearly everything is ruined. Jackets, shoes. My purses are in Heather's laundry room, filled with newspaper that I change twice a day. My dry cleaner is doing what she can with a few things. But it's more than just clothes, Grant. It's our appliances, our flooring, the drywall."

He touched the back of her hand. "Deep breaths, kid. We'll get through this together. We're coordinating everything with our insurance and the HOA. We'll get the same contractor. Sort of a two-fer. So you only have to carry half the load."

"That sounds good. Thank you."

"Welcome." He put the last shrimp taco on her plate. "Eat up. You're wasting away."

She smiled. "It's been forty-eight hours. Believe me, it would take a whole lot longer than that for me to waste away."

"Hey, I'm a doctor. I know what I'm talking about."

"I don't remember you being this bossy."

"Campbell's a bad influence."

Once again, Heather found herself in her car, wishing she could turn around and go home. Unfortunately for her, she wasn't alone. With Tori staying with her and with her having agreed to meet her friends for brunch, it only made sense for them to drive together. A truth that left Heather trapped and nervous.

"You okay?" Tori asked.

"No. Why did I say I'd join you? I was happy by myself."

"You missed our brunches."

"Yes, but that pain was familiar and I could deal with it. Now I have the never-fun fear of the unknown."

Tori laughed. "It's just us, hanging out, eating eggs."

"She'll be there."

Campbell's new and possibly perfect girlfriend. Heather knew in her head Nora wasn't the reason he'd told her they were, to quote Taylor Swift, never ever getting back together, but it was easier to blame the mystery woman than to face her own failings.

"She's not awful," Tori admitted. "Under other circumstances, I think you'd like her."

Heather briefly glared at her friend. "Don't say that. I don't want to like her."

"Because you still want to get back together with Campbell? Even though you won't move in with him or even discuss the L word?"

"I might move in with him. Or rather let him move into my place."

Tori stared at her. "You'd live with Campbell?"

"Maybe."

An easy admission considering the man was not only over her, but involved with someone else. Only Heather thought maybe she was telling the truth. She could, almost, see herself committing more to him.

"That's huge," Tori said.

"And irrelevant what with him dating Nora." She sucked in a breath. "Are they living together?"

"Not that I know of."

"But they're sleeping together."

Tori groaned. "I haven't asked, but the odds are good."

"I can't do this. Let's just go to McDonalds for breakfast. I'll buy."

Tori pointed straight ahead. "No wavering. You can do this. You'll feel better after you've been brave."

"I doubt that."

But Heather dutifully drove the rest of the way to Life's a Yolk. As they reached the door of the restaurant, she clutched Tori's arm.

"I'm not sitting across from her." Bad enough to be at the same table—no way she was going to spend the entire meal staring at Nora.

"I promise to sacrifice myself," Tori promised. "Deep breaths. You'll be fine."

Heather doubted that, but there was no turning back. She followed her friend inside, her radar immediately going on alert as her gaze settled on Campbell, already at the table, a petite blonde in the seat next to his. Grant sat across from them.

More quickly than she would have liked, they were approaching the table. Campbell's gaze locked with hers. Before she could bolt for safety, he gave her a welcoming smile that made her forget to be anxious. Grant turned, then stood.

"You made it," he said, pulling out a chair for each of them, then hugging them both. "About time you joined us," he whispered in Heather's ear.

Tori sat across from Nora, allowing Heather to take one seat over. Grant resumed his seat. Campbell leaned forward.

"Heather, this is Nora. Nora, our friend Heather."

Nora was as pretty as Heather had feared. She had delicate features and big blue eyes. Her smile was genuine as she said, "I'm so excited to finally meet you. I've heard so much about you."

Heather glanced at Campbell. "Why? Don't you have bet-ter things to talk about?"

Everyone laughed.

Nora kept her gaze on Heather. "I mean it. You started your own successful business. I'm so impressed."

The compliment didn't make her feel the least bit comfort-able. "What do you do, Nora?"

"I run a large preschool center in Renton."

Campbell put his arm on the back of her chair. "She was an early childhood development major."

Of course she was.

"I planned on being a teacher," Nora continued, "but I took a few fascinating business courses. I wanted to work with kids and be on the business side of things, as well."

It was a lot of information that Heather didn't particularly want. She was torn between changing the subject and saying something bondy—the latter of which made no sense. Still, she found herself blurting, "My father's a teacher."

Tori, who knew what had happened, was unfazed, but Grant looked surprised and Campbell stared at her as if she'd suddenly grown horns.

"Your father?" he asked. "Your birth father?"

Nora looked confused. "Is this a big deal?"

Heather wished she'd kept her mouth shut. Fortunately, Tori came to her rescue.

"Heather just connected with her birth father. He's so happy to have her in his life. Grant, you look grumpy. Did you just get off work?"

Grant stared at her in confusion. "I'm not grumpy."

"Sometimes you are. I just want to know so I can distract you, if necessary."

"No one's grumpy."

And as easily as that, conversation shifted. Heather relaxed a little. Tori was the best.

Just then Daphne and Brody walked in. Everyone said hello and coffee was poured. There was no more mention of Heather's father.

As they discussed the menu, Heather tried not to glance at Nora. But it was difficult to act natural and yet try to ignore her.

The server took their orders. Heather ordered the vegetable omelet with a side of hash browns. The server turned to Tori, but before she could speak, Campbell said, "You forgot no spinach."

Heather glanced from him to their server. "Um, he's right. No spinach, please." She looked back at him. "Thanks. I wasn't paying attention."

He smiled at her. "No problem."

She told herself he was just being nice and not to read anything into the moment. A moment they weren't having.

"Isn't he wonderful?" Nora asked, leaning against him. "So thoughtful. Remembering you don't like spinach is a very Campbell thing to do." She looked up at him. "This is why I adore you."

Adore? They'd reached the adoration stage? What did that mean? Were they already in love? Heather did her best not to grimace.

When all the orders were placed, Daphne pointed at Tori. "I might have a lead on a house. A client of mine can't decide if she wants to sell hers or not. She's moved into a retirement community but is afraid she won't like it, so she's thinking she wants to keep the house as a fallback plan. It's big and furnished. I'll have an answer in two days."

Tori glanced at Grant. "So we'd be sharing?"

"You said you were okay with that," Grant said.

"It's weird, but we can make it work."

"I'm not promising," Daphne told them. "Keep looking, but I'll call as soon as I know."

"Any housing that takes a large dog would be great," Tori said, smiling at Heather. "You're going to get sick of me."

"Never. Stay as long as you like."

Campbell looked surprised. She wanted to say that her resistance to living with him had nothing to do with sharing space and everything to do with him turning into her mother.

"You live alone?" Nora asked her. "I mean until the great flood."

Heather nodded. "I have LC, my cat and the foster kittens, but otherwise it's me."

"Heather enjoys her personal space," Campbell said easily. "She didn't mind me being gone for two or three days."

Nora wrinkled her nose. "Really? I know Campbell loves what he does, but him being away so much is really hard."

"It's not for very long," Heather murmured, thinking she'd always enjoyed the chance to do her own thing. "But I was happy when you came home."

"You were."

"I don't like being alone," Nora admitted. "I want another heartbeat around. I'm one of five girls so I've always shared a room. Even now I have a roommate, more for company than for help with the rent."

Heather caught Daphne's wide-eyed stare and knew exactly what she was thinking. *Shades of Krissa*, Grant's emotionally needy ex-wife. Even Brody looked a little startled.

"Pet heartbeats work for me," Tori said cheerfully. She glanced around the table. "Hmm, why is it Heather, Daphne, Grant and I have always had pets and Brody and Campbell never did?"

"They're heartless," Grant said cheerfully, pouring himself more coffee.

"I travel," Campbell pointed out.

"The kids are enough heartbeats for me," Brody said.

"I've never been a pet person," Nora murmured. "We didn't have them when I was growing up."

"You probably shouldn't have said that," Campbell teased. "Daphne has two cats and Heather is totally team cat. Her cousin started a cat supply company called Clandestine Kitty and Heather has always had cats. Tori has Scout, her Labradoodle."

"Mini Labradoodle," Tori added. "She's wonderful. Oh, and Heather fosters motherless kittens."

Nora's eyebrows rose. "Like newborns?"

"Usually a week or two old," Heather told her.

"It's a thing," Brody added. "You have to bottle-feed them and make them go to the bathroom. We've all learned how."

"The ones I have now are about four weeks old, so I'm going to start weaning them and litter box training them."

"You have to teach them to use a litter box? I thought cats just knew."

"It usually doesn't take long." Heather glanced around the table, thinking they should change the subject. Fortunately, their food arrived. By the time the plates were distributed and everyone had sighed over the shared cinnamon custard yum yum, conversation shifted on its own.

When brunch was finished, they all walked out together. Daphne paused by Heather's car.

"You doing okay?" she asked quietly. "You seemed comfortable, but I wasn't sure."

Heather looked toward where Campbell and Nora were talking to Brody. "It wasn't horrible. I felt bad we ganged up on her about not wanting a pet."

Tori snorted. "She deserved it. Who isn't an animal person?"

Daphne laughed. "Lots of people don't want pets and that's okay."

"You're so reasonable. She can't be alone for five minutes and she doesn't like kittens. What does he see in her?"

Something, Heather thought sadly, watching as Campbell took Nora's hand as they walked to his SUV. Their shoulders bumped companionably and he lightly kissed her before he opened the passenger door.

"The point is," Daphne said, "you did great, so now we can all hang out together." She hugged both of them. "I've missed this."

"Me, too," Heather admitted.

Daphne waved goodbye and joined Brody. Tori got in Heather's car, but Heather stood outside, watching Campbell and Nora drive away.

She wanted to be the one with him. She wanted his kisses and his smiles. The fact that she wouldn't have them ever again was on her. He'd been in love with her and she'd left him. She had no one to blame but herself. But knowing that and accepting it were two different things. Eventually, she would be fine, but for now, there was still the aching sense of loss and the pain of what could have been.

nine

Daphne had an hour left before the chicken cacciatore was finished. Then she could put the pot roast in the slow cooker for tonight. She already had split pea soup in the pressure cooker. Now that she'd finished with the vegetables and potatoes for the pot roast, she could make cookies.

Normally, she enjoyed her every other Sunday batch cooking. The kids arrived about four in the afternoon and it took at least an hour for them to settle in. After their initial greeting, she and Brody checked that they had the right clothes, schoolbooks and homework, along with special toys and in Cadin's case, his favorite pillow. That was followed by a family dinner and board games. No TV on their first night here. She and Brody had discovered the week went better when they took the time to reconnect.

She liked having the kids for the week. They were bright and funny and she enjoyed their company. It was just that today she was so tired. Actually, the being tired wasn't new. She hadn't been sleeping well lately and she and Brody still weren't speaking much. Or spending time together. After brunch yesterday, they'd gone their separate ways. She'd headed to the office and had no idea what he'd done.

She knew it was wrong, but she found it easy to bury herself in her job rather than face whatever was going on in their relationship. They were on a downward spiral and she didn't know how to make that stop.

She got the first batch of peanut butter cookies into the oven, then put a couple of large bowls on the counter. When the Crock-Pot dinged, she dished the chicken cacciatore into glass containers. Once everything had cooled, she would store it in the refrigerator for a midweek meal.

She took out the cookies, and put in the next two trays. After setting the timer, she washed the Crock-Pot stoneware inner container. She'd just put in the meat and started the machine when Brody walked into the kitchen.

They stared at each other in silence for a few seconds. He shoved his hands into his jeans.

"You're busy," he said.

"The kids are here for the week. I'm getting meals ready."

The timer dinged. She pulled out the cookies and set them on cooling racks.

He looked at the cooling cacciatore, the cookies on trays and the Crock-Pot.

"You don't have to do all this," he told her. "We've talked about finding a meal service."

"I don't mind cooking. It relaxes me." Most days. Today she'd rather take a nap.

"What can I do to help?" he asked.

Her first instinct was to say "nothing." But he was reaching out and she should accept that.

"If you'd take the cookies off the trays, please."

While he did that, she got out more containers for the split pea soup. The pressure cooker beeped that it was finished. She got ham out of the refrigerator and began to dice it to add to the soup.

"What else?" Brody asked.

She glanced around, trying to find an easy task for him. "All that's left is washing the bowl and paddle from the stand mixer so I can make chocolate chip cookies."

"I can do that."

He walked the items to the sink. Daphne watched him work, hating how quiet they were together. Where was the easy conversation, the affectionate teasing?

"I miss us," she blurted.

He turned to face her. "I miss us, too." He drew in a breath. "I want us to have a baby. I've always wanted that. It's just right now, things are complicated."

She told herself to believe him. This was the man she loved and she should trust him. But how could she when he thought she'd had an affair? They were stuck and she didn't see a way out.

"Can we let it go?" she asked impulsively. "Just for the week? Can we pretend everything is fine and not fight and go back to how we were? Next Sunday we'll deal with all this, but for now, can the bad stuff not exist?"

His mouth twisted. "We can't ignore our problems."

"I agree. We do need to face them, but it's just one week, Brody."

His reluctance was tangible but he nodded slowly. "Sure. We can deal with this after the kids are gone."

"Good." She smiled at him. "So what's new with you?"

He mentioned a design modification on the hydraulic system and how the new guy couldn't keep up.

"You said he wasn't a good fit after his interview," she said. "HR should have listened."

He set the clean bowl and paddle by the stand mixer. "Somehow they don't want to hear that from me." He hesitated. "How was your meeting with Renee?"

"I wondered when you were going to ask about that."

He leaned against the island. "It felt like a no-win for me."

"Why?"

"You love your job. If I show interest in the other place, you'll think I'm trying to push you to switch jobs."

"You wouldn't do that."

"These days we don't seem to assume the best about each other."

He was right, she thought sadly. "I'm sorry."

"Me, too," he said. "So how did it go?"

"The business model is interesting. While the work would be different from what I do now, there's plenty of overlap."

"And fewer hours."

"I don't mind how much I work."

His gaze was steady. "Sometimes I worry that you'll burn out."

She laughed. "That's not going to happen."

He didn't smile back at her.

"Brody, I'm fine."

He turned away. "Like I said, I worry."

She wondered what else he was thinking. His point about her schedule not being conducive to having a baby was a good one. She didn't want to put her child in day care for ten or twelve hours a day, six days a week. But cutting back wasn't company style. She was a partner now, there were expectations.

He pulled her close. She stepped into his embrace, trying to remember the last time he'd hugged her. At least a couple of weeks, she realized sadly.

She lightly kissed him. "I've missed us," she told him again.

"Me, too."

He kissed her again, softly at first, then deepening the contact. After a few seconds he pulled back and glanced around the kitchen. "Can you take a break?"

She smiled at him. "I haven't started the next batch of cookies. The Crock-Pot is going to be busy for a while and the soup can sit for at least half an hour."

"Good."

He took her hand in his and led her to the stairs. As they walked into the bedroom, she told herself pretending everything was fine wasn't the worst thing in the world. Their problems would still be there in a week, but until then, she planned to enjoy having things back the way they always should have been.

Tori blinked, trying not to cry. The restoration people had been through her condo, sucking up water and removing the things that couldn't be salvaged. The drywall and carpets were gone. The appliances were in the dining room, waiting to be hauled away. Her sofa, stained and misshapen, was next to a warped table. The smell of dampness permeated everything, even with the windows open.

"I knew it would be bad," she whispered, trying not to have a meltdown. "But this is so much worse."

Grant put his arm around her. "We'll get it fixed."

Rationally, she knew he was right, but her heart told her the condo would never be the same.

Next door, his place was just as bad. There was still drywall in his spare bedroom—most of it hanging off the studs.

"It happened so fast," she said.

"There was nothing you could have done."

"I know, but it's still a shock."

He'd picked her up at work so they could meet with the appraiser. Their shared insurance agent had arranged for her to assess both units at the same time. Once she filed her report, they'd have money to start repairs.

"Hello? Anybody here?"

They walked back to the living room. A tall, middle-aged woman gave them a sympathetic smile.

"Tori Rocha and Grant Brown?" she asked.

"That's us," Grant said, shaking her hand.

"Desiree Johnson. The appraiser."

Tori shook her hand, as well. "Thanks for coming so quickly."

"You're going to have a lot of work to do here," Desiree said, looking around. "I heard what happened. Water damage is the worst. Let's get started so I can go back to the office and file my report."

They went through both units. Desiree took pictures, measured rooms and made notes. The more they looked around, the more damage Tori saw. With every passing minute, her heart sank a little more until she wanted to curl up in a ball and cry.

"I'll get right on this," Desiree told them when they'd finished. "It's going to be a while until you can move back in."

Grant nodded. "We're staying with friends, but also looking for a six- or eight-month lease."

They walked downstairs together. Desiree went to her car, while Tori followed Grant to his SUV. They'd just gotten inside when Tori's cell rang with a call from Daphne.

"Hi," Tori said, activating the speakerphone. "I'm with Grant. We just met with the appraiser."

"Oh, good. You're together." Daphne sounded excited. "My client wants to rent the house. She's happy that I know you. She's fine with both dogs, as long as you pay a pet deposit. The house is fully furnished and you can move in as soon as you pass a credit check."

Grant looked at Tori, who nodded.

"Sounds good," he said. "Where is it?"

"Medina."

Tori hadn't realized it was in such a ritzy neighborhood. "So we'll be hanging out with rich people?"

"In an eight thousand square foot house."

Tori gasped. "Are you kidding?"

"Nope, but don't worry. She's not charging market rate. She's thrilled to have renters she can trust not to trash the place. Why don't you go take a look? I'll text you the address."

"Let's do it," Grant said.

Daphne texted them the address, the code for the door along with the surprisingly reasonable monthly rental amount.

"Medina," Tori said. "I won't fit in."

"You'll be fine," Grant told her with a grin. "If anyone asks, you can say we're the new caretakers."

Laughing eased some of her tension. Too much had happened too fast, she thought. She missed her life and routine. Heather was sweet to take her in, but the big sectional wasn't exactly the same as having her own bed.

They drove to the upscale neighborhood. There were "regular" size houses, along with huge estates on massive lots. Their rental place was one of the latter, a Mediterranean style sitting on a manicured acre, with wrought iron fencing and lush landscaping. They parked and went to the front door where she punched in the code.

The foyer was bigger than her condo living room and soared up two stories. The formal living room had seating for twenty, as did the huge dining room. The kitchen was the stuff of dreams, with a massive Sub-Zero refrigerator and freezer, two islands and an eight-burner stove. The eat-in alcove overlooked a pretty garden. There was a giant family room and a big library. An oversize mudroom led to the four-car garage.

There was a large fenced area for the dogs and a covered patio with a built-in outdoor kitchen. Upstairs were four bedrooms, all with their own bathrooms, a game room with a pool table and a home theater.

Tori walked into the master bath and nearly swooned at the gorgeous marble and fancy fixtures. "I could park my car in the closet."

"You'd have trouble getting it upstairs."

"Ha ha." She looked around. "The house is amazing."

"I agree it would work."

She stared at him. "It would work? Come on, there's a home theater and a pool table."

"You play pool?"

"No, but I could learn. What do you think?"

His dark gaze met hers. "We should take it, if you're okay with us living together."

She ran her hand along the cool marble vanity. "I was worried about that," she admitted, then grinned. "But the house is so big, we'll hardly ever see each other."

They walked back toward the stairs. Tori paused by a large bedroom with a comfy window seat. The bathroom came with a nice claw-foot tub and a walk-in shower.

"Scout and I want this one, if that's okay."

"Sure. Zeus and I will take the one in the corner."

"Not the master?" she teased.

"Let's leave that for the owner."

In the kitchen Tori opened several cupboards. There were plenty of dishes and cookware, along with every kitchen appliance she could name. She called Daphne.

"We want it," she said. "Can you email us the application?"

"I already did," Daphne told her. "Get the applications back to me as fast as you can. I'll run your credit and confirm the payment. You should be in there by the end of the week."

★ ★ ★

Heather crossed the bridge to Blackberry Island. The summer weather was perfect. The light breeze barely stirred the water of the Sound as she followed a string of cars, vacationers flocking to sample the wines, enjoy the beaches and views and stay at the picturesque Blackberry Island Inn.

Once she'd cleared the bridge, she turned off the main road and took the back way to her cousin's house. Although she'd put it off, it was time to tell her mother about Fletcher. She'd asked Sophie to provide interference, and her cousin had agreed to host a lunch for the three of them.

Amber, Sophie and Kristine were the daughters of three sisters. Amber was older by a few years, but Sophie and Kristine had gone through school together. When Sophie's single mom had been killed in a car accident, Sophie had gone to live with Kristine's family. While Sophie had created her Clandestine Kitty empire, Kristine had married her high school sweetheart and had three boys. Fifteen years ago she'd started her own bakery, now a thriving business on the island.

Unlike her cousins, Amber had never wanted a career. She'd claimed she would have gone to college if she hadn't gotten pregnant, but from Heather's perspective, her mother had never tried to better herself. She'd changed jobs every couple of years, complaining she wasn't appreciated. Nothing was ever Amber's fault and the world constantly disappointed her. As Heather had gotten older, Amber had pushed her only child to take on more responsibility. By the time Heather was sixteen, she was supporting them both, working as many hours as she could while still going to high school.

She'd found herself trapped on the island, unable to get away without abandoning her mother. Fate, in the form of Elliot and Sophie, had intervened. Elliot had helped her get into USC and had paid for her first year of college and had helped her get scholarships for the rest. Sophie had bought Amber a condo—on the condition that Amber let Heather have a life of her own.

Now, as she drove toward the house Sophie shared with her long-time partner, Dugan, Heather's shoulders tensed and her hands gripped the steering wheel. She wanted nothing more than to escape to the safety of the mainland. Being around her mother always felt dangerous. Telling herself she was an adult who could take care of herself didn't seem to ease her fears, and that was on a normal visit home. Today she was going to tell her mother about Fletcher. It wasn't a recipe designed to make her feel calm.

She pulled into the driveway of the large oceanfront house. There was a huge screened-in enclosure on the south side. Dugan had won Sophie's heart in many ways, but building the cat sunroom onto the side of his house had sealed the deal.

The front door opened before she reached it and Sophie raced out to greet her, her long hair flying behind her.

"You made it! I've missed you so much."

They hugged, hanging on for a few seconds.

"How was the drive? How are you?" Sophie grinned, looking much younger than her forty-eight years. "I'm having lunch catered, so be impressed."

"You're always impressive," Heather said with a laugh. "And it's only catered because you don't like to cook."

"That's true."

They went inside. Heather felt her smile fade as she saw her mother waiting in the foyer, her arms folded across her chest.

"You're here," Amber said, her tone more neutral than welcoming.

Heather crossed to her and gave her a non-touching, semi-hug. "Hi, Mom. How are you doing?"

"Not well. The tourists are everywhere and my back hurts. Not that anyone cares about my aches and pains."

Heather stepped back. "You look great."

A lie, but the right thing to say. Amber had put on weight and her less than positive outlook had left its stamp on her face. Her mouth turned down in a permanent frown and there were lines between her eyebrows.

Her mother pointed at Heather's sandals. "Those look expensive. It must be nice to be able to buy whatever you want. I could have started a business, too, if I'd been able to go to college. But I got pregnant and then you left and here I am, with nothing."

Sophie rolled her eyes. "Amber, please. Don't you want to get the greetings over with before you dive into your pity party?"

Amber grimaced. "You're always so mean." She turned to Heather. "What did you bring me?"

Heather pulled out a box of Fran's caramels from her bag. "I got the light and dark chocolate ones," she said quickly. "Sometimes you like both."

"Thank you," Amber said, then added, "These are mine. I'm not sharing."

Sophie patted her arm. "We wouldn't expect you to. Let's go have lunch."

The table was set for three with a beautiful strawberry, bacon and blue cheese salad in the middle, next to a platter with grilled caprese sandwiches. There was a vegetable plate and a dozen miniature cupcakes.

"Oh, Sophie, this is lovely," Heather said. "Thank you."

"It's not like she made it herself," Amber grumbled.

"That's true," Sophie said cheerfully. "Food cooked by other people tastes better."

They sat down, with Sophie at the head of the table and Heather across from her mother. Heather put a half sandwich and some salad on her plate, only to realize she couldn't possibly eat. She put her fork down, then cleared her throat.

"Remember when we all did Ancestry?" she asked.

Sophie, who knew what was coming, smiled. "I was hoping to be a little more exotic in my DNA, but I'm just boring Northern European with a little Irish thrown in for interest."

"It wasn't as much fun as I thought," Amber said between bites of her sandwich. "Maybe they messed up my test."

Heather cleared her throat. "Yes, well, I discovered something unexpected. My birth father."

For a second Amber didn't react. "Your what?" Then her eyes widened. "You mean that jerk who seduced me and left me pregnant, on my own?"

"That's exciting," Sophie said, her voice calm. "Have you been in touch with him?"

Amber stared at Heather. "Why would you—" Her stare turned into a glare. "You have! What? Did you call him?"

"I met him. He lives in the area."

"Here? Where?"

Heather hesitated. "On the mainland. He's married with two girls. He's a high school history teacher and he seems nice." She managed a smile. "He said you were pretty and funny and he talked about your smile."

Amber's mouth twisted. "He ruined my life. Why would I care what he thinks about my smile? I wonder how he got from being a rodeo cowboy to a teacher."

"He wasn't a rodeo cowboy, Mom. He was, um, helping around the venue." Which seemed kinder than saying he'd been cleaning out stables. "He was in WSU at the time. It was a temporary job."

Her mother ate more of her sandwich. "Yes, I remember him saying something about college and I said I wanted to go, which I couldn't do. You'd think if he liked my smile so much, he would have gotten in touch with me."

Sophie frowned. "You always said you didn't know his last name or where he lived. That it was just a magical night."

Amber glared at her. "I never said it was magical. He seduced me. And now he's happy with his perfect life. Typical."

"I think it's great," Sophie said. "You can get to know him. Plus, your medical history."

"He owes me child support."

Heather looked at her mother. "What?"

"Back child support. He owes me. I had to raise you on my own while he was living his life, doing whatever he wanted. He owes me."

"Mom, please. I just wanted to meet him so I could get to know him."

Her mother's eyes filled with tears. "So you can love him more than you love me? That's what this is about. You never wanted to be close to me. I'm just a burden."

Sophie slammed her hands on the dining room table. "Amber, stop it. This is one lunch with your daughter. Surely, you can act like a human being for an hour or two. If not, you know where the door is."

"You're such a bitch."

"Yes, but I'm okay with that."

Amber did her best to stare down her cousin, but Sophie never blinked. Eventually, Amber turned away.

"Whatever. I don't care about your birth father. Why would I? It was a long time ago."

Heather shot Sophie a grateful look, then rubbed her forehead as she felt the beginnings of a headache. This was why she never wanted to come see her mother. Amber could suck the good out of any situation. The visits had been better when she and Campbell had been together, she thought absently. He'd always had the ability to manage Amber. He was charming, attentive and had the rare skill of teasing her into a good mood.

When lunch was over and Amber had left, Heather helped Sophie clear the table. Her cousin wrapped up several sandwiches and put the rest of the salad in the container it had come in.

"Take this," she said firmly. "You didn't eat."

"It looked delicious," Heather told her. "But I just couldn't. Not with my mom being her usual self."

"She is a challenge."

"I don't know how you stand living so close to her."

"Ground rules," Sophie said. "If she gets in one of her moods, I leave or ask her to. Dugan does great with her. It's a guy thing."

"I guess."

Sophie put her hands on Heather's shoulders. "Listen to me. This thing with your dad is good. Don't let her take that from you. He sounds like a nice guy."

"He is."

Sophie looked into her eyes. "You're allowed to have a relationship with him. In fact, it's encouraged. Get to know him and your sisters."

Heather flinched. "I can't think of them as my sisters."

"Half sisters, then. Open your heart to the possibilities, at least. Again, I say, don't let your mom screw this up."

"You're always on my side." Heather hugged her. "Thank you."

"Anytime. Be happy, kid. You've earned it."

Heather was less sure about that, but she knew she wanted to spend more time with her dad and yes, meet his daughters. As for what came later, well, she would just have to wait and see.

ten

Everything Tori owned in the world—not counting soggy furniture and ruined appliances—fit in her car with room for Scout. Depressing but true. Yes, she and Grant were lucky to rent that amazing house while their condos were being repaired, but honestly, she would trade the killer kitchen for her own modest space. Unfortunately, lacking superpowers, she would have to wait out the construction.

"I hope you like the new house," she told Scout, who was busy hanging her head out the back window. "It's big and there's a nice fenced yard. Plus, you'll get to live with Zeus."

Scout was either unimpressed or too busy sniffing everything to respond.

Maybe she should have waited for Heather to get home from Blackberry Island, she thought. Having someone to say goodbye to would have been nice. But she wanted to get settled, so had told Heather she would be moving out that afternoon. An idea that she was now questioning. Did she really want to be in that big house by herself? Okay, Grant would be there for a couple of hours before he left for work, leaving her alone. At night.

She told herself not to think about that. Besides, she would have both dogs, so there was no reason to be scared.

At the house she was surprised to see several cars in the driveway. Grant she expected, but Campbell was there, too, along with Daphne. As she parked, Daphne came out and waved at her. Tori got out and went around to collect Scout.

"What are you doing here?" Tori asked, hurrying toward her friend.

"Helping you move in." Daphne pointed to the open back of her SUV. "I know the house is furnished but you need a few things for it to feel homey."

There were two giant, fluffy dog beds, a huge bag from Sephora and totes overflowing with linens. Nestled in the corner was a Dyson blow-dryer box.

"You can't give me all this," Tori said, stunned at her friend's generosity.

"It's not all for you." Daphne sounded smug. "Some is for the dogs and a few things are for Grant." She lowered her voice. "You know how guys get if you leave them out."

"I do."

Grant and Campbell joined them.

"Hey," Grant said, smiling at Tori. "You made it."

Zeus raced out and bolted for Scout. The two dogs wiggled with excitement, then darted for the grass to play.

"How are you feeling?" Grant asked.

Tori wrinkled her nose. "Overwhelmed." She turned to

Daphne. "Don't get me wrong. I'm so grateful you arranged the rental. It's stunning. But everything's happened so fast."

"I get that." Daphne hugged her. "You'll feel better when you're settled."

It didn't take long to empty all the vehicles. The dogs joined them to check out their new home. Daphne helped Tori make her bed. They put half the towels in her bathroom and the rest in Grant's. The new dog beds were placed in the family room.

"You don't want them in the bedroom?" Daphne asked when they'd all gathered in the kitchen.

"The dogs sleep with us," Grant said, then paused. "That came out wrong. My dog sleeps with me and Tori's dog sleeps with her."

"Not all the time," Tori joked. "When you work nights, Zeus sleeps with me, too."

"Cats take up a lot less room," Daphne murmured.

Campbell sat at one of the stools by the island. "How come no one took the master?" He winked at Tori. "I would have thought the bathroom would have you arm wrestling him for it."

"I know. That tub, the shower."

"The closet," she and Daphne said together, then laughed.

"It didn't feel right," Grant said. "That's the owner's room. We're happy with our tiny secondary bedrooms."

"The room you have is as big as my master back home," Campbell complained.

"Loser," Grant joked.

"Hey, you're the one who's homeless."

"And yet I live here."

Daphne smiled at Tori. "I have to run. If I'm not there to supervise Brody and the kids, something will get broken for sure." She pointed to the beautiful deck and backyard. "We should have a little housewarming celebration. We can barbecue and hang out."

"Sounds perfect." Tori hugged her. "Thank you for everything. You're amazing."

"Thank you for noticing."

Campbell stood. "I should head out, too. I'm meeting Nora for dinner."

"Tell her hi," Daphne said. Tori nodded.

She and Grant walked them out, then returned to the house. He glanced at her.

"You going to be all right here by yourself tonight?"

No, Tori thought, then forced a smile. "Of course. This is a very safe neighborhood and I'll have both dogs with me."

"You sure? It's a big house."

Yes, a big, strange house that probably had lots of big, strange house noises to keep her awake. But there was no way she would admit to nerves. She was an adult. She would be fine.

"It'll be great," she said, as much to herself as to him.

He didn't look convinced. "I'm sure Campbell and Nora would be happy to—"

"No," she said forcefully, interrupting him. "You're not asking your brother to babysit me. As if."

One eyebrow rose. "As if? What? Are we back in that old chick flick you like so much? *Clueless*?"

"Don't you dare mock *Clueless*. In fact, I'll stream it tonight, so there."

Back in the kitchen they had an awkward moment of staring at each other, as if both unsure how this living together thing was supposed to happen.

"So I, um…" he began.

Tori knew one of them had to take charge. "We'll finish

unpacking, then order pizza at five. Plenty of time to eat before you go to work."

He relaxed. "Sounds good."

"I'll want extra-large so I can have it for breakfast."

He grimaced. "That's not exactly healthy."

"So says the man who still eats Froot Loops."

"Hey, don't mess with my favorite cereal."

"I'm just saying."

He held out his arms. She stepped into his embrace and leaned against him.

"It's been a lot," he said quietly. "Too much. But now we can relax while the condos are fixed up. Before you know it, we'll be home."

"I want that." She looked at him. "I'm not a fan of change."

"I know. You're being very brave."

"Then can we get olives on the pizza? As a reward."

He grimaced. "Only on your half. Olives? On a pizza? You're so weird."

"You're weirder."

He chuckled. "I'll accept that."

Heather missed having Tori around more than she'd expected. Her condo felt empty without her friend and Scout. Sunday morning she took care of cat duties. Despite the kittens being weaned and making progress on their litter box training, she still had to mix formula in with the wet food and then make sure everyone got enough to eat. After that there was food to wash off tiny kitten faces. That was followed by a trip to the litter box and humorous attempts to cover up their business. Finally, both full and empty, they were ready to play.

This was the part of cat stepfatherhood that LC enjoyed the most. He was good for a quick chase, or batting a crinkly ball. He could pounce and roll with the best of them.

Heather put up the gate that would keep the kittens contained while giving LC a way to escape, then headed for her car. A short seventy minutes later she was at her father's house. As before, every fiber of her being told her to run home where yes, her life was small, but it was safe, and wasn't that better?

Yet, instead of starting the engine and making a quick U-turn, she marched toward the front door, only to have it open before she could knock. Her father and Jillian rushed out to greet her, but more significant were the two girls who followed.

"You made it," Fletcher said, giving her a quick hug. "We're happy to see you."

"More than happy," Jillian said warmly, hanging on a little longer. "The girls are beyond excited. They could barely sleep last night." She turned back to her daughters and smiled. "Heather, these are our daughters. Ella is eleven and Layla is nine. Girls, this is Heather."

They looked exactly like their mother, Heather thought, surprised by the resemblance. From their bright orange-red hair, to their freckles, to their smiles. Only their eyes, hazel like hers, seemed to come from their father.

The older girl, Ella, stepped forward. "Are you really our sister?"

"I think I am. A half sister, though. I have a different mother." She managed a shaky smile. "And I'm a whole lot older."

"That's okay," Layla said shyly. "We don't mind."

"Let's go inside." Jillian started for the door.

They settled in the living room. The girls flanked their mother on the sofa, while Fletcher and Heather each took a club chair.

"Did you know about us?" Ella asked.

"No. I didn't know who my dad was until a few months

ago. Once I found out we might be a DNA match, I looked him up on Facebook."

"There are pictures of us there!" Layla clapped her hands together. "Did you see us?"

"I did." No need to mention they'd freaked her out.

"You've been alive our whole lives." Ella leaned toward her. "And we didn't know."

"But you know now." Jillian smiled at her daughter. "It's very exciting."

"It is. I'm going into middle school next month."

"That's a big change." Heather hoped her comment wasn't too inane. Except for Brody's three, she didn't spend much time around kids.

"It is. I'm nervous."

Jillian put her arm around Ella. "You'll do great."

"I want to make a lot of friends."

"That's a good goal." Heather turned to Layla. "What grade are you going into?"

"Fourth. Want to see my room?"

Ella jumped up. "Mine, too! Mine, too!"

Fletcher shook his head. "Let's keep things calm," he told them. "Take a deep breath and let it out slowly. We're going to channel our excitement."

"I'd love to see your rooms." Heather glanced at Jillian. "If that's okay."

"Of course."

The girls led the way. Layla's room was done in shades of purple, with white lace curtains and stencils of fairies on the wall. The bookcase was bigger than the dresser. A desk was tucked into a corner. Stuffed animals covered the bed.

"The fairies are so beautiful," Heather said.

"Mommy made them."

Heather glanced at Jillian. "You're an artist."

"Stencils. It's not that difficult."

Ella's room reflected her older sister status. Instead of a twin bed, hers was a queen with drawers underneath. The aqua paint was dark by the baseboards and faded to nearly white at the ceiling. Silver stars dotted one wall. Her desk was larger and her standard closet had custom built-ins.

"Your room is so pretty," Heather said. "And very grown-up."

"We did it this summer," Ella said proudly. "Mommy and me. Daddy made the closet and Layla helped with the stars."

"It was a combination birthday and graduation present," Fletcher added.

His explanation made Heather uncomfortable, as if he felt they had to justify the expense. Ella was his daughter—he could do what he wanted. Only she would guess that like for most families, money was tight.

She smiled at Ella. "You'll be so proud to bring your friends home."

Ella beamed. "I am."

They took her on a quick tour of the rest of the house, which didn't take long. The only surprise was a craft room in the attic.

"Fletcher made this for me," Jillian said, pushing open the door to the surprisingly large space. There were dormer windows and open shelving. A big sewing machine sat at the far end and there were several works in progress on the large worktables in the center.

"I have craft envy," Heather said with a laugh. "I love this. When I was growing up, I used to quilt. I don't have time for it anymore."

She picked up a little crocheted bear. It was about six inches tall, with a sweet face and a bow by one ear.

"This is adorable. Did you make it?"

Jillian nodded. "It's a style of crochet called Amigurumi. I make different animals and dolls."

"She sells them on Etsy," Fletcher said proudly.

"It's not a big business," Jillian added. "Nothing like what you do. But it's fun and it's a little extra money I can make while I'm home with the girls. When they're in school, I work part-time at a local craft store."

Heather saw more of the little crocheted toys and immediately thought of Clandestine Kitty. Sophie was always on the lookout for custom products and these toys could be perfect if Jillian could make little cats that matched a customer's.

They trooped downstairs. In the kitchen Ella grabbed Heather's hand. "Do you have any other brothers and sisters?"

"No, I'm an only child." She paused. "Or I was. Growing up it was just my mom and me."

"Now you're our sister." Layla reached for her other hand. "Can we meet your mom? Is she our mom, too?" She frowned. "Is she our half mom?"

The thought of these girls being around Amber made Heather shudder. No way that was happening.

"I think we should get to know each other first," she said carefully.

Layla nodded. "We're having a special lunch because of you."

"Are you? That's so nice. Thank you." She looked at Jillian. "You shouldn't have gone to any trouble."

"Yes, well, it's not what you think." Jillian's tone was apologetic. "Around here, a special meal is takeout."

"We're getting Panda Express!" Ella hopped in place.

"I love Panda Express."

Fletcher smiled at her. "It's a family thing. I hope you don't mind."

"I'm not picky."

"I would have cooked," Jillian said, "but I was outvoted."

"You've been tired," Fletcher pointed out. "We all like Panda Express."

"No problem," Heather said quickly. "Next time, dinner's on me."

The words came out before she could stop them. Dinner was on her? What did that mean? Was she planning of making a habit of seeing these people?

But no one seemed to think what she'd said was extraordinary. Fletcher kissed Jillian, then touched Heather's arm.

"Back in a few."

The girls reluctantly released Heather and went out the back door with their dad. Jillian washed her hands.

"All we have to do is set the table and put out drinks." She chuckled. "Easy duty."

"I'll help."

Heather put out plates and glasses while Jillian poured lemonade.

"Did you tell your mom about Fletcher?"

Heather carefully set down the pitcher. "Yes. I, ah, had lunch with her and our cousin. She was surprised I found Fletcher."

"She was upset." Jillian didn't seem to be asking a question.

"She was in shock." Heather wondered how much to say. "My mom tends to look at things as a victim. Nothing is ever her fault and everyone else gets all the breaks. She can't be happy for anyone. Not even me."

Jillian's expression softened. "That has to be hard for you. I would imagine she's ambivalent about you meeting your birth father."

That was one way of putting it. "She needs a little time." Not that time would help, but why put a damper on the day?

"We're all finding our way." Jillian motioned for her to

take a chair, then sat across from her. "Fletcher and I are so grateful you reached out. You're a very unexpected blessing."

Heather felt her eyes widen. A blessing? "I'm not exactly the blessing type," she blurted.

Jillian laughed. "That's not true." She glanced at the back door, then returned her attention to Heather. "Your dad would tell me to leave you alone, but I have to know. Is there someone special in your life? You said you weren't married and you work a lot, but surely there's someone." Her expression turned impish. "I'm dying to meet him."

Heather tried to keep her tone upbeat. "Sorry to disappoint, but I'm not seeing anyone right now." She paused. "I'm not like you. I'm not good at relationships."

"I don't believe that."

"You should. I was dating this great guy. Campbell. He's a pilot for Alaska Airlines and was crazy about me. He wanted..." Her throat tightened. "Well, the usual stuff and I couldn't do it. I couldn't commit or move in with him or tell him I loved him."

"Did you love him?"

"I don't know." Heather fidgeted with her glass of lemonade. "I think about that. Did I love him? What is love, anyway? And why do we have to say the words?"

"Because words matter. Loving someone is a gift to them and to ourselves. We were put on this planet to give and receive love. It's our higher calling."

Those were about the scariest words she'd ever heard. "I'm too broken to have a normal romantic relationship."

Jillian shook her head. "I don't believe you."

"You haven't met my mother."

"No, but I've met you. That first day, you were so scared. But you showed up, anyway. And you came back. That's the definition of strength."

"Or idle curiosity."

"You're not here because you're curious. You want a connection, Heather. I can see it."

"That makes me feel both hopeful and terrified."

"We're not going to hurt you. We're excited to have you in our lives. We want to get to know you and have you be a part of our family."

"I don't know if I can handle that."

Jillian's smile returned. "The fact that you want to tells me you're a lot less broken than you think."

Fletcher and the girls returned with the food. Ella and Layla each insisted on sitting next to her. Once everyone was in their place, they joined hands and Fletcher said grace. When he specifically thanked God for bringing her into their lives and both girls squeezed her hands, as if saying they were grateful, too, her eyes burned. Not with tears, because she never, ever cried, but with some strange, unfamiliar emotion. If she had to put a name to it, she would guess it was some uncomfortable combination of loss and hope. Hope for how a normal, happy and yes, loving family could be. And loss because she'd never experienced it. Having not been loved by her mother, would she ever be able to love someone else, or was she destined to protect herself by shutting the doors to her heart forever?

eleven

Daphne kept her eye on both boys as they paddled in the designated area. They were at the north end of Lake Washington. Stand-up paddleboards required decent balance, core strength and an ability to control the board. Elijah was experienced, but Cadin was still learning.

She'd been trying to teach him that when he felt like he was losing his balance, he needed to lower his center of gravity, rather than flail his arms. Crouching down and widening his stance usually helped, but not always. Every time he fell into the water, she waited anxiously until he reappeared.

So far, he was doing great. By next summer he would be as good as his older brother. Alexa was still too small to manage a board on her own, so she went with her dad or with Daphne.

The afternoon was hot. Daphne checked her watch.

"Thirty more minutes," she yelled.

Elijah groaned. "Not yet."

"You'll look like a lobster soon. Besides, we only took the ninety-minute rental."

Before everyone got on their boards, she'd slathered the kids with sunscreen and had insisted they wear long-sleeved T-shirts designed to reflect the damaging rays. No one was getting burned on her watch.

The week had flown by. The kids had activities every day and a babysitter during their rare downtimes. She'd cut back on her hours as much as she could to hang out with them. She glanced at Brody, who was helping Alexa get comfortable holding the paddle.

They'd done as she'd asked—put their problems behind them—at least in the short-term. They'd been friendly with each other, had gotten through entire conversations without any accusations and had even made love a couple of more times. She was feeling pretty good about them. Maybe they could build on this week and get back to how things used to be.

When their time was up, they turned in their paddleboards and paddles. Daphne insisted everyone rinse off at the outdoor shower. She pulled her SUV key from her fanny pack. Once the vehicle was open, she passed out towels for everyone. She tossed Brody the key and climbed in the passenger side while the kids flung themselves into the rear seat.

"That was fun," Cadin said. "I'm getting good on the board."

"You're still falling." Elijah's tone was superior.

"You're both doing great." Daphne deliberately kept her voice quiet. "Alexa, you think you'll be ready to try paddleboarding on your own next summer?" She was small but surprisingly coordinated.

"I'm going to grow a lot this year," Alexa told her. "I'm going to be tall like you."

"I'll love you even if you're not. Are you all packed to go home?"

A chorus of "no" and "not yet" had her smiling. "Then you know what you're doing as soon as we get home."

"We'll hurry," Elijah said with a sigh. "We know the drill."

"The drill," Daphne mouthed to Brody. "Did you teach them that?"

He grinned.

At home there was a flurry of activity as the kids packed for their week with their mom and stepfather. Daphne spent her time finding things like the other athletic shoe and a missing tablet. She did a quick walk-through of the house to make sure nothing was forgotten. Brody texted Whitney to confirm the drop-off time. Sooner than she would have liked, she was hugging each of them and promising to miss them very much.

"I'll see you next Sunday," she said, helping Brody load the back of the SUV.

She waved on the front porch until they disappeared, before going back inside. Albert and Vanessa were waiting on the stairs. Vanessa looked sad at the kids' departure, but Albert's kitty body language hinted that he believed life would be much better without the invention of children.

Daphne cuddled him close. "You need to relax. If you let yourself, you might grow to like them."

His look of disbelief made her smile.

"Snob."

He meowed in agreement.

Her phone buzzed with a text. She set down the cat and saw a link from her mother.

Your father and I found this place. What do you think?

Daphne clicked on the link, then stared at a listing for a ten-bedroom chalet up in the Cascade Mountains.

There's room for all of us, including the kids. You have them for Christmas this year. Your father and I would fly up and you could invite some of your friends. Grant and Tori are always fun. And Campbell and Heather.

Daphne scrolled through the listing. The cost made her swallow hard, but she knew her parents would kick in a fair amount. If everyone else paid the price of a regular hotel room, they could swing it. The house was incredible. Three levels, six bathrooms, four fireplaces, a hot tub, nearby ski slopes and a sledding park.

"Count me in," she murmured before texting, Campbell has a new girlfriend. Nora.

That's right. You told me. Too bad. They made a great couple. Poor Heather. Her mother really did a number on her.

Because Daphne and Heather had been best friends since grade school, and her mother had known Amber all her life. When Daphne and her mom had the usual fights, a simple "Want to go live with Amber and Heather" was enough to make her see reason.

Let me talk to Brody. If we want the place for the holidays, we'll have to move quickly. I'll get back to you later tonight. If he's interested, we'll reserve it and I'll discuss the plans with everyone else.

Perfect. Love you, darling.

Love you, too, Mom.

Daphne went into her home office and booted her laptop. The pictures were even more impressive on the bigger screen. There would be space for everyone, and the main floor bedroom would be perfect for her parents. Brody, Daphne and the kids could take the top floor with everyone else downstairs. Or vice versa. The point was there would be plenty of separation and togetherness.

"You're working."

She looked up and saw Brody in her office doorway. "What? No."

"You were smiling. Emailing Miguel?"

And just like that, all the good feelings from the week bled away.

"Brody, don't." She turned her computer so he could see the screen. "My mom texted. She knows we have the kids for Christmas this year and she's been thinking about having a family trip somewhere we can all be together. She and Dad found this great house for rent. It has enough bedrooms for all of us. We could even invite Tori and Grant and Campbell and Nora."

Hopelessness made her sag in her seat. "You're never going to let it go, are you? No matter how many times I tell you nothing happened. You're never going to believe me."

His gaze was steady, his expression unrepentant. "How am I supposed to let it go when you won't admit there's a problem?"

She slammed her laptop shut and stood. "You're right. There is a problem and that problem is you. You're determined to think the worst of me. You're ripping us apart and I don't know why. What's your end game? How is that a win?"

She believed he loved her and most of the time they were good together, so why was he doing this?

"I want my wife back."

"I didn't go anywhere," she shrieked. "I've been right here all along. You just didn't notice." She pushed past him. "I'm going to work."

"Now?"

She didn't bother slowing. "There's no point in staying home. I might as well get in some billable hours."

She thought he might come after her, insist they talk it out, but he didn't. As she got in her car and drove toward downtown, a voice in her head whispered that she wasn't helping the situation by leaving. But turning back wasn't an option. If someone was going to bend, it had to be Brody. He was playing some kind of game with her and she had to stay strong and refuse to engage. Otherwise, they were doomed.

Tori opened cupboard after cupboard, searching for a toaster. She found an air fryer, a pressure cooker, a very fancy-looking stand mixer along with enough plates and bowls to open a restaurant, but no toaster. Or toaster oven. At this point she wasn't going to be picky.

As she continued her search, she glared at the coffeemaker, confident it was going slow on purpose. Obviously, it knew she hadn't been sleeping well in her new surroundings and was taunting her. Just like the toaster that had to be somewhere.

"Am I asking too much?" she asked loudly, slamming a drawer shut. "It's not like I'm trying to cure some terminal disease."

"Probably for the best," Grant said, entering the kitchen in jeans and a T-shirt. "What with you not having any experience with science."

She glared at him. "Is that meant to be funny?"

He studied her. "You like my sense of humor."

"Not always."

His gaze sharpened. "You're not sleeping."

"Shut up."

"You get cranky when you don't sleep."

"I'm not cranky," she muttered. "I'm murderous. There's a difference."

"Not a good one for me. What's the problem?"

"There's no toaster. I just want a frozen waffle with peanut butter and I can't find the toaster." She pointed to the miles of cabinets. "I swear I opened every single one of them. Did you want to use an immersion blender, because I know where that is."

Grant moved close and put his hands on her shoulders. She thought he was going to pull her in for a hug, which she figured she would fight, but instead, he turned her slowly to face the long wall with the stove. He pointed.

"So that thing in the corner is a..."

She stared at the toaster sitting on the counter. "I hate you. I mean that. I hate you with every fiber of my being."

"Always gracious. You need coffee."

"I made coffee. The slowest machine in the history of the universe."

"We should contact the press to do a story on something so record breaking."

She thought about elbowing him in the ribs but wasn't sure she could do it hard enough to cause serious damage.

"I'm going to make fruit salad," she said instead, pointing to the berries, peaches and plums sitting on the counter.

"I'll do that. You shouldn't be around knives when you're like this."

"Fine, but cut up the fruit small. No big chunks and don't forget to put lemon on the peaches so they don't get yucky."

He flashed her a smile. "I promise to make fruit salad to your exacting standards."

They both moved toward the flatware drawer, bumping into each other. Grant opened it, then waved for her to go first. She took a butter knife, then collected frozen waffles from the freezer.

They ran into each other, literally, again as she opened the cupboard to get a plate while he was searching for a bowl. She jumped back.

"This kitchen is huge. Stop being where I am."

"It's like bad first-time sex," he joked. "Our rhythm is off. Don't worry. We'll figure it out."

Did he mean sex or working in the kitchen together? Her mind stumbled over the question. There was no sex. They didn't have sex. They were friends and that had never been an issue. So why was he talking about it? She didn't want to go there with him. There had already been too many changes.

"I can't do this," she blurted. "I can't live here with you. Too much is different. I don't know how to do this. How can it work? You're transitioning to days. We had a routine. Now nothing's the same and we're living together. Do we eat meals together? Am I expected to cook? What about groceries? How do we pay for food and utilities? Rooming with Heather was easy and this isn't."

Her voice rose as her chest got tight. Scout and Zeus both looked up from their beds by the breakfast table.

"I just want my life back. I want my condo and my routine and knowing what's going to happen next."

Grant took her hand and led her to the stools by the island. He pulled one out.

"Sit."

"I'm not your dog."

His expression softened. "Tori, please sit for a minute."

She wanted to tell him no but instead planted her butt where he pointed and crossed her arms over her chest.

"My problem is unfixable."

"I know." His voice was gentle. "Everything is different and that's uncomfortable."

"Don't be reasonable. It's so annoying. I'm being a total bitch and you're using your coaxing voice. It makes me want to hit you."

He ignored that. "We'll get a calendar. One of those big wall ones where we can write down our schedules, so we know when we're here and when we're not."

"You'll write down your schedule," she muttered. "Mine doesn't change. I have no life."

He went on as if she hadn't spoken. "On the days we're both home for dinner, we'll eat together, alternating who cooks. Takeout every third meal."

Okay, that was possibly reasonable, she thought grudgingly. Grant was a decent cook, especially at grilling. And there was that big built-in barbecue out back.

He held her hand in his. "We suffered a huge loss, Tori. In a matter of minutes our homes were damaged and everything we owned was soaked. Yes, most of it's replaceable, but going through something like that is traumatic. More for you than for me, because you were there when it happened."

She briefly closed her eyes. "I don't want to think about that."

"I know. Now we have to coordinate the repairs, choose new appliances and finishes. It's daunting. You're not sleeping, so you're exhausted physically and emotionally. It's okay. You feel what you feel. I know it doesn't seem like it, but things will get better."

"You're just saying that so I don't kill you. Or cry."

"I'd prefer the latter to the former," he told her. "As for us living together, we'll figure out a new routine. We do great together. We're going to be fine."

She looked at him. "Do you really believe that?"

"Yes."

"Fool."

He chuckled. "I'm an optimist. So are you, most of the time. But we have each other and that's what matters."

She pulled her hand free and stood, then wrapped her arms around his waist and leaned against him.

"My life sucks."

"No, it doesn't," he said, holding her tight.

"Okay, maybe *sucks* is strong, but there's stuff."

"There is."

"I'm usually good with change."

"You will be again." He drew back so he could look into her eyes. "We're family, Tori. That's going to make this okay."

And just like that, her mad faded. She nodded. "You're right. But I still want that calendar. It's a really good idea."

"It'll be here by the time you get home. Ready for breakfast?"

She nodded. "Thank you for understanding."

He winked. "I'm a great guy."

"Five minutes ago I would have stabbed you for saying that."

"Five minutes ago I wouldn't have risked it."

Elliot walked into the conference room, several folders in his hand. Heather eyed them, surprised he had that much to discuss. She'd thought everything was going well at work. Did he see things differently?

He sat across from her, placing his mug of coffee next to the folders.

"More kittens?" he asked, his tone more conversational than judgmental. "Don't you still have three at home?"

She shifted uneasily. "Yes, well, they're almost fully weaned and are exploring their little world. In a couple of weeks, they'll be ready for adoption."

"Meaning you can't possibly not be fostering motherless kittens?"

"It's my thing."

"Should I ask what you're hiding from or let it go?"

"I'm not hiding."

"Distracting yourself, then. You don't want to think about something."

Campbell, she thought instantly. He was the reason she'd agreed to take on two additional kittens. Between work and caring for her fosters and getting to know her father and his family, she barely had time to think about how she'd blown it with the one guy who actually got her.

"Let's talk about work," she said brightly.

Elliot studied her for a second before nodding. He opened the top folder.

"Our office manager is leaving in six months. We need to find a replacement."

Heather grimaced. "I don't accept that she's leaving."

"Her husband's being transferred to Atlanta. She wants to go with him. She's given us plenty of notice. I want to go back to the recruiting firm we used before."

Heather wanted to whine, but knew he was right. The sooner they hired a new office manager, the smoother the transition would go. But she wasn't looking forward to the process. Like her cousin Sophie, when it came to key positions in her business, she had trouble trusting new people.

"While we're on the subject of people leaving," he began.

She cut him off with a sharp, "No!"

"I'm cutting back my hours."

"Why? You love your work."

"I'm sixty-seven." He smiled. "Heather, we've talked about

this. When you first started, you needed me to bounce ideas off of and to carry some of the load. But that's no longer necessary. At this point, I'm dead weight."

She winced. "Never said the D word in the context of you leaving. I need you too much."

"You really don't, but I'll make my retirement gradual. Starting next month I'll only be working twenty-five hours a week."

"Twenty-five hours? That's what you call gradual?"

His smile returned. "It is. And in early November, Mona and I are going on that cruise through the Panama Canal."

"I know about that trip," she said grudgingly, telling herself not to mention that it was for two whole weeks. "I hope you have a lovely time."

"I'm sure we will." He looked at her. "You'll be fine."

"I won't. I need you."

"The idea of me, but you've been running 206 Marketing Group yourself for a while. You're strong, Heather. Brilliant and determined. And even after I retire, I'll still be available whenever you need me."

"Can we still have lunch every other week?"

"I promise."

"I can't picture the company without you."

Elliot was the one who had inspired her to study marketing and he'd helped her pick the right job from the multiple offers she'd received after graduating.

"You've been like a father to me," she admitted.

"You have no idea how happy and proud that makes me. You're like one of my daughters, Heather. That won't change."

"It will a little."

"I'll concede that, but we'll still be close. Speaking of fathers, how's it going with yours?"

"Good. I met his daughters." She told him about visiting

their house. "They're sweet and excited to have a big sister." She paused. "I get that Fletcher is my biological father, but I'm having trouble wrapping my mind around half siblings."

"You're afraid," he said bluntly.

"Maybe a little."

"Amber is unique," Elliot told her. "I understand why you're worried but you're not that little girl anymore. You can protect yourself. Does she know about Fletcher?"

Heather nodded. "The conversation didn't go well."

"I'm not surprised. She's incapable of being happy for anyone. Even you."

That was true. Heather remembered when she'd finally found the courage and strength to go to college. Part of the terms of Sophie buying Amber a condo had been that Amber not stand between Heather and the opportunity she'd been given. Something Heather hadn't found out until years later. But her mother had been unable to resist trying to destroy Heather's chance at success.

Heather had never told Sophie, but the first year she'd been at college, her mother had sent horrible emails about how ungrateful Heather was, how she didn't deserve to go to college and how Amber would never forgive her for the abandonment. Heather had finally emailed back, saying if Amber didn't stop, they would never speak again. There had been no contact for nearly a year, then Amber had reached out, still bitter but less hostile. And so they'd gone on.

"I know in my head no one will ever act like her," Heather admitted. "But in my gut, I can't believe it, so I react." Often to her own detriment.

"Amber will always be Amber. You get to grow and change. You've come a long way, Heather. Give yourself credit. Now that you're aware of your negative patterns, you can make different decisions. Take one step of faith, then another. Most people won't let you down."

"You make it sound easy."

"It doesn't have to be difficult."

"Oh, I don't know. I seem to like throwing up barriers to happiness."

"Maybe stop doing that, too."

She nodded, then tapped the stack of folders. "Ready to move on?"

"I am."

She was, as well. In work, and very possibly, in her personal life. At least that was the dream.

twelve

Daphne left work just before six. Early for her, but she was determined to get home in time to have it out with Brody, once and for all. They hadn't spoken since Sunday. She'd taken to sleeping in Alexa's room, a dumb move on her part because now she didn't know how to go back to sleeping with Brody. Of course come the weekend, the problem would solve itself when the kids returned. Unless she moved to the basement sofa.

"No," she said aloud, turning onto their street. "We have to get back to being a couple."

But when she pulled up to the house, she saw both Grant's and Campbell's SUVs parked on the street. She would guess they were there to watch a baseball game. So much for having a talk with her husband.

She walked in through the garage. The faint noise of the game drifted up from downstairs. Albert and Vanessa ran to greet her. She petted them both, wondering if she should go say hi to the brothers. But if she didn't, they would wonder what was wrong. Only she didn't know how Brody would act, which made her uncomfortable, and why was this so hard?

She walked quietly down the stairs, only to stop when she heard Brody say, "I didn't think it would be so difficult. Whitney and Daphne are nothing alike, but I'm back where I was before."

"Then that's on you," Campbell said with a chuckle. "Sorry, bro, but you're who they have in common."

"I'm serious," Brody told him. "Things aren't right and I don't know how to fix them."

Daphne stopped on the stairs. No way she could announce herself now, she thought frantically, not sure what to do. Leaving was the polite choice, but she wanted to hear what Brody was saying.

"Marriages go through phases." Now Grant was speaking. "You have good days and days when you get on each other's nerves."

"This is more than that," Brody muttered.

Daphne's stomach clenched and heat burned on her cheeks as she waited for him to tell his brothers about her supposed affair. Instead, he said, "I don't know how to get through to her."

"You keep trying." Grant's tone was firm. "Look, Daphne's great. She's smart, she's successful, she's beautiful, but more important than all of that is the fact that she's crazy in love with you. We've all seen how she looks at you. Plus, she adores the kids. How many newly married stepmoms would be willing to go from visitation every other weekend to joint custody? But she was all for it. Face it, she's better than you deserve."

His kind words eased some of her tension.

"Hang in there," he continued. "Things will turn around."

"So speaks the divorced man," Campbell said bluntly. "Those who can't get it right give advice?"

"I have clarity now," Grant said easily. "I know what went wrong in my marriage."

"The fact that you married her in the first place and then stayed?"

There was the sound of two beer bottles clinking.

"You got that one right," Grant said with a chuckle.

"Maybe I'm getting clarity." Brody's voice was low and she had to strain to hear him. "Maybe marrying Daphne was a mistake."

The unexpected statement, the attack of the words, the way they shredded her heart and embedded in her soul, left her gasping for air. She swayed. If she hadn't been gripping the railing, she would have fallen to the concrete floor.

The brothers were still talking. She had the vague sense that Campbell and Grant were telling Brody he was wrong, but none of that mattered.

Brody thought their marriage was a mistake. He thought they didn't belong together. She tried desperately to grasp the meaning of all that, to realize that his belief that she had an affair was much worse than she'd realized. They weren't fighting—he was thinking about being done with her.

Her body went cold, then flushed all over. She was having trouble keeping silent and knew she couldn't stay on the stairs much longer. At some point one of them was going to head upstairs and she would be found. The fear of the humiliation, of having any of them see her so vulnerable, propelled her into action.

She turned as quietly as she could and walked to the top of the stairs. On the main floor she sagged against the wall. She couldn't stand upright—the pain was too great and she had to press a hand to her belly to keep the wound from ripping her open. She looked around, frantic for a place to hide where she would regroup mentally and figure out how to keep breathing.

Maybe marrying Daphne was a mistake.

The words replayed themselves over and over, sometimes quietly, sometimes so loud the volume made her wince. Her eyes burned, her breath came in gasps and she knew a serious breakdown was seconds away.

She started for the second floor, but knew she could easily be found up there. The main level offered nowhere to hide. She was too in shock to drive, and walking somewhere was out of the question.

In desperation, she hurried into the garage and curled up in the back of her SUV. No one would look for her here. If Brody didn't check the garage, he wouldn't even know she was home. She would have time to figure out what it meant and how she was supposed to keep going, now that she knew the truth.

She sobbed for what felt like hours. Her body shook and for a while she wondered if she would throw up. Emotions hit her like baseball bats, bruising every inch of her.

He didn't want her anymore, didn't want them. He genuinely believed she'd slept with Miguel and there was no way to change his mind. She was going to lose the only man she'd ever loved, the life she adored, because of something she'd not only never done, but had never considered. And there wasn't anything she could do to stop what very much felt like the inevitable.

"This is what? The maid's quarters?" Heather asked, following Tori through a giant kitchen into a three-room suite.

"I guess. We didn't get a map or anything, so we're figuring it out as we go." Tori motioned to the beautifully decorated living room. "There's plenty of light and I closed the air-conditioning vents so they won't get cold."

"You're sweet."

Tori set down Heather's large tote. Heather carefully lowered the box containing her two three-week-old kitten fosters. Both girls, so neither had been named Russell Wilson.

"Thanks for letting me bring my crew," Heather said, lightly stroking both black cats.

"Of course. They're babies."

"They are. The other three are too busy playing with each other and LC to notice when I'm gone."

"He's still enjoying being a stepdad?"

"He loves them way more than he likes me."

Tori hugged Heather. "LC loves you in his own quiet way. He just doesn't want you to know."

Heather laughed. "He's amazingly talented at pretending he loathes me."

"You have to admire the skill set."

They carefully closed the door as they left. Scout was patiently waiting. Heather petted her as they went back to the kitchen. She and Tori put two galvanized tubs onto a patio table then filled them with ice. Water and soda went into one while beer, white wine and rosé went into the other. There were stacks of cups and napkins, recyclable plates and flatware. Out on the lawn, under several huge umbrellas, the caterers were setting up.

Heather looked at the chalkboard with the menu. Appetizers included taquitos, stuffed jalapeños and chips, salsa, guacamole and queso. Entrées ranged from red snapper to tacos and quesadillas. Oh, and a salad bar.

"How many people are coming?" Heather asked.

Tori worried her bottom lip. "About forty. The guest list got out of hand really fast. We were just going to have a fun housewarming party, but then I wanted a few friends from work and Grant wanted his hospital friends, plus our family, so it's a lot."

Heather studied her friend. There were still shadows under Tori's eyes. "You're not sleeping well, are you?"

"I'm doing better. Every night is a little easier. That big meltdown I had last week actually helped. I think getting my emotions out in the open allowed me to start working through them. I'm not a hundred percent, but I feel better."

"I'm glad. You went through a lot." Heather smiled. "We talked about doing gag gifts—all water based—but it seemed cruel."

"Too soon." Tori touched her arm. "You doing okay?"

"I'm fine. Why?"

"The party."

Heather got what her friend meant right away. The party itself wasn't the issue. It was who would be attending. Two specific guests, to be honest.

"I'm fine. Campbell and Nora will be here and I'm fine."

Tori smiled. "So you think you're fine?"

"I am."

Grant walked out onto the patio. "Hey, Heather. How's it going?" He hugged her. "What do you think of the house? Tori and I look good here."

Heather grinned. "Even on your salary, there is no way you could afford a place like this."

"Yeah, that's true. But it's fun to hang out even temporarily. Tori said you brought kittens."

"Two."

"Dibs on the feeding. I need to keep my fostering skills sharp."

"I'll let you know when it's time."

Zeus flopped down next to Scout in the shade of a big tree.

"You and Grant aren't the only ones who will miss this place," she said, pointing to the dogs.

Tori laughed. "I know. I keep picturing Scout staring at me as if asking what went wrong in our lives that we had to move back to that tiny condo."

Calls of "Hello!" and "Anybody home?" came from the open

gate on the side of the house. Tori had already put up signs directing the guests to the backyard. There were plenty of tables and chairs, all in the shade. Closer to the fence were a giant ring toss game and bean bag tic-tac-toe. A piñata hung from a tree.

Daphne and Brody arrived with some people Heather didn't know. She greeted her friend and Brody, then waited while Grant introduced three nurses from the hospital.

"I'll never remember all the names," Tori whispered.

"I know."

"We thought name tags would be too corporate."

Heather turned to Daphne, expecting to see her smiling, but Daphne's expression was tight, her body language stiff.

"You okay?" Heather asked.

"Yes, of course. The backyard looks great. Are you enjoying living here, Tori?"

The words were appropriate, but there was something sharp about her tone. Heather glanced at Brody, but he seemed fine as he joked with his brother and the nurses.

"Are you sure you're all right?" Heather asked quietly.

Daphne looked away. "Yes, of course. I don't know why you'd even ask. Oh, look. We're having Mexican food. Will there be margaritas?"

Before Heather could insist that Daphne tell her what was going on, Sam, from 206 Marketing Group, and his girlfriend walked in with Campbell and Nora right behind them. Heather instinctively took a step back, but Nora rushed toward her, arms outstretched.

"Yay, you're here," the pretty blonde said, hugging her. "I was hoping you would be. You look great. Campbell said you have new kittens?"

"Um, yes." Heather slid out of the embrace, hoping she looked casual and not panicked. "They're three weeks old. They'll need to eat in a couple of hours, if you'd like to help."

Nora's eyes widened. "I'm not really a pet person, but that

would be amazing." She hugged Heather again. "You're so nice. I knew you would be."

Heather found Nora confounding and wanted to remind the other woman that she was the ex-girlfriend. Something Nora should already know but apparently didn't care about.

Campbell took Nora's hand and pulled her back. "Watch the enthusiasm. Heather doesn't like to be touched."

Tori glared at him. "That's not true. Don't make her sound freakish."

"I'm standing right here," Heather said mildly, knowing Campbell was kidding, but appreciating Tori's defense.

More people arrived. Heather used the distraction to move into the backyard, away from Campbell and Nora.

Grant joined her. "Got a minute?"

"Sure."

He drew her to the side of the yard. "A couple of doctors I know from work are single." One corner of his mouth turned up. "You're a lesbian, right?"

"Very funny."

"Just keeping things light," he said. "Seriously, I want to introduce you to Emer. He's a gifted surgeon and recently divorced. He's a good guy and now that he's ready to get back in the game, I thought of you."

"There's a game?" she asked, her voice teasing. "Are there rules?"

"Sometimes." Grant's gaze was steady. "It seems like you've changed your mind about not committing to anyone. Am I wrong?"

She told herself not to immediately look at Campbell. "Maybe I was too quick to throw away something good."

Grant's expression turned sympathetic. "He really loved you. I don't say that to make it hurt more, but to let you know that you mattered to him."

"He mattered to me, too. I just couldn't bring myself to

admit it. Not in time." She drew in a breath and told herself to pretend to be normal and brave. No one had to know she was faking both.

"Now he's with Nora," she added. "She's adorable. Who wouldn't want to go out with her?"

"She's wild about him. Puts it all on the line."

Something she'd never been able to do. "I'm sure that feels good to him. He knows where he stands."

"So yes on Emer?"

She nodded. "I'll do my best to be charming."

"Charm comes naturally to you."

With that surprising compliment, Grant walked away. Heather watched him go, thinking she'd never once in her life thought of herself as charming. Smart, sure. Determined? Absolutely. But charming?

She headed toward Daphne. Grant intercepted her, a good-looking guy with prematurely white hair at his side.

"Heather, I'd like you to meet a friend of mine, Emer. He's going to tell you he's a hot-shot surgeon, but don't believe him. He's adequate at best."

"It's the fear of blood," Emer joked, holding out his hand to shake hers. "Just when I think I've got the whole cutting people open thing nailed, I get queasy. Nice to meet you."

"Likewise," she murmured, thinking Grant was moving a little too fast. He could have mentioned that his doctor friend was at the *party*!

She told herself not to panic and to try to remember she might be charming.

Grant excused himself, leaving them alone. Heather stared into Emer's dark blue eyes, not sure what to say. Or how to act.

"You know what I do," he said with an easy smile. "What about you? Bear trainer? Astronaut? Oh, I know. Internet influencer."

She laughed. "No to all. I own a marketing company."

"I was really hoping for the bear trainer."

"Sorry to disappoint."

"I wouldn't say that." He pointed to the long table filled with appetizers. "Want to grab something to eat?"

"Sure."

They filled their plates. She poured herself a margarita while he got a beer. They settled at a table by a tree.

"How do you know Grant?" Emer asked when they were seated. "Old boyfriend?"

"No. The old boyfriend is his brother Campbell."

"The pilot. Good guy."

Heather ignored the slight twinge his words caused. "He is."

"You've obviously stayed friends."

"Yes, but he'd be stuck with me regardless. My best friend Daphne is married to Grant and Campbell's brother Brody and my other best friend is tight with Grant. It's a strange but interesting dynamic, and in the end we're all family."

At least that was how she preferred to think of them. Hanging with her friends more meant figuring out where she belonged in the group, or more specifically, how to coexist with Campbell and Nora.

"Family's important," he said.

"I agree. Do you have kids?"

"No. We never got around to that. You?"

She shook her head. "I have a cat who hates me. And I foster motherless kittens."

He stared at her. "What does that mean?"

"I take in kittens and raise them until they're old enough to be adopted." She held out her arm and showed him the countdown on her digital watch. "The two I brought today will need feeding in forty-six minutes."

"That's a big commitment."

"I've been doing it for a while and all my friends help. Motherless kittens aren't considered viable until they're eight weeks old, so it can be heartbreaking if one of them doesn't make it. But it's rewarding when everything goes well."

"I wish I could stay to watch the feeding, but I promised my mom I'd help her hang some pictures." His expression turned sheepish. "She doesn't want my dad to get up on a ladder, so I need to go over while he's golfing."

The sweetness of his admission made her defenses drop just a little.

"You're a good man."

"I try to be." His gaze met hers. "Would you like to go out to dinner in three weeks?"

She blinked. "That's oddly specific."

He hesitated. "Sorry. It's just I'm going to be out of town. Not on vacation or anything. Just, you know, gone."

Until this second, she'd quite liked Emer. Now she wasn't sure.

"Okay," she said slowly. "Still confusing." And she was a little less sure about dinner.

He looked away, then back at her. "It's not bad or any-thing." He mumbled something she couldn't hear, then ex-haled sharply as his shoulders dropped. "It's because of what I said about my parents. I didn't think that through, but I didn't want you to think I wasn't interested when I had to leave. As for the three weeks, I'm going to South America to do surger-ies through a nonprofit. But saying those two things together makes me sound like some, I don't know, do-gooder guy, and that's not sexy. I can be a jerk as much as the next guy."

Heather's lips twitched, then she laughed. "You think being a jerk makes a guy sexy?"

"No, it makes me sound normal. Everyone can have a bad day."

In her heart of hearts, she knew she was still dealing with

Campbell issues, and there was a chance she would never be like everyone else when it came to trusting a man and risking her feelings, but if there was any hope of having a decent romantic life, a guy like Emer seemed like a great place to start.

"I'd like to have dinner with you in three weeks," she told him.

"Yeah?" He gave her a slow, sexy smile. "Excellent."

They talked until he had to leave.

"I'll be in touch," he promised.

"From South America?"

"There's internet."

He headed out. Heather stayed in her seat, wondering if she could find her way to being interested in Emer. Until now she'd never been that concerned about being like everyone else, but maybe it was a path she should consider.

Tori joined her, setting a plate of food between them.

"We over ordered on tacos," she said, taking one.

"You'll have leftovers for a week. I'm jealous."

Her friend grinned. "I could probably be persuaded to send you home with some."

"Just bring them to work and we'll have them for lunch."

"Good idea." Tori studied her for a second. "So... Grant's friend. Any thoughts?"

"He was nice. I liked him."

"Liked as in...?"

"We're going to dinner when he gets back from his trip."

Tori's eyebrows rose. "Wow. That's huge."

"It's dinner."

"With a guy. Does this mean you would consider dating him?"

Heather did her best not to look at Campbell. Given the choice, she would pick him. But he wasn't an option anymore.

"Dinner kind of is a date," she said instead.

"You know what I mean."

"I do." She held in a sigh. "I get that I have issues. They've come between me and what I want. I refuse to spend the rest of my life wanting what I can't have, so the logical solution is to be different."

"Good plan. I'm sorry you're still in love with Campbell."

"What? I never said that. You know me—I don't do love."

"You just said that you lost Campbell because of your issues. Like he still matters." Tori's expression turned sympathetic. "Now he's with Nora and they're everywhere and it totally sucks."

"Excellent recap," Heather murmured, then sighed. "I don't know what I feel about him exactly. I just know that he's done with me and I want to move on. I want…" She paused, trying to figure out the rest of the sentence. "I want more. Romantically, I mean. I have a great life. My work, you and Daphne, the cats."

"Your dreamy condo with the lake view."

Heather laughed. "Yes, that, too. In my head I totally understand why I protect myself. I can have a rational discussion about how my mom damaged me. I can even think about healing and trusting. But I'm so scared."

She shrugged. "I don't like being afraid all the time."

"So you said yes to Emer."

"He seems nice and even if it doesn't work out, maybe going out with him will move me a step closer to being a little like everyone else."

"And help you get over Campbell."

"That, too." Heather took one of the tacos. "When I first contacted my dad, I was a little judgy of the age difference between him and Jillian. But they're completely in love with each other. The affection, the caring, it's tangible. Right there in the room with them. I can't explain it, but I know what they feel is real. I didn't know love could be like that. Their daughters are happy and sweet and totally adorable."

"Who's adorable?" Campbell asked, walking up to the table and sitting down. "You were talking about me, right?"

His smile was easy, his posture relaxed. Campbell had always been confident about his place in the world—something Heather envied. She was fine in business situations, but when it came to more intimate settings, she wasn't so sure of herself.

"We were talking about Heather's dad and his family," Tori told him. "Not everything is about you."

"Yet, it should be." He looked at Heather. "How's it going with your dad?"

"Good. We're getting to know each other. It's a process."

"There are two daughters, right?"

She nodded. "Ella and Layla. They're very enthused about having a new sister."

"How do you feel about it?" he asked.

"Open to the possibility," she admitted. "I like them. It's nice having family that isn't my mother."

He studied her without speaking. She had no idea what he was thinking, nor was she going to ask. Campbell had an uncomfortable habit of telling the truth and right now she didn't want to risk taking a hit.

"Did you like Grant's doctor friend?" he asked.

"Emer," Tori said. "His name is Emer and he's a surgeon."

Campbell smiled at her. "Thank you for clarifying."

"I live to be helpful."

He turned back to Heather. "So yes on the doctor?"

Why did it matter to him if she met someone? He had Nora and even if he didn't, he'd made it painfully clear he wasn't interested in her.

"We've just met so we're not picking out our wedding invitations until Tuesday. I talked to him for maybe fifteen minutes, Campbell. What do you want from me? He's nice. He asked me to dinner and I said yes."

His dark eyes were unreadable. "Grant says he's a good guy. I want you to be happy."

How incredibly altruistic of him. But even as a sarcastic response formed, she told herself not to react. Knowing Campbell as she did, she knew he *would* want her to be happy. Not with him, of course, but in general.

"I'll report back," she said.

"Good." He touched her wrist. "It must be about kitten time."

She glanced down. "Two minutes and twenty-eight seconds."

"Nora wants to learn how to feed them. I thought I could show her." His dark gaze locked with hers. "I won't mess up."

"I know." She waved toward the house. "Go ahead."

He nodded and rejoined Nora, who listened while he spoke, then clapped her hands together in obvious delight.

"You okay?" Tori asked.

"Never better."

"You know when you lie, your face gets all scrunchy."

"Does not."

"But you were lying."

"I'll get over him. I just didn't think it would take this long or hurt this much."

"Boys are stupid."

"Yes, they are. But we seem to be stuck wanting to have them in our lives."

thirteen

When Tori suggested a girls' night for the three of them, Daphne nearly turned her down. She wasn't in the mood to hang out with her friends. It took all her energy simply to get through her workday. She wasn't eating, wasn't sleeping and the second she stopped concentrating on her job, she felt sick.

Brody's words had taken root in her heart, sucking all the happy out of her. No matter how she tried to tell herself everything was fine, they were there, mocking her, torturing her.

Maybe marrying Daphne was a mistake.

There was no getting around his blunt statement, no making it not as bad as she thought. Her husband, the person she loved and adored and had planned to live with for the rest of her life, thought their marriage was a mistake. That he'd gotten it wrong when he'd picked her.

Which was why she'd nearly told Tori she was busy. Only she knew she needed a break from work, and going home wasn't an option. She couldn't face Brody without blurting out that she'd overheard him, and she wasn't ready to have that particular conversation.

Instead, she texted that she was looking forward to hanging out. They agreed to meet at Heather's and order Chinese. Daphne debated telling Brody where she was going but decided it didn't matter. She would get home at her usual time so her plans didn't affect him.

A little after six she pulled in next to Tori's car. She'd stopped for wine. Tori had said she would bring cupcakes.

They would have fun tonight, she told herself. She needed a little friend time. Lately, she only seemed to see Heather and Tori in large groups.

Tori opened the door and grinned at her.

"You made it. Yay! Now we can order. I'm starved."

Scout greeted Daphne with happy whines and enthusiastic tail wags. Daphne petted the dog.

"I've missed you, too, pretty girl."

"Wine," Heather said, hugging her. "Exactly what we need."

Daphne handed over the bottles, then stepped out of her heels. She followed her friends into the living room. Tori pointed to Heather's phone.

"Now will you push the order button?"

Heather laughed. "You should have eaten lunch."

"I was working. By the time I looked up, it was nearly four and I didn't want to spoil my dinner."

Heather tapped on her phone. "Done. It will be here in forty-five minutes. Can you last that long or do you want some crackers?"

"I can wait. Just don't let me have more than one glass of wine before I eat."

Heather started for the kitchen. "Wine all around?"

"I'll just have water for now," Daphne said, settling on the large sofa. "I haven't eaten much either and I'm afraid it'll upset my stomach."

LC jumped up next to her, purring loudly. She stroked the cat.

Heather brought her water, while Tori carried two glasses of the white wine. When her friends were seated, they exchanged a look.

"What's going on?" Tori asked. "You haven't been yourself lately. You're quiet, you seem upset."

"I'm fine." Daphne's response was automatic. "Just, you know, busy."

"It's more than that." Heather's tone was firm. "I've known you all my life. We want to help."

Daphne's first instinct was to deny that anything was wrong, only she doubted they would believe her. Plus, she was getting a little tired of handling everything on her own.

"It's Brody," she admitted. "We're having problems."

Her friends exchanged another look.

"What does that mean?" Tori asked. "You seemed fine at the party."

"We're good at pretending in public. In private, we're barely speaking." She thought about what she'd overheard, then wished she hadn't when tears filled her eyes. "Brody regrets marrying me."

"No, he doesn't!" Heather was at her side in a second. "He adores you. We can all see it. You're the most in love couple, just like my dad and Jillian."

Tori nodded frantically. "You are. I'm always bitter about it. He loves you."

"I appreciate the support, but you're wrong." Daphne cleared her throat so she could speak. "I heard him."

She told them about overhearing him with his brothers. "He said the words. I was there."

"Then you're missing context," Tori said firmly. "He's your husband."

For now, Daphne thought grimly. "There's more. We've been fighting for a while—about a bunch of stuff."

Tori frowned in confusion. "But you haven't said anything. Is it serious?"

"At first, no." A lie, but one Daphne was comfortable with. "But things are getting worse."

"Everybody fights," Heather said. "Living together creates friction. Or so I've been told."

"I snap at Grant all the time now," Tori added. "We're in the same space and it's weird."

"This is different," Daphne whispered. "He won't have a baby with me."

"What?"

"No way."

She swallowed. "It's true. I brought up us getting pregnant and he said it wasn't a good time. He thinks we should wait."

Heather frowned. "Waiting isn't the same as saying no."

"I understand that, but with everything else going on, I can't help wondering if he ever wanted kids with me." The tears returned. "I love his three so much. I want to be their step-mom, but I also want to be someone's real mom. I want to have a baby and help it grow up to be a good and happy person."

She wiped her cheeks. "But Brody doesn't want that with me."

"Did he say why he's not ready?" Heather asked.

"He blamed me. He said I work too much and now we share custody. He said it's a bad time to add one more thing."

"He's not wrong," Tori said slowly. "I'm not saying he isn't a pinhead, but you do work more than anyone I know."

"Even more than me," Heather added. "You're at what? Sixty or seventy hours a week? Plus everything else. When would you have the time?"

"It doesn't take long to make a baby," Daphne said.

"I'm talking later. Will you put your child in day care ten hours a day?"

"No, we'll have a nanny. We already have help when Brody's three are with us."

Which meant someone who was not her would be with her child most of the day, she thought uncomfortably. With her schedule, she was out of the house early and back late. She had to make up for leaving the office at a reasonable time on their custody week. With a baby, there would be no off weeks.

"I could work some from home," she said more to herself than them. When she wasn't seeing clients or in meetings. "Remote work is possible."

"Have you told Brody that?" Heather asked.

"We haven't been talking much."

"Then start there," Tori told her. "You're good at coming up with a plan. Show him that having a baby would totally work." Her voice softened. "Daphne, the man is crazy in love with you. We can all see it."

"He thinks I'm having an affair."

Her friends stared at her wide-eyed.

"For how long? And why?" Heather asked. "How come you haven't said anything?"

Daphne stared at the floor then back at her friends. "The affair thing has been going on for a few weeks. I didn't say anything because... Because..." A thousand excuses filled her brain, some the ugly truth and some a lot more attractive.

Tori leaned toward her. "Just say it."

"I was embarrassed. My husband thinks I'm having an affair. I'm not, of course, but he thinks that. I thought it would blow over, but it's gotten worse."

Heather smiled at her. "I get it. When we're kids, talking about the personal stuff is so easy, but as we get older, it's harder to talk about it."

"You'd never have an affair," Tori said. "When? While you're driving back and forth to work?"

Despite everything, Daphne smiled. "I know, right? It's crazy. I wouldn't do that."

"Why does he think that?" Heather asked.

"He's being a jerk." Daphne rolled her eyes. "He thinks I'm sleeping with one of the partners. Miguel. So frustrating. We're friends. We mostly talk shop. We have lunch, sometimes a quick drink in one of our offices. It's nothing."

Tori frowned. "That sounds like nothing. Why is Brody so upset?"

"Miguel sent me flowers. My assistant thought they were from Brody so I wasn't comfortable throwing them out. I put them on a shelf and forgot about them. Two days later Brody dropped by and saw them. He got all weird and now insists I'm having an affair."

Tori tilted her head. "Why would Miguel send you flowers?"

"I have no idea."

"But he must have had a reason. Were they a thank-you?"

"No. He said he was buying flowers for his mother and thought of me. That's hardly romantic. Besides, why does the reason matter?"

"Because guys don't just randomly send their friends flowers," Heather said. "He obviously thought it was an acceptable thing to do."

Daphne didn't like where the conversation was going. "We're just friends."

"You said that." Tori looked at Heather, then back at her. "When you go to lunch, is it just the two of you?"

"Sure, but I go to lunch with a lot of people."

"Men?"

"Some." All right, Miguel was the only guy she lunched with regularly, but so what?

"Does Brody know you have lunch with this guy?"

"I don't report every detail of my life to him."

"What do you talk about?" Tori asked. "Personal stuff?"

"Work, mostly. Who he's dating."

"Your marriage?" Heather asked.

Daphne suddenly felt interrogated. "Why all the questions? He's a friend. You sound like Brody."

Heather looked at her. "I'm sorry. I guess it's the flowers. No platonic guy friend has ever sent me any."

"Me, either," Tori added. "Is he sexy?"

"Miguel?" Daphne hesitated, then went with the truth. "He's incredibly good-looking. Anyone would find him sexy. But I don't care about that. I want my husband and only my husband."

"So you don't flirt," Tori said.

"No."

"Ever?"

Daphne regretted ever bringing up the topic. "No. No flirting, no touching, no hand-holding. Nothing! We split the check, we talk about work and sports and movies. I'm not having an affair with Miguel."

"You kind of are," Tori told her. "I'm not saying you slept with him, or did anything technically wrong, but you're spending time with another man, having personal conversations on a regular basis. You're getting some of your emotional needs met by him and you're keeping the lunches a secret from Brody. And even from us."

"I told you why I didn't say anything about Brody being upset. This has been blown out of proportion. Heather, who do you have lunch with? Can you get me a list? Any men? Same for you, Tori. It was just lunch!"

Daphne drew in a breath and consciously lowered her voice. "Sorry. This is all just so frustrating."

"Okay," Heather said in her "let's humor our friend" voice. "You're right. It was lunch. I'm sorry Brody won't accept that."

Daphne looked at both of them. "You don't believe me, either."

"I'm team Daphne," Tori told her.

"Me, too." Heather smiled. "We've been friends since we were four. I'll always have your back."

Even when you're wrong.

Neither spoke the words, but Daphne heard them all the same. And if the two women she trusted most in the world didn't believe her, what hope did she have of convincing Brody?

"It would be nice if you were friendly," Heather told LC as he bathed in a patch of sunlight. "These people are my family and I want to make a good impression."

LC never looked up as he carefully licked his paw, then wiped his face, over and over again. Then he started on the other side of his face.

Before she could complain he wasn't paying attention, she heard footsteps and giggling in the hallway, followed by someone knocking on her front door.

"You made it," she said, feeling nervous and excited at the same time. "Come in."

Ella and Layla burst inside, bundles of energy that danced in place as they hugged her tightly. Jillian also hugged her, but without the in-place jumping.

"You'd think they'd been cooped up in the car for hours," she said with a smile. "It's the thrill of being with you."

"I'm not usually thrill-worthy," Heather admitted with a laugh.

"You are to us." Her dad pulled her close. "Good to see you, Heather. Thanks for letting us invade."

"You're not an invasion. You're..." She hesitated only a second, then firmly said, "You're family."

The girls ran to the French doors.

"You can see the lake!" Layla's voice was filled with wonder. "It's really close."

"It's beautiful." Jillian joined her daughter. "May we go outside?"

"Of course."

They all went out onto the spacious L-shaped deck. There was a covered seating area with plenty of sofas and chairs. Around the corner was a gas barbecue and a table for six. The lake view was unobstructed.

"I have a little bit of a northeast view," she explained. "So less Seattle skyline, but also less sun. Some of the condos face full west and fight the sun all summer. Here, by five, my whole deck is in shade and I still have a water view."

"Perfect," Jillian said, leaning against Fletcher. "Your little girl has done well for herself."

"She's worked hard." He smiled at her. "I had nothing to do with your success and yet I'm ridiculously proud. I hope that's all right."

"It is."

Fletcher's happy acceptance was very different from Amber's frequent complaints that if she'd had the same opportunities, she could have done even better. While her mother had been dealt some tough blows in life, she'd also turned her back on any chance of bettering her situation. Amber didn't believe in doing the work, no matter the potential reward. Complaining was so much easier.

They settled on the sofa and chairs.

"How was the drive?" Heather asked, passing out cans of sparkling water.

"Easy," Fletcher said. "We did some shopping on the way."

"School starts Tuesday," Ella told her. "I can't wait for middle school."

"You're practically a teenager!" Heather said.

Ella beamed.

"I'm going into fourth grade," Layla said loudly.

"Good for you."

Jillian smiled. "Sometimes there's a little competition."

"That seems about right."

Layla shifted so she was next to Heather. "I wish I could take you to school with me and show everyone my new sister."

"I'll be busy working that day."

"Maybe another time?"

Heather saw a little of her father, and therefore herself, in the girl. The same hazel eyes, the same shape of her smile. Everything else was pure Jillian.

"Maybe," she said.

LC strolled out to join them. The girls shrieked when they saw him, but carefully stayed in their seats. He surveyed the group, ignoring Heather, of course, before lightly jumping next to Jillian.

"You're a handsome boy," Jillian said, offering her fingers for inspection. LC sniffed them, then lowered his head so she could pet him. LC shot Heather a little stink eye before starting to purr.

"He likes you, Mommy," Layla said, clapping her hands.

"LC is very particular," Heather told them. "When I first moved to Seattle, I wanted to adopt a bonded pair of cats so they'd have company while I was working. Willow was sweet and friendly. She just wanted to be around people and share the love. LC was more reserved."

Jillian smiled at her. "You fell for Willow and took LC so she would have a friend."

"They were siblings who'd been together their whole lives."

"They weren't kittens?" Fletcher asked.

"No. Their original owner had to go into assisted living. They were about six. I adopted them from a shelter."

She touched LC's tail. He immediately drew it closer to his body so she couldn't reach.

"They'd already lost their mom and were in a strange environment. I couldn't separate them, even though LC has never warmed up to me."

As if to prove her point, the cat curled up in Jillian's lap. He shot Heather more stink eye before gazing up at Jillian and cranking up the purr.

"I feel guilty," Jillian said with a laugh. "I'm not doing anything to deserve this, I swear."

"Happens all the time."

Ella inched closer to her mom, then softy petted LC. He licked her fingers.

"He gave me kisses! Mommy, did you see?"

"I want cat kisses," Layla said.

"Go slow," her dad told her. "You don't want to scare him."

Layla stretched out her hand. LC rubbed his face against her fingers.

"He likes me!"

"What happened to Willow?" Fletcher asked.

Heather did her best to keep her expression upbeat. "We lost her two years ago. It was very fast. LC and I were devastated."

The sisters looked at their mom.

"That's sad," Ella said.

"It was. LC stopped eating. I was afraid I would lose him, too. I wasn't sure how to help him and I guess me, too. I brought in a litter of foster kittens and we both perked up."

"How does that work?" Fletcher asked.

"I volunteer with an animal rescue organization. Spring and summer are considered kitten season. I started with pregnant cats, which is pretty easy. The mama cat does all the work. Now I mostly work with motherless kittens anywhere from one to three weeks old and I raise them until they're ready to be adopted."

Jillian studied her. "You take care of everything? Feeding them, making them go to the bathroom, training them on the litter box?"

Heather nodded. "LC helps. He's a very good foster dad. Right now I have kittens that are ready to be adopted next week, along with three-week-old kittens. The older ones are a good example for the younger ones."

The girls stared at her with identical pleading expressions.

"Can we see the kittens?" Ella asked, her tone reverent. "Please? We'll be very careful."

"If it's all right with you two," Heather said.

"Fine by us. Kitten play time, then lunch." Fletcher smiled. "Unless you girls decide you're not hungry. Kittens are pretty irresistible."

"That's kind of my point," Heather said with a laugh. "Little girls and kittens often fall in love with each other."

Jillian squeezed Fletcher's hand. "We're prepared for the possibility."

Inside, Heather had everyone wash their hands.

"The older ones have already been picked by families," she said, crouching to eye level with Ella and Layla. "The two little kittens are four weeks away from being adoptable.

They're still bottle-feeding and are very fragile, so you have to be extra gentle."

"We will be," Layla said earnestly. "We promise."

LC led the way to the kitten room. He easily jumped over the low gate to check on his charges.

Russell Wilson, Zerlina and Tilly were awake and pouncing on each other. They barely noticed as the humans joined them on the carpet.

The two younger female kittens, both black, were curled up together in a bed.

"They're so small," Ella said softly.

"They are, but they're growing fast. I'll start them on wet food this week and they're already getting the idea of the litter box." She stroked the kittens. "Hey, guys. Want to get up and play?"

The kittens stirred, then opened their eyes.

"The one with the purple collar is Molly," she said. "The one with the pink collar is Polly." She smiled. "I wasn't very creative with their names. The new owners will change them, of course."

The kittens stretched. Polly fell over, then stood again and managed to get out of the bed. Molly followed. Heather gave the girls feather toys to entice the older kittens to play. She shifted back to give Layla and Ella more room. Jillian moved next to her.

"I'm impressed how you've taken all this on," she said. "It's a lot of responsibility."

"With a routine, it's not that hard, and I have help. I take the kittens to work, and my employees pitch in."

"You have a nice life."

Heather hadn't thought about it in that way, but she supposed she did. There were disappointments—everyone had them. In her case, most of them were about herself. But she was doing better. Look at her today—letting her father and his family into her house was a big deal and she was feeling a little bit proud.

"My cousin Sophie is the one who got me into fostering cats," she said. "Oh, speaking of Sophie, her customers at Clandestine Kitty pay big bucks for custom items. I was thinking of those little dolls you crochet."

"The Amigurumi?"

"Yes. Would you be interested in designing a couple of customizable patterns? No pressure. I haven't talked to Sophie."

Jillian glanced at Fletcher, then back at her. "No, I couldn't commit to that. Not right now."

Her voice was a little sharp but before Heather could worry she'd said something wrong, Jillian smiled and touched her arm. "I have a lot going on with the girls and my part-time job. I wouldn't want to commit to a new project. But I'm flattered that you asked."

Heather told herself Jillian's answer was no big deal. Sure, it was a way to make money, but not everyone had to be doing more. Some people were simply happy with what they had. A philosophy she'd never understood but tried to accept in everyone else.

fourteen

Tori stared at the calendar in the walk-in pantry. Or rather, at the most recent entry in Grant's tidy handwriting. 7:30 Date.

She tried to make sense of the information. The obvious explanation was between this time yesterday and right now, Grant had met a woman and asked her out. On. A. Date.

She heard his SUV enter the garage and walked out into the main kitchen to wait. Emotions churned in her belly. Confusion, mild anxiety, neither of which made sense. There was also a hint of being left behind. And strangest of all, a faint whisper of hurt.

Grant stepped into the kitchen. His scrubs had a couple of stains on them and he looked tired. But his mouth curved up when he saw her.

"Hey. You're home."

"My car in the garage should have been a big clue."

He chuckled. "You're right. It's just we don't usually get home at the same time. This is nice."

Zeus and Scout came running. Both dogs demanded serious affection, whining and wagging their tails.

"I've already let them out," she said. "I was about to feed them." She'd also brought home a rotisserie chicken and salads from the grocery store. Enough for both of them. Although tonight it would be a table for one.

"I can feed them," he said.

She glanced at the clock. It was already after six. "Don't you have to get ready for your, um, date?"

He glanced away. "Yes, well, I probably should."

She looked at him until he met her gaze. "Did you want to say more?"

"Not really." He shifted uneasily from foot to foot and kept looking past her.

"Are you embarrassed or just plain weirded out?"

"Both," he admitted, then sighed. "I have a blind date with a friend of a friend. We're meeting for drinks."

"You don't sound excited."

"I'm not." He shrugged. "It's been a long time since I've been out with a woman. The situation feels awkward and forced."

His discomfort made her feel a little better and there was no way she was going to figure out why.

"Think of this as practice. You don't know the woman, so what do you care if it goes well? But you'll put on something other than scrubs, get out into the real world and remember what dating is like. Next time will be easier."

He brightened. "You're right. And if we hit it off, we could have sex."

An unexpected zing stabbed her heart. "That's evolved."

"It's been a really long time."

"Which is your own fault. I get all men think about is sex, but talking about it is so tacky."

"Yet honest."

"Honesty is overrated."

"You don't believe that." He glanced at the clock. "I'll feed the dogs then jump in the shower. What are you doing tonight?"

Before she could figure out what to say that wasn't some version of "trying not to think about you being with someone, although why I care is beyond me," her phone buzzed.

"Excuse me," she said, reading the text.

Hey, it's me. I'm feeling out of sorts. Want to get dinner and talk?

Heather's question was exactly what she needed.

Love to. I have a rotisserie chicken and a few salads, along with chocolate ice cream that will make you weep.

Sounds perfect. I just fed everyone so I have a few hours before I have to be home. LC is happy to babysit and judge me. See you soon.

She turned back to see Grant setting down two dog food bowls. Both Scout and Zeus waited politely until they were given the release command.

"Heather's coming over for dinner," she said.

"Have fun."

"You, too." Or not, she added silently.

Thirty minutes later Heather arrived, a bottle of Merlot in hand.

"Thanks for saving me," she said as she hugged Tori then walked into the house. "I'm so in my head, I'm driving myself crazy."

"I can offer a fun distraction in about thirty seconds."

"What?"

Tori grinned. "Let's make it a surprise."

They went into the kitchen. Tori had already carved the chicken. The sides were on the table and she'd gotten out wineglasses, knowing her friend never arrived empty-handed.

They'd just taken their seats when Grant walked in. He waved absently at Heather, then faced Tori.

"How do I look?"

"Anxious and slightly nauseous."

His eyebrows drew together. "I'm serious."

"So am I. Are you feeling okay?"

He groaned, then turned to Heather. "How do I look?"

She frowned. "You're being weird. You look fine. Did you hit your head?"

Tori stood. "It's okay. He's not having an episode. I was just messing with him." She glanced at her friend. "Grant's going on a date."

"With a woman?"

"I haven't changed teams, so yes. A date with a woman."

"A blind date," Tori added.

"That's brave."

Grant's expression turned pained. "Could one of you say if I look okay?"

Tori studied the dark-wash jeans, the leather loafers and the deceptively casual but wildly expensive long-sleeve shirt he'd put on. The soft blue fabric suited him. His hair had grown out just enough to have a bit of a sexy wave.

She motioned for him to turn. Yup, from the back he looked just as good. The man had a great butt.

"She'll be dazzled," Tori said, taking her seat and serving herself chicken.

"You sure? I don't want to look like I'm trying too hard."

"Accept that the evening will feel awkward," she told him. "Set the bar for success really low and then everything else will be a win."

Heather glanced at her. "That's good advice."

"I've dated a lot."

"You and I are having a serious conversation before I go out with Emer."

"Tell me when and I'll be there. I can even bring charts."

Heather laughed. "You know how I love a good chart." She motioned to Grant. "You probably need to leave."

"Or I could stay with you two. We'd have fun."

"You need to have fun with a different grown-up," Tori told him. "Now, go be a good date. You can tell me all about it in the morning."

Grant hesitated a second, then nodded. "I won't be late."

"Be late," Heather told him. "Have sex on the first date. You'll sleep better."

He grumbled something under his breath and left. Tori watched him go, trying not to react to Heather's playful comment.

Of course Grant should have sex, she told herself. He was a really good guy who deserved someone special in his life. It was just that if he found his one true love, where did that leave her? Not romantically, she didn't care about him that way, but in her life?

"You okay?" Heather asked, reaching for her wine. "You have a funny look." She set down the glass. "Oh, God. You have a thing for Grant."

"What? No. Of course not. We're friends. I was just thinking when he gets serious about someone, everything will change. We won't be the non-couple friends anymore."

Heather's expression turned sympathetic. "I know what you feel."

Of course she did. She'd been cut out every time she'd broken up with Campbell.

"There have been too many changes already," Tori grumbled.

"Maybe you and I could be the non-couple friends. That way the numbers would be even."

Tori laughed. "An interesting idea. But what about if you fall for Emer? That will leave me non-couple friendless."

"The odds are slim." Heather studied her. "You sure you don't have feelings for Grant?"

"Not in the way you mean. Like I said, it's the change." She thought about what Grant having a girlfriend would do to the group dynamics. "And losing what we have."

Heather's brows drew together. "What does that mean? Why wouldn't Grant stay your friend?"

"Because right now we're each other's support. He gets the oil changed in my car and I'm designing his new kitchen. We have a routine. When he finds someone, it's like he'll go away."

"And people you love can't always be trusted to stay."

Tori nodded. "It doesn't make sense, but that's how it feels. I'd never been close to my sister. Her choice rather than mine. I think the seven-year age difference was just too much. Mom's death was so sudden. I was fifteen and scared. Sable had no interest in taking care of me, but she wouldn't force me into foster care, so I moved in with her."

Tori remembered how there'd been no room for her in the small apartment Sable had shared with a girlfriend. Tori had slept on the sofa and done her best to be invisible.

"She made it clear that the day I turned eighteen, I was on my own."

Tori had lost her mom and her home and had cried herself to sleep every night for weeks. Then she'd told herself she needed to get her act together and had gotten a couple of part-time jobs—mostly to keep herself busy. Between keeping up her grades and working, she hadn't had much time to think or mourn.

She'd turned eighteen in May. Sable had allowed her to stay until the day she graduated from high school. She'd rented a room from a nice older lady for the summer. She'd already been accepted to USC and between what her mom had left her in insurance money, financial aid and a couple of scholarships, college had been paid for.

She'd arrived on campus scared, alone and determined to figure out how to have a life. She and Heather had been roommates. Their junior year, Daphne had joined them to attend law school and the three of them had rented a house together.

"Grant adores you and wants to stay friends as much as you do," Heather pointed out. "That won't change, even if he gets a girlfriend."

Tori nodded because she wanted to be done talking about the possibility of not being friends with Grant. Thinking about the situation and her helplessness was too depressing.

"So... Emer," she said, her voice teasing. "That has to be fun to think about."

"More nerve-racking than fun, but he was nice." Heather's tone turned wistful. "I miss being in a relationship. Even when Campbell scared me, I still liked him." Her mouth twisted. "Not enough to stay, of course."

"That did make things difficult. How do you feel now, with Emer? Would staying be a possibility?"

"I don't know him well enough to say. But if we're talking generically, I'm starting to see possibilities. The wins in the love column are piling up. Sophie and Dugan, my cousin Kristine and Jaxsen. My dad and Jillian."

"It does seem like you're opening up your heart more with your new family. You like your sisters."

Heather sipped her wine. "I do."

"Why do you say it like that? I thought you were excited about them."

"I am. Sort of." She leaned forward. "They're my half sisters and I never knew about them until the Ancestry thing. We've all been living our lives, having no idea the other person exists. It's tough to grasp."

"But they're thrilled about you."

"They are. The family came over last weekend. For a quick visit, I thought, but they spent the day. They met LC and the kittens, we went out to lunch and played in the park. It was nice."

"Normal," Tori murmured. "You need a little normal in your life."

"I guess. It wasn't just that we had a good time. It was that I wasn't scared or nervous they'd want too much. It gave me hope."

Tori smiled at her. "No one else is going to be like your mom."

"I can't tell you how I need that to be true."

After dinner they curled up on the sofa with the dogs and talked until nearly nine. Finally, Heather said she had to feed the kittens.

Tori walked her to her car, then waited while the dogs did their business, all the while aware of the passing time. Grant's date must be going well, she thought, waving as her friend drove away. If not, he would have been home by now. After all, they were only meeting for drinks and how long did it take to chitchat and down a cocktail?

Unease settled in her stomach as she went into the house

and carefully locked the door behind her. As she, Scout and Zeus climbed to the second floor, she told herself she was happy for Grant. He deserved someone in his life, and it had been over a year since he'd done the deed so yay him if he was getting some. Only she couldn't quite make herself believe what she was thinking, and her earlier fear returned. If he found someone special, she would be the odd person out. And then what? They were the only family she had.

Daphne left work a little before three. Her low-grade nausea had faded enough for her to consider eating. More significantly, she knew she couldn't keep her worry locked up inside anymore. If Brody was done with her, she wanted to know and start making plans. Not that she could imagine a world without him, nor did she want to. He was the one. The man of her dreams. Or he had been.

Her lack of sureness had less to do with her own feelings than with his. They'd been at an impasse for so long—she wasn't sure they could find their way back. He didn't believe her about the affair, and she didn't trust that he'd ever wanted a child with her. Sometimes it felt as if their relationship was a beautiful crystal ornament, perfect in every way. Then a tiny crack appeared and another and now she worried that one day, it would simply shatter.

She stopped on her way home to buy ingredients for chicken soup, along with a fresh baguette. She also got a couple of eclairs. If all went well, she and Brody could enjoy them together. If the evening went to shit, she could lock herself in Alexa's room with the eclairs and a bottle of wine.

By four she'd cut up the vegetables. Her electronic pressure cooker stood at the ready. Once she'd put everything inside, she gave it a thorough stir, then locked the top and pressed the buttons to start the cycle.

She went upstairs, Albert and Vanessa at her heels. She showered, taking the time to deep condition her hair. The cats chased the drips of water on the shower door and rolled around on the bath mat. She dressed in yoga pants and a T-shirt, then blew out her bob.

Downstairs the pressure cooker had finished the cycle and was slowly cooling down. She would give it another half hour, then open it. Until then, she would make a salad. A few minutes later Brody walked into the kitchen, his expression two parts surprise, one part concern.

"You're home." He set his backpack on a chair. "It's barely five. Are you sick?"

She stared at him, trying to remember how it had been before their marriage had started to crumble. Even after two years, she'd still felt butterflies every time she saw him. When he smiled, she'd been unable to keep from smiling back. Just the lightest brush of his hand across her shoulder was enough to make her want him.

She'd fallen hard and fast and had given him all she had. She'd believed in him, in them. Now she wasn't sure.

"I needed to take a break from work," she told him. "So I came home early and made dinner."

His expression remained quizzical. "So you feel okay?"

She knew what he was asking and how she should answer. But her physical well-being wasn't really important right now.

"Are you finished with our marriage?" she asked, fighting sudden tears.

Under other circumstances, his extreme look of surprise and dismay could have been comical.

He swore quietly as he took a step toward her, then stopped. "Why would you ask that? I'm the one who's here, trying to make things work."

She ignored that because she thought it might be a distraction from the bigger question.

"I heard what you said," she told him, her voice shaking. "Last week, when your brothers were over." Tears spilled down her cheeks. "You said you thought marrying me was a mistake."

His shoulders sagged. "I'm sorry. I didn't mean it. I was frustrated and I vented." He moved toward her. "Daphne, we're so stuck and I can't figure out how to fix things. Half the time I don't know what's wrong. Yes, I'm angry and upset, but I love you and I want us to stay together. Do you want that, too?"

His answer eased some of her fear. "Of course. I've been showing up every day. I love us and our life and your kids." Now that she was less afraid, she was able to deal with some of her anger. "But we can't move on until you understand I didn't have an affair. I didn't even come close."

She thought briefly about what Tori and Heather had said, but pushed that away. They'd been reacting to the surprise, not thinking things through.

He leaned against the island. "I want to believe you," he admitted. "But when I close my eyes, I see the two of you together and it rips me apart."

She glared at him. "What do you picture? Us sitting across the table from each other, eating salad? We go to lunch. It's lunch. There's no wine, no touching, nothing the least bit intimate. Nothing, nothing, nothing!"

Brody stiffened. "You *go* to lunch? You're still seeing him?"

"I…"

She pressed her lips together, not sure what to say. The hurt look in Brody's eyes, the uncomfortable sensation of having been wrong, made her want to lash out.

"Yes, we've had lunch," she said stiffly. "You were acting weird and I wasn't going to let you dictate my life."

Which had sounded better in her head than it did when she said it out loud. Worse was the clarity of knowing she was in the wrong on this one. That by acting out of spite, being so determined to not let him influence her decisions, she'd hurt him. Worse, she'd given him yet another reason not to trust her.

"So you're proving a point?" His voice was deceptively soft and calm.

"Brody, don't," she began. "You're right to be upset. I reacted badly to the accusations. I shouldn't have done it."

"But you did." He stared at her. "You're not the one who should be asking whether I want to be in the marriage. I should be asking you."

The tears returned. "Brody, don't. Please. It's not like that."

"You're still seeing him. You knew it upset me, you knew it hurt me and honestly scared me, and you're still doing it. So how I feel, what I worry about, doesn't matter?"

"That's not true." She felt horrible. Her face was hot and the nausea had returned. "It wasn't like that. I acted childishly. I won't see him again." The tears fell faster. "I really am sorry."

"While I appreciate that, it doesn't make up for what I've just figured out. We're not a team. You'll do what you want, our marriage be damned."

He walked out of the kitchen, leaving her alone. Daphne sank onto the floor and leaned against the cabinets. She pulled her legs to her chest and rested her head on her knees. Tears turned into sobs and she cried until she was empty.

She'd hurt Brody and she'd damaged their relationship—all in the name of pride and pique. Things had been bad before and now she'd made them worse. The image of that cracked ornament filled her mind, and she wondered how much more damage it could sustain until it shattered so badly it could never be repaired.

The next day Daphne walked into Miguel's office. He was on the phone, but waved her in. As he finished up his call, she looked at the photos and sports memorabilia on the shelves. There were signed baseballs and footballs, a hockey puck from the Seattle Kraken, pictures of him with famous sports figures. Miguel had quite the celebrity life.

He hung up and rose. "Sorry. Needy client." His smile widened. "You don't normally make it all the way to my floor, but I like it."

She closed the door, then faced him. "I can't have lunch with you anymore. Not just the two of us."

"Brody doesn't approve."

"No, he doesn't. He's my husband and I don't want to hurt him." Which sounded better than admitting it was possible she'd been the one to make a mistake.

"I don't want to make this sound more complicated than it is," she added. "But I want things to work out with him and us having lunch gets in the way of that."

His dark gaze was steady. "I'm sorry to hear that. Of course I want whatever's best for you. I'll miss our lunches, though."

"Me, too." Seeing him was often a bright spot in a busy day. But while she liked Miguel, she *loved* Brody and she'd been wrong to hurt him.

She started for the door, then paused. "Thank you for understanding."

"Of course. And Daphne, if you ever need to talk, you know where to find me."

She faked a smile. "In a box seat at a Mariners game?"

He chuckled. "There, too."

She nodded and left. On her way back to her floor, she told herself she was doing the right thing. That she owed it to Brody to not have Miguel in her life. But as she rode the elevator, she couldn't help wondering if her action was going to be way too little, way too late.

fifteen

Heather felt ridiculous as she texted Fletcher that she'd arrived. She never should have agreed to have lunch with him at his school, but he'd wanted her to see where he worked and the teacher prep days were, according to him, the perfect time. So here she was, taking time off work so she could hang out with her biological father.

Her instinct to bolt was as strong as ever, but along with that was an unexpected longing to stay and continue the process of getting to know him.

Fletcher walked through the high school's open front doors. The second he spotted her, his smile broadened into something so welcoming and happy that she had to smile back.

"You made it," he said as he hugged her. "I'm so glad. I know you'd rather be working but I appreciate you indulging me."

"Of course. This will be fun."

He led her inside where she signed in at the front desk. Fletcher took her on a brief tour of the surprisingly modern building.

"Everything looks new," she said as they walked past the huge auditorium.

"We had a complete update two years ago. It was an ugly eighteen months of teaching out of portable classrooms, but it was worth it. We have high-speed internet and energy-efficient windows. The lighting's much better." He winked at her. "Wait until you see the teachers' lounge. It's very fancy."

On their way to his classroom, they passed a couple of teachers. Fletcher stopped to introduce her to them.

"This is Heather Sitterly, my daughter. She's a successful marketing entrepreneur." His voice was filled with pride, his expression adoring.

Heather dutifully shook hands and smiled, feeling a little embarrassed by his exuberance. Yes, she worked hard and the company did well, but she wasn't used to parental gushing. Not that she was going to complain—his obvious delight was a nice change from her mother's reaction to her achievements.

They made their way to his classroom. Heather fussed over the new desks, the big windows and the posters depicting historical events. He showed her how he could link his laptop to the screen and put up graphics and lesson plans.

"We have a student portal. I can post homework assignments and suggestions for projects. If someone's home sick, I can forward lesson plans. We also have a parent portal."

"Is that a good thing? Don't some email you too much?"

"A few, but mostly it's good to have contact. Students do better when they feel they're part of a community." He glanced at his watch. "Ready for lunch?"

"Sure. Where do you want to go?"

His expression turned quizzical. "I don't go out. Jillian packed a lunch for both of us."

Right, she thought. Because eating out every day would be expensive. "Sounds good."

They went into the large teacher's lounge. There were several sofas at one end, with tables and chairs at the other. Big windows opened onto a small walled garden. It was still warm outside and the sliding glass doors stood open.

Fletcher collected a large bag from the refrigerator. They took one of the tables outside. He set out sandwiches, a big container with green salad, another with chips and a third with dressing. There were cookies, plates and napkins, along with a thermos.

"Strawberry lemonade," he said, setting two plastic glasses on the table. "Jillian made it herself."

"Along with the cookies."

He grinned. "How did you know?"

"Jillian's the cookie-making type."

"She is. Did your mom make cookies when you were a kid?"

"Amber isn't much of a baker. My cousin Kristine owns a bakery, though. It's hugely popular, plus, she ships all over the country."

They sat across from each other. They split the turkey and ham sandwiches. Heather dished out the salad, then reached for her handbag.

"I nearly forgot." She pulled out the report she'd printed out that morning. "We have our official DNA results."

Fletcher didn't bother glancing at the paper. "I already know what it says."

"You're right. It's confirmed—you're my biological father."

"You okay with that?"

"I am."

"I'm glad. We're all excited to have you as part of our family." He hesitated. "The girls want to meet Amber."

Heather tried not to flinch. "That's not a good idea. She's not a kid person."

"I wouldn't mind seeing her again. It's been a long time."

Danger signs flashed in Heather's head. "I know how you remember her, but she's not exactly the same person she was. My mom had a tough time of it. She was a single mom. She married briefly, but things didn't work out. She always felt that because she had me, she never had the opportunities she deserved."

Fletcher's mouth turned down. "That's on me. I should have gotten her number. I should have been there for both of you."

Heather had no idea what her life would have been like if he had. Would he have kept her mom from slipping into her world of self-pity and narcissism?

"You didn't know she was pregnant," she told him.

"If things had been different," he began.

She cut him off with a shake of her head. "Don't beat yourself up about things that could have been. We can't change the past."

"I know." He studied her. "Would meeting us upset her?"

"I'm less concerned about her reaction." Heather paused. "My mom isn't a happy person. She looks at every situation from the perspective of how it affects her. If something good happens to me, she wants to know why it didn't happen to her."

She paused, knowing she was saying it all wrong, but not sure how to explain. "I started working part-time when I was fourteen. By the time I was sixteen, I was paying all the bills. We lived in my grandmother's house, so we didn't pay rent. Just insurance, taxes and utilities. She had a job, but her money was for her. One time she hurt her back. I was working the breakfast shift at a local B&B. I would bring her home breakfast."

She moved her fork from one side of her plate to the other. "The first time I placed the order, the cook put my name on the to-go box. I'd ordered it and I paid for it. But when I got home, my mom was furious. She wanted to know why my name was on her order."

She looked at him. "I don't want the girls around her. She'll be mean and they won't understand why. I know it's bad to say that about my mom, but you have to believe me. Any meeting won't go well at all."

He frowned. "I'm sorry for what you went through and I believe you. But I'm having trouble reconciling this with the woman I remember."

"I can't explain it, either."

"I appreciate that you want to protect your sisters." His expression was kind. "That must have been difficult for you."

She tried to smile. "I have trouble letting people in." She paused. "Men, mostly." One man in particular, she thought.

"I want you to be happy."

"Thanks. Me, too."

He picked up the second half of his sandwich. "Jillian mentioned a shared birthday party."

Heather immediately stiffened. "What does that mean?" she asked, even though she was pretty sure she already knew.

"Your birthdays are only a week apart. She thought it would be fun to have a combined party. Our friends, your friends. We could have it at the house. It wouldn't have to be expensive. I'd like to get to know the important people in your life."

No. Just no. Blending their friends? It was too much.

"I don't know," she hedged.

"Think about it. Like I said, just at the house, so nothing fancy and no pressure."

"You're freaking me out," she admitted.

"I don't want to do that but I hope you'll consider the idea."

She nodded slowly, thinking they'd been doing so well. But that was what always happened to her. Everything was great, then the other person wanted to go to the next level. No one wanted to stay where they were. While in her head she knew progression was normal, it felt threatening.

"Let's change the subject," he said, his voice gentle. "We've agreed to let the girls get a kitten. Actually, we'd like both of them so Layla and Ella can each claim one and the kittens can play with each other."

"Oh, that's great. Molly and Polly are so sweet. I'll let the rescue know, then forward you the paperwork."

She would also pay the adoption fee, so the money didn't come out of what she assumed was an already tight budget. And she'd send the kittens home with supplies.

"Are they thinking up names?"

Fletcher laughed. "Constantly. It's quite the process."

"They're going to love them."

"They are and you made it happen."

She shifted uneasily at the praise. "I didn't do anything."

"You have no idea how much you do. While I have nothing to do with the woman you've become, I'm so proud of you."

"You keep saying that."

"Because I mean it."

"Your daughters are very lucky to have you as their father."

"I'm glad you think so."

She did. Once again, she was left wondering how things would have been different if she'd met this man thirty years ago. But as she'd told him, the past couldn't be changed. Which left only today and all the days that followed.

Daphne had covered the kitchen table with newspaper and sacrificial sheets. She'd set out paint and brushes.

"This morning we're going to paint the flowers," she told

Elijah, Cadin and Alexa. "Later this afternoon we'll glue on the pictures. Once the glue is dry, I'll spray on the sealer and we'll put on the magnets."

She'd looked online for craft projects and had decided on salt dough flower magnets. Earlier in the week, they'd made salt dough. After rolling it out, they'd used cookie cutters to make flower shapes. Daphne had carefully cut out the center. Once they'd baked, they'd dried for a few days.

The plan was to each paint four and cut out pictures of themselves. When the magnets were finished, they would leave a couple here and take the rest to their mom's. She'd drawn outlines of the flower shape on paper and had painted a few options to give the kids ideas. Now they crowded around her to see what she'd done.

"I like the stars," Alexa said, sliding onto her lap. "And the suns and moons."

"You can't put stars and moons on a flower," Cadin complained.

"Sure you can. It's called art expression." Elijah's tone was superior as he sat beside Daphne. "An artist at summer camp talked about it and we did lots of projects. Even using chalk on the sidewalk." He sounded faintly scandalized.

"I like that one." Cadin pointed to a dark blue flower covered with white flecks. "It looks like the night sky."

"I'm glad you think so. That's what I was going for." Daphne grinned at him. "Making the tiny specks of white is messy but fun."

"I want to do one like that," he said eagerly as he sat on her other side.

"Me, too." Elijah passed out paintbrushes.

"I want to do one with the moon and stars. And a striped one."

"Then let's get started."

She had the kids put on their craft aprons, then poured water into plastic bowls for cleaning brushes between colors. By the time they finished, they each had four flowers drying on the counter and plenty of paint on their hands.

Cleanup went quickly. Elijah directed his siblings to scrub *all* the paint off their skin. Daphne promised they would glue on the photographs after dinner and put on the magnets in the morning, before they went back to their mom's. They raced outside to play soccer in the backyard—a good way to burn off energy after sitting for so long.

She'd just finished wiping down the kitchen table when Brody walked in.

They stared at each other without speaking. Sadness gripped her as she acknowledged that their easy conversation had been lost over the past few weeks. Now silence was the norm.

"The kids painted the magnets," she said, pointing to the drying flowers.

"They did a good job. You were patient with them."

"I like when we all do crafts together."

"This was a fun project for them. You've always been good at that kind of thing."

She shrugged. "My mom and I did all kinds of things when I was growing up. Heather and I started quilting in high school but neither of us kept it up."

"You could start quilting again if you wanted."

"I don't."

Brody glanced out the window, then back at her. He started to say something, only to stop. Frustration gripped her.

"I'm not going to have lunch with Miguel again," she said abruptly. "Not because anything was going on, but because it hurt you and was disrespectful. I should have stopped when you made it clear you were upset. I'm sorry about that."

He looked at her. "I wish I was enough for you."

"What?" The word came out as a yelp. "What does that even mean?"

"You could do a lot better. I don't bring much to the table. I've got three kids from a previous marriage. I make about half what you do. Sometimes I don't know what you see in me."

"You're not making any sense. I love the kids and who cares which one of us makes more. We're blessed to have all that we need, financially, with money left over. Brody, I didn't marry you for money. I married you because I love you and I wanted to spend my life with you."

He looked at her, his expression troubled. "If I made more, you wouldn't have to work so much."

"I work the hours I do because I love my job and that's what's expected by the firm. We could get by on less money. I really don't understand why you'd say you don't have anything to offer me. I'm not looking for a meal ticket. I want a partner. I thought that's what we were to each other."

"You don't need me."

The unfairness of the statement made her want to throw something. "How can you say that? I do need you. I want us to have a life together. I want us to raise your kids and have a baby and—"

She paused. "I'm not suggesting we have a baby now. I'm saying when things are more stable. You were right to say we're not ready. But in the next few months."

He looked away. "Sure. Let's do that."

His lack of enthusiasm, the way he suddenly seemed disengaged, cut down to her heart. He was saying the words, but he didn't mean them. Had he given up on them?

A question a braver version of herself would ask, only she didn't have the strength to hear what she thought would be an uncomfortable truth. Not right now.

"The kids are in the backyard," she said instead. "You should go check on them."

He nodded and left. Daphne went into her home office and closed the door. Only then did she allow herself to feel the pain and let the tears fall.

Tori spread out several sheets of paper. She'd done 3D renderings of both their kitchens in advance of the meeting with the designer who would shepherd them through the remodel.

"Both layouts are good," she said. "We'll keep those. My kitchen is a little smaller, so I want to keep the style simple and contemporary. I want to take the cabinets to the ceiling for extra storage. The additional cost should be minimal. We'll replace the under-counter cabinets with deep drawers on both sides of the range."

She pointed to another sheet of paper. "Grant has more space, so I'm thinking a slightly more detailed cabinet door in a darker color. Masculine without being off-putting for resale."

"Why would I move?" Grant asked.

Tori ignored him. "Again, the cabinets should go to the ceiling." She set down another 3D picture. "In the butler's pantry, I want glass doors on the uppers and under-cabinet lighting. It makes a huge difference."

Candace, their designer, looked from the designs to Tori and back. "These are excellent."

"She's a graphic designer," Grant said.

"You hardly need me at all."

Tori shook her head. "I couldn't manage the remodel on my own. I can tell you I want to make some changes in the lighting, but where to source everything? No clue."

They sat around a large table in a cabinet shop, surrounded by kitchen mock-ups and door options. They would order semi-custom cabinets—choosing the style and the finish, but sticking with standard sizes.

Candace collected several samples. Tori chose a simple

Shaker style for herself, painted creamy white. She laid out three doors for Grant.

"This first one is similar to mine, but with a bit more detail." She pointed to the quarter round. "Do you like it?"

Grant shifted uneasily. "It's nice. What do you think?"

She sighed. "You were like this when you wanted to get your place painted." She glanced at Candace. "He took me to the paint store, made me pick three shades of white, then wouldn't choose."

"It could be worse," Candace said with a laugh. "He could have wanted beige."

"Beige is dependable," Grant told them.

"I love the espresso finish," Tori said, rubbing her hand along the smooth surface. "But it would be too dark for the space."

She picked up another sample that was a gray with nice brown undertones. "What about Storm?"

"I like that," he said. "With the cabinets like you have."

"You don't want something different?"

"Nope. This one."

Tori nodded. "Okay, done."

They selected quartz countertops. Or rather, she did and Grant nodded.

Candace wrote up the order and they each put down a deposit.

"I'll send you an ETA," she told them. "By the time they're ready, your contractor should have all the drywall and flooring replaced. You'll be home before you know it."

"Sounds good," Grant said. They headed for his SUV. "That was easier than I thought it would be."

She got into the passenger seat. "Maybe because you didn't do any of the work."

"You're right. You were great. Thank you." He glanced at his watch. "I'll thank you with lunch."

"Somewhere good because you seriously owe me."

He grinned. "I know just the place."

He took her to STK Steakhouse in downtown Bellevue. The upscale restaurant was busy, but they were given a nice window table.

They agreed they would each order a salad and split the STK Sandwich—a glorious creation with shaved rib eye, caramelized onion, gruyere and horseradish cream.

"I also need French fries," Tori told him.

"Whatever you want."

Once they'd placed their order, Grant leaned toward her. "I meant what I said, Tori. You were amazing, and I appreciate all your work."

"Thanks. I enjoyed it. Kitchen design is different from my day job."

He studied her. "You okay? You seem… I don't know. Down maybe."

"I'm not down. Just dealing with so many changes. I still have nightmares about the sprinklers going off."

"You do?"

She nodded. "You weren't there, so you missed the trauma, but it was awful. While I'm grateful for the rental house, it's not home." She paused, thinking she shouldn't get into the other things that were bothering her. Unfortunately, Grant knew her too well.

"Tell me," he said, his voice gentle. "I want to know."

"You're dating." She held up a hand. "I want you to find someone, but it's weird. What if you fall madly in love and don't want to be my friend anymore?"

His dark gaze locked with hers. "That will never happen."

"She could hate me and if the sex is really good, you'll side with her."

"I'm not interested in anyone who hates you."

"You say that now, but you don't know how great she is in bed."

"Wouldn't matter. You're important to me. Whoever I find has to understand that. Besides, I'm not looking to get serious."

She wanted to believe him, but wasn't sure. "You've been going out a lot."

He grinned. "Tori, I've been on two dates."

"With two different women. You're like a modern-day Casanova."

"I wish, but no. It's been a long time since I dated and I don't seem to be very good at it."

She told herself to be sympathetic, while secretly cheering. She'd meant what she'd said—that she did want Grant to find someone. Just not, you know, right away. She needed some continuity in her life.

"You didn't like either of them?"

"No chemistry."

"Maybe your standards are too high."

Amusement brightened his eyes. "You're saying I should settle for the sake of sex."

"Maybe."

"Speaking of sex," he said. "What about you? You haven't gone out with anyone in a while."

"I'm not in meeting-guys mode right now. I have enough going on." Plus, the whole Kyle debacle had been so upsetting. "Although, if you're so worried about me, why did you set Heather up with Emer and not me?"

Their server returned with their salads and drinks—iced tea for him and a mocktail made with watermelon water, mint, cucumber juice and soda for her.

Grant waited until they were alone to say, "Because if it goes badly, I can deal with Heather being mad at me, but if you were upset by something I'd done, I couldn't handle it."

His blunt honesty nearly made her melt. "That's the sweetest thing you've ever said to me."

"You matter, Tori. I mean that." His smile returned. "We're the non-couple friends. Even if we both find other people, I want us to stay close."

"Me, too."

They looked at each other. For a second she felt something strange inside. Kind of a weird tightness in her chest and a sense of some great truth just out of reach.

"Nora's visiting her mom for a couple of days," Grant said as he dug into his salad. "I thought I'd invite Campbell over for dinner."

His words were so at odds with what she might or might not be feeling, that it took her a second to respond. "Um, sure. Just let me know when. Oh, and you'll be cooking that night."

"I figured. I'm actually better than you in the kitchen."

"In your dreams."

"I grill better."

"Because I don't grill."

He grinned. "You're saying if you did, you'd be good."

"You know it."

And just like that, order was restored. Tori had no idea what had just happened, or not happened, but it was gone now and she was never going to think about it again.

sixteen

Heather hung up the phone and immediately walked to Tori's office. Her friend looked up from her computer. Her quick smile faded.

"What's wrong?"

Heather closed Tori's door and sank into the visitor's chair. She waved her cell as emotions churned inside. Bad ones. Ones that made her want to run far, far away.

"Jillian called me."

"Your stepmother?"

Heather winced. "Do we have to call her that? Can't she be Fletcher's wife?"

"You still call him Fletcher?"

"That's his name."

"What about Dad?"

"That is never happening." Dad? Dad? "We're not close. I barely know him."

"Your closeness doesn't change who he is, but I get not being ready to use a more intimate term. I was just asking. So Jillian, aka Fletcher's wife, called and you're upset. She must want something."

"She has a doctor's appointment and asked me to go with her. She wants someone there to help listen and Fletcher has school."

Tori's mouth twisted. "So it's bad. The doctor's appointment. You don't need someone else for a checkup."

"That's what I'm thinking."

Jillian didn't look sick or act sick, but maybe she was good at faking it. And for some reason she didn't want her husband to go with her. Heather understood needing emotional support, but...

"Why me? She has friends. She seems like the type to have a lot of friends. Is this her attempt to bond? Because if it is, I don't like it. I have no interest in bonding over some illness."

She paused. "That sounded harsher than I intended but you know what I mean. My God, if she thinks her being sick will make me like her more, she's wrong. She's turning into my mother."

"It's not about bonding," Tori told her. "She seems more emotionally intelligent than to try that. Nothing you've said made her sound like a victim. Take a breath."

"I'm breathing."

"You're getting upset. I know it's a strange request, but she really does sound like a genuine person. She knows you're smart and capable. Maybe she asked you along because you're not that close. Maybe she doesn't want to deal with a bunch of drama while she's scared, but she doesn't want to go alone. You can be another set of ears and be supportive without falling apart."

Heather hadn't thought of that. "It could be that," she admitted. "Maybe. If it's that, then I'm okay with it." Honestly, nothing with Jillian's health would be upsetting. She barely knew the woman.

"You could ask her," Tori said.

"That would be awkward. I'll find out when I go with her." Heather sighed. "It's not just the doctor thing. Fletcher told me they want to adopt the two kittens for the girls."

"That's good news."

"Why don't they adopt random cats from a shelter? Why do they have to be the cats I'm raising?"

Tori looked confused. "Isn't the point of fostering kittens having them grow up and get adopted?"

"Of course. And yes, I know they'll take care of Molly and Polly. I'm just saying why can't they pick someone else's foster kittens so mine can go to someone I don't know?"

Tori frowned. "That makes no sense. You should appreciate knowing your kittens will have a great life."

"I feel like all of them have a great life. It's just so intrusive."

Tori's expression turned knowing. "Oh, I get it. You're freaked out about Jillian and now you're in reaction mode."

"I'm not. You're wrong. They're just too much and there are too many of them," Heather snapped. "Jillian wants to have a joint birthday party. Her friends and family, my friends and family. One big party. Together!" Her voice got louder with each word. "It's too much. I can't do this."

"You're so lucky," Tori whispered, her eyes filling with emotion. "Most people have to get married to find more family as an adult, but here you are with a whole new one and all you had to do was spit in a tube."

Heather's ranty feelings collapsed as she realized how small and ungrateful she must sound to her friend. All Tori had ever wanted was to belong.

"I'm sorry," Heather said, her voice more quiet. "I went too far."

"You feel how you feel. I know it's hard for you to trust people and it sounds like Fletcher and Jillian aren't big believers in boundaries. Do what you're comfortable with and say no to the rest." Tori managed a faint smile. "Personally, I'd jump in with both feet, but that's just me."

Heather studied her. "Your heart was broken by your mom dying and your sister tossing you out when you turned eighteen, yet you're totally open to love and friendship. Why is that?"

"I don't know." Tori leaned toward her. "I guess because I had so many good years with my mom. I knew she loved me and would do anything for me. My sister didn't mean to be cruel. She was in her early twenties and raising me was too much for her. I remember what it was like and want to get back to that. Or find a new version of loving someone and being loved. You didn't have that with Amber. There were no good memories to call on."

She paused. "I'm not saying she was horrible every second, but she kept getting worse. In the end she tried to trap you into giving up your life to care for her. She never wanted what was best for you and when good things happened, she was resentful. That's different. My fear is I'll never find love again. Your fear is you'll be guilted into being powerless. That you'll be forced to surrender who you are for someone who wants not just your time, but your very existence."

Heather stared at her friend, stunned by her clear, honest, uncomfortable-to-hear assessment of their problems. Heather was terrified of someone trapping her, by any means, and taking not just what she had, but who she was. Of someone reducing her to so much less. The price of staying safe was to only let in a very few people. Those who had been vetted over time and had proven their worth. Tori, of course, and Daphne. Her cousins. Otherwise, she felt safer keeping people at arm's length.

As for the love Tori desperately wanted, most days Heather would rather walk through fire. It would be more difficult for a friend to hurt her, but a man could take everything. A man could slip into her heart, make her trust him then slowly erode every piece of her self-worth until there was nothing left.

"You'll always have me," Heather told her. "And Daphne."

Tori smiled. "I know. I love you guys so much."

Heather felt the words rising up inside her. Just four of them. Words she'd never said aloud to anyone who wasn't her cousins. She couldn't. She didn't. But somehow she couldn't stop them.

"I love you, too."

Tori reached across her desk and grabbed Heather's hand. "You're a really good friend and I appreciate that. You're always there for me. I want you to know I'll always be there for you, too."

"I know that."

"Go with Jillian and find out what's wrong. Trust her to be a decent human until she starts to prove otherwise. If it turns out she's secretly Amber, you'll have time to run. If you can't, no matter where I am or what I'm doing, I'll come drag you to safety."

Her chest was tight, her eyes a little burny. "You're killing me," she said. "You know I hate this emotional crap."

Tori smiled. "You hate it less than you think."

"I'm getting a rash."

"You're not. You're growing and changing. Soon, you'll be able to admit you were in love with Campbell."

Heather snatched her hand back. "I wasn't! I don't do love."

"You just said you love me."

"That's different. We don't have sex."

Tori laughed. "It's not the sex that scares you. It's the caring." Her humor faded. "I know this is going to sound weird and you're going to tell me I'm wrong, but I believe that you admitting how you felt about Campbell will be the first step in healing. The reason you can't get over him is you've never acknowledged what he meant to you. What's the saying? Name it and claim it?"

Heather had been kidding about the rash, but suddenly she felt weird and prickly. As if her own skin didn't fit anymore.

"I wasn't in love with him," she said firmly.

"Okay, sure."

Heather glared at her. "You're mocking me."

"A little. Maybe a lot. Just let the thought sit. If I'm wrong, then I'm sorry. But if I'm right, maybe you can start to let go. Wouldn't it be nice to go out with Emer knowing you might be interested in him rather than because you need a distraction?"

Heather hadn't thought about that. Emer had been a nice guy. But her in love with Campbell? Why would she do that to herself?

"Relationships suck." She stood. "I'm going to bury my emotions in work. Clients, I understand."

"And you're very good with them. I, on the other hand, will continue my brilliant video editing. Later, I will eat salad for lunch and feel smug about my insights."

Heather laughed. "You know even if I do decide I was in love with Campbell, I can never tell you."

"That's probably wise. The endless refrain of 'I told you so' would get so annoying."

"The deli stops delivering in twenty minutes," Irena said, her voice concerned. "Why don't you let me get you a sandwich?"

Daphne gave her assistant what she hoped was a pleasant smile. "I'm fine."

"I don't usually get up in your business, but you obviously don't feel well and I swear you're getting thinner by the day. You need to eat."

Irena was right, Daphne thought grimly. She'd lost her appetite, wasn't sleeping and hadn't felt right in a while. She would guess the cause was the ongoing trouble in her marriage.

"Do you think it's the flu?" Irena asked. "Do you have a fever?"

"No, I'm just tired and I'm not sleeping well. Plus, my stomach's been off. I'm not nauseous exactly, just a little queasy, if that makes sense. Smells are bothering me and—"

She stopped talking as her assistant suddenly grinned like a fool.

"Really?" Irena asked eagerly. She closed the door and approached the desk. "I'm so happy. I was hoping, but you know, some couples aren't interested, so I wasn't sure and it seemed rude to ask."

Daphne stared at her. "I have no idea what you're talking about."

"You're pregnant."

Daphne had never been a fainter but at that exact second, the walls of the room seemed to rush toward her as the light faded to a pinprick. A heartbeat later her vision returned, even as she struggled to catch her breath.

"What? No, I'm not."

She couldn't be. Pregnant? She and Brody were barely having sex. She'd gone off her monthly shots to give her body a rest but they were using condoms. And again, not much in the sex department.

Irena's happy smile never faded. "I've had three. I know what I'm talking about. You have all the symptoms. It's either that or menopause and you're way too young for that. But you're the boss. If you say no, it's no." She lowered her voice. "I won't say a word to anyone, but if you want to talk, I'm here."

Okay, this was getting uncomfortable. Daphne quickly saved her work, then stood.

"You know what? I do need a break." She glanced toward the window and saw it was sunny outside. "I'm going to take a walk and get some lunch. I'll be back in an hour."

"Excellent. No soft cheese, no unpasteurized dairy or juices, no fish high in mercury. Oh, and you'll need to give up caffeine. I'd say do it over a few days so you don't get that killer headache."

"Still not pregnant." Daphne pulled her bag from her desk drawer. "See you in a bit."

Outside, she took deep breaths and waited for her heart to stop pounding and the vague sense of panic to go away.

"This is ridiculous," she murmured, taking out her phone and scrolling through her calendar. She'd gotten her period, what? Two weeks ago?

She continued scrolling and scrolling. The fluttery panic became a drumbeat in her head as she found the entry. Her last period had been six weeks ago. She was two weeks late.

Oh God, oh God, oh God. No. Just no. She couldn't be pregnant. Not now. Not with everything so horrible between her and Brody. She leaned against the building and told herself she was fine. This wasn't happening.

But what if it was? He would never believe he was the father. He would assume she had slept with Miguel and they would spend the whole pregnancy fighting. Once the baby was born, he would insist on a DNA test, which would prove the kid was his, but by then, the damage would be done. She would never be able to forgive him for not believing in her. They would divorce and there she would be, a single mother, with no husband, no stepkids. She would lose everything that mattered to her.

The on-again, off-again queasiness returned. After taking a couple of deep breaths, she shoved her phone into her bag and walked purposefully down the street. There was only one way to solve this problem.

Thirty minutes later she stared at the stick she'd peed on and waited for the answer. Per the instructions, there would be a control line on the right. If a second line appeared, she was pregnant. If not, she wasn't. She set her phone for three minutes and waited.

The seconds ticked by. Her phone beeped at three minutes. Daphne waited another ninety seconds before allowing herself to sink back onto the toilet as she accepted the news.

She wasn't pregnant. Relief bubbled up like champagne. No baby, no reason to fight with Brody, no DNA test. She was fine.

She wrapped the test in several paper towels, then shoved it far down the trash bin and washed her hands. For the first time in days, she was actually hungry. She hurried into her office and pulled out her phone. It was too late to order up from the deli downstairs, but she could have something delivered from a nearby restaurant. Soup and a sandwich, she thought, feeling as if she hadn't eaten in days. Maybe a burger with extra fries.

Once the order was placed, she walked out to Irena's desk. "I'm having food delivered," she said. "If you'd bring it in when it gets here."

Her assistant looked at her. "You look better."

"I feel great." Daphne smiled. "I think I just needed a little fresh air. I've been cooped up too much lately. I need to get out more."

And to know that she wasn't pregnant. That was the happiest news of all.

★ ★ ★

Tori let herself into Heather's condo, Scout at her heels. Heather and Elliot had a client dinner, so Tori had volunteered to feed the kittens and LC. She would stay and play with them for an hour or so.

LC came running when she called. He wound his way around her legs, purring loudly, before rubbing against Scout.

"How are you, handsome boy?" Tori asked as she got out his food. "Did you have a good day?"

She dished out his canned food, changed his water, then made sure Scout followed her to the kitten room so she wouldn't help herself to LC's dinner.

Molly and Polly were both playing, tumbling over each other. Tori stepped over the low gate and greeted the kittens, who began to purr. She sank onto the floor and petted each of them before picking up a feather wand to continue the play action. Hunt, eat, sleep, she thought humorously. The happy life cycle of a cat. As their meals were delivered on a dish, no actual hunting occurred, but a good play session was a fine substitution.

Scout stretched out to observe. Both kittens raced over to bat at Scout's wagging tail and climb all over her. LC joined them, sitting off to the side for his post-dinner groom.

Tori smiled as she watched the kittens play. They were healthy and happy and totally secure in their world. That was how it was supposed to be. She supposed she could say the same about herself. Okay, there were a few bumps in the road, like the whole flooded condo thing and her sense of being overwhelmed. And she still hadn't figured out how to reconcile her sense of wanting Grant to be happy with her concern about being left behind if he fell madly in love. She supposed the solution was to put herself out there, dating-wise, and find a good guy. A real good guy, not a fake one like Kyle.

Why couldn't she find someone normal? Funny and kind, with a nice family. She would so love to be a part of a big family. He wouldn't have to be good-looking—she didn't care about that. But he needed to have a job and be a decent human being. Chemistry was important. She'd tried muscling through a lack of chemistry with Kyle, but even taking the whole married thing out of the equation, she knew now that had been a mistake.

She wanted someone she looked forward to seeing. Someone she could joke with and hang out with. Oh, and he had to like dogs and get along with her friends.

"That's a list," she murmured. "Maybe I am asking for too much."

Only she knew she wasn't. Elliot was great. Not for her, but he was exactly what she was talking about. The same with Sam from market research. Sure, he was obsessed with Russell Wilson, but she could live with that in a guy. Not that she was interested in Sam. He was a little young and there was no chemistry.

Brody was terrific, and so was Campbell. Again, not for her, but they proved her list wasn't impossible. There they were, meeting nearly all her criteria. And Grant, of course. She smiled. Funny, sweet Grant, who took care of her and made her laugh and worried about her. He adored Scout, had a big, close-knit family. For extra credit, the man was a doctor and incredibly good-looking. As for them having chemistry...

"Nope, no chemistry," she whispered.

Sure, they hugged and he kissed her on the cheek, but there wasn't any sexual energy between them. Okay, yes, she'd noticed his butt once or possibly twice, and she might have speculated about him in bed, but that was just pretend. They were friends. Good friends. Non-couple friends. Grant was her rock and there was no way she would risk what they had by, you know, sleeping with him. Nor did she want to. That was the most important point. She didn't want to sleep with Grant. It would be too weird. It wasn't as if she had feelings for him.

That decided, she got up and prepared the wet food for the kittens. Once they'd eaten, she cleaned up their messy faces, then herded them toward the litter box where they did their business. After that she played with them until they got sleepy. They headed for their bed of blankets, LC trailing after them. She petted the three of them and rose.

"Your mom will be home soon," she told the trio, before collecting Scout and driving to her rental house. Grant's car was already in the driveway.

"It's me," she called as she walked inside, Scout pushing past her to greet Zeus.

"In the kitchen."

She found Grant, still in scrubs, unpacking a grocery bag. He grinned.

"I have a taste for hot dogs." He held up a hand. "I know, not healthy. So I got the kosher ones you've approved, along with a kale salad. I figure the kale has to counteract the hot dogs."

He dumped several limes on the counter. "I thought we'd make margaritas first with that tequila we like." He grinned. "What do you think?"

She took in the slightly too-long hair, the easy smile, the broad shoulders. She thought about how he gave the greatest hugs, was always there for her and the weird little flutter she sometimes felt low in her belly...like now.

The truth she'd been unable to see slammed into her. If she hadn't been leaning against the counter, she would have fallen on her butt.

She was in love with Grant. Totally and completely, down to her toes in love with him. She wanted to have sex with him and get married and have his babies. She wanted to be

Mrs. Grant Brown and be a part of his family and grow old with him.

"Tori?" He frowned. "You okay?"

No, she wasn't. She was terrified. She couldn't love Grant. They were the non-couple friends. Her loving him messed up everything.

"I'd rather have Tater Tots than kale salad," she said.

His grin returned. "Sold. You know I love a Tater Tot. I'll preheat the oven."

"Great. I need to feed Scout but I want to change first."

He pointed to the stairs. "Go. I'll feed her and start on the margaritas." He smiled again. "It's going to be a good night."

"It is," she managed before ducking out of the room and racing upstairs. When she was safely in her bedroom, she leaned against the door.

"No, no, no. This is so bad."

Loving Grant had disaster written all over it. Because of his horrible marriage, he wasn't looking for anything permanent. He saw her as a friend and had never hinted he had the least bit of interest in her that way. He was actively dating other women and trying to have sex with them. One day he would succeed and then what? How was she supposed to handle him telling her it had happened? Because he would. Oh, not the details, but he would absolutely talk about getting laid.

"I can't be in love with him," she whispered. "This is worse than Kyle and all the other bad boyfriends put together."

Because he would for sure break her heart. This would end badly for her. And there was nothing she could do about it.

The only solution was to make sure he never found out how she felt, because while she knew she could handle whatever pain was coming, she wasn't sure she could survive Grant's pity.

seventeen

"Are you mad?" Jillian asked when she opened her front door. Heather had spent the drive up trying to figure out what she was feeling. Confusion, yes. Annoyance? Probably. But most of her emotions seemed to fall in the "I couldn't handle you turning into my mother" column.

"Is this a game?" Heather asked bluntly. "Are you playing me?"

Jillian's shoulders slumped. "I'm sorry. I should have been more clear. I wasn't thinking. I wanted someone to come with me today and while you're great, we've only just started to get to know each other and I thought you would be concerned but not devastated if it's something bad."

Her words were close enough to what Tori had said to help Heather relax a little. She studied Jillian's face.

"You don't look sick."

"I have metastatic breast cancer." She stepped out onto the front porch. "We should leave. I'll drive."

Heather stared at her, unable to take in what she'd been told. "You have breast cancer? Right now?"

"I have cancer every single day."

Heather slid into the minivan's passenger seat. Thoughts swirled. None of this seemed possible.

"Are you getting chemo? You look fine. Aren't you too young? I don't understand."

Jillian started the car. "I was diagnosed three years ago. Metastatic breast cancer is also known as Stage IV breast cancer. It's cancer that has spread to other parts of the body. Usually the liver, lungs or bones. For me, it's the bones."

She glanced at Heather. "I'm getting treatment and it's working. In theory, I could live decades and be fine." She paused. "Relatively fine."

Breast cancer? "How can you be so normal? I'd be terrified."

"I was. Some days I still am. But I take care of myself and do what my doctors tell me. Like I said, I could live longer than you." She stopped at a signal. "I'm having pain in my side. It's probably nothing, but I want to be sure."

Fear gripped Heather, making her stomach knot and her body go cold. "You think it's back?"

"I don't know." The light turned green and she drove forward. "I haven't told Fletcher or the kids. I don't want to scare them unnecessarily. They've already been through so much. But *I'm* scared, so I asked you to come. I'm sorry for putting you through this."

"It's okay."

Later, when she was back home and by herself, she would process what Jillian had told her. For now, there was only getting through the moment.

"What, ah, are they going to do?"

"Just an exam and a couple of X-rays. That's the first step in detecting bone cancer."

"You're hoping for a pulled muscle?"

"That's my fantasy."

Jillian offered her a quick smile before she pulled into the parking lot of a tall medical building.

"You can wait in the reception area," Jillian said as they walked inside. "I shouldn't be long."

"I'll do whatever you want."

Jillian's smile returned. "No scary procedures to watch. I promise."

They reached the elevator. Without thinking, Heather took Jillian's hand and squeezed it. "I'm going to be right here for you."

"Thanks."

The receptionist greeted Jillian by name, then Jillian was whisked away. Heather sat and stared blankly at the wall.

Jillian had cancer. Jillian had metastatic breast cancer, which probably meant for the rest of her life she would worry about every ache and pain.

Heather had no frame of reference for that. All she knew for sure was Jillian had wanted to protect her family from the worry and pain until she had more information. The very definition of an unselfish act of love. Jillian wasn't like her mother—she was the opposite.

Heather wrapped her arms around her midsection and told herself to keep breathing. Whatever happened, it would be fine. Jillian had good doctors. She'd survived this long. But even as she tried to reassure herself, her throat tightened and her eyes burned. She didn't cry—she never cried. But she came really, really close.

Time ticked by slowly. Heather googled metastatic breast cancer on her phone, then wished she hadn't. She worried about what was happening and what the doctor was saying.

She wondered if the cancer was genetic and if the girls carried the gene.

Forty minutes later Jillian returned to reception, her expression relieved and happy. Heather sprang to her feet and hurried over.

"You're okay? You're good?"

Jillian hugged her. "She thinks I pulled a muscle gardening last weekend."

"Thank God! We are so stopping at Starbucks on the way back to the house. I need sugar and caffeine. I really need liquor but it's ten a.m. and I have to work."

Jillian linked arms with her. "I would love to go to Starbucks. We'll get Frappuccinos. With extra whipped cream."

They got into the elevator.

"And while we're there, we'll talk about our shared birthday party."

Heather shook her head. "You just spent the better part of a week worrying you had bone cancer and now you want to talk about a birthday party?" One she hadn't agreed to, but somehow this didn't seem like the moment to mention that.

"That's how I get through it."

That stopped Heather. She stared at her stepmother. "You're incredibly brave."

"Thanks. Some days. Other times I can barely get out of bed."

"But you do get out of bed to take care of your family."

Jillian frowned. "Of course. They need me."

Because that was who she was, Heather thought. That was who most people were. As they got in the minivan, she had the thought that instead of worrying that everyone had the potential to turn into her mother, she should consider that most of them were a whole lot more like Jillian.

"I am so ordering you extra whipped cream," she said. "And a cookie."

★ ★ ★

"You look great," Tori said, trying not to clench her teeth. Or whimper.

Grant stood in the family room, his expression uncertain. "You sure? I could go change."

"You already have. Twice. You're turning into a teenage girl. You look fine. Besides, isn't the purpose of the date to get out of your clothes?"

Dang, she was good, she thought grimly. Her tone had the perfect blend of exasperation and teasing. Grant, dressed in dark-wash jeans and a cream-colored shirt, was going out with one of his women for the third time and everyone knew what the third date meant, especially when the woman in question had said how much she was looking forward to them getting *closer*.

Ugh. Why had Grant told her that? But he had and honestly, it had been all she'd been able to think about today. The fact that in a couple of hours, Grant would be getting naked with someone who wasn't her.

He sank onto the sectional. "I'm nervous."

"You'll be fine. You have condoms?"

He glared at her. "Yes."

The single word was like a punch to the gut. "That's the most important part." She forced herself to lean back in the cushion and smile as if she found him amusing.

"Any questions? Do you remember what goes where?"

"Very funny."

"Just checking. It's been a long time since you've seen girly parts up close. Not counting the porn, of course."

He groaned. "I don't watch porn."

"Uh-huh. All guys watch porn." She glanced at her watch, then at him. "You should get going. Being late won't make you sexually attractive."

He rose. "What are you doing tonight?"

Oh, mostly I'll be sitting here trying not to picture you having sex with someone else.

"Looking at furniture. I want to get some ideas about sofas."

"While you're at it, pick one for me."

"You're an adult. You should pick out your own furniture. I don't work for you."

Her tone came out a little sharper than she'd planned. Grant glanced at her.

"You okay?"

She held in a sigh. "Yes. I didn't mean to snap. It's just sometimes I get overwhelmed with having to replace literally everything we own."

"I know. It's tough." He circled the sofa and put his hand on her shoulder. "Don't work too hard."

"I won't. Have fun."

"Thanks."

With that, he waved and left. Tori stayed where she was until she heard his car backing down the driveway, then she jumped to her feet and screamed. Not for long, but loud enough that both dogs stared at her.

"Sorry," she muttered. "I'm having issues."

They watched her for a second, before putting their heads back down. Tori walked into the kitchen. She needed sugar and salt and possibly alcohol, although she was by herself, so maybe she should stick to the bad-for-her carbs. She'd bought Chinese food for dinner, but wasn't in the mood.

She grabbed a bag of microwave kettle corn and got that going, then checked out the ice cream selection in the freezer. There were a couple she liked. So she would start with the popcorn and then see if she wanted anything else.

She carried her bowl back to the family room and threw herself onto the sectional next to the dogs. She flipped channels on TV until she found the original *Jurassic Park* movie.

Death by dinosaur should be a nice distraction for the reality that sometime in the next hour or so, Grant was going to be touching some woman's breasts.

"I hate my life," she muttered between bites. "All right, not my *whole* life, but the stupid falling-in-love-with-Grant part. Why did I do that? Why couldn't friendship be enough? Friends are good. We're great at being friends."

She forced herself to pay attention to the movie and tried not to watch the clock. Around nine, just when the T-rex was gobbling up the mean finance guy, she heard a car in the driveway.

Her first thought was to run upstairs. She didn't want to see Grant looking all smug and manly. Her gaze returned to the clock as she realized that it was a little early for him to be getting home. Especially if they'd done the deed. Wouldn't he want to hang around and do it again, or at least snuggle?

Her indecision cost her precious seconds. By the time she knew she should bolt for the safety of her bedroom, he was walking into the house.

She put the half-empty popcorn bowl on the coffee table and reminded herself to be strong. If nothing else, making sure Grant never found out how she felt about him should be motivation enough to keep from reacting to whatever he said.

"Hey." He walked into the family room. "You're still up."

"It's barely nine."

"Is it?"

She studied him, looking for clues. He didn't look happy or even slightly smug. If anything, she would guess he was frustrated and possibly a little disappointed. Hope flared, but she ignored the sensation.

"What happened?" she asked, then wished she could call back the words. Maybe Grant had slept with that other woman and had simply left afterward, which meant she'd been upset not only because of the sex thing but also because she would learn something icky about him. Good men at least asked to stay and cuddle.

He sat on the sofa. "Nothing."

It took her a second to realize he was answering her question.

"So you didn't do the deed?"

"Not even close."

"A performance issue?" she asked.

He leaned back against the cushions and shook his head. "We met at the restaurant. She was giving me all the signals. At least I think she was. It's been a while. And when we were done eating, she invited me back to her place."

She did her best not to flinch. "Did you accidentally turn the wrong way?"

He met her gaze. "I didn't want to sleep with her. I don't know why. I miss sex. I like her. She's nice and pretty and I should have been all over her. But I told her I had an early morning."

Tori tried not to let her relief show. Once she was alone, she would do the dance of giddy happiness, but for now she needed to be his friend.

"Was it a chemistry thing?" she asked.

"I guess." He swore under his breath. "Is it possible I haven't had sex in so long, I've lost interest?"

"I doubt that. If you'd been attracted to her, you would have taken her up on her invitation. Although I have to say, you might want to get in touch with your inner dog."

He sat up and stared at her. "My what?"

"Your inner dog. You know how guys can act badly. Like a dog?" She patted Scout. "No offense."

"You mean I should have done it, anyway? Just taken advantage of what was offered?"

No and no. Except as his friend, she should probably not say that. "Maybe you need to push through the moment, so to speak."

Wait! Why was she telling him this? Shouldn't she be pointing out how it's so much better to wait for the right person?

"That's not me." He sagged back on the sofa. "I'm not looking to fall in love, but I do want some kind of connection. I was never the guy who wanted to get laid for the sake of it."

Could his answer have been better? she thought glumly. Heaven forbid Grant have flaws that would make it easier to fall out of love with him. Nooooo. He had to be perfect.

"Dating sucks," he said.

"Yes, it does."

He stood. "I didn't have much dinner. Are there any leftovers?"

She nodded. "I bought Chinese food for twenty. Most of it's still in the refrigerator."

"Great."

He circled around the sofa, pausing in front of her, then bent over and kissed her on the head, which was so annoying. What was she? His five-year-old niece?

He headed for the kitchen, then glanced at the TV. "Oh, great. *Jurassic Park*. The first one. Did the kid already throw up?"

"Yes."

"But that's my favorite part."

"Your favorite part of the movie is vomit? You're so weird."

He chuckled. "That's why we're friends."

It was, and wasn't that bad news for her?

The relief of not being pregnant didn't seem to help Daphne sleep any better or ease her stomach. She told herself she would give it another couple of weeks and if she was still not back to herself, she would see her doctor. In the meantime, she would power through.

Saturday morning she and Brody headed to the local soccer field to watch Elijah and Cadin play their first game of the fall season. Although Whitney had the kids this weekend, they'd promised to cheer on the boys.

The short car ride was silent. Daphne tried to think of something to say, but she was too tired to come up with sparkling conversation.

"Will you find us seats?" Brody asked as they got out of the SUV. "I want to say hi to the kids."

"Sure," she said, heading for the stands without looking back at him.

She greeted the parents she knew as she climbed up to about midway. She'd barely sat down when she saw Whitney headed in her direction, eight-month-old Maisey in her arms.

At the sight of the happy baby, she felt a fist close around her heart. Longing filled her and while she was happy she wasn't pregnant now, when everything was so awful with Brody, she couldn't help wishing for a child of her own.

"Hi," Whitney said, sitting next to her. "Thanks for coming. I know there are a thousand things you'd rather be doing on a sunny day, but the boys will be thrilled to see you."

"Of course."

Whitney grimaced. "Alexa is home with a stomach bug. Nothing serious, but I thought she should rest. Evan's with her. They're going to watch both *Frozen* movies and then both versions of *Mulan*."

Maisey waved her arms, obviously asking to go to Daphne. Whitney chuckled.

"Take her. I could use a break."

"I'd love to." She reached for the baby. "Come here, pretty girl. How are you? You're growing so fast. What a smart girl."

Maisey settled on her lap, babbling happily, feet kicking out. Her weight was warm and comforting and she looked adorable in a T-shirt and bright yellow overalls covered with applique raccoons.

"She's amazing," Daphne said. "How can you stand to let me hold her?"

"For you, this is a treat," Whitney said with a tired smile. "For me, it's 24/7. It's great to have a breather."

Daphne studied Brody's ex-wife. "You okay?"

"Sure. Just exhausted. The weeks with all four kids are challenging." She touched her daughter's arm. "I love her and I'm glad we had her, but I'll admit, after six years, I'd forgotten what it was like to have a baby in the house. She took forever to sleep through the night and still isn't a great sleeper, so I'm up a lot with her. Between that and work and rushing home so she's not in day care too much, it's a challenge. Evan's been working from home a couple of days a week to watch her, but when she starts walking that won't be an option."

"You don't want to hire help?" Daphne asked.

"We can't afford that. Evan does okay with his job, but we don't make the money you and Brody do."

"Sorry. I wasn't thinking." Daphne felt herself flush. She'd never really considered Whitney's financial situation, although she should have realized Whitney and Evan weren't making as much. Even with shared custody, Brody paid child support. Less, but a monthly check went out.

"It's okay. You're a high-powered lawyer. You went to college and law school. I was in community college when Brody and I met. I planned to finish but somehow never did. I have a job, not a career." Her tone turned wistful. "Sometimes I'm envious of what you do."

"Being a lawyer?"

"Going to a fancy office, having nice clothes and a new car."

"If it makes you feel better, I work at least a sixty-hour week. Sometimes eighty."

Whitney's eyes widened. "That much?"

"I cut back the weeks we have the kids, or I bring work home and do it after they're in bed but I still put in a ton of hours."

"And you have that part-time nanny."

Unexpected guilt made Daphne look away. "Yes, we do have that."

"Must be nice." Whitney smiled at her daughter. "If you guys have a baby, you'll get someone in full-time, right? Oh, how I envy that." She looked at Daphne. "But it's all about trade-offs. I wouldn't want to work as much as you do. I want to be home with my kids as much as I can."

She shrugged. "Once I had Cadin, I stayed home until Elijah started kindergarten. Then I got a job." She smiled. "It didn't go well. I sat in my car and cried the day I dropped off Cadin and Alexa at day care. It broke my heart."

Daphne had no idea what to say. "I'm sorry."

"Everyone deals with something." She stood and waved. "Over here."

Daphne followed her gaze and saw Brody had started up the bleachers. His gaze settled on Maisey. His mouth flattened into a straight line.

His obvious displeasure at the sight of her holding the little girl nearly made Daphne cry. Couldn't she hold Maisey without him assuming there was a hidden meaning?

"Hi," he said as he settled next to Daphne. "Where's Evan and Alexa?"

"Alexa has a little tummy trouble," Daphne told him. "Evan stayed home with her."

"Not you?" he asked his ex.

She grinned. "I took the night shift. He can handle a few hours of lying on the sofa, watching movies."

"He's a good dad," Daphne murmured, thinking Brody was, too. He would do anything for his children. Unfortunately, he was less interested in doing anything for her. He wouldn't let go of the whole Miguel non-issue and he obviously hadn't warmed to having a baby.

Once again, she sent up a prayer of gratitude that she wasn't pregnant. The last thing their relationship needed now was more stress.

eighteen

Heather alternated between anticipation and trepidation as she drove to the restaurant where she would meet Emer. They'd been texting every few days for the past three and a half weeks. Nothing significant—just "Hi, how's it going" texts. He'd worked sixteen-hour days in South America, so hadn't had a lot of free time, and she was still trying to convince herself that dating someone who wasn't Campbell was a good idea.

But wanting someone she couldn't have sucked and she knew that she had to move past him. Maybe Emer could help.

He'd chosen a nice lakefront restaurant in Kirkland. She left her car with the valet and walked inside to find he was already there. He smiled.

"You made it." He took her hands in his and lightly kissed her cheek.

"I did."

They were seated by the window. He set his menu down and gazed into her eyes.

"You look great."

"Thank you. So do you. So how was your trip?"

"Long hours, lots of surgeries." His smile returned. "I won't get into the details. Probably best not to start dinner with talk of organs and blood."

She laughed. "I agree. Are you still tired?"

"I'm catching up on my sleep. I had a couple of days off before I had to go back to work. I basically slept the whole time."

"That's a big commitment, giving up that much time. I'm impressed."

"You foster kittens."

"Hardly the same."

Their server told them about the specials. They each ordered a glass of wine. When they were alone again, Emer asked, "How are things with you?"

Heather thought briefly about Jillian's cancer. Not a good first date topic.

"Good. I recently found my birth father. His girls are eleven and nine and they're going to take my current kittens."

"You found your birth father?"

She nodded and explained how she'd connected with Fletcher. "It's been interesting getting to know everyone. His wife, Jillian's, my age, so that's strange, but I like them." She smiled. "The girls are thrilled to have another sister."

His gaze was steady. "How do you feel about all of it?"

"Confused sometimes, but happy. I still can't wrap my mind around the fact that I have half sisters. Apparently, there's a new kids' movie coming out about three sisters. They've both texted me that we *have* to go see it together."

"You were an only child until you found out about them?"

"Uh-huh. Just my mom and me. And cousins we're close to." She paused. "Her cousins, so my second cousins, I think. I can't quite figure that out."

"Not first cousins once removed?"

She laughed. "I never knew what that meant."

The server returned with their wine and took their orders. When she'd left, Heather asked, "Where did you go to medical school?"

"UCLA."

"I got my bachelor's at USC. But I grew up on Blackberry Island."

He grinned. "I grew up in Wenatchee and couldn't wait to move to a city. My undergrad is from the University of Washington, then I moved to LA."

"Did you like it?" she asked with a laugh. "The weather was amazing."

"It was. You have to love all that sunshine."

"I agree." She picked up her glass. "I can't figure out a subtle way to transition into this so I'll just go for it. Tell me about your divorce."

His relaxed posture never changed. "Not much to tell. We were married five years. Around year three, we started fighting. It got worse and worse until we realized we didn't like each other anymore. The divorce was a relief to both of us."

"Still, a breakup is never easy."

"It's not." He paused. "We had great chemistry, but I'm not sure we were ever friends. That's the big lesson I learned. Next time I want to be friends as well as lovers."

"Makes sense."

"In the spirit of just going for it, tell me about your breakup with Campbell."

Heather hadn't seen that coming. "Oh. Well, um, we were together for a while and then we split up." She set down her glass. "I'm the one who ended things. He wanted things to progress and I didn't."

"It's tough when you aren't in the same place. I get that."

She realized he thought she'd simply not cared about Campbell as much as he cared about her, which wasn't the real problem. She had cared. Still did. Her inability to trust, to allow someone in, had made her back off. But on a first date she should probably keep her deepest flaws to herself.

"You still see him," Emer added. "Is that tough?"

"No. He's part of the group."

"And the girlfriend?"

"Nora," she said, doing her best to smile. "She's sweet. It would be impossible not to like her so I surrendered to the inevitable."

His gaze was steady. "I don't think I could hang out with my ex and her new boyfriend."

"But there's a difference," she pointed out. "My problem was never that I didn't like Campbell. I still enjoy his company." Even if watching him fall in love with someone else was painful. "We're part of the same circle of friends. We deal."

"That's very healthy." He grinned. "I say that as a medical professional."

"Then I'll treasure the compliment all the more."

They talked through dinner. A couple of times she nearly asked about Jillian's condition, but decided to hold back. For one thing, she felt uncomfortable talking about her health issues without her permission. For another, she didn't want to hear anything bad. Her online research had made her both more and less anxious and she'd reached a very precarious acceptance. She didn't want to hear anything that would tip her toward the negative.

When they'd finished, they walked out together. As they waited for their cars, Emer pulled her to the side.

"I'd like to see you again," he said. "If you're interested."

He was nice, she thought. She'd enjoyed his company, but hadn't been blown away. Still, she wanted to heal from Campbell and find someone special, and dating was awkward. Given time, maybe she could fall for Emer.

"I'd like that, too," she told him.

"I'll text you."

"You could even call."

"Really?" He grinned. "You'd talk to me on the phone. Score!"

She laughed.

He leaned in and kissed her. The brush of his mouth against hers was nice. She hoped for tingles and a whisper of desire, but it didn't happen.

Next time, she promised herself. She would feel all that next time. Because she wasn't giving up on the possibility of being happy.

"You didn't have to come all this way," Heather said.

Fletcher had asked if he could stop by, reassuring her everything was fine. It was five on a weekday. He must have had a miserable drive through traffic.

"I wanted to see you," he told her.

They were in her office, at the table in the corner. She'd put out cans of soda for each of them.

When she sat, he said, "Jillian told me what happened." His worried gaze settled on her face. "You must have been upset."

"I had a few difficult moments before I took her to the doctor," she admitted. "Finding out about her breast cancer didn't help."

"She should have told me she was having pain. I would have been there for her."

Heather didn't want to get in the middle of their marriage, but also understood Jillian's point.

"She didn't want you to worry. I was happy to go with her and I'm glad she's okay."

"Are *you* okay?"

Heather sighed. "When she first asked me to take her to the doctor, I thought she might be manipulating me. Then, when I heard about the cancer, I was scared. I always thought stage IV cancer was a death sentence. But according to my research, that's not true. She could be fine."

Well, not fine, exactly, but she could live a long time.

Fletcher smiled sadly. "You can't take this in all at once. I was the one who found the lump. We were, um, while I was—"

Heather held in a shriek. "Sex, yes, let's move on."

He managed a chuckle. "I mentioned it to her and she said it was nothing. Not just because she was so young, but there was no family history. I insisted she schedule a mammogram. It was cancer."

His voice broke on the word. He cleared his throat before continuing. "I thought they'd take it out and we'd go on with our lives. At worst, they'd take a breast. I'd be okay with that and could help her through whatever she needed."

"But it wasn't fine," Heather whispered.

"No. The cancer had spread." He opened his soda and took a drink. "I can't explain the fear. It was everywhere, every second. I lay awake at night and listened to her breathing, wondering how many more nights we'd have together. I prayed that God would take me instead."

His pain was palpable.

She touched his hand. "It doesn't work like that."

"Or God wasn't listening." He gripped her fingers. "She's my world, Heather. I love her more than I've loved anyone. I would do anything for her."

"I know."

She might not believe in much, but she believed in their

love. They were two of the lucky ones—people who found their true partner. Like Sophie and Dugan, and Kristine and Jaxsen. A few weeks ago she would have added Daphne and Brody to that list, but now she was less sure. Love was complicated, at least it was for some people.

Not for Campbell, she thought sadly. For him it had been easy. She'd been the problem. But not anything to dwell on this second.

"She loves you, too," Heather told her father. "I can feel it when I'm with you two."

"I'm glad. It's just so hard. I worry about her and the girls."

"It's an issue for them?"

"Possibly. They'll need regular checkups when they get older."

That news hit Heather nearly as hard as Jillian's cancer.

"I want them to be okay."

Tears filled his eyes. "I do, too." He released her and brushed his palms against his eyes. "Sorry. I get emotional."

"Of course you do. This is serious stuff."

"It is." He looked at her. "I used to joke that one of the advantages of falling for a younger woman was that I would go first. We'd laugh about that, then I'd tell her she needed to find someone when I was gone. That she was too good at loving someone to be on her own. Then she'd get mad and say she wouldn't want another man after me."

The tears returned. "Now it's not a sure thing. It could be her going first. I couldn't handle that."

Heather circled the table and sat next to him. She wrapped her arms around him and hung on tight.

"That's not happening today," she murmured.

"I know, but sometimes all of this seems like it's going to break me."

"Yet, you wouldn't change anything." Heather knew that

for sure. Whatever the outcome, her dad would never regret loving Jillian.

"You're right," he admitted. "I want every second I can get, no matter what happens in the end. She's worth it all. The way she handles everything—her grace, her caring spirit. She's so brave and determined. I know she gets down and scared and she mostly keeps that to herself. She's the best woman I know."

Heather believed him. Jillian had shown remarkable courage at the doctor's. For all she knew, she could have been told that her cancer was back and this time it was going to kill her. Yes, she'd been worried, but she hadn't been… Amber.

Unlike her mother, who only ever had imaginary slights, Jillian was dealing with a real, terrifying medical condition with grace and compassion. They could all learn from her.

Daphne's heart pounded as she straightened and flushed the toilet. So much for her lunch, she thought, rinsing her mouth at the sink. She wasn't sure she'd thrown up because of a change in hormones. Shock was the more likely culprit.

Twelve days after the first pregnancy test, she still hadn't gotten her period, so she'd locked herself in the bathroom at work to take a second one.

Which had turned positive. And then she'd thrown up.

Now she leaned against the wall, her eyes closed. She had no idea what to think, what to do, who to talk to. She couldn't tell Brody because he wouldn't believe the baby was his.

Tears burned and her heart ached. How could this be happening? Why now?

She wrapped the offending stick in paper towels before burying it in the trash. After washing her hands, she returned to her office. Thankfully, she had no appointments that afternoon. She sent a quick text to Tori and Heather.

9-1-1. I have to talk asap. I can be home in thirty minutes.

She only had to wait a few seconds until dots appeared. Tori's answer came first.

On my way. Should I stop for anything? Ice cream? Donuts? Vodka?

I just need my friends. But if you want to stop for lunch for yourself, that's fine.

Heather answered. I'll get sandwiches from Jersey Mike's on the way. What does everyone want?

The ham and provolone for me, Tori texted.

Daphne didn't think she could eat anything, but considering she was pregnant and had just barfed up her lunch, she should probably try. She wasn't sure of her dietary restrictions, but she was pretty sure she was supposed to avoid processed meats.

I'll take a veggie sandwich. No meat.

Why? Heather asked, then added. Never mind. I'll bring it. See you in forty-five.

Thanks, you two. I mean that.

Daphne told Irena she was leaving for the afternoon. She got home before Tori arrived. Albert and Vanessa rushed to greet her. She petted both of them.

"I know. I'm never home anymore. I'm sorry. But I will pay attention to you all afternoon. I promise."

She quickly changed clothes and had just returned to the main floor when Tori rang the bell. They hugged. Tori kicked off her shoes and held out a small white bag.

"I brought ice cream. In case the sandwiches aren't enough." Her voice was concerned, her gaze probing. "I'll wait until

Heather gets here to ask what's wrong. But you're so pale and thin, you're scaring me."

"I'm not sick," Daphne promised. "Or dying."

They set the kitchen table. Daphne put out soda and sparkling water. Albert and Vanessa meowed for attention until Tori crossed to the family room sofa and sat down so they could rub on her. Heather arrived a few minutes later.

She slapped the bag of sandwiches and chips on the table and glared at Daphne. "I'm your friend, so whatever it is, I'll be there, but please, I beg you, don't tell me you have cancer."

"I'm not sick," Daphne said. "I swear. I'm healthy."

Tori joined them. "Then what's with the high alert?"

Daphne blinked back tears. "I'm pregnant."

Tori and Heather exchanged a look.

"But isn't that good news?" Tori asked, grinning broadly. "You wanted kids and now you're pregnant." She hugged Daphne. "Aren't you excited?"

Heather watched the two of them. "It's not the baby," she said slowly. "It's Brody."

Tori stepped back, her smile fading. "Oh, right. Because he knows about you sleeping with Miguel."

Daphne groaned. "For the fortieth time, I never had sex with Miguel."

"She's right. It was an emotional affair." Heather pulled out a chair.

"You two are nightmares," Daphne muttered, taking her seat. "And yes, Miguel is a huge issue." She put her elbows on the table and rested her forehead in her hands. "Brody won't believe the baby is his. What should be a beautiful time bonding over our child will be ruined by him questioning me. By the time the baby's born and we can do a DNA test, the damage will have been done." She raised her head, tears in her eyes. "Me being pregnant is going to destroy our marriage."

"Maybe he'll be fine with it," Tori said quickly.

"He won't believe me." Daphne's voice was small.

"What do you want to do?" Heather asked. "Have an abortion?"

"What? No! I want the baby. Just not with Brody and me barely speaking. I can't get through to him. And now I'm pregnant and I can't see a way out." She felt hopeless. "I have to keep the pregnancy from him for as long as I can."

"At some point he's going to notice the belly." Heather unwrapped her sandwich.

"You should see your doctor," Tori advised. "Confirm the pregnancy. Find out what you need to know. Especially because you'll be having a geriatric pregnancy."

Daphne stared at her. "Excuse me?"

"You're thirty-five. You'll be thirty-six when the baby's born. In reproduction terms, you're at the older end of the spectrum." She paused. "I didn't mean anything by that."

Heather tried not to smile. "I'm sure she needs a minute to revel in the term *geriatric* pregnancy."

Because it wasn't enough that Brody wouldn't believe he was the father, she thought grimly. Now she had to worry about being too old?

"On the bright side," Tori said, her tone hopeful. "You're going to be a mom."

Daphne thought about the tiny life growing inside her. She was pregnant. In eight months or so, she would have a baby. She had to stay strong and remember what was important.

"I'm going to be a mom," she repeated, the words finally sinking in.

They both smiled at her. She grabbed their hands. No matter what, her friends would be there for her, and she would be there for her baby.

nineteen

"We love them so much," Ella said, tears in her eyes. An equally emotional Layla nodded.

Heather felt unexpected tightness in her throat. Each girl sat on the floor, holding a kitten. She'd delivered them a couple of hours ago, along with cat food, toys, two litter boxes and the litter the kittens were used to and a couple of beds. She added water and food dishes, a certificate that gave them a complimentary visit at their local vet. She'd already paid for the shots the kittens would need over the next few months. Once the kittens were fully vaccinated, their medical bills should be minimal, so she was happy to take care of the first year.

"They've found a good home," she said gently.

"I love Bella best," Layla said, kissing the kitten she held. "But I love Stella, too."

"I love them the same," Jillian told them, smiling at Heather. "And you did a good thing."

Heather wanted to say that the kittens were fosters who were going to be adopted by someone and why not her dad's family. But she knew Jillian was thanking her for more than the kittens.

"I want lots of pictures," Heather said, coming to her feet. She was meeting Tori later that evening to listen to a local band they liked.

The girls put down the kittens and rushed toward her. She wrapped her arms around them as they clung to her.

"We love them," Ella whispered. "And we love you."

"We do."

The unexpected admission startled her. She had no idea what to say or do, although running seemed the smartest option. But thin little arms made it impossible to move, so she stayed where she was and let the words sink in.

When they finally released her, Jillian gave her a quick hug.

"Thank you for everything," she said quietly. "Not just the kittens."

Heather nodded. "I'm always available. You know how to get me." She paused, thinking of her father, who was still at work. "Tell Dad I said hi."

"I will."

Heather drove home, telling herself that love was easy for other people and she should just go with what her sisters had said. They were sharing information, not asking for anything. They weren't a threat. She should be grateful they were so welcoming.

She'd wanted to meet her father. He could have refused to have anything to do with her. Instead, she'd found a warm welcome and people who were rapidly becoming important to her. That was a good thing. She wasn't going to let her sisters saying the L word freak her out.

When she got home, she fed a disgruntled LC, who glared at her as if asking what had happened to his kitten family.

"I'm sorry," she told him. "You know this is the pattern. At eight weeks they find their forever families."

He walked over to his food and settled down to eat, careful to keep his back to her.

"I'm going to take a break from fostering," she added. "Just a few weeks."

She wasn't sure, but she thought maybe his shoulders hunched at the announcement. Poor LC.

"This would go better if you liked me."

That comment earned her a disdainful glance.

She was still smiling as she went to get ready for her evening with Tori.

At eight, she parked at the upscale bar. The lot was filling fast—big crowd tonight. She was looking forward to hanging out with Tori. In a few days she would go on another date with Emer. While he wasn't the man of her dreams, he was nice and at least seeing him proved she was moving on. All in all, she was kind of in a good place.

Inside, she looked for an empty table. Tori had texted to say she would be a few minutes late, so Heather wanted to get them good seats. The open tables by the wall would put them too close to the speakers. Maybe something in the middle of the room where—

She froze in place as she saw a familiar couple at a table for four. As she watched, Campbell smiled at Nora, then cupped her face and kissed her. Without wanting to, Heather remembered the feel of his lips on hers. Campbell was a man who enjoyed kissing and was better at it than anyone else she'd ever dated.

She knew how his warm fingers would feel against her cheek and the way his tongue would tease hers. Longing joined a jolt of pain as she watched them, unable to turn away. Longing for so much more than a simple kiss.

She told herself to get out before they saw her. At that moment, Nora looked up. Her mouth curved up into a happy, welcoming smile as she jumped to her feet.

"Heather!" She waved both arms. "Hi!"

Trapped, Heather could only watch her approach.

Nora hugged her. "I didn't know you'd be here."

"I could say the same."

"Campbell loves this band." Nora looked past her. "Are you with Emer?"

"No, I'm meeting Tori. She should be here any second."

Nora linked arms with her. "Sit with us. We got here early, so we have the best seats."

Sit with them? Spend the evening that close to Campbell, knowing he was in love with someone else? Her stomach lurched. She couldn't do it.

Heather disentangled herself and faked a smile. "I'll go wait for Tori by the door. When she gets here, we'll be right over."

Nora's beamy smile returned. "I'm so glad you're here."

"Me, too."

Heather was careful not to look in Campbell's direction as she waited by the entrance until Tori walked inside. She grabbed her friend's arm.

"We can't stay," she said quickly. "Please. Campbell's here with Nora and they want us to sit with them and I can't do it."

Tori studied her. "Are you all right?"

"No. Help. We need to think up a reason to leave."

"I got this. Give me a second."

Tori turned away. Her shoulders rose and fell several times.

When she faced Heather again, tears filled her eyes. As Heather watched, two rolled down her cheeks.

"How did you do that?"

Tori sniffed. "I thought about how I didn't have any family and what if you didn't want to be my friend anymore. Where are they?"

Heather pointed.

Tori walked to the table and offered a shaky smile. "Hey, guys. I'm sorry, but I can't do this tonight." Her voice cracked. "I'm fine. It's just a guy and I need to—"

Heather quickly put her arm around her. "It's okay. I'll get you home and we can talk."

Campbell stood, his expression fierce. "Did someone hurt you?"

Tori shook her head. "It was just me being stupid. You know how I always pick the wrong guy."

Heather gave Nora a sad smile. "Rain check."

"Of course. We'll miss you."

Heather and Tori walked outside. Tori took a couple of deep breaths, then smiled. "Your place?"

"Sure. LC is sulking without the kittens. He could use some Tori time."

"I'll follow you home."

When they settled on the sofa with cocktails and LC cuddled with Tori, Heather drew in a breath. She should just say it, she told herself. Speaking the words would be painful, but a growth experience.

"I'm in love with Campbell."

Tori continued to pet the cat. "I'm waiting."

"No, that's it."

Tori looked at her. "That's what freaked you out? But you've been in love with him forever." Her voice gentled. "We've talked about this."

"Yes, but I thought I didn't do romantic love. But now I know that I do and he's gone."

Tori frowned. "Are you seriously telling me you just now realized how you feel?"

Heather nodded, feeling miserable. "I saw him kiss her and it was like he stabbed me in the heart." She clutched her drink as she relived the moment. "I never told him how I felt."

"How could you if you didn't know yourself? You really are messed up, aren't you?"

"Apparently. I was such a fool."

Tori's expression turned sympathetic. "And now the whole Nora thing makes it worse. I'm sorry."

"Me, too." Heather thought about the ups and downs of her relationship with Campbell. "I kept getting so scared he would turn into my mother."

"Amber has a personality disorder. She's not normal."

"Apparently, neither am I."

"You're very close and hey, you've admitted you were in love with Campbell. That's a good thing. Now you know you're capable of the feeling, you can fall in love with someone else and be happy."

If only it were that simple. "Don't I have to fall out of love with Campbell first?"

"Oh. Right. Yes, there's that. What about Emer? He could help."

"Maybe. I'm not feeling much chemistry."

"Maybe you're numb from losing Campbell." Tori pressed her lips together. "Sorry. Not helpful."

"I've never been in love before. How do you get over it? Should I start journaling or get one of those adult coloring books? Or should I keep seeing Emer and hope he'll be a distraction?"

"You're not the coloring book type. Journaling isn't a bad idea, but I'm not sure you have the patience."

Heather didn't want to have to process her emotions, but this could be one of those times when what she wanted didn't matter.

"I guess I just go through it and see where I end up."

"I'm here for you."

Heather smiled. "I know." She thought about what her sisters had said to her. She cleared her throat, then said, "I love you. You're a great friend and I'm lucky to have you in my life."

Tori's eyes filled with tears. "I love you, too, and now you're going to make me cry for real." She reached out her free hand and squeezed Heather's fingers. "We'll get through this together. And when you're over Campbell, you'll find someone amazing."

"I hope so."

In the meantime, she would let herself feel the pain—not only of losing the man she loved, but of knowing she had no one to blame but herself.

"I need coffee," Tori said as Grant held open the door to Life's a Yolk.

"I told you to have some before we left," he said easily. "You get crabby without caffeine."

"*You get crabby without caffeine,*" she mimicked. "You are the most annoying man on the planet."

"We both know that's not true." He pointed. "There."

Tori saw Daphne was still pale. Beside her, Brody looked anything but happy.

Ugh, so they hadn't worked out their issues, she thought sadly. At some point Daphne had to tell him she was pregnant and if he didn't believe her… Tori couldn't imagine how horrible Daphne must be feeling.

She followed Grant to the table. He held out a chair for her. Nora and Campbell turned toward her.

"Are you all right?"

"You okay?"

They spoke at the same time, their voices filled with concern. Tori stared at them blankly, wondering what on earth—

Crap! Last night at the bar she'd pretended great upset because of a guy.

"I'm fine," she said cheerfully. She waved at Daphne and Brody.

Grant sat next to her. "Why wouldn't you be okay?"

Campbell stared at him. "You didn't know?"

"Know what?"

Tori held in a groan. "I'm fine. Let's talk about something else."

Campbell ignored her. "Some guy broke her heart."

Grant turned to her. "How did I not know this? When do you see him? You're always home."

"I'm not always home. I go out."

"Not on dates."

Now Campbell and Nora looked confused.

"You were crying," she said.

"You were crying?" Grant echoed. "When?"

"Last night." Nora leaned toward him. "We went to hear that band Campbell likes. Heather and Tori were there and I asked them to sit with us. Tori couldn't stay because she was crying."

Tori felt everyone staring at her. She had no idea what to say and vowed next time she faked romantic trouble, she would think it through more carefully.

"I, ah, heard from somebody I used to date," she said, struggling to come up with something believable. "Talking to him made me realize how many mistakes I've made with guys and it was overwhelming."

Grant looked more confused than convinced.

"There are a lot of toads in my past."

"Enough to make you cry?"

"Apparently." She pressed her lips together. "I really need all of you to stop staring at me. Let's talk about something else."

Fortunately, their server arrived with coffee. Daphne didn't refuse hers, but Tori saw her carefully push the mug to the side. By the time they'd all ordered, conversation had shifted.

Brody turned to Grant. "How was your date? Was sex everything you remembered?"

Grant looked past his brother. "Nothing happened."

"Performance issues?" Campbell asked with a grin.

"That's what I said!" He and Tori shared a high five.

"I'm going to ignore that," Grant muttered. "It didn't feel right. We didn't have a good connection."

"It's been over a year." Brody looked amused. "How much of a connection do you need?"

"I don't want it to be just bodies."

"That's so sweet." Nora pressed her hands together. "I love that."

"You need help." Brody shook his head. "Anyone know someone we can set him up with?"

"I don't need help."

"All evidence to the contrary."

Tori held in a smile. "Poor Grant. Can't find the right woman."

"He should date you." Nora smiled. "You're such a cute couple."

The words exploded in her brain, causing Tori to shrink back in her chair. Had Nora said that to be funny, or did she suspect that Tori was in love with him? And if she knew or thought she knew, would she say something else, humiliating Tori in front of everyone she adored?

Campbell laughed. "You look horrified," he teased. "I guess we have our answer."

Grant looked equally uncomfortable. "It's not like that."

"He's right," she said quickly. "We're the non-couple friends. I like where we are." She glanced at him. "Why mess up a good thing? Right?"

"Exactly. Sex would change everything. I'm not risking our friendship for that."

Nora didn't look convinced. "I think you belong together."

"Not happening," Tori said, picking up her mug. "Not now, not ever."

"So that's a no?" Brody asked with a grin.

"It's a no," Grant said. "The Rams are playing later. Who's watching the game?"

Talk turned to football. Nora asked Daphne about work and the whole Tori-Grant dating thing was forgotten. At least by everyone who wasn't her.

She smiled and nodded, telling herself she was fine. That her secret was still her secret and she'd been spared the mortification of everyone's pity. That would be the worst, she thought. All her friends feeling sorry for her. Grant would feel awkward and then everything would change. Better to stay exactly where they were.

Only she couldn't help thinking that he'd been very quick to dismiss the idea of them as a couple. Probably because he'd meant what he said. He couldn't see them as anything other than friends, which meant falling in love with him was one of her dumbest ideas ever.

Heather's anger grew with every mile. By the time she reached her mother's condo, she was furious. She ignored the elevator and took the stairs two at a time, then banged on the front door.

Amber opened it. "What on earth… Heather? What are you doing here?"

Heather pushed past her, entering the spacious, airy condo with a view of the Sound. The kitchen, messy with dishes in the sink and food on the counters, had been remodeled two years ago. In fact, the entire place had been redone. Amber had insisted and Heather had paid for it.

Because her mother whined and complained and made herself the victim. Heather supposed she was equally at fault, because she had trouble telling her no. Until today, the only time she'd really stood up to her mother had been the day she'd left the island to go to college and she'd only managed that with support from Sophie and Elliot.

Heather walked into the living room, then turned to face her mother. "What do you want from Fletcher?"

Amber frowned. "What are you talking about?"

"You texted me, asking for contact information. Why, after thirty-five years, do you need to speak to him?"

Her mother's expression turned speculative. "Why should you be the only one in touch with him? He could have been my one true love. I thought we should talk."

"He doesn't have any money, Mom. He's a high school teacher with a family. Jillian works part-time. He has nothing for you to take."

Amber stepped back, her eyes wide. "How can you say that to me? What a horrible thing to think. Take it back!"

"It's what you do, what you've always done. You assess every situation with an eye to how it can benefit you. The only reason you didn't come after me when I left for college was because Sophie bought you this condo. Then Kristine bought you a car. You lived rent-free in your mother's house for years, and even paying insurance and property tax was too much. Somehow, you convinced me that I had to support you. Who does that? I'm your child."

Amber's small eyes narrowed. "What's wrong with you? You're acting crazy. You burst into my home and start yelling at me. Well, I won't stand for it. Either change your attitude, young lady, or get out."

"I'll leave, but first we're going to deal with Fletcher and his family."

Amber's breath caught. "You're defending him. You care about him and his brat children."

"He's my father and his children are my half siblings. They're as much a part of my family as you are."

Tears filled Amber's eyes. "How can you say that? I'm the one who raised you. I'm the one who took care of you from the day you were born. Where was he? Living his fancy life, going to college and not having to worry about anything. He didn't care that I never got to go to college or live my life. I was stuck being a single parent. That's on him and he should pay."

Heather had heard all this before. Oh, not the part about Fletcher, but the rest of it. How her mother's life had been ruined because of getting pregnant. She'd grown up knowing she was the cause of all her mother's many disappointments.

Maybe that was why she'd found it so hard to tell Amber no. Guilt was powerful and she'd learned early she had to do everything possible to make her mother happy.

Until today, she'd never defended herself. It took too much energy and wasn't a permanent solution. In the end, Amber out-stubborned everyone around her. Heather wouldn't go so far as to say Amber found joy in making other people miserable, but she seemed to feel a level of satisfaction.

But this was different, she thought grimly. This time she was fighting for her father, her sisters and Jillian. They had no idea what Amber was capable of. Fletcher would be confused by her avarice, Jillian would think she could be healed by love, and the girls, well, they would be permanently scarred.

"I've always wondered which was real, Mom," she said quietly.

Amber eyed her warily. "What are you talking about?"

"Sometimes you go on about how it was you and me against the world. How you were always there for me and it was a magical time. Then you slip right into how you were stuck being a single mother and your life was ruined. Pick a side."

"You have too much attitude." Amber pointed to the door. "Get out."

"I will as soon as we get this straight. Leave them alone."

"You're taking their side? You're defending that man?"

Tears returned, but this time Heather thought they might be genuine. Her mother pressed a hand to her chest.

"You care about him. Are you spending time with him? With them?"

Heather braced for the storm. "I am. Like I said, they're my family as much as you are."

"They're no one. Where were they when you were growing up? At every birthday? When you graduated high school. I'm your mother." She covered her face with her hands. "I gave you everything and now you're rejecting me for some family you barely met."

"I'm not rejecting you."

She dropped her hands. "You're yelling at me for something I haven't done. You think I'm a horrible person."

"You want Fletcher to pay child support."

"He should. I had nothing."

"You had *everything*. Everyone has always taken care of you. Your mother, your cousins. You're a capable, healthy person, but you've never made the effort. Grandma offered to pay for community college or trade school, but you wouldn't go. Sophie gave you a dozen chances, then had to fire you because you were stealing. You lived on your mother until she had to sell the house to get you to stand on your own. You would have stolen my future, if you could have."

She waved her arm, indicating the condo. "Sophie bought you this. I remodeled it." She stared at her mother. "I have to hand it to you. You're amazing. You manipulate all of us, taking as much as you can and never giving back."

"My life was ruined and I was on my own," Amber yelled. "He just left me, not caring if I was pregnant."

Heather folded her arms across her chest. "I've always wondered, Mom. How is it you slept with a guy without knowing his last name? Seriously, did you just pick him up in a bar to get laid?"

The slap landed hard on her cheek. Heather staggered back a step.

Amber's voice was low and thick with fury as she said, "Whatever else you think of me, I am your mother and you will treat me with respect."

"Gladly," she said. "The day you act like my mother and not some victim out for what she can get." She picked up her purse. "Here's the thing. Fletcher doesn't owe you anything. More to the point, he doesn't have anything. But if you don't believe me, if you go after him, you will have to come through me first."

Her mother pressed a hand to her throat. "What are you saying?"

"I've taken care of you since I was a kid. Every time I saved enough money to leave the island so I could get a fresh start, you took it. When I was at college, you asked me for money. While I was working two jobs and keeping my grades up for my scholarships."

Her mother looked away. "I had back issues."

"Whatever. Since I got out of college, I've been sending you money every quarter. I paid for the condo remodel. You've been hinting you want a new car." Heather shook her head. "You're a leech and I never cared for myself, but I care now, because of them."

"You love them." Amber went pale. "You love them more than you love me."

Not hard to do. But she didn't say that. There was no point. "Stay away from my father and his family or you and I are done. Look at me, Mom. Look at me and know that I mean every word. The checks will stop and I will turn my back on you for the rest of my life. I've given you everything you've asked for without wanting anything in return."

Peace, she thought grimly. A break from the demands and whining. But those had been silent requests.

"Now there's a price. Leave them alone."

"You don't know him," Amber said bitterly. "You're excited because they're new, but you don't know what he's really like."

"Neither do you." She started toward her door.

Her mother followed. "You're dead to me. I never want to hear from you again. You hear me? You ruined my life. You're ungrateful and horrible and I'm sorry you were born. You want to cut yourself off from me? Fine. It's done."

Heather stepped out onto the landing. Amber slammed the door behind her. Seconds later she heard her mother burst into tears.

The guilt was automatic and probably justified. She'd been harsh—honest, but a case could be made there'd been a more delicate way to get her point across.

Still, as she took the elevator to the main level and walked out to her car, she felt an odd sense of relief. Oh, there would be repercussions. Amber wouldn't end things, as she promised.

That would require her to be self-sufficient. She could probably get Kristine or Sophie to pay for a few things, but these days Heather was the reason she never had to get a job to support herself.

So she would be back and they would start over—dealing with their twisted, uncomfortable relationship. But even knowing that, Heather felt a little lighter. Whatever curiosity her mother might have about Fletcher, whatever desire to poke and foul, would be tempered by a harsh financial reality. Funny how she'd never been able to stand up for herself, but had found it almost easy to stand up for her family.

twenty

"You know the worst part about my shitty life?" Daphne asked from her comfy chaise. "It's boring."

Tori, next to her but actually risking sun, raised herself on one elbow. "You think your life is boring?"

Heather, on her other side, didn't bother opening her eyes. "Sure. How do you stand the sameness? Your husband thinks you're having an affair, you're pregnant and can't tell him because he'll think it's the other guy's, you're being courted by some new company and don't want the job so are dodging phone calls from one of your mom's closest friends, which is not going to end well. You're right. It's a yawn."

Despite her sense of being trapped in a situation she couldn't fix, she smiled. "When you put it that way..."

They were in Tori's backyard, taking advantage of a warm,

sunny Saturday. Brody had the kids, and she had a pile of work waiting, but an afternoon with her friends had been more inviting.

"Boring is the wrong word," she admitted. "Tedious and repetitive are more appropriate."

"Examples, please," Heather said as she reached for her lemonade. A drink Tori had offered so Daphne wouldn't have to watch them indulge in something she couldn't have.

"I got home late the other night. I'd been busy and not paying attention to the time. I missed putting the kids to bed." She sighed. "Which I love. Sometimes they don't cooperate, but there's a nice ritual to it. We talk, we read books."

"You felt bad," Tori said.

"Brody was on me the second I walked in, accusing me of being with Miguel and implying I don't care about the children." She closed her eyes as she remembered his anger. "In return, he didn't bother to clean, so dishes were piled everywhere. We fought, he walked out and I spent the next hour scrubbing dishes."

Tori squeezed her hand. "I'm sorry."

"Me, too." She unclenched the fist around her heart long enough to admit, "I don't think we're going to make it."

Tori was instantly in a sitting position. "Don't say that."

Heather joined Tori. "Daphne, are you serious?"

"He doesn't trust me and I'm out of ways to say I didn't sleep with Miguel. He's going to be awful about the baby." Sadness chilled her. "How are we supposed to have a child together when he won't believe it's his?"

Her friends looked at her, then back at each other. "I'm sorry," Heather said. "I don't know what to say."

"Me, either." Daphne's mouth twisted. "I love him, I love the kids. But we're caught in a nightmare." She looked at them. "I never wanted to be a single parent. I want Brody and I don't know how to keep him."

"You know we'll be here for you," Tori said.

"I do and I appreciate it." But it wasn't the same.

She pointed at Heather. "Back to your chaise. I'm fine. Let's talk about something else. How's Emer?"

Heather lay back down and sighed. "Fine. We went out again."

"And?"

"I don't know. It was okay. There's no chemistry."

"Don't do it," Tori said, sitting back up again. "You should pay attention to your feelings."

Daphne was less sure. "You can't trust your feelings while you're still in love with Campbell."

Heather glared at her. "Do you have to say that so bluntly? Can't we talk about me having feelings? Do you have to say *love* just like that?"

Tori nodded. "We can say *feelings* if it makes you more comfortable." Scout jumped up on the chaise and Tori petted her. "Maybe Daphne's right. Maybe you won't see possibilities in another guy until you get over Campbell a little more."

"I've thought about that, and I don't like it."

Despite everything happening in her own life, Daphne smiled. "That's my girl. Live in denial. It's nice here."

"Have you heard from your mom?" Tori asked. "I'm still so proud you told her off."

"Thanks and no. Not a word. I warned Sophie and Kristine that she might be more difficult than usual. Sophie hasn't heard from her, but Kristine checked on her and told me Amber didn't say a word about what happened."

"You okay?" Daphne asked. "Aside from the inevitable guilt?"

"I'm mostly sad. For her and the small life she chose. For me for not standing up to her before. I worry about my dad and his family, but I'll do my best to protect them. I want to ask why she has to be that way, but I know there's no answer."

"Oh, there's an answer." Tori grinned. "It'll cost you about twenty grand with a therapist, but there's an answer."

Heather laughed. "I guess my interest does have a limit. What about you? Anything new?"

Daphne glanced at Tori in time to see her gaze shift and her body tense. Daphne went on alert.

"What?" she demanded. "There's something. Tell us? You walked in on Grant doing it with someone?"

"He wouldn't bring someone into our home."

"Interesting." Heather sat up. "I'm going to stare at you in an uncomfortable way until you tell us."

Tori opened then closed her mouth. "I can't."

Daphne didn't say anything, nor did Heather. Seconds later Tori blurted, "I have feelings for Grant."

"Of course you have feelings," Heather said. "You're friends."

But Daphne knew that wasn't what Tori meant. Being friends wouldn't cause her to squirm or blush.

"Oh, my God, you're in love with him!"

"What?" Heather sprang to her feet. "You love Grant? I can't process that. I'm not saying it's bad, but what happened to being the non-couple friends? My world view is shattered."

She sat back down. "You're in love with Grant."

Tori groaned. "Please stop saying that. What if he comes home and hears you?"

"So you haven't told him," Daphne said.

"What? Are you insane? No, I haven't told him. I shouldn't have told you." She pointed. "Heather is freaking out. Imagine what Grant would do."

"Maybe he'd drag you to his bedroom and make love to you."

Tori's expression turned wistful for a second, before returning to panicked. "I wouldn't want that because I don't want our relationship to change."

"Lying to our faces," Daphne murmured. "I'm so disappointed."

"Fine. I *want* it to change, but I know better. It wouldn't work out."

Heather exhaled. "I can talk now and I have to say I can see it. You two are great together. Why not get sexual and make it permanent?"

Daphne smiled. "Tori has a list of reasons why not. Don't you?"

Tori hung her head. "Yes. First of all, if Grant was secretly lusting after me, he would have done something already."

"You're lusting after him and you haven't done anything," Heather pointed out.

"It's different for guys. I'm right there. All. The. Time. He hasn't made a move. He talks to me about the women he wants to sleep with. Not exactly signs that he's secretly in love with me."

Daphne had to admit she had a point.

"Second, the aforementioned perfect relationship. I like having Grant as my non-couple friend. If I said something, the dynamics would shift and not for the better." She swallowed. "You guys are my family and I need you. But I'm only a part of the larger group because of Grant. I love having him and Brody and Campbell as my family, too. I won't risk losing that."

Heather sighed. "You're not wrong to worry about that. I dumped Campbell because I'm an idiot and I lost the group."

"You didn't," Daphne said automatically, then paused. "I'll admit the Nora issue is a complication."

"See." Tori shook her head. "I love him and it's killing me to listen to him talk about dating other women. But I can't tell him how I feel. I'm totally alone in the world. You guys are all I have and I just can't risk losing my family."

"Are you all right?" Jillian asked as she led the way into the living room.

"Never better," Heather lied.

After mulling over her mother's threats, she'd decided to warn Jillian about the possibility of contact from Amber. Her dad and Jillian were simply too nice to deal with her mother on their own.

"Your timing is perfect," Jillian said with a smile. "I have something to discuss, as well. But you go first."

Heather sat on the edge of the sofa cushion, not sure how to explain the reality that was her mother.

"You know Fletcher and my mom had a one-night stand and I'm the result," she began.

Jillian laughed. "Of course. While I'm sorry she had to raise you on her own, I'm so happy they got together and now we have you in our lives."

Niceness, Heather thought grimly. So much niceness.

"She's not like other people. My mother is difficult. She twists everything around to be about herself. She's always the victim."

"You've talked about this before. What's wrong, sweetie? How can I help?"

"She's threatening to get in touch with you." She held up a hand. "I know that doesn't sound bad, but it is. She's not someone you want in your lives and you sure don't want her around your girls." She hated to think of her mother draining the joy from Ella and Layla, not to mention the whole child support threat.

"I'm serious about this," she continued. "If she gets in touch with you, call me right away. I don't care what time it is or what I'm doing. Call me."

Jillian's expression softened. "You're really worried."

"Yes."

"And you're taking care of us. Oh, Heather, you are such a joy for us."

Heather had never been called a joy before and wasn't sure

what to do with the concept. She didn't think of herself as a particularly happy person, let alone a joyous one, but sure.

"Do you promise?"

"I do. I will call and text if we hear from Amber. But honestly, I don't think you have anything to worry about."

"I wish that were true." She shifted back on the sofa. "How are you feeling? You look good."

"I feel good. We're all doing great." She laughed. "We love the kittens. The girls get up twenty minutes early every school day to feed them and play with them, and the second they're home, they're all about them."

Her expression turned sheepish. "I have a couple of play sessions with them every day myself. They're just so sweet and nice to have around." She pointed toward the hallway. "Right now they're crashed on Layla's bed. They're so cute."

"I'm glad everyone is happy with them."

"You did a good job fostering them. You're very nurturing."

Heather held up both hands. "Don't make me better than I am. I'm great with cats, I do well with my friends and my employees, but that's kind of where my skill set ends."

She was a disaster when it came to romantic love, but why go there?

"The girls adore you," Jillian said. "You're the sister they always wanted."

Heather grinned. "Somehow I doubt that. Very few little girls dream of finding a sister who is twenty-plus years older."

"Okay, that's true, but you're important to them."

Words that just a few months ago would have caused her to freak out, Heather thought. Now she was comfortable knowing her sisters liked her. She liked them, too.

"I feel the same way. They're great kids. You and my dad should be proud."

"We are." Jillian paused. "Okay, I'm just going to say it. Your dad and I have never been happy with the arrangements we've made should something happen to us. We have friends who have three kids of their own and while they've said they would take the girls, it's not ideal. Fletcher and I wondered if you'd consider being their guardian."

At first, Heather didn't understand. Guardian? Then the rest of what she'd said sank in. The *if something happened* translated to *if they were dead*. Because Fletcher was in his fifties and Jillian had stage IV cancer so what was a *probably not* for other parents was much more a possibility for them.

Jillian was asking if she would consider taking the girls and raising them. Being responsible and making decisions and helping them recover from the most terrible loss ever. Jillian was asking her to love them and nurture them.

She couldn't do that. She didn't know how—she never had. When feelings got too intense, she ran. She didn't cry, she'd only ever said "I love you" recently and even then hadn't been that comfortable. Children needed things she didn't have.

"No," Heather said sharply. "I couldn't." She stared at her stepmother. "You don't understand. I'm not like you. I wasn't raised like you. If you'd met my mom and saw what she was like…"

Because that was the real fear. That she would do to Ella and Layla what Amber had done to her. Not on purpose, but because that was all she knew. She could subconsciously act the same way, not even seeing it until the damage was done. What if they felt about her the way she felt about Amber? What if she destroyed them?

"Heather, we know you. I understand this is a big ask, but you're the one person we trust the most with our children."

Heather stood, trying to catch her breath. She felt more than panic, more than terror. Horror clutched her heart.

"No," she repeated. "No, I can't. I won't. You want too much. I don't know you or them. Not like this. You shouldn't trust me and you shouldn't ask. You look at me and you think

I'm fine, but I'm not. I can't promise to love them the right way. I'm too broken."

Campbell had been right about her.

"I couldn't be with the man I loved because I wasn't willing to trust him. He's an adult who's capable of taking care of himself. Think of what I could do to two innocent children. No. Just no. Don't ask me again."

She ran out of the house. When she got back to her condo, she sank onto the floor, her back up against the corner. She pulled her knees to her chest and huddled there, telling herself to breathe and that everything would be fine.

"We appreciate this, but we want you to be sure."

The sixty-something-year-old volunteer paused, waiting for an answer. Heather faked her best smile.

"I'm happy to help with kittens," she said.

"You're one of our best fosters," the volunteer told her.

It didn't take long to load a box of four two-week-old orphans into her car, bags of supplies in her trunk.

After two days of dodging calls and texts from Jillian and her father, not sleeping and being unable to outrun the chanting in her head that she was absolutely the last person on earth who should be responsible for children, she'd realized she needed a distraction or she would completely lose it. Foster kittens offered the easiest one. Tori frequently accused her of fostering to avoid her emotions. This was one time Heather was happy to tell her friend she was right.

Her phone buzzed as she pulled into her parking space. Assuming it was her dad, she ignored it and got the kittens inside. LC glared at her when she closed the door, preventing him from inspecting his new charges.

"Let's give them a couple of days to get settled," she told the cat. "Then you can meet them."

He stalked away. Her phone buzzed again.

"Leave me alone," she muttered before glancing at the screen. Only the text was from Tori.

Everything all right?

Heather sighed. She hadn't been herself at work and of course Tori had noticed. Heather had lied and said she wasn't feeling well.

Great, she texted back. I was getting another litter of kittens. I don't want to move them on their first day so I'm going to work from home.

Why? It's Saturday and you said you were taking a break from kittens.

"You were right. I use foster kittens to distract myself."

Heather, what's going on?

Nothing. I'm great. Have a good weekend.

She half expected Tori to demand an explanation. But all she got was You, too.

She made a quick trip to the grocery store. She'd barely unpacked the bags when her doorbell rang.

Her stomach sank. She didn't want to deal with her father or Jillian. Not now, maybe not ever. But it was Tori at the door.

"What are you doing here?"

Tori pushed past her into the condo. "I'm not leaving until you tell me what's wrong."

Heather held in a groan. "I'm fine," she lied.

"You've been acting strange for days. You said you were sick, which I didn't believe. Then you got more kittens." Her friend shook her head. "You know you need a break from the fostering, so the fact that you got another litter tells me there's a problem. A big one."

LC came running. Tori picked him up and hugged him. "You're scaring me, so I'm not leaving until I know what's going on."

The doorbell rang again.

"I told Brody something was wrong, so that's probably Daphne."

Frustration mingled with appreciation for her friend's concern. "Should I expect anyone else?" she asked as she walked to the door.

"Just Daphne."

Only it wasn't Daphne waiting to be let in. It was Campbell.

Her mouth went dry and her heart started pounding. She tried to speak, but couldn't. God, he looked good. Tall and strong. She wanted to throw herself at him because for the very first time in her life, she needed to be held like she was fragile, and she trusted him to keep her from breaking.

"I heard there was a problem," he said as he walked in.

LC meowed and leaped from Tori's arms. He ran to Campbell and frantically rubbed against him.

"Hey, you." Campbell picked him up and stroked him. "How's it going?"

Tori put her hands on her hips. "Who called you? Grant or Brody? I should knock their heads together. This is a ladies-only moment."

"I'm a problem solver." Campbell sat on the sofa. LC snuggled against his chest, purring loudly enough to be heard across the room.

Heather was about to close the door when Daphne hurried in.

"Am I late? What's going on?" She hugged Heather, then studied her. "You're not sick. The last time we talked you weren't desperately in love with a new guy, so your heart isn't recently broken. What happened?"

"This is humiliating," Heather said. "I'm fine. You all need to leave."

Daphne sat next to Tori and smiled at Campbell. "Brody or Grant?"

"I'm not saying."

The three of them looked at her. Heather sank into a chair and wondered what to say. The truth seemed impossible, yet nothing else came to mind.

"We love you," Tori said gently. "We want to help."

Heather refused to look at Campbell, because there was no way he still loved her. Nora had hold of his heart and she didn't seem the type to let go. But she knew he still cared for her as a friend.

Maybe she should just blurt out the truth. It wouldn't make her look good, but maybe seeing disdain in his eyes would help her get over him.

LC's purr filled the room.

"Traitor," she murmured. "You know Jillian has metastatic breast cancer, right?"

Daphne and Tori nodded while Campbell looked confused.

"What's that?"

Tori quickly explained.

"Is she okay?" he asked Heather.

"For now. She could live years. But it could get really bad."

"That's scary, plus you're just getting to know her. I'm sorry."

His concern hit her hard in her heart. "Thanks, but that's not the problem. It's not just Jillian. My dad is in his fifties and while he's healthy, he's an older father."

Everyone waited.

"Jillian asked me to be the girls' guardian if something happens to them. To basically raise them." She swallowed. "I didn't handle it well. I told her no, of course. No one who knows me would want me raising their kid."

"I'd trust you with my child," Tori said.

"Me, too," Daphne said, her gaze pointed. "I'd talk to you first and get your agreement, but Heather, you'd be a great mom."

"Have you met me?"

"Since we were babies," Daphne said.

"She scared you," Campbell said quietly.

Heather forced herself to look at him. "She did." She searched his eyes for judgment, but found none.

"You're afraid because of how you were raised," he continued.

"I'd never hurt them on purpose, but what if I don't know it's happening until it's too late?"

"That's ridiculous," Tori said. "You'd be fine. Did they think about logistics?"

"What logistics?" Heather asked.

"Your sisters. There's not enough room in this condo. Plus, if they've just lost their parents, they won't need more change. So would you move up there? Live in their house? You have a life here. Friends, your business. Are they expecting you to drop everything to care for their kids?"

She paused. "I didn't mean that to sound harsh, but this is huge. You're their sister, but you've only known each other a couple of months. They should have taken more time."

"She's right," Daphne said. "If something happened to Brody, his kids would have their mom. The odds of both of them being killed seem unlikely, but with your dad and Jillian, it's more precarious. They shouldn't have sprung that on you."

"You're not your mom," Campbell told her.

"I never want anyone to hate me the way I've hated her."

"I thought you just didn't want kids."

The room went still. Even LC's purring seemed to fade. She looked at him, not sure what to say.

"You're not your mom," he repeated. "You could never be like her."

"I wish I could believe that."

"They were wrong," he told her. "They moved too fast. They were only thinking about themselves."

"They're trying to protect their children."

"You're his daughter, too."

While she appreciated that he was taking her side, she wished he wouldn't. If Campbell would look at her like she was scum, it might help her get over him. Or at least want him less. But telling him not to be nice wasn't an option.

"It's done." She shrugged. "I ran and I haven't talked to either of them since. You're right. This happened too fast. I found out I have another family and suddenly they want me to be their daughters' guardian? I need to regroup. Not see them for a while."

"Makes sense." Daphne petted LC. "You know you're not the bad guy, right? This is on them."

"They were just asking," Heather pointed out.

"Why do you keep taking their side?" Tori asked.

"I don't know. I feel guilty but I know I'm not wrong." She sighed. Her watch beeped. "And I have kittens to feed."

Tori rose. "I'll help."

"Me, too." Daphne smiled. "I do love a kitten."

"I have to go." Campbell put LC on the sofa. "I have a flight in a few hours." He touched her arm. "Will you be all right?"

"Of course."

"I'm around if you need me."

If only that were true, she thought. But Campbell was speaking as her friend, nothing more. Maybe it was time to accept that friendship was as good as it was going to get.

twenty-one

Daphne had put off a second meeting with Renee from *Velkommen* as long as she could but when her mother had called to complain, Daphne had accepted a lunch invitation.

When she arrived at the restaurant, she spotted Renee at a corner table. She walked over and greeted her.

"I want to apologize for being so persistent," the other woman said with a laugh. "But I can't help myself."

"And you have my mother on your side." Daphne managed a genuine smile, thinking her life would be easier if she didn't love her mom so much.

Driving over she'd come up with a plan. She would listen politely for a few minutes, then tell Renee she was happy with her current job and had no plans to leave.

"She wore you down?" Renee asked.

"I'm not sleeping well these days so it was easier than it should have been."

Renee studied her. "Are you all right?"

There was a question. Daphne thought about answering honestly. *Not really. My husband thinks I had an affair, which I didn't. I'm working too much and I haven't slept well in weeks. Oh, and I'm pregnant but I can't tell Brody because I'm afraid he won't believe it's his. Other than that, I'm peachy.*

"I'm good," she said. "Just busy. Work is suddenly crazy and getting the kids settled in their fall schedule is a challenge. Next up, the holidays. Life is a whirlwind."

Renee's concerned expression softened. "And here I am, trying to convince you to change course. I should feel guilty."

Daphne laughed. "But you don't."

"Not really. I still think you're perfect for us, so I'll do my best to convince you. But let's order lunch first."

Daphne scanned the menu, looking for food she could eat. What she wanted was a juicy rare burger and eight cups of coffee, but she chose the grilled chicken salad with a side of vegetable soup and a club soda.

"Did you research our firm?" Renee asked.

"I did. Your mission statement is impressive and I couldn't find any negative reviews. Your clients adore you."

"We adore them, too." Renee smiled. "I've been trying to get an idea on your salary without asking directly. My guess is low-to-mid-six figures."

Daphne kept her expression neutral. "You're in the range."

"We can't compete with that. You would be looking at about a thirty percent cut in pay with us."

"That's a lot." But not a surprise, she thought. *Velkommen* wasn't a high-powered law firm.

Renee leaned toward her. "But we can offer you other benefits—such as time with your family. Forty hours a week.

Technically, we're all on call, but in all the years I've worked here, I've never needed legal counsel at three in the morning."

"That's comforting."

"We'll start you at four weeks of vacation. I've brought a brochure that explains our benefit program. It's very generous. Working from home a few days a week would also be an option." Renee's eyes twinkled. "In case you decide to give your mother that grandchild she craves."

Daphne did her best to laugh naturally. "Lately, she has a one-track mind."

"She wants to be a grandmother."

Their food arrived which, thankfully, shifted the conversation. Pregnancy and kids were not topics she wanted to dwell on.

"The next step is for you to meet the senior team," Renee said. "No pressure. We'd get together casually, to see if there's any chemistry. After all, we work closely together. We want to get along."

"Renee, I don't want to waste anyone's time. I'll admit there are some things that tempt me, but I have no intention of leaving my job."

"I'm talking coffee and Danishes at our office. We'll spend an hour getting to know each other." She held up her hand. "I've heard what you've said. But please, what could one more hour of your time hurt?"

Daphne shook her head. "You remind me of my mother."

"Thank you. That's a lovely thing to say."

They both laughed. Daphne gave in to the inevitable and pulled out her phone. "Fine, but let's make it midafternoon. My mornings are usually a scramble."

Plus, she didn't want to explain why she wasn't drinking coffee. An afternoon meeting would avoid that problem and because they were all working, no one would offer her liquor.

As she walked to her car, she allowed herself the brief fantasy of considering the offer. She'd never worked a forty-hour week in her life. What did people do with the extra time?

In her case, she could get home early enough to have dinner with the kids every night they were there. She and Brody could meet friends or go to a movie. She'd be around more for the baby, and they'd be less reliant on a nanny. Plus, some days she could hang with her cats and work from home.

Only she'd spent the last eleven years with one goal—to make partner. She'd put in the time. She'd volunteered for projects no one else wanted, come in sick, tired and, when she was younger, hungover. She'd had a clear vision of her future and she'd finally achieved it. Was she willing to walk away from all that within the first year of getting her name on the letterhead?

And what about the pay cut? Right now she and Brody were financially comfortable. The house would be paid off in less than five years, they drove new cars and had fully funded their retirement and the kids' college accounts. A 30 percent cut in pay would mean having to budget a little more.

She drove across the 520 bridge as she realized the ridiculousness of that last thought.

Everything came at a price, she thought. Time versus money. Making partner versus life balance. Seeing the kids, spending time with her baby, or working the eighty hours she loved.

And what if she and Brody didn't make it? How would that influence her decision? As a single mother, the job at *Velkommen* made a lot more sense.

Not anything she wanted to think about, she told herself. Because if she went there—if she considered the fact that her marriage was over—she would totally lose it. And partners at her firm did not cry in the office. They were professionals who left their problems at home. Even if that home was falling apart.

★ ★ ★

"People are staring," Grant said mildly.

"I don't care." Tori continued to drape herself across the 48" Wolf range. It had eight burners and two ovens. It was pure stove heaven. Too big for either of their condos, but when else was she ever going to get this close to something so magical?

"You don't even cook that much."

"Who needs to cook? It's art."

"So you'd frame it?"

"Very funny."

With a sigh of regret, she straightened and gave the range a pat. "Ours could have been a great love. I would have been true to you."

Grant scrolled through the contacts on his phone. "I'm finding that doctor I know in the psych department. You need help. Just a quick chat to make sure you didn't shake something loose up there."

"I'm ignoring you," she said, walking toward the exit.

"You say that like it's news."

He beat her to the door and held it open. They stepped out into the cloudy afternoon, having ordered new appliances. They'd gone with budget-friendly options that would be covered by insurance. Tori's limited remodel fund was being spent on the extra upper cabinets in her kitchen and a cool custom master closet redo. Not only didn't she have the room for a Wolf range, she'd have to sell her car to get it. But it had been pretty.

She glanced back at the store. "I'll miss you forever."

"How about if I buy you a Frappuccino to take your mind off your pain?"

"Sold!"

They crossed the street to Starbucks. This time of day the store was quiet with only a few customers. Grant ordered her a mocha Frappuccino with extra whip and himself some iced tea lemonade combo that would have made her gag.

"Are you happy with the choices?" he asked, sitting across from her at a small table. "I know they're not Wolf-worthy."

"They'll be fine." She flipped through screens on her tablet until she found her list. "I think we're done with the kitchens. We have flooring, cabinets, countertops, appliances and backsplash. Now bathrooms."

He groaned. "More decisions?"

"Oh, please. You just sit next to me, wide-eyed, agreeing to whatever I say. What if I pick something awful?"

"You won't." He studied her. "I heard what happened Saturday. You worried about Heather?"

And Daphne, she thought. But she wasn't sure how much Grant knew about their marriage, and she knew he had no idea Daphne was pregnant. How sad that Daphne was in such a bad place during what should be a happy and shared experience.

"I'm not worried exactly," she said. "She's been through a lot. Finding her birth father, his family. It was going really well, then suddenly everything got all twisted."

"I get them wanting to look out for their kids, but they need to get to know each other first."

She nodded in agreement. "How are things with Nora and Campbell?"

"Not talking about them."

"Why not? He shares stuff with you."

Grant smiled. "Yes, and I'm not telling you what he says."

"Why not? Who am I going to tell?"

"Heather and Daphne."

"You're so annoying," she muttered. "So they're happy?"

He eyed her. "Where are you going with this?"

"I was just wondering. I mean Nora's sweet, but Heather's my family."

"You want her to get back together with Campbell?"

"Don't you?"

"No."

"Why not?" Tori glared at him.

"She dumped him twice. The first time was at Brody's wedding. That's cold, even for her."

"I'll admit the timing was unfortunate, but she was scared. It's hard for her to trust people. I just miss them being together. Although I do like Nora. But when she's around, Heather can't always hang with us."

Although the whole Heather-Campbell-Nora thing wasn't as confusing as her feelings for Grant. Why had her heart changed the rules? She'd been so happy as just friends.

"Nothing's forever," he said.

"That's grim."

"I meant situations will always change. Look at Brody and Daphne. They got married and got into a routine then suddenly they go from kids every other weekend to every other week. That had to be hard on Daphne."

"She loves his kids."

"She's great. I'm just pointing out that they haven't been married long and adding three kids to the mix is a challenge."

She felt he was trying to tell her something. "Is Brody unhappy?"

Grant looked away. "He's realizing that he should have waited before changing the parenting agreement. Whitney had been on him for a while to take more time. Once she had her baby, she was scrambling. Daphne was happy to have the kids more and she's great with them, but it's been a strain."

"Did he tell Daphne he feels bad about it?"

"I don't know."

"He should."

Maybe that would help, she thought. Of course there was still the whole emotional affair. Something she wasn't going to mention until she was sure he knew about it. Oh, the complications of family.

"She works those long hours," Tori added. "I love my job, but I don't want to do it eighty hours a week."

"I'm with you."

She sipped her drink. "So how's your dating life?"

"I'm taking a break."

Hope flared, which was stupid. He wasn't taking a break because of her.

"You just got started. You've been on maybe three dates. At this rate, you'll never get laid."

His gaze narrowed. "Thank you for your support. Maybe I'll pick up someone in a bar."

"Have you ever done that?"

"No, but I'm a good-looking doctor. It shouldn't be hard."

"You play the doctor card a lot."

His smile was smug. "I do what works."

"Actually, you're not doing anything right now. Maybe you should hire a professional. You know, for the first time back in the pool, so to speak."

His look of horror was comical. He glanced around, then leaned close. "Are you suggesting I get a hooker?"

"Just to get you over the hump."

"There's no hump. What hump? I'm fine." He sat back in his chair. "There's something wrong with you."

"So says the guy who hasn't had sex in what? Two years? I wouldn't be so judgy if I were you."

"When was the last time you got some?"

She sighed. "It's been a while. Pre-Kyle." And she wasn't interested in finding anyone else right now. Yet more fallout from realizing she was madly in love with Grant. "My life sucks."

"No, it doesn't."

"Okay, parts of my life suck."

He touched his drink to hers. "Back at you."

★ ★ ★

Heather paused briefly in the hallway, squared her shoulders and told herself she could handle this, then opened the door to her office and stepped inside. Fletcher stood by the window, looking out at the green space. When she entered, he faced her.

He looked older. The lines around his mouth seemed more pronounced and his shoulders drooped. Sadness filled his eyes.

"I wasn't sure you'd see me," he said. "You've been avoiding my calls and texts."

He was right, she thought, motioning to the small conference table. But not just his—Jillian's as well, she thought. They sat. She held herself stiffly, her shoulders square, her spine rigid.

"I thought we should clear up a few things."

He waited, as if expecting her to say something, but she had no idea what that would be.

"I'm sorry." He looked at her. "Jillian shouldn't have brought up the guardianship. We're in agreement on the subject, but it was too soon. We'd said we would wait and when we did it, we would do it together. She shouldn't have blurted it out like that."

"You don't know me," Heather said, her voice sharp. "You think you do, but you don't. It's been less than three months. You don't offer your children to someone you've known less than three months. You think we're a family, but we're not. We're people who are related and yes, it's been going well, but it takes time to form a relationship."

She wished she could put more space between them. At this small table, they were too close.

"We should have taken things more slowly," she continued.

"Heather, don't say that."

"I *am* saying it." She folded her arms across her chest. "You expect too much from me and I can't do it anymore. I can't see you or talk to you."

He flinched at her words. Guilt flooded her along with an unexpected sense of loss.

"At least for a while," she amended. "I need to think this through."

She thought he would get angry or try to convince her. Instead, his expression softened with compassion.

"Oh, child. I can feel your pain from here."

He stood and circled the table. After pulling her to her feet, he wrapped his arms around her and hung on.

"You're right," he said softly. "We did move too fast. We should have listened when you said relationships were difficult for you. We should have listened when you said it was hard for you to trust. We promised we didn't want anything then asked for more than anyone ever has. I'm so, so sorry."

His quiet words, the security of his hug, found their way into her heart. She hung on to him.

"I know you're scared," he told her. "And I'm sorry for that, too. We never meant to push you away. You've become a part of us and we miss you. The girls are always asking after you. We did this all wrong and I want to make it right."

He drew back and looked into her eyes. "We don't want to lose you, Heather. We take it back. We have a plan for the girls and odds are it will never be an issue. Please forgive us and come back to the family."

She put some space between them. "I want to. I miss everyone."

He nodded slowly. "But you still need time. I understand. Just don't take too much. There's a hole in our hearts now that only you can fill."

"I'm supposed to go to the movies with Ella and Layla," she began.

He cut her off. "Don't worry about it. I'll tell them you can't make it. They'll understand."

They were kids—would they really? For weeks they'd been talking about seeing that movie together. But doing that, getting involved, seemed too risky.

He gave her a sad smile. "I miss you already."

With that, he left. Heather watched him go, knowing she'd done what she had to so she could protect herself, while at the same time wondering if she was fooling herself.

"Grant's on a date," Tori said. "With a woman."

"Is the woman part a surprise?" Heather asked, pausing by a plaid sectional.

"No, but saying it somehow makes me feel worse." Tori shook her head. "I can't do plaid and it's too big for my condo."

"I was thinking for Grant's living room."

"Maybe." She threw herself onto one of the cushions. "It's comfortable, but I still feel awful."

"Join the club," Daphne said, sitting next to her friend.

They were out sofa shopping, or at least looking at options. A distraction, Daphne thought—something she needed right now.

"We share pain." Tori grabbed her hand. "But on the misery scale, I win." She frowned. "I don't feel very victorious."

"You don't win," Heather said, joining them on the sectional. "I win because I'm incapable of learning."

"You have a degree from USC," Daphne pointed out. "I'm pretty sure you're capable of learning."

"Not that kind. When it comes to emotional intelligence, I'm in the dull-normal range."

"Harsh," Tori murmured. "And not true."

"My father came to see me."

Daphne looked at Tori, who seemed surprised, too.

"When?" Daphne asked.

"A couple of days ago. I was too upset to talk about it." She leaned back. "This is nice. I don't love the plaid, but it's comfortable. Maybe Grant could order it in leather."

Daphne stared at her. "Could we please stay on topic? What happened with your dad?"

"He apologized for the whole guardianship thing." Heather shrugged. "He agreed it was too soon and he said they took back the ask." She paused. "He said they missed me and didn't want anything to change."

Daphne watched her friend. "Which should have made things better, but didn't."

"No. I appreciate the effort, but they're asking for things I don't have. I told him I needed time to process."

"You pulled back," Daphne said flatly.

Heather looked at her. "I didn't have a choice."

"Nooo," Tori wailed. "Don't do that. You love them."

Heather glared at her. "I don't do love."

"You told me you love me."

"That's different."

"How?" Daphne asked. "It's not romantic love. It's friendship love." She smiled. "I assume you don't just love Tori."

Heather glared at her. "Fine. I love you, too."

"That was so warm. And I love you." Her smile faded. "You're doing it again. You're doing exactly what you did to Campbell. It was great and you were happy. Then he wanted to take things to the next level and you got scared, so you ran."

Heather studied the fabric. "This is totally different."

"Daphne's right." Tori shook her head. "You're repeating the pattern. You're cutting them off because you can't handle the emotion, then in a few weeks you'll be sorry and it will be too late." Tori's eyes filled with tears. "Don't lose your family over this. They made a mistake and they corrected it. That's what people do. They grow and learn."

"She's not listening," Daphne said, watching Heather.

"It's not the same," Heather told them.

"Yeah, it is. This is what you do. You think you can only go so far. That's the story you tell yourself because you get scared. They're not Amber."

"They tried to give me their children," Heather snapped. "That seems a little Amber-like."

"No, it's not," Tori said. "It's the exact opposite. Your mom only thinks of herself. Your dad and stepmom are thinking of their children. They're trusting you to take care of the two human beings they love more than anyone else. They believe in you. I know it's not what you want, but it shows how highly they think of you. They're trusting you with treasure."

Daphne lightly touched her belly. Right now the child she carried was little more than a theory and a reason to be afraid of her future with Brody. But once he or she was born, that would change. She knew how much she loved Brody's three—imagine how her heart would grow when she held her own baby.

"You're going to be sorry," Tori repeated softly. "Because I think you love them and want to be a part of their lives. You need to stop running, Heather. You need to face your fears or you're going to lose everything important. This is your family."

Daphne waited for Heather to make a comment about Tori's lack of courage when it came to Grant, but Heather surprised her by nodding slowly.

"I know you're right. I've been thinking the same thing. I just don't know if I can do it." She gave a strangled laugh. "So I'm the most miserable."

"Not even close." Daphne thought about everything going on in her life. "I have a job offer."

They both stared at her blankly.

Tori leaned forward. "From *Velkommen*? They sound amazing and I think you could be happy there, but you just made partner. Are you considering it?"

"No."

Heather raised her eyebrows. "You are! Because of..." She glanced around, then lowered her voice. "The baby?"

"I'm not considering it. Why would I? It would be a cut in pay, but fewer hours and a lot less stress. I like what the company is doing. My work with wills and trusts means I'd be an asset for them. I would be doing interesting work. But I worked too hard to get where I am. Why would I give that up?"

"I'm confused," Tori admitted. "So why are we talking about this?"

"I'm pregnant. What happens when I have the baby? Do I put him or her in day care for ten hours a day? Technically, I could work from home some of the time, but the firm frowns on that. Plus, could I work with a newborn around? So I have a kid I never see that someone else raises?"

Heather touched her hand. "Are you worrying about the job offer because it's easier than wondering what's happening with Brody?"

Daphne nodded. "I don't know if we're going to make it."

"He still doesn't know about the baby?" Tori asked.

"No. I can't tell him." She briefly closed her eyes. "You know what he'll think."

"But you're having a—"

Daphne glared at Tori. "Do not say the word *geriatric* to me."

Tori tried not to smile. "I won't but my point is you're probably going to have amniocentesis, right? They can determine paternity then. So Brody will know before the baby's born and he'll be happy."

Daphne hadn't thought of that, probably because she hadn't spent much of her life thinking about getting pregnant. Her mood brightened.

"You're right. He'll know it's his baby. I still have to get through the ugliness of telling him, but if I wait until close to the test, it won't be too horrible."

Hopefully, the test was relatively early in her pregnancy so she didn't have to wait too long. Or have Brody figure out what was going on before she could tell him herself.

"I feel better," she said. "I have a plan." She looked at Heather. "You could have a plan, too. You could have a little faith."

"I'm unconvinced."

Tori sighed. "You have a plan and Heather is going to come to her senses and get back together with her family, which means I'm right. I'm the miserable one."

"You could tell Grant how you feel," Daphne said.

"That is never happening."

twenty-two

Tori rinsed the conditioner from her hair and turned off the shower. She had a list of things she wanted to get done as quickly as possible because she had a new book she wanted to start. Sundays were her best reading days.

She stepped onto the bath mat and reached for her towel. The rain was supposed to be done by eleven, so that afternoon she would take Scout on a long walk around the neighborhood. Looking at all the big, fancy houses was fun, and Scout enjoyed sniffing new things.

She'd barely wrapped her towel around herself when the sharp, high-pitched sound of the fire alarm filled the house. Her heart thundered in her chest and she screamed as she braced for a sudden spray of water.

"Grant! Grant!" She ran down the stairs, Scout at her heels.

Her ears hurt from the sound and her body was cold with terror.

"It's happening again!"

"Tori? It's okay."

She barely heard the words. Zeus was barking, the alarm was blaring and any second now water would pour down. Then as suddenly as the noise had started, it ended. She raced into the kitchen and saw black smoke billowing from the toaster.

"What did you do?" she demanded.

"The bread got caught and I wasn't paying attention." Grant's expression was sheepish. "Sorry. I was looking at my phone and didn't notice until the alarm went off. I guess they're all connected."

"You guess?" Her voice was a shriek. "You *guess*?" She eyed the ceiling. "What if the sprinklers go off? I can't go through that again."

She turned the fan on high. The smoke was sucked up and out of the kitchen. She pressed a hand to her chest.

"My heart is pounding so hard." She smacked his arm. "Don't do that again."

"I won't." He pointed to the ceiling. "If it helps, we won't have a problem with sprinklers going off."

She glared at him. "You can't know that."

"There aren't any."

"What?" She stared at the ceiling. Sure enough, she didn't see any. "Oh. Okay. Well, that's better." She flipped off the fan and turned her attention back to him. "Stay off your phone when you're cooking."

She expected him to say something funny or tell her she was overreacting. Instead, he stared at her with the strangest look on his face.

"You were in the shower." His voice was low and husky as he spoke.

"Duh. I'm in a towel and my hair is wet. Where else would I have been?"

She had more to say. Sarcasm was one of her superpowers. But somehow, as her gaze locked with his, she couldn't think of any specific words.

The room was so quiet, she could hear her heart beating. She felt the hard floor under her bare feet and was suddenly aware of the fact that except for the towel, she was naked. Something she had a feeling Grant had noticed, as well. Or maybe that was just wishful thinking.

"Tori."

He spoke her name with an edge of longing that made her insides quiver. Given her newly discovered feelings, she was already weak where he was concerned.

"You should probably go upstairs and get dressed."

"I probably should."

Only she couldn't seem to move. Before she could figure out what was wrong, he was walking toward her. When he was right in front of her, he cupped her face in his hands and lightly pressed his mouth to hers.

The kiss was so soft—a barely there brush of skin on skin that made her weak. He drew back so he could look at her face.

"What are you thinking?" he asked.

"I can't think."

"Me, either."

He kissed her again—this time like he meant it. The feel of his lips was exquisitely arousing. This was what she wanted, she thought as he pulled her close. This man, this touching.

She wrapped her arms around his neck and leaned into him. His hands roamed her back as his tongue teased hers. Wanting grew until there was only fire and need. She felt his erection against her belly.

He drew back enough to pull off his T-shirt, then he grabbed her hands and put them on his bare chest. His skin was warm, his body muscled.

"Tori," he whispered, kissing her cheeks, her temples, her mouth. "Tell me what you want."

"You."

His dark gaze locked with hers. She saw desire and need and all kinds of other delicious things. He gave her a slow, sexy smile.

"I want you, too. I have condoms in my bedroom."

"How convenient."

He grabbed her hand and they raced upstairs together.

The next few minutes were a blur of sensations as they touched each other everywhere. His hands shook as he put on the condom. She'd already come once, compliments of his skillful fingers. She reached between them and guided him inside.

He sucked in his breath as he entered her.

"I'd forgotten this could feel so good," he said, then groaned.

She had, too, she thought, watching him find his rhythm, then lose himself in her. She held him as he shuddered his release, feeling fiercely protective of this moment and this man. There would be time for second thoughts and self-recrimination later. For now, this was plenty.

By the time she got back into her bathroom, her hair was dry with a couple of weird kinks from lying on it. She dressed, then wet her hair and blew it straight. Once done, she had to face what had just happened.

She and Grant had had sex. Yes, she was all tingly with the post-orgasm glow, but there were complications. Questions. Was it a onetime thing? Did they pretend it never happened? Could she do that? Did she want to do that? What was Grant thinking? What did he want? Did he know she was in love with him? Should she ask him to talk about what they'd done, or would that be too weird? She had about four thousand other things to ask, but those seemed like enough of a starting point.

She walked out of her bathroom only to find the man of the hour standing in the doorway of her bedroom. He gave her a happy, very satisfied smile that made her toes curl even as her heart warned her to be careful. Seconds later his expression shifted to more concerned.

"Are you okay? You ran."

She stopped in the middle of her bedroom. "I didn't run. I scurried."

"Whatever you want to call it, one second we were enjoying the aftereffects of the most amazing sex ever and the next you were gone." He walked toward her, stopping when he was close enough to put his hands on her shoulders. "Why? Do you regret what happened?"

The most amazing sex ever? The man had been without for a while, so she was probably getting more credit than she deserved, but still. A little of her freak-out-ness faded.

She stared at his familiar face. "No regrets."

"You sure? Because as great as that was, you and our friendship matter more."

"I think so, too." She smiled. "But it was nice."

He reeled back in mock dismay. "Nice? A toasted bagel is nice. That was incredible."

"You're just grateful you finally got some."

Instead of laughing, he shook his head. "No. Don't say that. I wasn't getting off. I was making love with someone I like and trust. Someone who's important to me."

The man did have a way with words, she thought, slipping a little further down the "in love" path.

"I'm glad you think that," she told him. "I feel the same way. It's just, I have questions."

"Me, too." His dark gaze settled on her face. "Was it a onetime thing or do we want to continue? Would being lovers get in the way of the great relationship we already have?"

Lovers. Just his speaking that word made her shiver.

She knew what he wanted—in life if not specifically with her. He'd been burned in his marriage and the idea of forever with someone scared him nearly as much as it scared Heather. So if she got involved with him, there was no happily-ever-after. There would just be this. What was the old cliché? Friends with benefits. So the real question seemed to be—could she accept only part of what she wanted with Grant?

He gave her a lopsided smile. "For what it's worth, I want us to be lovers."

The shivers of desire returned. The things that man did to her, she thought, wondering how badly this would end for her.

"Me, too," she whispered.

His eyes brightened. "Yeah?"

She nodded. "But I have ground rules."

"Sure. Anything. Say the word and it's done."

She laughed. "You're very eager."

"You have no idea."

Her humor faded as she thought about what was important to her. "No ghosting me, and no dating other women while we're doing this."

His expression tightened. "Tori, I would never do that."

"I know, but I want to be clear."

He moved close and lightly touched her cheek. "I'm not that guy."

She stepped back. "Let me finish."

"Okay."

"No one can know. Not until we figure out what we're

doing and what it means." Not to mention how long it would last. If it ended in a week, there was no reason for their family to get involved.

"Agreed. Telling them could be a complication."

"The cooking plan doesn't change. Just because we're having sex doesn't mean I'm suddenly going to be taking care of you."

His lips twitched. "I promise to uphold my end of the bargain."

That was pretty much all she had. She looked at him and thought about what they were proposing. There was a better than even possibility that she wouldn't like the outcome, but she couldn't resist him.

"We'll both get tested for STDs," she said. "Until then, you need to carry a condom."

"Done."

She stepped into his embrace. "The last time was a little fast. Want to see if we can slow things down a bit?"

He lowered his mouth to hers. "We'll be the slowest of the slow."

"You say that now."

They were both still laughing when he kissed her.

Heather sat in her car, looking at the familiar house with the porch and the big windows. It wasn't fancy, but it was a home and the people who lived there loved each other. They also claimed to love her and yet she'd walked away. Because she was afraid.

Oh, they'd been totally wrong with the whole guardian thing, but that wasn't the problem. After months of missing Campbell, she now also missed her dad and Jillian and her sisters. She lay awake at night, telling herself she'd made the sensible decision—that everyone eventually turned into her mother and she couldn't take the chance. Every morning she knew she was lying. The problem was her, or rather the fear she always let win.

She'd realized that there was nothing she could do on the Campbell front, but she could do something about her family. If they still wanted her in their lives.

She knocked on the front door. It was early afternoon on a weekday, so only Jillian should be home. Heather figured they had the most to say to each other.

Her stepmother opened the door and stared at her. Heather had been hoping for a welcoming smile, but Jillian's expression was guarded.

"I wasn't expecting you," she said, making no move to let Heather into the house.

"I know."

One of the kittens darted out onto the porch. Heather turned and grabbed her, scooping her up into her arms.

"No way. You're not getting out today." She looked at Jillian. "Can we talk?"

Jillian held the door open wider. Heather slipped inside and set the kitten on the floor. The other one raced into the living room and jumped on her sister. They tumbled across the area rug before speeding down the hall.

Jillian pointed to the formal living room. "We can sit here."

So not the kitchen, Heather thought. And no offer of lemonade or cookies.

They sat across from each other. Heather had spent the drive trying to figure out what she wanted to say, only she couldn't remember anything she'd wanted to discuss.

"I'm sorry," she began.

"No." Jillian glared at her. "Just no. I get that I was wrong to ask. Your reaction made that clear. Plus, Fletcher was furious. Sometimes I get impulsive. We were going to do it together

300

but I went ahead, and let me be honest when I tell you I had no idea you were going to be so horrible."

Her gaze sharpened. "How dare you? Be pissed at me. Don't speak to me. That's fine. Ignore your dad, but don't you ever, *ever* treat my girls like that. They adore you. They talk about you all the time, they want to be like you when they grow up. They think you're magical. And you disappeared, just gone. Do you know what that did to them? Do you know how they cried when their dad told them you weren't taking them to the movies? You hurt my children."

She turned away. "I was willing to trust you with their lives and you hurt them."

Each word was a stab to her heart. Heather shrank in her seat. Her chest was tight, her throat dry with shame.

"I'm sorry," she whispered.

Jillian whipped her head back. "Do you think I care about that? You're sorry, like that matters? You hurt my family. I thought you were becoming part of us, but it was some kind of game for you. Why did you get in touch with your dad in the first place? You never wanted a relationship with him. Are you using us to piss off your mother?"

The attack was so harsh and so unexpected that Heather didn't know what to think. "No. I wouldn't do that."

"I can't really know that, can I?"

"I'm sorry," she repeated, realizing how meaningless the words were. "I reacted. I couldn't do what you asked and knowing what you expected terrified me. I was afraid I'd hurt the girls and I did."

"Because you were only thinking of yourself," Jillian snapped. "The whole point of raising children is to think about what's best for them. That's the responsibility you take on."

Her shoulders sagged. "Which you didn't want, did you? I keep forgetting that. We live such different lives. I always wanted a family, to be a mom. I wasn't interested in a career or external success. I wanted this."

She waved at the room. "A life with a good man and children. They are my reason for being, so when you hurt my girls, you cut me to the core."

Heather struggled to find something to say that wasn't "I'm sorry."

"You're not me," Jillian said. "And I'll never be you." She drew in a breath. "This is so messed up. I'm just so angry with you."

"I know."

"You're probably pretty pissed at me."

"Not anymore."

"You should be."

They stared at each other. Heather forced herself to sit with all the ugly emotions she felt. This time she refused to run.

"I feel terrible about the girls," she said slowly. "You're right about everything. I should have explained to them personally. I didn't know what to say and yes, I was only thinking of myself."

She looked at Jillian. "You're right—I'm not like you. I've always been terrified to let myself get close to people and I never dreamed of having a family. I don't let people in because I'm afraid of how much they'll take from me. I'm afraid of being sucked in and then having them steal my life."

"I can't wait to meet your mother."

"I'm hoping you never will."

"Oh, I will." Jillian sighed. "Heather, you're full of crap. I'm sorry, but it's true. You're telling yourself a story that has nothing to do with reality."

The blunt statement caused Heather to draw back. "I have no idea what you're talking about."

"This whole not-letting-people-in thing. You're as close to

your girlfriends as I am to mine. You care about your employees. You're in love with Campbell. You're incredibly nurturing. Look what you did for the girls with the kittens."

"That's just cats. Cats are safe."

"You didn't do it for the kittens. You did it to make your sisters happy. I don't pretend to understand how you were raised
or what horrible things happened to you, but I do know who
you are today. The sad part is you can't see it, so you think
the worst and live a small life. You're so busy looking for reasons to be afraid that you can't see all the wonderful opportunities you're missing."

She paused. "We shouldn't have asked you to be the girls'
guardian. You're right. It was too soon. You need to be comfortable with us and I was pushing."

Heather was still trying to deal with Jillian's assessment of
her character. "You're worried about them. I get that."

"In the context that I don't want anything from you, can
you see how much faith we have in you?"

Heather nodded. "You thought I could love them and take
care of them, and the very first thing I did was hurt them."
Her eyes began to burn but she reminded herself that she didn't
cry. "I really am sorry."

"I know. Me, too." Her stepmother looked at her. "So what
happens now?"

"I don't know what you mean."

"Are you done with us or do you want to try this again?"

Heather didn't bother thinking about her answer. "I want
to try this again."

"Me, too."

Jillian rose. Heather did the same. One second they were
staring at each other, the next they were hugging so hard.
Heather hung on, thinking she never wanted to let go.

She'd come so close to losing all this. Too close. Later, she would think about what Jillian had said—that she was so busy telling herself the wrong story and being afraid, that she was missing out. She didn't like the implication, but she had a feeling it was true.

"I have to go get Layla," Jillian said when they'd released each other. "Want to come with me?"

The thought of facing her sisters made her want to cringe, but she forced herself to nod. "I would."

They walked the few blocks to the elementary school and waited with the other parents.

"When does Ella get out?"

"In an hour."

"Do they start at different times, too?"

Jillian grinned. "Of course. Why would the school district make it easy?"

Kids streamed from the building. Heather spotted Layla right away. When the nine-year-old saw her, her steps slowed. She looked from her mom to Heather and back.

The apprehension on Layla's face was yet another blow to Heather's heart. She'd been so wrong, she thought sadly. So thoughtless and cruel. She walked toward her.

"I'm sorry," she said, dropping to a crouch when she reached her sister. "Oh, Layla, I was wrong and I hurt you and I apologize."

Her sister watched her warily. "You didn't call or anything. You were just gone."

"I know. That's terrible." She pressed her lips together, fighting tears. "I got scared. Sometimes it's hard for me to love people, so I hold back. That's what I was doing. Only it was really a dumb plan because I already love you, so I ended up hurting both of us and isn't that ridiculous?"

She shifted onto her knees as tears filled her eyes. She who never cried, who wouldn't allow herself, had no power against what she was feeling. Regret, of course, but more significant, love.

"I've never had a sister before, so I didn't know how to act. It's always only been me, so I didn't know what I was supposed to do. I understand better now. I'm hoping you can forgive me and give me a second chance. I promise I'll keep working on getting it right."

She had more to say, but Layla flung her arms around her. Heather hugged her back, feeling how small she was. So little and defenseless. The enormity of what she'd done crashed in on her, shaming her.

I'll do better, she promised herself. She had to—her sisters were on the line.

Layla looked at her. "Don't cry. It's not just you anymore," she whispered. "Me and Ella are your sisters forever."

"And I'm yours."

twenty-three

Daphne typed quickly, pausing to review her notes every few minutes. A client wanted a complicated will and several trusts. With the birth of new grandchildren and one of her sons getting a divorce, changes were needed.

The work required intense concentration, making Daphne grateful she was sleeping better. Having a plan for telling Brody about the baby had eased a lot of her worry. Yes, there would be an ugly few weeks until they could do a DNA test, but he wouldn't think the worst through her entire pregnancy. Now all she had to do was tell him she was pregnant. Something she was going to put off as long as possible.

Someone knocked on her half-open door. She was surprised to see Miguel stepping inside. She hadn't seen him since she'd told him they couldn't have lunch anymore.

"Hi." She motioned to the seat opposite her desk. "You're never on this floor. Does one of your athletes want help with a will?"

"Not that I've heard of." He sat down and smiled at her. "I thought I'd check in."

Which was just like him, she thought. Although she hadn't really given him any thought in the past few weeks, now that she saw him, she found herself wanting to blurt out everything happening in her life. Miguel was a good listener who always saw her side. He was easy to be with, something that couldn't currently be said for her husband.

"You're doing well?" he asked.

"I am. You?"

She waited for the obligatory "Fine" but what he said instead was, "I miss you."

She blinked. "I'm sorry, what?"

"I miss you," he repeated, his gaze direct. "I miss us."

His words stunned her. Us? As in they were an *us*? "What are you talking about?"

He smiled. "You have to ask? I miss our lunches. Talking to you, hanging out."

She missed it, too. Only saying that seemed…wrong.

No, not wrong, she quickly amended. Just uncomfortable. They weren't an us, they couldn't be. They were only friends.

"I thought we were going somewhere," he said quietly, his gaze locking with hers.

She had a bad feeling he didn't mean a day trip to Tacoma. In his mind, lunch hadn't just been lunch.

Thoughts swirled. Mostly confusion, along with some very annoying guilt. She had nothing to be guilty about.

"Do you mean emotionally?" she asked, her voice quiet.

He flashed her a sexy smile. "I suppose that would have worked, as well."

The truth slammed into her. "You thought we were going to have an affair. You thought I was going to sleep with you."

"We have a lot in common, Daphne. We'd be good together."

"I'm married."

"I like a challenge."

This couldn't be happening. He honest to God thought they'd have sex? She wasn't sure which was worse—his arrogance or his assumption that she would cheat on her husband.

But even as she dealt with the outrage, a teeny, tiny voice in her head whispered that there had to be a reason he'd thought that. Miguel was a smart man who knew a lot about women. He wouldn't assume she was interested out of the blue.

She thought of their lunches, of the occasional drink after dinner, of how they laughed together and IM'd during video meetings. Had they really been *only friends* as she'd claimed?

"No," she said clearly, as much to herself as to him. "Never. Not with you, not with anyone. If I was unhappy with my husband, I would leave. I wouldn't have an affair. It's a weaselly way to deal with a problem."

She stood. "You misunderstood. We were friends, Miguel. Just friends."

His expression turned regretful as he rose. "I'm sorry you think that."

"I don't want this to be a problem."

He crossed to the door, then looked back at her. "It won't be. If you change your mind…"

"I won't."

He nodded and left. Daphne sank back in her chair. She felt queasy and embarrassed and confused. She'd meant what she said—she would never have an affair, and she hadn't. Nothing physical had happened.

She wanted to dismiss Miguel's musings as delusions, but she couldn't. Not when Brody had thought the same thing.

One of them assuming there had been an affair was easily ignored, but when they both thought it, she had to pay attention.

She thought about Heather and Tori saying she was having an emotional affair. Ridiculous. Only what if it wasn't?

"I didn't do anything wrong," she whispered, her previous good mood draining away.

Except what if she had? What if Brody had been right all along and everything that had come after was her fault, not his? What if nothing was as it seemed?

Could we meet somewhere and talk? It won't take long, and I promise it's not scary.

Heather sent the text. She'd been debating the action for a week. She could argue either side of the situation, but she had a feeling that the part of her that said "No! Don't do it!" was wrong.

No matter how she tried, she couldn't unhear Jillian saying that she wasn't as broken as she claimed. That telling herself the wrong story was messing up her life.

She'd poked at the possibility, had told herself Jillian was wrong and had, for seconds at a time, tried to live as though she was right. Because what if Jillian's theory was true? What if, without even noticing it, she'd recovered from her childhood? What if she was more normal than she'd thought? Think of all she was missing by not embracing who she really was.

I can come by now if that works.

She stared at her phone for several seconds before typing, Great. See you in a few.

She held her phone to her chest, then looked at LC, who was lounging on the sofa.

"Campbell's coming over," she told the cat. "You might want to do a quick groom."

He ignored her, as per usual.

Heather sat at the island counter and tried to plan menus for the next couple of weeks, only she couldn't focus. She ended up pacing until she heard a knock on her door.

"Hi," Campbell said, walking into her place, looking as handsome and sexy as ever.

"Hi, yourself. Thanks for coming over."

"Sure." He looked at her quizzically. "You okay?"

Before she could answer, LC flung himself at Campbell. He picked up the cat and held him. LC's loud purr filled the room.

"Big guy," Campbell said affectionately. "You look good."

"He has those new kittens to care for."

"How's that going?"

"Good. They're growing and thriving. LC is a great father."

Campbell put down the cat. "He is." His gaze returned to her. "What's up?"

She motioned to the sofa. "Everything's fine." She waited until they were both seated to say, "I'm glad you're with Nora. You look happy when you're around her."

His expression turned wary. "I don't know how to respond."

She told herself she was stronger than she knew and that Campbell had always been good to her. She owed him the truth.

"You don't have to say anything. I'll talk." She rested her hands on her lap. "My point was I know you're together and I know that it's serious. I'm happy for you."

She offered a self-deprecating smile. "I mean that. I want you to find what you're looking for." She wanted him to still be in love with her even more, but that wasn't an option. She had to be realistic and she needed to get to the point.

His expression was unreadable. "Thank you."

"You're welcome." She pressed her lips together. "You and I were together for a while. I know I was difficult, emotionally, always holding back and running whenever you wanted to go to the next level. You once said you felt like the only one in the relationship."

She looked at him. "I want you to know that wasn't true. I didn't show it and I sure didn't say it, but you mattered to me. I was in it, too, even when I couldn't articulate what I was feeling."

"Which was pretty much all the time." The words were harsh, but his tone was gentle.

She nodded. "Yes. You wanted normal things. A relationship with someone who cared. A future. I wanted that, too, but the fear was bigger."

He relaxed a little. "You thought I'd turn into Amber. You thought one day you'd wake up and I'd be a human black hole."

"Exactly."

"No one else will ever be like your mother."

"I'm starting to think that might be true," she admitted. Now came the hard part. "I want you to know that I'm sorry for what I put you through. And I want you to know that I did love you and I deeply regret what was lost."

His expression tightened. She quickly raised a hand.

"I'm not asking for anything. Like I said, you're with Nora and that's where you should be. This is about me apologizing and saying you weren't in it alone. I was there, too. I just had a really crappy way of showing it." She paused. "In a way, we're a family. I don't want to lose that. I'm sorry for how I acted, or rather, couldn't act. I wish you only the best. I really did just want you to know."

He studied her. "You've changed."

"I've had a few painful lessons. I don't want to be afraid all the time." She thought about what Jillian had said. "It's possible I've been telling myself the wrong story."

She turned her palms up. "That's what I wanted to say."

"Thanks for letting me know." He stood.

"Thanks for letting me tell you."

He stroked LC, then walked to the door. He turned back, as if he had something to say, then gave her a quick smile and left.

Heather sank back in her seat. She'd thought she might feel better, but she didn't. She felt sad and empty and a little foolish. Now that she was done, she could admit that she'd been hoping for some kind of reaction from him. Which was dumb. He'd told her more than once he was over her. She needed to start listening better.

And she would, she told herself. Starting right this second. Yes, she loved Campbell, but so what? It was time to get over him and move forward. The sooner she healed, the sooner she could find a good guy and fall in love. She wanted what her dad and Jillian had. She wanted forever. So she needed to get over herself and make that happen.

Daphne woke to a horrible cramping in her belly. She'd been deeply asleep and had to struggle to consciousness, not sure what was happening. As she tried to focus on something other than the stabbing pain, she thought groggily she must have gotten her period, but she couldn't remember it ever being that bad. She needed to—

She sat up and pressed her hand to her mouth to keep from crying out. Not only from how much it hurt but from the reality crashing in on her. She was *cramping*. She was pregnant—cramping was bad.

As she moved, she realized she was lying in a pool of blood. She could feel the warm liquid between her thighs. Tears filled her eyes as she scrambled to her feet. Blood rushed down and soaked the area rug. She shoved her bathrobe between her legs, then hurried to the bathroom.

She turned on the light and started for the toilet only to pause. Was she having a miscarriage? Nothing about this felt normal or right, but she didn't know what to do. Sitting on the toilet seemed disrespectful and wrong, but there weren't any other options.

Another cramp made her groan. She hobbled to the cabinet under the sink and pulled out a box of pads, then made her way to the toilet, pulled away her robe and sat down. Blood stained the fabric. A lot of blood. Her underwear was ruined and she'd left a dark red trail from the door.

Tears poured down her cheeks as she wrapped her arms around her midsection. Even as she told herself she was fine, she knew. The baby was gone.

Brody knocked once, then let himself in. "Daphne? Are you okay?"

His hair was mussed. He wore pj bottoms and a T-shirt and looked scared and confused. "There's blood in the bed." He glanced down at her robe. His eyes widened. "We're going to the hospital."

She brushed her cheeks. "No, I got my period."

"That's too much blood for just a period."

"In your vast experience?"

He looked at her. "It's a lot of blood."

It was. Too much. Another cramp made her moan.

"It's just bad and I wasn't prepared," she said. "Can you get me clean underwear?"

He retreated to the bedroom and returned with a pair of panties. She mopped up as best she could, put the pad in position, then stood. There was no rush of blood, nothing other than the cramping that was already easing a little. As if the hard work had been done.

Her eyes burned, but she blinked away tears. The blood was hard enough to explain—if she had to make up some reason for crying, she would totally fall apart. Brody didn't need to know the truth—not now and not like this.

"You sure you're okay?" he asked.

She nodded. "I just have to get cleaned up, then I'll take care of everything else."

"I'll change the sheets."

"The mattress pad is going to be wet, as well. There's another one in the hall closet."

Thankfully, the one they used was moisture resistant so the mattress should be all right.

She washed her legs, then pulled on yoga pants and a T-shirt. Albert and Vanessa circled her, meowing. She gave them a brief pat. The pain in her belly had dulled to an ache. Her heart felt heavy, her spirit crushed, but she forced herself to act normal as she cleaned the floor. The rug by the bed was destroyed, but thankfully, the hardwood cleaned up easily. While Brody made the bed, she put the sheets and mattress pad into the washer to soak. She would wash everything in the morning.

She returned to the bedroom to find Brody waiting for her.

"You sure you're all right? I think we should go to the hospital."

She knew there was no point. She wasn't pregnant anymore. She couldn't be. No embryo could survive what had just happened.

"I'm okay," she lied. "Just uncomfortable. I'm going downstairs for a bit. You go back to sleep."

He studied her. "You're not yourself."

"Brody, I'm fine. Just go to sleep."

She went downstairs, the cats at her heels. When she reached the family room, she curled up on the sofa with a throw. She didn't bother with lights or TV. She sat in the dark, the cats snuggled close, and gave in to tears.

After weeks of uncertainty, resisting the fact that she was pregnant, telling herself it was a bad time for a baby, the choice had been taken from her. She wasn't pregnant anymore and there was nothing she could do to change that.

"I'm sorry," Dr. Stone said, her voice sympathetic. "Based on your hormone level and my exam, you were pregnant."

The information wasn't news, but Daphne started to cry, anyway—something she'd been doing steadily for the past thirty-six hours.

"Sorry," she said, trying to get control. "I'm really emotional lately."

"Not a surprise. Your body is dealing with a lot, and the elevated hormone levels don't help. How's the cramping?"

"Pretty much gone. Now there's just the bleeding, which is better."

The fifty-something-year-old doctor helped her into a sitting position. Daphne adjusted the cotton exam robe.

"Take it easy for a few days," her doctor advised. "Wait a couple of weeks before resuming sex. You're late for your birth control shot. I would suggest getting one now. By the time it's effective you'll be physically ready for sex." She glanced at Daphne. "It may take a bit longer emotionally."

Not a problem. She and Brody still weren't having sex.

"Wait four months before trying again," the doctor continued. "At your age—"

Daphne cut her off with a groan. "Please don't say *geriatric pregnancy*."

Dr. Stone laughed. "You've been doing some reading."

"Actually, a friend mentioned it to me. I'm only thirty-five. Apparently, that's ancient in the childbearing world."

"It would be easier if you were twenty-two."

"There's no way I was ready to have a baby at twenty-two."

"Mother Nature doesn't care about that." Dr. Stone put

down her tablet. "I'm sorry, Daphne. Losing a child is difficult. The fact that it was so early in your pregnancy doesn't make it any easier. You're going to feel a lot of emotions. That's normal. Give yourself a break."

"I will."

When Daphne got back to work, she quickly packed up her briefcase.

"I'm glad you're taking a few days off," Irena said. "You've been working crazy hours lately."

"I haven't been sleeping well." Daphne did her best to smile. "And you're right. I've been working too much."

Something she'd realized the night she miscarried. She'd been pushing herself too hard for too long. She'd arranged for a few days away from the office and had made reservations for herself at Salish Lodge. It was only about forty minutes away, but right now she needed time to think, not distance. But she did have to tell her husband she would be gone.

When she got home, she packed for the hotel, then waited for Brody to get home. He walked into the kitchen a little after five.

"You're home early," he said. His body was tense, his expression concerned. "Are you all right?"

She studied his familiar face, wondering how much had been lost. They'd been so in love, so good together. Now she didn't know what they were.

"I saw my gynecologist today. She said I'm doing well and not to worry." Which was both the truth and an omission, but now wasn't the time to tell him about the baby.

He relaxed. "That's good to hear."

"I'm going away for a few days. Just to a local hotel. I'll be back before we have the kids on Sunday. I need time to think and figure out what's been going on between us. Can you take care of the cats or should I take them to Heather's?"

He stared at her in disbelief. "You're leaving me? Just like that?"

Exhaustion tugged at her. She wasn't going to cry—there weren't any tears left—but she wasn't sure she could get through the conversation they obviously needed to have.

"I'm not leaving. I just need to be alone to think."

"About leaving. You're giving up?" His fear and worry morphed to something else. "Or are you going away with him?"

"Oh, Brody. It was never that." The hopelessness of being unable to convince him settled on her. "I know you can't believe me, but I've never slept with him and never wanted to. I'm sorry I hurt you. I'm sorry I hurt us. I need some time alone. I need to rest and think. That's what I'm doing and I hope you can understand."

He didn't speak.

She sighed. "I'll take the cats to Heather."

"You don't have to move the damned cats. I can take care of them. The cats are fine. It's us I'm worried about. I want to say I'm losing you but part of me says you're already gone. Are you?"

"I'm not. I love you."

"If you loved me, you wouldn't leave."

There was an edge to his voice. Worry, she thought. Pain and fear. Later, she would feel those emotions, too, but right now there was nothing.

"I'm sorry," she told him. "For hurting you over and over again. It was never my intention. But here you are, feeling it, anyway."

"Don't go."

"I have to. I'll be back Sunday."

She started for the garage. She half expected him to come after her, to demand that she stay, but he didn't.

She drove directly to Salish Lodge. Once she'd checked in,

she walked to her suite. The sun had set so she couldn't see the view, but she went out to the balcony overlooking the Snoqualmie River, anyway. She could hear the falls and feel the cool breeze on her face. She sat quietly in the dark until she began to shiver from the cold.

Back in her room, she unpacked, then ordered a light dinner from room service. While she waited, she opened her laptop and typed, *What is an emotional affair?*

Her screen filled with articles. She read the first one. The beginning of the second paragraph made her pause.

The three main elements of an emotional affair are exchanging personal information, keeping the relationship a secret from your significant other and being sexually attracted to the other person. An emotional affair exists without physical intimacy but it can be just as destructive as a physical affair.

Daphne reread the words a second time, then a third. Her mouth went dry, her heart began pounding. She thought of Brody's accusations. She thought about Miguel thinking they were going somewhere. She thought about her denials and the pain she and Brody had suffered, then she covered her face with her hands.

"Dear God, what have I done?"

twenty-four

"I didn't like the part with the boy," Ella said, dipping a French fry into ketchup. "He was nice, but it should have just been a story about the sisters."

"No love interest for you?" Heather asked, her voice teasing.

Ella flushed. "It's fine to have a boyfriend, just not in a movie about sisters."

"Boys can be mean," Layla said firmly. "A boy at school always pulls my hair and trips me. Mommy had to talk to the principal, and if he does it again he has to go to an anti-bullying workshop."

Seated in a busy Red Robin on a Friday night, Heather wasn't sure what to do with all the information being thrown at her.

The afternoon had started out simply. Wanting to atone for her bad behavior, she'd offered the girls a sleepover in addition to going to the "sister movie" they'd wanted to see. They'd jumped at the chance. Jillian had texted her that she and Fletcher were excited to have an evening for themselves.

She'd offered her sisters the option of a hotel with adjoining rooms—one for them, one for her, but the girls had wanted to stay with her.

You have a big bed. We can all sleep in it together.

Ella's text had been clear enough, with Heather not sure she was ready to share her bed with two preteens. Jillian had followed with a phone call.

"Let me know if it's too much. It's kind of a thing. When they have sleepovers, everyone fits in one bed."

"Sounds great," Heather had lied. Yes, the concept made her uncomfortable, but the sleepover wasn't about her. It was about being there for her sisters. She'd hurt them and even though the wound would heal, they would always remember what she'd done. It was up to her to prove she could be trusted.

So she'd picked them up at two, then brought them to meet her new batch of kittens. The little fur balls were nearly four weeks now, with open eyes and inquisitive natures. They'd fed them, then headed to the movies with burgers to follow.

"There are anti-bullying workshops for kids your age?" Heather asked.

Layla nodded. "I went to one on how to deal with bullying. I learned about reframing the situation and standing up for myself."

"Does the boy scare you or annoy you?"

Layla considered the question. "Mostly annoy."

Heather thought about how in her day, everyone would have assumed he had a crush on Layla and let it go. Amusing for the adults, but leaving Layla being tormented. She supposed it was hard to know the right thing to do.

"How's middle school?" she asked Ella.

"Good. I have my friends from before plus new ones. I'm doing really well in math." Her smile widened. "If I keep up my grades, next semester I'll move into the accelerated class. It's on the STEM track."

"Right," Heather said slowly, trying to decipher the letters. "Science, technology, engineering and math."

Ella nodded. "I'm not that into engineering, but I want to study technology and math for sure. Maybe science, too."

"Well, I certainly didn't inherit those talents," she said with a laugh.

They debated dessert, but agreed they were too full. "We can have ice cream at home later," Heather told them.

At her condo they greeted LC and had a long, happy play session with the kittens before piling on the sofa to watch more movies. Her sisters wanted a *Despicable Me* marathon because the movie was about three sisters and finding family. They were still surprisingly awake at nine, which was, according to Jillian, their regular bedtime.

Heather sent a quick text saying all was well, then started *Despicable Me 2*. Close to ten, the girls started getting sleepy. She left them watching the movie while she fed the kittens one last time. LC helped with cleanup. By the time the kittens were settled for the night, her sisters were zonked on the sofa.

"I thought we were going to be awake the whole, whole night," she said softly, shaking each of them. "Come on, time to brush your teeth and get into bed."

"What about the movie?" Layla asked over a big yawn.

"We can watch it from bed."

"You have a TV in your bedroom?" Ella was instantly awake. "Mom and Dad won't let me."

"You'll have to wait until you're living on your own."

"That's a long time away."

"It'll be here before you know it."

She ushered them into her bathroom. They took turns

washing their faces and brushing their teeth. She did the same, then pulled on yoga pants and a T-shirt. LC monitored from the tub surround.

Heather collected the TV remote and put it on her nightstand, then made sure her phone was close by and charging. She was about to climb into bed when Layla grabbed her hand.

"We have to say prayers."

Oh. Heather couldn't remember ever saying prayers before bed. She hadn't been raised with religion. But she dutifully sank to her knees, the girls flanking her.

"How do we do this?" she asked.

"We each take a turn," Ella told her. "We give thanks for what we have and ask for blessings for other people." She whispered conspiratorially. "It's not a time to ask for stuff for ourselves. Nighttime prayers aren't a visit to God's mall."

"Good to know."

Layla folded her hands and closed her eyes. "Dear God, thank You for my family and for school. Today was a really good day. Please keep Mommy and Daddy safe and keep Mommy healthy." She opened one eye and smiled at Heather, then closed her eye again. "Thank You for our sister, Heather. We love her very much. Oh, and please bless Bella and Stella and tell them we'll be home in the morning."

Ella went next, her words similar to her sister's with extra thanks for her math ability.

"It's your turn," Ella whispered.

Heather flushed. She felt uncomfortable and oddly exposed, which made no sense. If God existed, then He would probably be happy to hear from her. If He didn't, then what did the prayer matter?

"Dear God, thank You for this good day and for my family." She paused as her throat tightened with unexpected emotion. "Thank You for bringing my sisters into my life. They're a

322

true joy to me and I love them. Please keep my dad and Jillian safe and healthy. Oh, and ah, bless my mother."

That last bit wasn't very heartfelt, but seemed right.

"Amen," Layla and Ella said together.

"Amen."

They stood. Heather pulled back the covers, then got into the king-size bed. Her sisters settled on either side of her. LC surprised her by joining them. She expected him to curl up next to one of the girls, but he actually settled on her lap. Of course his back was to her and when she patted him, he gave her full-on stink eye as if warning her not to push it, but he stayed where he was.

Heather rewound the movie until they found a spot they agreed they had all been watching. Not ten minutes later her sisters were fast asleep. She kept the movie going, in case one of them woke up. By ten-thirty, it was obvious they were out for the night.

She turned off the TV and slid down in the bed. LC protested, but stayed on top of her. She'd left the light on in the master bath so her sisters wouldn't wake up in the dark and not know where they were.

Having two bodies pressed against her was unfamiliar enough to keep her from getting sleepy. She'd always preferred to sleep alone. Even when she and Campbell had been together, she'd rarely spent the night. And him staying here hadn't been an option.

Remembering how she'd practically pushed him out into the night after they'd made love caused her to flinch. She'd been a horrible girlfriend. Why had the man put up with her?

Not a question she could answer, but he had been there, no matter what. Now she could only hope Nora appreciated what a great guy she was getting.

Layla rolled over in her sleep and rested her head on Heather's shoulder. The nine-year-old was small and defenseless. And Ella wasn't much bigger. The world was dangerous—they shouldn't have to navigate it alone. Yes, they had their parents, but Fletcher was in his fifties and Jillian's cancer could get bad at any time.

What if the worst happened? Would that other family have room for two more kids? Plus, wouldn't the parents already be busy? Would they help the girls get over the devastating loss of their parents? Would they make sure they brushed their teeth and prayed every night?

She told herself she was catastrophizing. Nothing bad was going to happen. And she was in no position to care for her sisters. She could be the backup parent or something, check in from time to time.

Without wanting to, she remembered how Layla had looked at her when she'd gone to meet her at her school after breaking her heart. She'd been so sad, so wary. She hadn't known she couldn't trust Heather, hadn't known someone she loved could be so careless with her feelings.

Heather's cheeks burned with shame. She'd been selfish—just like her mother. Jillian had made the point that parenting was supposed to be about thinking of your children. That was why she'd wanted certainty about their future. Heather was her age, healthy, with financial resources. At the time, Jillian had assumed Heather cared about her daughters, only she'd proved her stepmother wrong.

She lay in the dark, trying to tell herself everything would work out. That her sisters would be fine, but she couldn't know for sure. Life often took unexpected turns. Once again, her mind turned to how Layla had responded to her that day. She contrasted that with how her sister was with her now. She'd been forgiven so easily—did she deserve that?

Waves of emotions crashed over her. There was so much feeling and nowhere to put it. She was upset but wasn't sure why. She was cold and hot at once and her chest was so tight.

LC, still on her belly, shifted to his side. She felt the rumble of his purr. She was trapped by the three of them, but somehow that was okay. She pulled an arm out from under the covers and lightly petted him. He rubbed his cheek against her hand.

"I won't expect this in the morning," she murmured. "I know it's a onetime thing."

She relaxed back on the bed, accepting she wouldn't get much sleep, but that was okay. She was with her sisters and she knew they would always have each other's back.

"I'm nervous," Tori admitted as they walked toward Campbell's condo.

"Why? You've eaten dinner before."

She rolled her eyes. "Very funny."

Grant smiled, then leaned in and kissed her. She jumped back.

"You can't do that. If Campbell sees you kissing me, he'll know something's different."

"You think?" Grant teased. "He's not very observant."

"He'll notice kissing."

He stopped on the sidewalk and faced her. "I like the kissing."

Butterflies danced in her belly. "Me, too."

His mouth curved into a smile. "And the other stuff."

"Yeah, that's pretty good."

They stared at each other for several seconds. Tension crackled between them. Ever since they'd started doing the *other stuff* a week ago, life had been amazing. Their chemistry was off the charts, their laughter was more frequent, the sun was brighter and she was happier.

Grant was a god in bed. She figured the incredible frequency would calm down, but right now she was enjoying everything they were doing. If she was risking her heart because she was already in love with him, then that was on her. Later, when the newness had worn off, she would be sensible. But for now, she was all in.

He sighed heavily. "I'll behave."

"Thank you."

They knocked on the front door.

"Hi," Nora said with a smile that didn't quite reach her eyes. "Come on in. Campbell will say he's cooking, but really he's reheating dinner from a restaurant."

"Sounds like cooking to me," Grant said, lightly kissing Nora's cheek. He lowered his voice. "I don't like to judge."

Tori shook her head. "Ignore him. He thinks that qualifies as cooking because we take turns with meals while we're living together. Anything that keeps him from standing in front of the stove is a win for him."

"That's true," he said easily.

Tori hugged Nora. "You okay?"

Nora nodded a little too enthusiastically. "Great." She led the way into the kitchen. "They're here. I ratted you out about the meal."

Campbell was setting appetizers on a plate. He grinned. "As long as it tastes good, right?"

He hugged his brother, then Tori. "What would you like? Beer? Wine? Nora brought over a nice Merlot for dinner. We can open it now."

Nora looked at Tori. "Or Cosmos if you'd like."

"That sounds good."

"I'll take a beer," Grant said.

He and Campbell got their drinks and went into the family room. Nora collected vodka, limes, Cointreau and cranberry juice. She moved easily around his kitchen. No doubt because she spent a lot of time here. But something was off—Tori was sure of it. Normally, Nora sparkled but tonight there was a lot less bubble in her step.

"How's work?" she asked.

Nora juiced two limes into a martini shaker. "Good. Busy. We're training three new hires."

Tori glanced toward the family room where Grant and Campbell were talking, then looked back at Nora.

"Are you all right? You seem quiet."

"Fine." Nora smiled tightly as she measured out the rest of the ingredients. "My roommate wants to move out when our lease ends. I don't know if I should keep the apartment myself or get another roommate or move somewhere smaller."

Tori's gaze snapped back to Campbell. Was moving in with him an option? Were they that far along in their relationship? She couldn't help hoping things would work out between him and Heather. Not that she wanted Nora to be hurt.

"Moving sucks," Tori said. "Trust me, I just did it. It's stressful and unsettling." She paused. "Am I whining?"

Nora's smile turned genuine. "Just telling the truth. What you went through was bad. An unexpected disaster is worse than a planned move. You lost so much. How's the rental working out?"

Tori deliberately kept her attention on her friend. "Good. You saw the house. It's huge, so there's plenty of room. Grant and I already had a nice rhythm with the dogs, so that helped."

Nora added ice to the martini shaker, put on the lid and shook it for several seconds. As she poured the pink drinks she said, "I know this will sound old-fashioned or possibly sexist, but I don't think I would be comfortable living with a man I wasn't in a relationship with."

"I get it. With anyone but Grant, I couldn't do it." She gave what she hoped was a casual laugh. "But you know us. We're the non-couple friends. It's what we do."

"I still think you'd be good together."

"That will never happen," Tori lied.

"Too bad."

They went into the family room. Grant was in one of the chairs. Tori took the other one while Nora sat on the sofa with Campbell.

"We were talking sports," Grant told Tori. "You didn't miss anything."

"But I love sports."

"Since when?"

She laughed.

Campbell pointed at his brother. "I nearly forgot. I have someone for you."

Tori stiffened and just as quickly told herself to relax and act normal.

"Who is she?" she asked, trying to sound interested and happy. "You know how picky Grant is."

"I am picky," he said easily. "It takes a lot to get me interested."

She refused to look at him even as she felt a little *ping* of happiness.

"You should be grateful if anyone's interested," Campbell told his brother. "Anyway, Rachel is a pilot. Pretty, funny, smart. Divorced a few months ago. She's ready to start dating and I thought of you."

Tori gripped her glass so tightly, she thought it might snap in two. "She sounds amazing."

Grant leaned back. "Thanks, Campbell, but I'm going to pass. I'm not ready to get back in the dating pool."

"You were never in it to begin with," his brother complained. "Why don't you want to go?"

"Not the right time."

Nora jumped to her feet. "We forgot the appetizers."

"I'll get them." Campbell rose. "Sit. Talk."

"I'm fine."

They stared at each other.

"I'll get them," Campbell repeated, his voice gentle.

Nora sank back on the sofa. An awkward silence filled the room.

Tori could tell something was up. While part of her hoped they would work it out, part of her didn't. Because if Campbell was single, maybe Heather would have a chance.

twenty-five

Daphne slept most of the first twenty-four hours she was at the hotel. Once she felt more rested, she went for long walks, as much to clear her head as to get exercise. Sadness weighed her down but she didn't try to process her feelings. It was too soon and there was still so much more she had to deal with. Everything about her life felt as if it was in flux. Her job, her relationship with Brody, what she wanted for herself. The only thing she knew was that she'd lost the baby.

Dr. Stone had said miscarriages weren't uncommon and the reading Daphne had done on the internet had supported the statement. But what her head could understand wasn't what her heart was willing to accept. She hadn't wanted to be pregnant but now that the baby was gone, she felt bereft and more alone than ever before.

She debated calling Heather or Tori, but wanted to tell them in person. No one else knew. She hadn't wanted to tell her parents she was pregnant before Brody and that had never happened. So she had nowhere to turn for support.

Normally, she would have looked to Brody, but she couldn't. Not yet. As for telling him what had happened—she debated what to do. Explaining about the baby after the fact seemed cruel. Yet, he was her husband and it seemed wrong to keep the truth from him.

She was also wrestling with the realization that she'd had an affair. Not with sex, but the lunches with Miguel, the laughter, the complaining about her marriage, all that had been wrong. She'd confided in him, kept their meetings a secret and yes, been attracted to him. His bold assumptions had made her uncomfortable and she'd gotten self-righteous, but had that been genuine, or had she reacted out of guilt as much as shock? Miguel's conclusions hadn't come from no-where. She'd been right there, playing along.

She'd risked her marriage for something that didn't matter. Just as awful, she'd seen a side of herself she didn't like. She wasn't a cheater. And yet, she'd crossed a line that she didn't know how to uncross.

She returned from her second walk of the day about four-thirty. Her first thought was she should call Brody. She missed him so much. But speaking to him meant figuring out what to say and she had no idea what that would be.

Her stomach grumbled. She hadn't eaten since breakfast. She should go down to the restaurant or at least order in some-thing, but she couldn't decide what. Food was important—she was still healing. The bleeding had nearly stopped, but her body wouldn't return to normal for a couple of weeks. She had to take care of herself and that included eating.

"Later," she said, tossing the room service menu onto the

dresser. She'd just reached for the TV remote control when someone knocked on the door.

Brody stood in the hallway. When she'd arrived, she'd texted him her room number, but she'd never expected him to show up. Yet, there he was, looking like he hadn't slept. There were dark circles under his eyes and his mouth turned down at the corners.

"I know I should give you time, but I can't," he said, stepping into the room. "Not anymore." His dark gaze met hers. "Is he here?"

The raw pain in his voice cut her nearly as deeply as the words. Regret clutched her. Regret and sorrow and a thousand other emotions she didn't want to name. She'd missed him but how did that matter when she'd so obviously hurt him?

"No one's here but me," she told him. "I don't have lunch with Miguel anymore and I never saw him beyond work or our lunches."

"Then why did you leave me?"

The starkness of the question clawed at her. She'd done this, she told herself. She was to blame. She fought against tears as she realized it was time to tell her husband the truth. All of it.

She motioned to the sofa, then pulled up the desk chair so she could face him.

"I'm going to say a lot of things," she began. "I want you to let me finish before you ask questions, and I want you to consider the possibility that I'm telling the truth. You'll want to think I'm lying and I get that, but please be open to the possibility that what I'm saying is what happened."

He hesitated before nodding. "I'll listen."

Which wasn't the same as believing, but it was a start.

"You were right about it not being the right time for us to have a baby," she began. "There were too many changes. Having your kids more, me making partner. We haven't been married that long and we've had a lot of stressors."

She drew in a breath. "But I did want a baby and while I understand why you said 'Let's wait,' it felt like you were saying no. Like you'd never wanted a baby with me in the first place. It felt like you'd changed the rules and I got so angry."

"That wasn't what I meant. You know I want a baby with you."

She nodded. "I do know that. I wasn't thinking, I was reacting."

"And hiding. When things get tough, you retreat into your work."

"I know. It's my safe space."

He relaxed a little, as if the concession eased some of his concern. "I interrupted. Sorry. Please go on."

She would rather not, she thought. Because now came the hard part.

"Miguel was a friend," she said quietly. "He was easy to talk to and he made me laugh."

Brody stiffened but didn't speak.

"It really was just lunch." She swallowed. "But that doesn't mean it wasn't an emotional affair."

She looked away as she tried not to cry. "I didn't know at the time. I was so self-righteous because nothing ever happened, but now, looking back, I'm horrified. That's not how I see myself at all, but it still happened."

Brody watched her without giving anything away.

"I would never cheat on you. I believe that down to my bones, but Miguel and I were involved in a way I never realized. I hurt you. I hurt us. I'm mortified that I was so stupid and smug. I told myself you were wrong, that you were making up your outrage because you were trying to distract me from the fact that you didn't want a baby. I made you the bad guy when it was me all along."

Tears slipped down her cheeks. She brushed them away impatiently. "I'm so sorry. I was careless with what matters most to me. I lied to you and to myself and now I don't know where we are in our relationship and it's all my fault."

"It's not just you," Brody told her, his voice thick with sadness. "I was angry and I shut down. Instead of asking, I accused you."

"Rightly so. I was awful. I can't believe I didn't see what I was doing." She swallowed a sob. "Is it over? Did I destroy our marriage?"

"No. We couldn't move forward while you refused to see what was happening. I got to where I couldn't trust what I was feeling. I didn't know what to think."

"I'm so sorry."

"I know. Now we can start moving forward."

She hoped he believed that. "I don't want to lose you. I love you."

"Then why did you leave me?"

"I never slept with Miguel. I never touched him or kissed him."

He frowned. "We've been over this."

"Do you believe me?"

"That you never had sex?" He paused. "Yes."

She collected a box of tissues from the bathroom, then sat back down. After wiping her face and blowing her nose, she looked at him.

"I was pregnant."

His eyes widened and he half rose from the sofa before sinking back down. "I don't understand." His gaze dropped to her belly. "The blood. You didn't get your period."

The tears returned, falling faster now. "No. I miscarried our baby."

He crossed to her and pulled her to her feet, then wrapped his strong arms around her. She clung to him and released the pain and sadness she'd been holding inside. Sobs shook her body until she had trouble catching her breath. All she'd been through—the fear of what the pregnancy would mean, the fear of him leaving her and her having to raise their child on her own, the relief when she'd come up with a plan, the horror of realizing the baby was gone. Waves of emotions washed over her and she cried until there was nothing left.

And still he held her, so strong and steady. He murmured that they would get through this, that he was here and would always be here. When the tears had subsided, he pulled her down next to him on the sofa. She snuggled into him. He put his arm around her shoulders.

"Tell me," he said softly.

She explained about the first pregnancy test and how relieved she'd been it was negative. "You and I were barely speaking. You thought I was sleeping with Miguel. If I'd told you then, you would have thought it was his."

"You're right." He kissed her head.

"I felt tired and sick so I took another test. That one came back positive. I didn't know what to do."

"I'm sorry you had to go through that on your own."

"Me, too, but it's my fault. If there'd never been an issue with Miguel, I would have told you right away." She looked up at him. "It was so awful to think about what was going to happen when you found out. I didn't want to go through my pregnancy with you thinking I wasn't carrying your baby."

She sniffed. "But because I'm thirty-five, I'd probably have to have amniocentesis, which means we could determine paternity at that point. That made me feel better. I knew you wouldn't be mad for as long. So I was waiting until close to when I'd get the test to tell you."

She hung her head. "Then I lost it."

"Tell me what the doctor said."

"That there could be a dozen reasons. I'm healthy and there's no reason to think my next pregnancy won't go to term."

"But you have to recover."

"It'll take a couple of weeks for things to get back to normal." At least physically. She had a feeling her mental state was going to take a little longer.

"You must have felt so alone," he said. "I wish you'd told me."

She sniffed. "Would that have gone well?"

"Probably not." He lifted her chin. "We both messed up. I'm sorry for my part in it. I should have talked to you more."

"No, it was me. I was such a fool. The whole Miguel thing was a disaster. What was I thinking? I never wanted to hurt you."

"I know."

His steady gaze told her he was telling her the truth. That despite everything, he believed her, loved her and wasn't about to let her go.

"I love you, Brody. I'm sorry for what I did. I don't want to lose you."

"Not a chance."

She hoped he meant that. "I'm committed to us," she told him. "Heart and soul."

"Me, too." He kissed her. "When you're healed, let's come up with a plan on the baby front. We need to figure out when we're going to make that happen."

"I'd like that." She shifted to her knees, facing him. "And I'd like to come home, if that's okay."

"It's more than okay." He glanced at his watch. "Although it's way past time to check out, so we're kind of stuck with the room for a while. Want to grab dinner first? Then drive home?"

She smiled. "That would be nice. I haven't been eating much."

They stood. She wrapped her arms around him. There was still so much to talk about and understand, but at least they'd made a start. Hopefully, this step would be followed by others and eventually they would find their way to a place even better than before.

★ ★ ★

Tori studied the addresses on the street, not sure if she'd made a wrong turn. Finding new places had never been her thing, and her trusty GPS was not playing nice today.

"Turn right at the next intersection, then you will have arrived at your destination."

"You are so lying," she murmured, but dutifully did as the slightly superior voice told her.

"Oh, wait. There it is. Sorry for not trusting you."

She parked in front of the large apartment building and walked to the main entrance. She scanned the listings for Nora's last name, then buzzed to be let in.

"Hello?" The slightly wobbly voice didn't sound anything like her friend.

"Nora? It's Tori."

"Thanks for coming. Take the elevator to the third floor and turn right. I'm at the end."

Tori did as instructed and found herself walking down a nice open corridor. The building was in Issaquah, at the base of Cougar Mountain, an area with plenty of trees and walking trails.

The last door opened and Nora stepped into the hallway. Tori nearly stumbled in surprise. The normally perky, smiling, well-dressed person she knew had been replaced with an obviously miserable duplicate. Nora's hair needed washing, her skin was blotchy and her eyes swollen from what Tori would guess was way too much crying. Her T-shirt was stained and her sweatpants were far too big.

"What happened?" Tori asked as she approached. "Are you all right? Have you been sick?"

Nora ushered her into an open living, kitchen and dining room. Huge windows on two sides displayed the beauty of the changing leaves. Light spilled onto the hardwood floors.

The furniture looked attractive and comfortable, the kitchen pristine. Only Nora was a mess.

She sank onto the sofa and covered her face with her hands. "Give me a second. I thought I'd do better. It's just seeing you..."

She began crying. Tori sat close by, her hand hovering as she wondered if it was okay to hug the other woman or if she should keep her distance.

Nora grabbed several tissues from a box. She wiped her face and blew her nose, then cleared her throat. She offered Tori a shaky smile.

"All better."

"What's going on? You're scaring me."

Nora looked confused. "He didn't tell you? Campbell broke up with me."

Tori felt her eyes widen. "When? I haven't heard anything." Grant hadn't even hinted, which meant he probably didn't know. He wouldn't keep something big from her when they were together every second outside work.

"Two days ago." Nora waved her hand. "It's been coming on for a while. I always knew he wasn't as in love with me as I was with him, but he's such a great guy, I was willing to wait."

Tears leaked out. She brushed them away. "A few weeks ago my roommate told me she was moving out. I can afford it, but I don't like living alone. I was talking to Campbell about what to do."

She bit her lower lip, then looked at Tori. "I did that thing I always do. I hinted at what I wanted and I wasn't very subtle."

"You wanted to move in with Campbell."

"Yes." Her voice cracked. "I thought we would take things to the next level. He said he wasn't ready for that kind of a commitment. He said he wasn't sure where he saw us going."

Tori flinched in sympathy. "Not what you wanted to hear."

"No. I started worrying that he wasn't in love with me at all. That I'd been fooling myself."

Tori instinctively wanted to say that of course Campbell loved her, but the breakup told a different story.

"Things got tense." Nora tried to smile. "As you saw."

"You didn't seem to be yourself."

"I think I already knew what was coming. I just thought he was the one."

Tori hugged her. "I'm sorry. This sucks. We love having you around. You fit in."

Which was true. She felt awful for Nora and was determined not to be the least bit hopeful about Heather until she left the building.

"I wanted to thank you for always being so nice to me," Nora said, drawing back. "You always made me feel welcome, part of something special. It's hard to be the new person when all the relationships are so well established."

She wiped her face with the tissue. "I have friends, of course. Good friends. But it's not like what you guys have. You're a family."

Tori's heart began to hurt. "Don't talk like we'll never see each other again. We can stay friends."

"No, we can't. I was only ever a part of things because I was with Campbell. Now that we've broken up, things will never be the same. I'll just be the girl he used to date. You saw it happen with Heather. You try to have her fit in, but she doesn't. The brothers are the glue. They're the reason it all works. The women are disposable."

She touched Tori's arm. "I'm sorry. That came out wrong. I'm not talking about you. Grant would never want you to leave. But Campbell's done with me. It was never my family, it was his." She cleared her throat. "Anyway, I just wanted to say thank you for being so kind."

"Of course," Tori said, doing her best to keep speaking despite the loud buzzing in her head. Nora had just said something important and in a second or two its meaning would crash into her, but for now, she had to stay focused on the conversation.

"How can I help?" Tori asked. "Do you need ice cream?"

Nora's smile turned genuine. "You're so sweet. Thanks, but I'm good. I won't keep you. I just wanted to tell you how much I appreciate your kindness."

They stood, hugged, then Nora walked her to the door. Tori came to a stop halfway to the elevator.

Nora had been with Campbell so she'd become a part of the group. Campbell broke up with Nora, so she was out. Heather had broken up with Campbell and she'd stopped being a part of things, as well. If Daphne and Brody couldn't fix things, if they split up, then there wouldn't be any more Daphne. The brothers would go on without any of them.

She was only a part of the larger group because of Grant. They'd been the non-couple friends, only they weren't that anymore. They were lovers. But he didn't want anything serious. He wasn't in love with her. What happened when he was done? What happened to them and to her? She would always have Daphne and Heather, but not Campbell and Brody, and not Grant!

Her stomach flipped. By having sex with Grant, she was putting their amazing relationship on the line. If it ended badly, he wouldn't be her friend anymore. She'd lose their laughter, the late-night talks, the routine that meant the world to her. By changing the rules, they'd taken something safe and wonderful and risked it all.

She continued toward the elevator and rode it to the main floor. When she reached her car, she told herself she was overreacting. Everything would be fine. Only she knew she was lying.

She was in love with Grant. When he ended things with her, she would be destroyed. And then he would figure out she'd been in love with him all along and then he would be horrified and he would break up with her and she would have nothing.

Obviously, falling out of love with him was the best solution. But it wasn't as if she could flip a stop-loving-Grant switch. Maybe the solution was to stop having sex with him now, before she got too entangled in how much she loved him. Maybe they should go back to just being non-couple friends.

That had always worked for them. She'd liked being non-couple friends. She liked being his sexy, live-in girlfriend more, but her emotional well-being was at stake and sacrifices had to be made.

Whatever she decided, she had to do it fast—before he figured out about the whole love thing. Because she couldn't possibly survive losing Grant and half her family, all at the same time.

twenty-six

"You going to be all right?" Brody asked, his voice filled with concern.

Daphne shrugged on her coat. "I have to tell them eventually. I just want to get it over with."

"I should be with you."

She smiled. "I love you, but you couldn't handle all the crying. Plus, you need to stay with the kids."

Worry lingered in his eyes. "You're already dealing with enough. I want to help."

She and Brody might have gotten sideways in their relationship but since she'd admitted her emotional affair and had told him about the baby, they'd found their way back to each other. The first night he'd been home, he'd held her until dawn. She wasn't sure if he'd slept, but back in his arms, she'd finally been able to relax and get the rest she needed. He'd offered to go with her when she next saw her gynecologist. He'd insisted on cooking dinner every night. He was there for her. When she'd mentioned they couldn't make love for at least another week, he already knew. He'd looked up miscarriages online and understood how her body had to heal.

"You're a good man, but trust me," she said with a smile. "Stay where it's safe. I won't be late."

She was meeting Heather and Tori at Heather's place. Jillian had convinced Heather to have a joint birthday party on Saturday, so there was food to prepare and Tori had mentioned filling a piñata. While Daphne helped, she'd tell them about the baby.

He carried her Crock-Pot to the car, then kissed her. She waved as she drove away. She wasn't looking forward to the conversation, but she knew her friends would be supportive. And later, she would go home to the good man she'd married.

She pulled into a visitor spot. Seconds later Tori parked next to her. While Daphne took out the slow cooker, Tori pulled several shopping bags and a huge piñata from her trunk.

"I think I overbought," Tori admitted. "I have four large bags of candy and tons of party favors and little toys from that party place in Bothell." She lifted one of the bags. "This one has the ingredients for the chili and lime-roasted cashews."

Daphne slung one of the shopping bags over her shoulder. "Can the piñata support all that weight?"

"I guess we'll find out."

Heather greeted them at the door, LC at her heels. The cat meowed and rubbed against them.

"How much did you buy?" Heather asked Tori as she took bags from her.

"A lot."

Tori carried the piñata into the dining room while Daphne set the slow cooker on the counter. Heather eyed the Crock-Pot.

"You think it'll work?"

Daphne smiled. "I know it will. Make the sauce in the morning. You already have the frozen meatballs, right?"

Heather nodded. "Two bags of them. I got the brand you said."

"When you get to your dad's place, dump the meatballs in the slow cooker, add the sauce and give it a good stir. Put it on high. Two and a half hours later, they'll be done. Oh, and stir every thirty minutes or so." She patted the slow cooker. "They taste great and you can plug this in anywhere."

Tori leaned against the counter. "I mean this with love, Heather, but you aren't the birthday party type. Are you sure about this?"

Heather grimaced. "I'm nervous," she admitted. "When Jillian first suggested a joint celebration, I thought it was a bad idea, but I guess I've changed. I'm excited to meet Jillian's friends. Ella and Layla each invited someone, too, so that will be good."

She wrinkled her nose. "My dad insisted I invite my mom, so I worry about her legendary ability to ruin an event."

Daphne knew that to be true. "Brody and I will keep an eye on Amber. You enjoy the party."

"I'll help," Tori said brightly. "I love a challenge."

"Thank you." Heather drew in a breath. "I refuse to let my mom ruin the day."

"She won't." Daphne tapped the list Heather had made. "Now let's get cooking."

In addition to the cashews, they were going to make Parmesan Pesto Pinwheels and several dips.

"Is there any wine?" Tori asked.

"Sure. Red or white?"

"White, if you have it."

Heather glanced at Daphne. "I have several flavored waters or possibly some sparkling apple juice."

Daphne hesitated. "I wasn't sure when to say something. Or how. So I guess now works."

Heather and Tori looked at each other. Tori touched her arm.

"Is something wrong?"

"I lost the baby."

She managed to speak the words without crying, so yay her. Unfortunately, both her friends rushed toward her, engulfing her in a warm group hug that had her throat tightening and tears threatening.

"When?" Heather asked. "Oh, Daphne, I'm so sorry."

"Are you okay?" Tori stepped back to study her. "You look okay. How do you feel?"

"Sad. Physically better, but sad."

"Wait." Heather pointed to the family room. "Let's go sit down. I'll get the wine. We'll talk, then we'll cook."

Daphne settled on the sofa. LC immediately jumped up to join her. She petted him while Heather opened a bottle of Sauvignon Blanc. Tori opened a can of cashews and dumped them into a bowl, then got crackers from the pantry.

"Don't we need the nuts for tomorrow?" Daphne asked.

"I bought six cans. I don't think we'll miss one."

Once seated, Daphne sipped the wine, then set down her glass.

"I woke up cramping and bleeding," she said. "I didn't have any warning. The bleeding was heavy, so I knew I'd lost the baby."

She tried to speak without reliving the horror of the blood and pain that night.

"My doctor confirmed I'd miscarried. It's more common than I'd realized."

Heather studied her. "Does Brody know?"

"I told him a few days later." She didn't mention how she'd left and gone to a hotel. The information would make her friends worry about her marriage and there was no reason for that. Not anymore.

"He was devastated. Not only that I'd lost a baby, but that I'd been pregnant and hadn't told him."

"Because of the whole Miguel thing," Tori said.

Ah, that. "Yes, well, that's the other thing." Daphne stared at her lap, then looked at her friends. "You were both right when you said I'd had an emotional affair. I didn't want to believe it, but that's exactly what happened. I realized it after I lost the baby."

Tears threatened again. She drew in a breath and told herself to be strong.

"I was so stupid," she admitted. "I don't know what I was thinking. I love Brody. Why would I risk our marriage?"

"You were mad," Tori reminded her. "About Brody saying he didn't think it was a good time for you to get pregnant."

"I was. I thought he was backing out of a promise. I thought he'd lied to me from the beginning."

"Plus the kids." Heather sipped her wine. "I know you love them, but going from every other weekend to sharing custody can't have been easy on top of your eighty-hour weeks. It was too much. You probably got resentful and didn't realize it."

Daphne thought maybe Heather was right. "I was tired all the time and then Brody took away the one thing I'd been looking forward to."

"And there was Miguel," Tori said. "All handsome and sexy."

Despite her emotions, Daphne smiled. "Have you met him?"

"No, but I can't imagine you'd have an emotional affair with a guy who wasn't handsome and sexy."

"He wasn't worth what I put on the line. I risked everything that mattered to me."

"Did you tell Brody that?" Heather asked.

"I did. I admitted that I had an emotional affair, which was so humiliating. I never saw myself that way."

"Did he understand?" Tori asked.

Daphne thought about her conversation with Brody. "All he wanted was for me to admit what was happening. He knows I wasn't really interested in Miguel, that I wasn't realizing what happened." She thought about his loving support. "He hasn't just forgiven me, he's let it go."

Now the tears won and filled her eyes. "He's so good to me. I don't deserve him."

"He loves you."

She nodded as she wiped her face. "He does. He's a good guy. We're going to try getting pregnant again in a few months. So that's me." She picked up her wine. "How are you two doing?"

Heather smiled. "I'm good. Worried about tomorrow but otherwise fine."

Tori offered a wide smile that somehow didn't seem genuine.

"You know my life is perfect," she said a little too loudly. "I'm picking out fixtures and backsplashes."

Daphne studied her. "You okay?"

"I'm fine." Tori hesitated, as if she was thinking about something, then brightened. "Oh, wait. I have news." Her expression fell a little. "It's not, you know, cheerful, and maybe I shouldn't say anything."

Heather rolled her eyes. "Either think of a good lie or tell us."

"I don't lie well under pressure," Tori admitted. "And you can't tell anyone because I don't know how public this is."

"Now I'm intrigued," Daphne said with a laugh. "Tell us."

"Campbell broke up with Nora."

Daphne immediately glanced at Heather, who looked surprised and oddly uncomfortable.

"I didn't need to know that," Heather said quietly.

Tori's expression turned stricken. "So I shouldn't have said anything? I'm sorry."

"No, it's not you. How did you find out?"

"Nora asked me to come by so she could say that she appreciated how I'd made her feel welcome." Tori's mouth twisted. "She talked about how hard it can be for the new person to fit into the group because we all know each other so well."

Daphne sensed there was more, but couldn't figure out what. She touched Heather's arm. "Are you afraid this will make it harder to get over him?"

Heather sagged back against the sofa. "I was making progress, growing. But no matter what I do, I can't seem to let him go. He said he'd be at the party and I just assumed he would bring Nora. I was ready for that. Now I'll be wondering if we could have a chance." She sat up straight. "If you see me making a fool of myself tomorrow, stop me. Please. Drag me out of the room or shove a cashew in my mouth."

Tori hunched over. "I feel awful."

"Don't," Heather told her. "I was going to find out eventually. I'd rather hear it from you, where I'm safe, than in a crowd where there's no one to protect me."

She looked at Daphne. "Tell me he's done with me."

Daphne thought about how Heather had broken Campbell's heart more than once. How he wanted more than she was able to give. Yes, Heather was changing but Campbell wasn't the type to risk everything again.

"I think he's done with you."

Heather flinched, then nodded. "You're right. Fool me once and all that. I couldn't be what he needed and that's on me. He gave me more chances than I deserved."

But she still loved him. Daphne understood that helpless emotion. She would have been living it herself if Brody hadn't forgiven her for what she'd done.

Heather stood. "Let's start prepping the food," she said. "I need the distraction."

Tori watched her. "I'm really sorry."

"No." Heather hugged her. "I'm glad I know. I can handle this." She managed a smile. "If I feel myself weakening to the point where I want to say something to him, spending time with my mother will heal me."

"You excited?" her dad asked as he helped Heather unload her car.

In addition to all the food she'd brought, she also had the giant, very heavy piñata that she and her friends had filled.

"I'm looking forward to this," Heather said cheerfully, only partially lying. Tori had been right to say Heather wasn't exactly a party person—not when she was the guest of honor. There was also concern about her mother, not to mention seeing Campbell. Knowing he'd broken up with Nora shouldn't matter to her but did. She was a fool.

"Ella and Layla have been up since six," Fletcher said as they walked into the house. "They're hyper and speaking at a pitch that should be reserved for a military weapon."

"A little excited?" Heather asked with a laugh.

"You have no idea."

The front door burst open and the girls raced out.

"You're here! You're here! The party starts in two hours. We can't wait!" Ella danced in place as she spoke. "We've been helping Mom."

"Is that a piñata?" Layla shrieked. "Can we hit it? Is there candy inside?"

"You really need to entertain more." Heather smiled at her

sisters. "Hi. There are a couple of light bags in my car. Can you get them?"

"We can!"

They raced to her car. Heather looked at her dad. "I just bought you eight seconds of quiet. You're welcome."

Jillian met them at the door. "Happy birthday, October baby."

"You, too." Heather handed her the Crock-Pot. "There's more."

The girls ran past her, each of them holding a bag. "Mommy! Mommy! There's a piñata."

"I heard. I think the people three streets down heard." But she was smiling as she spoke.

They brought everything into the house. Fletcher took the girls outside to hang the piñata while Jillian and Heather organized the food.

"I'm so grateful it's sunny and warm," Jillian said as she started unpacking bags. "No way we could fit everyone into the house. We set up tables out back."

She shook a container of roasted cashews. "I'm looking forward to trying these."

"I sampled last night and they're delicious." Heather pulled out the frozen meatballs. "Daphne swears this recipe works. Where should I plug in?"

"How about the dining room?"

It didn't take long to get the meatballs going. Heather carefully stirred the sauce, then put on the lid and set the Crock-Pot on high. She returned to the kitchen.

"I have a schedule," Jillian said, waving several sheets of paper. "We need to cut up fruits and vegetables. Your pinwheels will get the oven at three forty-five. People will start arriving at four. We have burgers, hot dogs, ribs, salads and a giant cake."

"Sounds amazing."

Jillian put down the paper. "Thanks for doing this with me. It's more fun when there's a party for two."

Heather hugged her. "You did all the work. I'm just the hanger-on." She stepped back. "We need to talk about my mother."

Jillian waved the comment away. "No, we don't. We'll be fine."

"I'm worried about what she's going to say."

"Her words can't hurt me or Fletcher," Jillian said mildly. "But I understand you're worried so we have a couple of family friends who will keep an eye on the girls. Should your mother corner them, someone will swoop in and rescue them."

"I'll be watching, too."

Heather had revised her plan. Instead of avoiding Amber, she would spend time with her. It would be a great distraction from wishing she could be with Campbell. She wasn't supposed to know about the breakup and didn't want to make a fool of herself in front of him. She'd already put the man through enough.

Jillian stiffened. "You didn't bring your kittens. Don't they have to be fed?"

"They do." Heather patted her arm. "I asked one of the volunteers I know at the shelter to stop by and feed them. They'll be fine. Don't worry."

Normally, she would have asked someone from work, but they'd all been invited. Somehow, the guest list had grown to fifty people.

She and Jillian spent the next couple of hours getting everything ready. Right at four, people started arriving. Heather was introduced to friends of her dad and Jillian's, along with several of Jillian's girlfriends. Daphne and Brody arrived. Heather was pleased to see them relaxed with each other. Brody kept a protective hand on the small of Daphne's back.

Grant and Tori arrived. Tori hurried over.

"Your mom and Sophie just drove by. They'll have to find parking, so expect them in a few minutes."

"Thanks for the warning."

Heather braced herself for whatever was going to happen and promised later, she would force LC to cuddle with her for at least ten seconds. Any longer than that and he would claw her, but for those few heartbeats, she would feel his warm body in her arms.

twenty-seven

Heather waited by the front door longer than she'd anticipated, but finally she saw her mom and Sophie. She stepped out onto the porch.

"You made it."

"No thanks to her," Amber grumbled. "I asked her to let me off in front of the house, but she refused so we had to walk four blocks to get here."

Sophie hugged Heather, then grinned. "Your doctor told you to start getting some exercise. I was helping."

"I have a bad back. I can't walk distances like that." Amber glared at her cousin.

"All evidence to the contrary." Sophie linked arms with Heather. "I'm so thrilled to finally be meeting your father. The mystery is solved after all these years."

"Does he know I'm coming?"

Amber's voice was uncharacteristically hesitant. Heather realized her mother was nervous to be meeting the man she'd known for a single night, all those years ago.

"He does and he's excited to catch up." Heather moved close to her mom. "His daughters are thrilled and Jillian already refers to you as part of the family."

"I'm not interested in babysitting. I'm a guest in their house. They need to treat me like one."

Heather held in a smile. That sounded more like the Amber she knew. "They will," she said, holding open the front door. "Shall we?"

They'd barely stepped inside when Jillian hurried to greet them. She was smiling broadly.

"At last," she said happily. "I'm so pleased you could make it."

"Mom, this is Jillian, my stepmother. Jillian, my mother, Amber, and my cousin Sophie."

"Of Clandestine Kitty fame," Jillian said, shaking hands with them both. "Thank you for coming." She turned to Amber. "I have to warn you, our girls are a little overly excited about the party." She laughed. "I suppose that's their way of telling us we don't entertain enough."

"Children should behave," Amber told her.

"They should," Jillian agreed easily. "But then they don't and we love them, anyway." She leaned toward Amber. "I know you understand completely."

Heather would guess that Amber didn't understand at all, but it seemed her mother wasn't sure what to say and before she could think of something, Ella and Layla raced over. The girls danced from foot to foot, obviously trying to remember their manners while filled with excitement.

"Is it her?" Ella asked in a loud whisper.

"It is." Jillian put her hands on her daughters' shoulders. "These are our girls. Ella's eleven and Layla is nine."

Amber studied them for a second, before turning to Heather. "They look like you." Her tone was accusing.

"A little."

"It's because we have the same dad," Layla told her. She tilted her head. "If Heather is our half sister, are you our half grandmother?"

Amber blanched. "No. I'm not a grandmother."

"You looked a little like one," Layla said. "All soft and pretty. You look like you give good hugs."

An interesting interpretation of her mother's demeanor, Heather thought, not sure if Amber was going to bolt or scream. Color rose on her cheeks, then faded just as quickly.

"I prefer not to hug," Amber told them.

The sisters exchanged a look. "Why?" Ella asked. "Hugs are the best. Hugs make you feel better."

Layla smiled at Sophie. "I know who you are. Heather showed us your picture on your website. You have the best store. We have new kittens. Bella and Stella. They're sisters, like us. Right now they're in our room because of all the people."

Sophie nodded. "That's the best place for a kitten when there are a lot of people around. They could get scared and with the doors open all the time, they could run away. We wouldn't want that."

The girls' eyes widened. "No, we wouldn't." Layla swallowed. "We love them."

"Did you play with them before the party to get them tired?"

"A little."

"Maybe later you could take me to see your kittens and we could all play together."

Ella pressed her hands together. "Thank you," she breathed reverently. "Maybe you can teach us some games for our kittens."

"I'll do my best."

"Would you like something to drink?" Ella asked Sophie. She held out her hand.

Sophie took it. "I guess I'll see you two later." The sisters led her away.

"Impressive," Heather said with a laugh. "Sophie's great, but she's not much of a kid person. But your girls charmed her."

"I think the kittens might have had something to do with it." Jillian looked at Amber. "Shall we join the party?"

They fell into step together.

"You're a lot younger than Fletcher," Amber said.

"I am. I'm only a week older than Heather."

"You were what? Eighteen when you met?" Judgment chilled her tone.

"I was." Jillian stayed relaxed. "I knew right away he was special. He told me he was too old for me and that I should stay away. But I didn't want to."

Heather could feel her mother getting outraged and knew she had to step in. "I know what you mean, Mom. I was shocked, too. Some couples have age differences, but not like this." She hoped her little laugh wasn't forced. "But when you see them together for even a minute, you know they're so right for each other. It reminds me of Sophie and Dugan, or Kristine and Jaxsen. They just belong."

Her mother muttered something she couldn't hear. They walked out into the backyard. Most of the guests had arrived and the big, open area had filled up with people. There was plenty of conversation, laughter and kids running around. It was the kind of chaos that usually sent Heather running for a quiet room, but she found herself more relaxed than usual. Maybe because she knew at least half the people and the ones she hadn't met were friends of Jillian and her dad. Of course they'd be nice.

"There you are."

Fletcher appeared in front of them. He looked from Heather to her mother and back. The flicker of surprise in his eyes was quickly masked as he took one of Amber's hands in his.

"It's been a long time, Amber," he said, his tone gentle. "But I'd know you anywhere. Welcome to our home."

Amber flushed. "Fletcher. Ah, thank you for inviting me."

"To our daughter's birthday party? Of course you're welcome. Now you've met Jillian and you're probably wondering if I sold my soul to the devil to win her. I won't comment on that either way, but I will admit I've been very, very lucky with the women I've known." He leaned toward her. "I think that winning streak started with you."

Heather stared open-mouthed at her father. She knew he was nice and funny and kind, but she'd never seen him so... smooth.

Jillian stepped close. "Uh-huh. He's good with the ladies. You only see the gifted teacher and loving father, but there is a whole other side to that man."

"Remind him to use his powers for good," Heather murmured, equally impressed and uncomfortable.

Jillian laughed. "I will. Now go hang out with your friends. We'll take care of your mom for a while."

"Protect your soft underbelly."

Jillian touched her arm. "Your mother can't hurt me. I have Fletcher and my girls and you. My life is perfect. Any cruelty she speaks comes from a place of pain and while sad, isn't my responsibility."

She walked toward her husband and Amber, leaving Heather stunned and without words. Her life was perfect? Was that what Jillian had said? The woman had stage IV breast cancer and more bills than money and a thousand other problems Heather didn't know about. But even as she thought the words, she knew they didn't matter. Jillian meant what she said. Love was what mattered. Knowing Fletcher would walk through fire for her and that her girls worshipped her. In all that mattered, Jillian was the wealthiest woman in the world.

"Happy birthday."

She turned and saw Campbell. Immediately, her heart fluttered. She did her best to squash the feelings.

"Hi," she said. "Welcome. I'll warn you—the piñata is loaded to the point of being dangerous. When that thing goes, get out of the way because the kids are going to go crazy."

"Thanks for the heads-up." He smiled. "Great party."

"It is."

His dark gaze met hers. "You don't like parties."

"I'm working on changing my mind on that. Besides, this one is different." She pointed to the galvanized tubs filled with ice and drinks. "Want something? There is the obligatory soda selection, along with wine and beer."

"Sure. What are you drinking?"

"I've been so busy prepping, I haven't had a chance to get something."

"Now seems like a good time."

They both took cans of beer. Somehow, they made their way to a quiet part of the yard and sat down. She was aware of Campbell next to her. The need to stretch out her hand and touch him unnerved her and she searched frantically for something to say. Anything that would be a distraction.

"I'm sorry about Nora," she blurted, only to realize that was the absolute dumbest of opening lines.

He looked at her. "How did you find out?"

Heather winced. "Sorry. I shouldn't have said that. I don't think I was supposed to know."

"It's not a state secret."

"You weren't telling anyone."

"I was waiting. So how did you find out?"

"Nora told Tori. She wanted to thank her for welcoming her into the group." She paused. "I really am sorry. She was nice and I liked her."

One eyebrow rose.

"I'm sure I would have liked her if I'd gotten to know her better. I didn't not like her. I mean I barely knew her but all the qualities for liking were there."

The corners of his mouth twitched.

"What?" she demanded.

"You're trying really hard to be generous," he said. "I appreciate it."

"I'm not a total bitch."

"You never were. But you were more…closed off."

That did not sound attractive. "I'm not asking you what you meant by that."

"Nothing bad."

"You say that now." She looked at him. "Mind if I ask what happened? I thought you two were really happy."

He set his can on the grass. "We were." He paused, turning away, then looking back at her. "She wanted more than I was ready to give. She was pushing to take things to the next level and I wasn't ready."

His gaze dropped to the ground. "Believe me, I get the irony of that."

"Because that's what I said to you?" She shook her head. "There isn't any irony, Campbell. You weren't ready at that moment. But you could have been and eventually you wanted to be. When you and I were together, I wasn't capable of handling any more than we had. There's a huge difference there."

She sipped her drink. "Do you know that except for my cousin Sophie, the first time I told someone I loved them was about three months ago?"

He stared at her. "Seriously?" He frowned. "Wait, what?

Sophie and not your mom? You've never told Amber..." He picked up his beer. "Right. Because she would never say it to you. She wasn't that kind of mom and it wouldn't occur to you to say it. Those words would be too much like handing her a weapon."

She wasn't surprised he understood. He'd seen her mother in action. And being the kind of man he was, he'd always run interference.

"So who was it?" he asked, his tone casual.

"Who was what?"

"Who did you tell you loved them?"

She hoped he was asking because the thought of her saying it to another man would bother him. Then she told herself not to be foolish.

"Tori."

"Good choice."

She laughed. "Thanks. Later I said it to Daphne and now I'm just the kind of person who blabs it all the time. I've told my dad and Jillian, my sisters. I'm trying not to use the L word at work because it could upset my employees."

"You also said it to me."

His voice was quiet, his expression unreadable. She swallowed as she felt herself flush.

"Yes, well, in the past tense. But I wanted you to know." She waved her hand. "You were there. You remember my point."

"Thank you for making it."

She drew in a breath. "I really am sorry for what I put you through. Relationships are hard for me and you got the worst of my poor skill set. You're a good guy, Campbell. You deserve someone amazing. I really hope you find her."

"Thanks. I hope you find what you're looking for, too."

She had, she thought sadly. Then she'd let it get away.

"What do you think about setting up Nora and Emer?" she asked, mostly in an effort to change the subject. "She's great, he's great. I only went out with him a couple of times, but he seems very normal. Oh, he does volunteer surgery in other countries. That sounds very Nora-like."

He looked at her. "You're serious."

"I don't know. Maybe. What do you think?"

"I'll talk to Grant."

"There you are!" Amber walked up to them. "You left me alone with strangers."

Heather scrambled to her feet. "You were with Jillian and Fletcher."

"Yes, strangers." She turned as Campbell rose. "Oh, it's you. I haven't seen you in so long." She rolled her eyes. "Not since my daughter dumped you. How are you, Campbell? You were always my favorite."

"Amber." He squeezed her hand, then lightly kissed her cheek. "I've missed you, too. Let me get you a chair. This grass is so uneven."

"I know."

He stepped away. Amber watched him go.

"I wish you could get him back," she grumbled.

Me, too, but Heather knew better than to say that.

Amber looked around at the crowds of people. "They have a lot of friends."

"It's a shared group. That makes the guest list bigger."

Her mother wrinkled her nose. "Their house is a little shabby. Nothing like my condo."

Heather told herself to let her mother talk. Stating the truth— that the only reason Amber had a beautiful, waterfront condo was because Sophie had bought it for her—wouldn't help.

"They're raising two kids on a teacher's salary."

"Jillian should get a job instead of sitting on her ass all day, expecting other people to take care of her."

Waves of anger coursed through Heather. All Amber had ever done in her life was to expect people to take care of her.

She hadn't seriously held down a job in years. Heather had been paying her monthly bills since she got her first job out of college.

"Mom," she said quietly. "Don't. Just don't."

Campbell returned with a chair and a glass of wine for Amber, then excused himself. Her mother sank onto the chair and stared at Heather.

"You're done with me," she said slowly, pressing her free hand to her chest. "You don't care about me at all. You want them for your family and you wish I would die."

Heather longed to escape, but there was nowhere to go. She settled back on the grass.

"I wish that just once you could have a conversation about someone else without judging and assuming and making it all about you."

Her mother drew back. "I don't do that."

"You just said that Jillian should get off her butt and work. That's judging." She had to grind her teeth together to keep from mentioning the whole you-don't-have-a-job-either thing. "You always look for the bad and if it's not there, you make it up. No one's out to get you. In fact, pretty much everyone in your life takes care of you. The reason Jillian doesn't work is because she has metastatic breast cancer and sometimes she's sick or exhausted. She has a part-time job she goes to when she's feeling strong enough."

Heather sharpened her gaze. "It wouldn't kill you to be nice. Even if you have to pretend. Everyone is so careful about what they say about you, but you never return the favor. You just say horrible things and expect us to deal with it."

"That's not me at all. I'm a wonderful person." Tears filled her eyes. "Is that what you really think of me? I'm kind. I've had a hard life. Do you know what it's like for me to see him with her? That should have been me."

It took Heather a second to figure out what her mother was talking about. "You mean Fletcher?"

"Yes. If he'd bothered to call me, we could have fallen in love and then this would have been my life. He's a good man and she stole him from me."

Her mother covered her eyes. Tears leaked down her cheeks. Heather wanted to throw herself off the nearest bridge. She'd told herself not to get into anything with her mother and yet she'd done it. Now Amber was crying and from there it was a short road to a party-ruining scene.

"I'm sorry," she said, hoping she sounded sincere. "I was wrong to upset you."

"Yes, it was. A few weeks ago you accused me of horrible things. You threatened me. Now you're being mean again." She raised her head. "You don't like me."

"Of course I do. You're my mother."

"You don't take care of me anymore."

"I send you money every month. When you wanted to visit Grandma in Arizona, I flew you down there. When you said her house was too small, I paid for a luxury hotel room at that spa place you wanted to visit."

Which her mother had decided was so nice, she'd extended her vacation to three weeks and had racked up about four grand worth of spa treatments.

"You wouldn't fly me home first class," Amber said with a pout. "And I had to take a shuttle from the airport instead of car service."

"Because you changed your flight without telling me and they didn't have a driver on call."

Heather told herself to disengage. No matter what she did, Amber would never be happy. A happiness plan had to come from somewhere inside yourself—it couldn't be persuaded or prodded into a person who didn't want to change. Heather might be learning how to let people into her life, but she was still failing when to find a healthy way to deal with her mother.

"There you are!" Tori said loudly as she approached. "I've

362

been looking for you everywhere." She gave Heather a sympathetic look before turning to Amber. "How are you? You look great. It's been forever. I bet you had the best summer on the island. We had those gorgeous days and with your views…" She sighed. "Ah, what a life you live."

"Hello, Tori. Heather and I were talking."

"Then I'm interrupting. The food's out. Let's go fill our plates. I want to hear about everything you've been doing, then I'll tell you the funny story of my condo being flooded."

Before Heather knew what was happening, Tori and her mother were moving toward the buffet. She gave herself a few seconds of peace before rejoining the crowd. Her father spotted her and headed toward her.

"How's it going?" he asked.

"Everyone's having such a good time," she said, hoping he wouldn't notice she wasn't answering his question.

"You and Jillian worked hard on the party. Thank you for helping and for agreeing to it in the first place." He hugged her. "After you eat, I want you to meet a few people. You know me. I have to show off my oldest."

He looked at her with such love and affection. He asked for so little and gave so much.

"What did you think of Amber?" she asked quietly.

He glanced toward the food line, where Daphne and Brody had joined Tori in occupying her mother. She was blessed with great friends who watched out for her, she thought fiercely.

"She's not the girl I remember," he said slowly. "But I see flashes of the one I knew."

"We all pick our own path."

She heard loud shrieks and saw Layla and Ella running with their friends. Jillian was talking to several women about her age. They all laughed at something she said.

This was good, she thought. Happy. This was, for better or worse, her family. She grabbed her dad's hand.

"I'll do it," she said quietly. "Be the girls' guardian. I know I flinched the first time you asked, but I understand why you're scared and I think I've learned enough not to mess up too horribly. No matter what happens, I'll love them."

He blinked several times. "Are you sure? You don't have to do this. We were wrong to ask."

"You're my family. All of you. If something happens, I'll be there for them. I'll take over for you and Jillian and whenever I'm not sure what to do, I'll ask myself what you would have done."

He pulled her close and hung on so tight. She hugged him back.

"Can anybody get in on this?"

She laughed as she saw Campbell standing next to them.

"We're wrapping up the hugging portion of the program," she said, knowing he was teasing.

"Too bad."

Heather introduced them. Fletcher looked interested as he realized who Campbell was. She'd told him about messing up and how Campbell was the one who got away.

"Did you eat?" Campbell asked her.

"No, I was busy being tortured by my mother." She pointed toward Amber sitting with Sophie, Tori, Grant, Daphne and Brody. "The second shift has rescued me."

"Let's get you some food. Then I'll take the next shift."

"She always liked you."

He winked at her. "Of course she did. I'm kind of irresistible."

She laughed because she was supposed to, even as she knew he was 100 percent right.

twenty-eight

Tori told herself to suck it up and be strong. And brave. Or at the very least, protect herself from inevitable disaster. She'd managed to fake her way through the past few days, pretending all was well, stealing a few extra nights in Grant's bed, but now was the time for her to grow a pair and take care of business. Which was an oddly mixed metaphor and made her slightly uncomfortable. Regardless, she had to do it.

Grant was reading in the family room. She gave herself a second to study his familiar, handsome face that was a nice bonus but came in way second to his amazing heart.

She'd always liked him but now she knew him better than she had. She knew the things a lover did—how his eyes darkened when he wanted her and how his feet were ticklish and how he slept with his arm around her, holding her close. She knew he was protective and supportive and when Scout stole a piece of bone-in chicken from the counter, he'd raced after her faster than light to wrestle the dangerous treat from her.

And she knew she loved him. That he was the one for her, which was great and sucked at the same time. Because Grant wasn't interested in love and she didn't know how to make the emotions stop.

He looked up. Instantly, his mouth curved into a smile. "Hey, you."

"We have to talk."

He was unperturbed by her words. "Can we talk naked?"

"No."

"Okay. Just asking." He set down the book and patted the cushion next to him. "Let's talk."

She carefully settled in a chair across from him. If she sat close, she would get distracted by how much she liked being near him, and then she wouldn't be able to say what she needed to.

She cleared her throat several times, grasped her hands tightly, then blurted, "We can't have sex anymore."

His brows rose, but otherwise he didn't react. "Okay, why?"

"It's too dangerous."

"Our making love is dangerous?"

"Yes. To me."

He frowned. "My STD test came back negative."

She folded her arms across her chest and shifted in her chair. "Not physically. Emotionally. I need a family more than I need us to be lovers. I'm sorry but there it is."

He slid to the edge of the cushion. "Tori, I have no idea what you're trying to say. What family?"

"Mine. Us. This. We're a family. You, me, Campbell, Brody and Daphne. We're family. But here's the thing. If we break up, then I won't have half my family anymore. You won't want me around, so I won't just lose you, I'll lose Brody and Campbell, too."

He looked confused. "You're not losing anyone."

"Not now, but it could happen. Look at Nora. She's gone. Campbell broke up with her and she's no longer a part of the family. And what about Heather? She was totally one of us and now we never see her."

"You see her every day at work."

She groaned. "That's not the point. *We* don't see her. The group, aka the family. She's no longer welcome. Oh, sure, the occasional brunch, but it's not what it was."

"We all went to her birthday party."

"Yes, but then what? You three will always be together but my position is more precarious."

She stood and walked around her chair so it was between her and Grant. "What happens in a few weeks or months? I've never had a successful relationship and you're not interested in anything permanent, so we're doomed. This is going to end and badly. When that happens, you'll still have your brothers and your circle, but I'll be thrown out. Without sex, we're the non-couple friends. But now we're more than that and when you dump me, I'll be the woman you used to see, not the non-couple friend. I'll have no place in the group."

He studied her. "You're really upset."

"Of course I'm upset! That's my entire point. You're risking nothing and I'm risking everything and I just can't. I need a family. I'm not like you. I don't have anyone else. I know Heather and Daphne will always be there, but there's still you three."

She drew in a breath. "I want us to go back to how we were before. This never happened and I never loved you. That's the only way I can be safe."

"Wait, what?"

She held up her hand. "I don't want to talk about it. I've told you how I feel. Now I'm going to let you think about it for a while and then we'll have a conversation. All I ask is that you try to see what I've put on the line."

With that, she left the family room. As she grabbed her handbag, she called for Scout. She'd already made arrangements to hang out with Daphne and the kids that evening. She also had plans for the next three nights because she couldn't imagine facing Grant right now. At some point, yes, but first she needed to get a little stronger.

Daphne didn't usually have meetings with Miguel and his team but one had appeared on her calendar. It was in a midsize conference room, so he wasn't trying to speak to her alone. She downloaded the file and saw he'd planned a series of updates on several of his clients. She was in the ten-thirty to eleven-thirty slot and he wanted to discuss changes in trust funds and the possibility of a new will.

She collected the information he'd requested and familiarized herself with the files. Right on time, she walked into the conference room. Miguel and several associates sat at the table. There was an empty seat across from him, which was the obvious place for her to sit. It was where she always sat in meetings like this—it was no big deal.

Only she couldn't shake the feeling of everyone watching her, and she wondered if Miguel was going to say something flirty or suggestive, because thinking back on their previous encounters, he sometimes had.

"Daphne," he said with an easy smile as she sat down. "I believe you know everyone here."

"I do. Hello." She opened her laptop. "I know you're having a busy morning. Let's get to it, shall we?"

She went over the first trust, explaining the details of how the client in question had divided his estate among his three children, all by different mothers. Each of the mothers, as trustee for the child, would have access to the funds with very little oversight.

"That's the problem," Miguel told her. "One of the mothers has developed a drug problem. My client wants to remove the mother as trustee and substitute his mother instead."

Daphne explained what that would entail while privately thinking that conversation would not go well. But the client was right to be concerned about his child's welfare.

For the next forty minutes she and Miguel went line by line through the documents while his associates listened and made notes. She kept track of the changes and items she would have to look up. Normally, she worked directly with the clients, but several of Miguel's sports figures preferred a single point of contact at the firm.

When they'd finished, Miguel smiled. "Good meeting. I know it's early, but want to grab some lunch?"

"I have another meeting in fifteen minutes," she lied as she rose. "I'll get you the revised drafts tomorrow."

"I'll look for them."

She walked toward the elevator. As she waited, she thought about what had just happened. Yes, it was work and the lunch invitation was probably innocuous, but what if it wasn't? And what if she'd said yes? Would they be back where they had been?

She didn't want that. She didn't want to be the person who would have an emotional affair, but she had. And no matter how she handled herself in the future, that moment would always have happened. She would always have to face Miguel at work, and Brody would always worry.

She walked into her office and put her laptop on her desk,

then crossed to the window. She had a view of the Puget Sound. The clouds were low and it was raining but she could still see one of the ferries pulling into port and the container ships beyond.

She loved her job. She'd worked hard to get where she was. There were less prestigious firms where she could have made partner in six or seven years, but she'd chosen this one, knowing it would take longer, but be worth it in the end. She'd accomplished what she'd wanted. The seventy- or eighty-hour workweeks didn't bother her, but they did come at a price.

What happened in six months, if she got pregnant again? No, what happened nine months after that? How long could she reasonably take for maternity leave? What about her long hours? Sure, they would get a nanny, but she wasn't interested in having a child she never got to spend time with. Technically, she could work from home but culturally, it wasn't encouraged.

And what about Brody? He'd been right about her and Miguel. Oh, not them sleeping together, but the rest of it. Her marriage was important to her. He was a good man and she'd known from the first night they'd met that he was the one for her. So why hadn't she been acting like it?

She pulled her cell phone out of her jacket pocket and scrolled through her contacts. She hesitated only a second before pushing the dial button.

"Daphne! This is unexpected."

"Hi, Renee. Can we set up a time to talk?"

"He's pacing," Daphne said, leaning back in the sofa, her feet up on the coffee table, a glass of wine in one hand and LC in her lap.

"He is." Heather didn't bother keeping the amusement out of her voice. "I think it's serious."

Grant—honest to God pacing in her living room—glared at both of them. "I'm trying to get my thoughts together."

"You're a doctor. Shouldn't you be better at thinking on your feet?" Heather motioned to him. "No pun intended."

"You're not helping."

"That is true, but mostly because you haven't told us what's wrong."

He stopped and put his hands on his hips, then straightened his arms, then went back to pacing.

"It's Tori."

Heather looked at Daphne, who shook her head, indicating she didn't know what he meant, either.

"Tori's fine," Heather said. "I saw her like two hours ago at work. We had lunch together today. There's no problem."

"You're wrong." He dropped into a chair. "We're sleeping together. Or we were."

Heather sat up straight, nearly sloshing her wine over the rim. "What?" she asked, her voice a shriek. "You're sleeping with Tori and I didn't know?" She looked at Daphne. "Did you know?"

"Absolutely not."

Heather swung her attention back to Grant. "When? How?"

Tori and Grant? But she hadn't said anything or hinted. Why had she kept it a secret? Heather told herself to ignore the instant hurt and focus on what he was saying.

"It's been a couple of weeks, maybe longer. We didn't say anything because—"

"Are you ashamed of what happened?" Daphne demanded. "How dare you. If Tori's interested in you, you should be grateful. You don't deserve her."

Grant gave her a faint smile. "Pull in the claws. Keeping it quiet was Tori's idea. It just sort of happened and neither of us knew where it was going so she suggested waiting to tell everyone."

Tori sleeping with Grant? Heather couldn't grasp it. Not that they were together—they'd always been great together, even though they'd claimed to be the non-couple friends. But sex had a way of changing everything.

"I wish she'd said something," she told Daphne.

"Me, too. But she had a reason for keeping quiet."

Heather wondered if it was because she'd assumed it wouldn't last and didn't want to explain one more broken relationship.

"She was testing you," Daphne said flatly. "You were supposed to want to tell the world."

"I don't think so." He looked at them. "She told me she wants to go back to how things were. That she can't take the chance of us ending badly. That if it does, she'll be cut off from the group."

Heather nodded. "Sure. We're her family and you guys are at the center of it. Every time Campbell and I broke up, I was pushed to the outside."

"You weren't pushed," Grant began.

Daphne cut him off with a wave. "Oh, please. You're brothers. You're never going to take the woman's side. At the end of the day it's you three and then us. But we all have biological family and Tori doesn't. She doesn't want to be alone, with no support." She glared at Grant. "You don't have a great track record with women."

"He doesn't have one at all," Heather murmured. "You don't want to fall in love. You've said that. You want a nice monogamous relationship with no emotional risk and commitment."

He flinched. "Don't say that like it's a bad thing."

"Of course it is. Tori deserves someone who loves her. You're just using her for sex."

"Could you please wait to yell at me until I've told you why I'm here?"

Heather pressed her lips together. "Fine. Talk."

He stared at the floor for a second, then back at them. "The other night she said she wanted things to go back to how they'd been and that she never loved me."

"Whoa." Daphne set down her wine. "She said that?"

He nodded. "So here's my question. What does that mean? Was she saying that she was never in love with me or was she saying she was in love with me but we were going to pretend she wasn't?"

Heather looked at Daphne, who shrugged.

"I don't know," Heather told him, thinking there was no way she was going to admit she knew Tori had feelings for him.

Grant clenched his teeth. "It's your job to know. You're women and her best friends. You have to know."

"Why?" Heather asked. "Does it make a difference?"

"Of course it does."

"Nora was right," Daphne said with a laugh.

Heather glared at her. "Really? We have to talk about her?"

"No, it's okay. Nora said Grant and Tori should date each other. Tori explained how they were the non-couple friends, but she wouldn't buy it." She looked at Grant. "That's it, isn't it? You want her to be in love with you."

Heather swung her gaze back to him. "Is that true? And is it because it feels good to be loved, which makes you a dick, by the way, or because you're in love with her, too?"

"Hey, when did I become the bad guy?"

"I don't know, but it happened, so deal with it. Are you in love with her?"

He crossed then uncrossed his arms. "I don't know."

"Moron," Daphne muttered.

"Hey, I get to feel how I feel."

"Not if you hurt Tori," Heather told him. "You need to have a long talk with yourself and figure out where you are. If you're in love with her, tell her. If not, get your ass home and start being a non-couple friend. Don't you dare dump her over this. That would be everything she didn't want and you know it."

He groaned. "Why did everything have to change?"

"Because you couldn't keep it in your pants." Heather shook her head. "This is on you. You created the problem, now you have to fix it."

"You're not being very supportive."

"I don't have a problem with that."

Friday Tori sat in her car, staring at the massive house. She'd been parked for nearly five minutes and at some point she had to go inside. Grant was already home—his car was in the driveway. For all she knew he was looking at her out the window, wondering why she was such a weirdo.

She'd been avoiding him for days, hanging out with her friends after work or staying late at the office. She'd gotten home when he was already in bed, or at least in his room. But she couldn't do that forever. At some point she had to suck it up and face him, and today was that day.

She got out, then let Scout out of the car. Her dog took off toward the front door, eager to greet Zeus and Grant. Tori followed more slowly, unsure of what she was going to say to him. Or what he was going to say to her.

"It's me," she called as she entered the house.

Zeus came running. He greeted Scout, then circled her, frantic for pets and hugs.

"In the kitchen."

She thought about bolting for the stairs, but then what? Did she plan to stay in her room forever? She walked through the huge foyer and into the kitchen. Grant was sitting at the island counter. He'd already changed out of scrubs into jeans and a T-shirt. He looked good, which was hardly news.

She faked a smile. "Hi." She set her bag on the kitchen desk. "How was your day?"

"Good." He watched her as he spoke. "I've been waiting for you."

She glanced at the clock. "I'm home at my usual time."

He offered a brief smile as he stood. "No. I've been waiting for *you*, Tori."

"I don't understand."

"What you said before. I've been thinking about it a lot. About how we were friends before and how it's so much better now." His expression turned rueful. "Or it was before you decided we had to go back to just being friends."

Her heart twisted from worry that he was going to end things. "It's the best thing to do."

"It's not," he said quietly. "Because we're not just friends. I didn't get it before, but I do now. You're the reason I wasn't interested in dating anyone. You're the reason I put off getting involved and then couldn't find someone who appealed to me. I couldn't make the move because everything I wanted, everything I'd been looking for, was right there in front of me."

He moved closer. "It was always you. I was just too dumb to see it."

Her breath hitched in her chest. Was he saying what she thought he was saying?

"You want us to start dating?"

"No." He moved closer still, until he was right in front of her and she had to tilt her head to see his face. "I'm saying I'm in love with you and I have been for a while. I'm saying I love you, which feels like a little bit more than dating."

It was like hearing words while she was under water. She knew he was speaking but wasn't sure of the message.

"You're in love with me?" The weight of what he'd said hit her hard. Her legs began shaking. "Are you sure?"

"Very." The sexy smile returned. "Did you want to comment on that?"

She started crying, but that didn't matter. She flung herself at him and hung on tight. "You're in love with me."

"Yes."

"In a totally let's-have-sex-every-day-and-I-want-this-to-last kind of way?"

He drew back so he could look into her eyes. "I love you, Tori. In the most let's-have-sex-I'll-put-gas-in-your-car-and-take-care-of-you-when-you're-sick kind of way." He touched her face. "Why is this so hard for you to accept?"

"Because I've been in love with you for so long, but I didn't know. I think you're the reason I kept dating crappy guys. If I couldn't have you, why bother? And then when I got how I felt, I was so scared. You're my family."

He wiped the tears from her cheeks. "And you're mine." He kissed her. "You're not going to lose me and I sure don't want to lose you."

He pulled a small box from his jeans pocket and set it on the island. "In fact, I was kind of wondering if you were interested in marrying me."

Her heart stopped. Just stopped. She felt the absence of beating. She also couldn't breathe, couldn't think, could only stand there, looking between them and the blue square box.

"I don't know what to say," she admitted.

One corner of his mouth turned up. "Yes is the most traditional response."

She flung herself at him. He caught her and pulled her hard against him. "Yes, Grant. I'll marry you. I love you for always."

"I'm glad." His voice was gruff. "Because that's nearly as long as I'm going to love you."

★ ★ ★

"But I don't want to," Daphne said, aware of the whine in her voice.

"It's no big deal and you'll like the outcome."

She was unconvinced, but before she could say anything, Brody dug his thumbs more deeply into the ball of her foot and waves of relaxation washed through her. The man had a way of finding the parts that hurt and caressing them into submission.

"It's hard to have a serious conversation when you're doing that," she complained, but without a lot of energy. She and Brody had agreed they had to make some changes. She was working too hard and doing too much. When his kids were with them, the pace could be frenetic.

She pushed herself into a sitting position on the sofa and wiggled her toes. "Much better. Thank you."

"Anytime." He gave her a suggestive smile. "Any other parts of you need attention?"

She'd been cleared by her doctor to resume "all" activities. She and Brody had taken advantage of that several times over the past few days. She liked that they were back where they had been—connected and working together. But there were still issues to resolve.

"Let's finish the conversation first." She tapped the list. "You want us to hire someone to make the meals. I don't love the idea of someone cooking in the house."

"She's bonded and insured and comes highly recommended. I talked to her and she works with people in our situation all the time. The best plan is eight meals for six people. She'll come for one day every two weeks and cook. She has an opening on Tuesdays, the week we have the kids, so that's perfect. We'll be responsible for Sunday and Monday dinner, then we'll eat her food through Saturday. That leaves five meals for us to share and take for lunch."

"I do love a leftover for lunch." She glanced at the spreadsheet Brody had prepared. The price was reasonable and they got to choose the entrées.

"We freeze some of the food, right? Because it's not going to last for two weeks in the refrigerator."

"She'll label the dinners that should be eaten more quickly and which can be frozen. She can also provide desserts, cookies and bread that is ready to be baked fresh."

"That sounds amazing."

He waited, watching her. She sighed.

"Let's do it."

"You sure?"

"Your idea makes sense. I don't have time to cook as much as I'd like and this way dinner is easy. Rather than one of us prepping, we're spending more time with the kids. If we eat out, we can simply put that meal into the freezer for later."

He made a couple of notes. "So we're in agreement. The cleaners will come every week instead of every other week and we're hiring the home chef."

"Yes."

"When do we make an appointment for your gynecologist?"

To talk about them getting pregnant. Something he'd mentioned before. With the changes they were talking about, they were getting closer to being ready. But there was still the issue of her eighty-hour weeks.

"Before we talk about that," she began. "I have another topic."

She set down her pad of paper and angled so she was facing him. "I've been thinking a lot about my life and what's important. I love my job. I worked hard to make partner and I enjoy the work. I know I should be able to do it all, but I can't figure out how. I don't want our baby to be raised by a nanny. I want to be home at a reasonable time and maybe even work from home sometimes. I don't want to be the absent parent, and I want to hang with the kids and you."

He started shaking his head. "Daphne, you made partner. It was your big career goal. You can't walk away from that."

"You're right. It was my big career goal and I achieved it. Now it's time for a different goal. I talked to Renee a few days ago. She's setting up a meeting with the senior management team at *Velkommen*. If that goes well, they're going to make me an offer. It'll be about a thirty percent pay cut, but that's still plenty." She smiled. "We'll have to sacrifice private jets, but otherwise…"

"We've never flown on a private jet."

"I was making a point."

"You were distracting me." He studied her face. "Don't do this for me. I want you to be happy and if you change your job because of us, you'll get resentful and I'll feel guilty."

"I'm not doing it for you. I'm doing it for me, and for us and for the baby we want to have. I want to be around to hold my kid and go to school events. I want to figure out how to spend my evenings when I'm not always at work."

She thought about mentioning that Miguel was a small part of her decision, but knew saying that would only open fresh wounds.

"Brody, I nearly lost you because I was blind and stupid. I don't want to risk our relationship. I want us to be happy and have a life that's more than me working all the time. I don't want to realize in twenty years that I've missed everything. I made partner. No one can take that away from me. Now I have a different dream. One with you and the kids and a baby."

"I need you to be sure."

"I am." She smiled. "Oh, and they want to meet you. Apparently, there are a lot of family events at *Velkommen*, so you need to be vetted, as well."

He grinned. "I'll be on my best behavior." The smile faded. "You have to know this is the right decision for you."

"I want this," she said firmly. "I'm ready to make a change and this is a good one."

"Then tell me when and where, and I'll be there." He moved toward her and put his arm around her. "What do you think about me wearing a kilt?"

"Your family is Irish, not Scottish."

"The Irish wear kilts. I could research the family tartan. Wear those white knee socks. It would be a sexy look."

She leaned against him. "My understanding is traditional kilt wearing doesn't allow underwear. You better hope there isn't a breeze."

He laughed, then kissed her. "I love you, Daphne."

"I love you, too." She shifted so she could straddle his lap. "Want to go upstairs and practice baby making? Just so when the time comes, we know what we're doing?"

"That sounds like a plan."

380

twenty-nine

Heather held the spray paint can at arm's length, sweeping it back and forth until all the leaves were covered in a light dusting of gold. Ella and Layla watched from a safe distance. When the leaves dried, they would make leaf angels to decorate the house for Thanksgiving. She and her sisters had already spent the afternoon making leaf napkin rings. October had spilled into November and before they knew it, the holidays would be upon them.

"These have to dry," she said, capping the can, then closing the garage door. She'd opened it for ventilation, but as it was forty-two and raining, it was also creating a serious draft.

"Then we can make the faces and add the wings?" Ella asked.

"Yes. Your mom will help."

She and her stepmom were coordinating holiday crafts. Jillian was an expert, but Heather had discovered she also enjoyed creating with her sisters. It was a fun outlet and gave them a chance to just hang out and talk. She'd taken a hiatus from fostering kittens, at least until spring, when the season started up again, so had time for things like leaf angels. Jillian was teaching her to crochet. She was starting simple—with a small blanket—but had hopes to get fancy with possibly a scarf or even a hat.

They set the tray of leaves on the washer to finish drying. In the kitchen Jillian was pulling together ingredients for biscuits.

"Want to stay for chili?" she asked when she saw Heather.

"Thanks, but I need to head home. I feel bad that LC hasn't seen much of me this week."

Plus, her condo needed a thorough cleaning. Not the most exciting Saturday night, but necessary. Neither of her friends was available for fun. Daphne and Brody wanted a quiet night alone before the kids descended, and since Tori and Grant had declared their love, neither wanted to leave the house.

Young love, Heather thought, more sad than bitter. She wouldn't mind a little of that in her life.

"We have our Zoom call on Tuesday," she said as she hugged Jillian.

"We'll be there. I appreciate your friend drawing up the paperwork."

"Daphne's the best." Heather knew her friend would make sure the guardianship was legally solid and her sisters protected.

She hugged the girls, then went to say goodbye to her dad. On her way out, she pointed at her sisters.

"Sleepover next weekend," she reminded them.

They jumped up and down.

"Yes, please!"

"We can't wait!"

Heather was still smiling as she started the drive back to Seattle.

She'd barely pulled onto I-5 when her cell phone rang. She glanced at the caller and groaned, then pushed the talk button.

"Hi, Mom."

"Are you in your car?"

"I am. How are things?"

"Fine. The dishwasher's making a funny noise, but maybe it's not so bad."

"It should still be under warranty from the kitchen remodel. Can you call the service department about it?"

"I never know what to say to those people. They ask so many questions and they're so rude."

Heather told herself to just go with the flow. Yes, she could insist her mother deal with her own dishwasher problems, but to what end? Amber was never going to change.

"I'll put a call in to the service department on Monday," she said. "In the meantime, if you could text me some information on the problem."

"It's making a funny noise."

"Funny how?"

"It grinds."

"I'll tell them that. I need to know when you're available in the next couple of weeks."

"Where would I go?" Amber asked, a whimper in her voice. "I don't have any friends or anything to do. I just sit alone in this small condo, wishing I had family who cared about me."

Heather felt her grip tighten on the steering wheel. She consciously relaxed her hands.

"If you got out more, you'd meet people. Maybe you could get a part-time job."

"Oh, you'd like that, wouldn't you? You want your only mother to break her back with hard labor."

"I was thinking more of one of the wineries. Pouring wine and talking to tourists could be interesting."

"The tourists are all such idiots, then they get drunk."

All righty then, Heather thought, telling herself to look for the humor in the situation. Or at least remind herself that when she got home, she, too, could have wine and pretend she and her mother had never spoken.

"On that cheerful note, I'm going to go. There's traffic up ahead and I have to pay attention."

"You won't forget about the dishwasher?"

"I won't. Bye, Mom."

"Goodbye."

Heather ended the call, then cranked up the oldies station on the radio. There were very few problems that couldn't be if not solved, then at least mitigated, by some serious '60s rock music.

She sang along until she exited the freeway and drove the short distance to her condo. As she headed for the parking garage, she passed a familiar truck parked out front. Her breath caught in her chest as she drove by.

Campbell? Here?

She parked in her spot, then quickly checked her phone. No text from him, or voice mail. He'd never been the type to simply drop by, so why now?

She found him waiting by her front door. He leaned against the wall, looking relaxed. She walked toward him.

"Hi. Did I know you were going to be here?"

"Not unless you're psychic. I stopped by earlier, but you weren't here."

"I spent the afternoon with my sisters. We were making decorations for Thanksgiving."

"It's three weeks away."

"Crafts take time." She opened the front door and waved him inside. "Thanksgiving angels made of leaves don't happen overnight."

He grinned. "I don't know what that is, but I believe you."

LC came running. Campbell picked him up.

"Hey, you. How you doing? Are you lonely without kittens?"

"He's made it clear he prefers having other cats in the house," she said, setting her bag on the entry table. "I think it has something to do with having the attention off him. Then I'm less likely to annoy him by petting him or looking at him." She paused. "You know, in some ways, he reminds me of my mother."

Campbell feigned offense. "Don't say that."

"He wants a whole lot and doesn't give much in return. Although he did accidentally cuddle with me a few weeks ago. But then he made it clear it was a onetime thing."

"Steps taken," he said, lowering LC to the floor. "You have a minute?"

"Sure."

Housecleaning could wait. She would rather hang with Campbell, even if she didn't know why he was here.

They went into the living room. She sat down, then immediately stood. "Do you want something? A beer or—"

"I'm good."

She sank into the sofa and waited. Nerves fluttered, joining apprehension. She still had no idea why he was here and the odds of him wanting to say something great seemed unlikely. So what was the reason? Advice? Did he need her to look at a rash and tell him if he should go to the doctor?

"You're different," he said.

"You mean taller?"

He chuckled. "No. You've changed from how you used to be. You're more open and friendly."

"I'm trying. Discovering my dad and his family helped. Having sisters. I'm late to the game, but I adore them. And being friends with Jillian has been great." She shrugged. "Sometimes I think about how my life would have changed if I'd met him sooner. He would have been a good antidote to Amber."

"You wouldn't have been you."

"There is that, but still. Sometimes I wonder." She gave him a quick smile. "Not that we can change the past. So I'm still me. A little less emotionally rigid, although I do seem determined to take on motherless kittens whenever emotions threaten to overwhelm me."

"That's not a huge flaw."

"It's better than a cocaine habit."

He didn't laugh. Instead, he looked at her and said, "You telling me you loved me was the reason I broke up with Nora."

Guilt slammed into her. In her head, she knew it wasn't her fault, but her visceral reaction was one of shame and regret.

"Campbell, no. Please don't say that. I never wanted to hurt you or get between you."

"I know and I'm sorry. I said it wrong. What happened with me and Nora isn't your fault. It's not even about you." His gaze was steady. "Hearing you say those words affected me. I'd wondered if you felt anything when we were together. I wanted to believe you cared and sometimes I could convince myself you did. That if I just hung on a little longer, you'd come around. But then you'd get spooked and run and there was nothing I could do to make you stay."

She took a couple of deep breaths. "I hurt you. I'm sorry. I didn't do it on purpose." She held up a hand. "I know that doesn't take away the pain or make it right, but in my heart of hearts, I never wanted to make you feel bad. And I did love you. I just couldn't admit it to myself and I was nowhere near brave enough to take a chance on us." She tried to smile. "Like you said. Broken."

"No. You're not. I was angry and surprised when you showed up that time and I lashed out. I didn't mean it."

"You were telling the truth and I needed to hear it. I'm working on a plan to be happy, truly happy. I'm getting there.

I think I'm less broken now, but it's not like I'll ever fall fully into the normal spectrum when it comes to dealing with difficult emotions."

"But you're still going to be your sisters' guardian, aren't you?"

"How did you know?"

"It's the right thing to do."

She ducked her head. "Yes, well, they're family and if they lose their parents, they need someone who can take care of them. We all know I'm a screwup, but I'll keep trying."

"I'm still in love with you."

She blinked as she stared at him. "Excuse me?"

He smiled. "I would have thought the statement was clear enough. I'm still in love with you. That didn't go away and believe me I tried not to be."

Her body went hot, then cold and the room spun a little. "What does that mean?" Was he giving her information or something much more wonderful?

"I can't get you out of my head. You're the one I want to be with. I'm hoping you still love me and we can—"

She threw herself at him, wrapping her arms around his neck and hanging on. Hope and happiness and relief and love filled her. He hugged her back, squeezing hard and whispering her name.

They stayed like that for a long time. She breathed in the scent of him, absorbed the warmth of his body. Campbell still loved her. After all this time, after all she'd done, or rather hadn't done, he was still here.

She drew back. "Are you giving me another chance?"

"Yes."

"At a relationship with you?"

One corner of his mouth lifted. "Yes. It would be awkward if I wanted a relationship with someone else." He rubbed his thumb against her cheek. "Are you crying?"

"Probably."

"You never cry."

"I had a breakthrough."

He leaned forward and brushed his mouth against hers. She kissed him back, thinking she'd never thought she would have this again. Have them.

"I'll do whatever you want," she told him when he drew back. "We can date for a while, then discuss moving in together. We can move in together now. I'd say my place because it's bigger and has a better view, but either works. I'm ready, Campbell. For us, for a future. I'm still scared about having kids because of my mother. Oh, and you know she's still in my life, so that's unfortunate, but you get along with her, so maybe that's not so bad."

He pressed his finger to her lips. "Shh. We have time."

"I want you to know I'm all in. I love you."

"Good. So let's start hanging out regularly. When we get to the point that half my stuff is here, I'll move in." His dark gaze softened with affection. "I don't want you to think you have to keep changing for me. I loved you before, you know. The new you is nice, but I'm good if this is how you stay."

"What if you have a few flaws I want to discuss?"

His raised his eyebrows. "Not possible. I'm pretty damned perfect."

She lunged for him. He caught her and then they were kissing and holding on and everything, just everything, was exactly as it was supposed to be.

"When do you fly out?" Heather asked as she and Campbell drove toward Life's A Yolk for brunch. She'd had to use a little extra concealer that morning to cover the shadows under her eyes. The result of a night where she'd gotten very little sleep. Not that it hadn't been worth it. She and Campbell were still in their first twenty-four hours together and she'd wanted to enjoy every second of it.

"Early Monday morning."

"Then you should probably go home tonight," she said, trying to keep the reluctance out of her voice. "I want to spend the night with you, but we're going to have too much sex and you need to be rested for your flight."

"Can there be too much sex?" he asked, his tone teasing.

"When you're a pilot responsible for the lives of a couple hundred people, yes."

"Then I'll go home after dinner to sleep. I'm back Wednesday around noon. Want to meet at your place?"

"Yes, please." She'd already given him a key. "I'll rearrange my calendar so I can leave work early."

He picked up the hand she'd rested on his thigh and brought it to his mouth, where he kissed her palm.

"I like dating a powerful woman. It's kind of sexy."

"I'm glad you think so." She looked at him and felt her heart melting. "I'll miss you."

"On my flight?"

"Uh-huh."

"But you like being alone."

"Not as much as I used to."

They pulled into the parking lot and walked toward the restaurant.

"Does anyone know about us?" she asked.

"Not unless you were secretly texting with your friends."

She grinned. "So when would I have had time to do that?"

He chuckled and held open the door. "This will be a surprise." He paused to kiss her. "A happy one."

"You're back together!"

The shriek came from across the restaurant. All the customers turned to stare, but Heather only saw Tori and Daphne rushing toward her. She ran to them and they all hugged and jumped up and down.

"When did this happen?"

"You couldn't text, you couldn't call?"

Heather laughed. "It's been less than a day, so no. There wasn't time."

Daphne grabbed her arms. "Is it casual or something more?"

Campbell joined them. "We have declared our love and are discussing moving in together."

There was more shrieking and jumping. Brody and Grant waited for things to calm before joining them.

"You know, we have a table," Grant said mildly, even as he put an arm around Heather and kissed her cheek. "Welcome back. You're my favorite of all his women."

"Hey." Campbell poked him in the arm. "Don't make trouble."

Brody hugged Heather. "I know he's a step down for you, but it's nice that you're willing to overlook that."

She laughed. "Me, too."

They walked back to the table and took their seats. Seconds later their server appeared with an ice bucket and a bottle of fancy champagne.

"This was left in back with your name on it," she said with a grin. "No idea why, but I thought I'd serve it."

Heather looked at Campbell, who seemed as confused as she was. Daphne shook her head. Tori glanced at Grant.

"You did this."

"I did."

Heather realized they looked very relaxed together. And also, just a little smug. Her gaze dropped to her friend's left hand.

"Holy crap, you're engaged!"

The restaurant went silent. Tori held out her hand to show off the very large, very beautiful, diamond engagement ring. The other patrons clapped. Grant stood and bowed, then began pouring champagne into glasses.

"When did this happen?" Daphne asked. "And why didn't we know until now?"

"He proposed Friday night," Tori said. "And we wanted to tell everyone together." She pointed at Campbell. "I asked him if it was okay that Heather join us for brunch and he said he'd bring her. I didn't know that meant you were getting back together."

"I didn't think you should be the first to know."

"I get that."

The six of them picked up their glasses.

"Congratulations," Brody said. "To a long, happy, healthy life filled with joy and love."

Heather glanced at Campbell and saw him watching her. Under the table, they joined hands. Later, when Campbell went home to get some sleep, she would call her dad and Jillian and let them know the happy news, along with Sophie, Kristine and her mom. All the members of her family.

"What are you thinking?" Campbell asked.

"That if I hadn't gone looking for my father, none of this would have happened. I wouldn't have grown enough for you to want to be with me." She shook her head. "Worse, I wouldn't even have been able to see that I was in love with you. My life was so small and sad."

He kissed her. "Not anymore."

"No, not anymore."

★ ★ ★ ★ ★

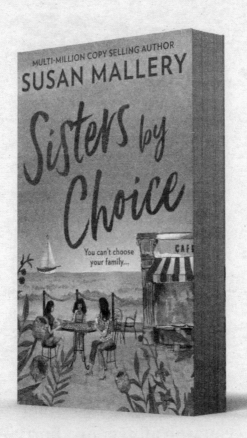

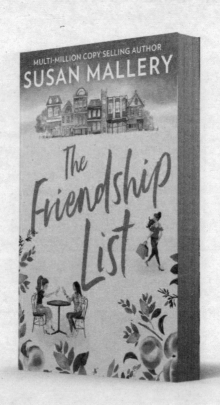

Spend Christmas with
SUSAN MALLERY

Festive romances from
New York Times #1 bestselling author

LET'S TALK
Romance

Follow us:

- **Millsandboon**
- **@MillsandBoon**
- **@MillsandBoonUK**
- **@MillsandBoonUK**

For all the latest titles and special offers, sign up to our newsletter:

Millsandboon.co.uk